Staffordshire Library and Information Services
Please return or renew by the last date shown

If not required by other readers, this item may be
renewed in person, by post or telephone, online or by
email. To renew, either the book or ticket are required

24 Hour Renewal Line
0845 33 00 740

Staffordshire
County Council

81063/16

Veronica Henry worked as a scriptwriter for *The Archers*, *Heartbeat* and *Holby City* amongst many others, before turning to writing novels. She won the RNA Novel of the Year Award in 2014. Veronica lives with her family in a village in north Devon.

You can discover more about the author at www.veronicahenry.co.uk

A HOME FROM HOME

Dragonfly Farm has been a home and a haven for generations of Melchiors — arch-rivals to the Culbones, the wealthy family who live across the river. Life there is dictated by the seasons and cider-making, and everyone falls under its spell. For cousins Tabitha and Georgia, it has always been a home from home. When a tragedy befalls their beloved great-uncle Matthew, it seems the place where they've always belonged might now belong to them, but the will also reveals that a third of the farm has been left to a total stranger. Gabriel Culbone has no idea why he's been included, or what his connection to the farm — or the Melchiors — can be. As the first apples start to fall for the cider harvest, will Dragonfly Farm begin to give up its secrets?

Books by Veronica Henry
Published by Ulverscroft:

THE BEACH HUT NEXT DOOR
HOW TO FIND LOVE IN A BOOK SHOP
THE FOREVER HOUSE
A FAMILY RECIPE
CHRISTMAS AT THE BEACH HUT

VERONICA HENRY

A HOME FROM HOME

Complete and Unabridged

CHARNWOOD
Leicester

First published in Great Britain in 2019 by
Orion Fiction
an imprint of The Orion Publishing Group Ltd
London

First Charnwood Edition
published 2020
by arrangement with
The Orion Publishing Group Ltd
London

The moral right of the author has been asserted

All the characters in this book are fictitious, and any
resemblance to actual persons, living or dead,
is purely coincidental.

A catalogue record for this book is available
from the British Library.

ISBN 978–1–4448–4549–5

Published by
Ulverscroft Limited
Anstey, Leicestershire

Set by Words & Graphics Ltd.
Anstey, Leicestershire
Printed and bound in Great Britain by
T. J. International Ltd., Padstow, Cornwall

This book is printed on acid-free paper

And pluck till time and times are done
The silver apples of the moon,
The golden apples of the sun

W B YEATS

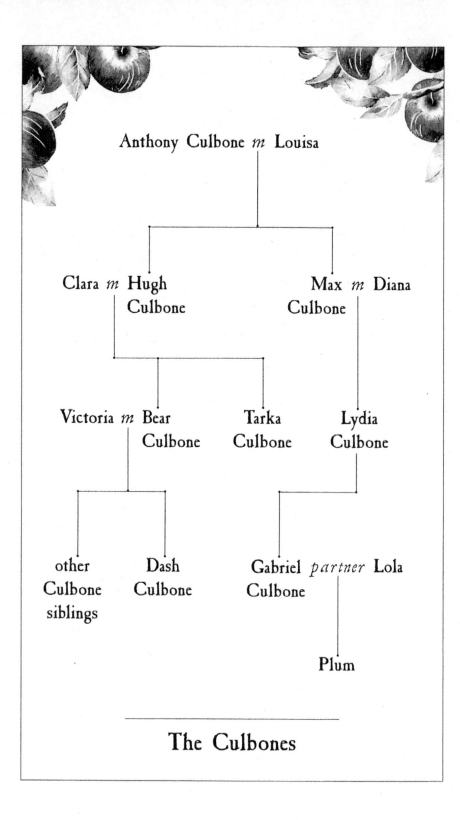

Anthony Culbone *m* Louisa

Clara *m* Hugh
Culbone

Max *m* Diana
Culbone

Victoria *m* Bear
Culbone

Tarka
Culbone

Lydia
Culbone

other
Culbone
siblings

Dash
Culbone

Gabriel *partner* Lola
Culbone

Plum

The Culbones

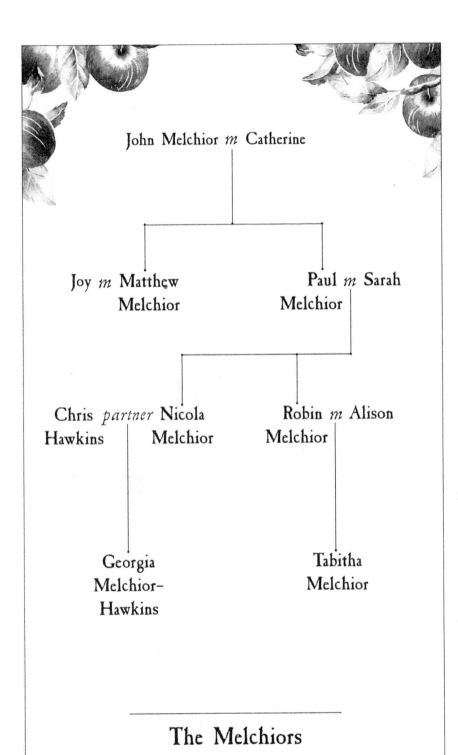

John Melchior *m* Catherine

Joy *m* Matthew
Melchior

Paul *m* Sarah
Melchior

Chris *partner* Nicola
Hawkins   Melchior

Robin *m* Alison
Melchior

Georgia
Melchior–
Hawkins

Tabitha
Melchior

The Melchiors

PART ONE

PART ONE

1

Crack!

There was nothing more satisfying than the sound of an axe splitting a log. Tabitha had spent all morning getting her swing just right, like a golfer, and now she had the perfect rhythm. It was better than any workout, and she was stripped down to a camisole and shorts, dripping with sweat. Not a ladylike glow, but good honest salty sweat, running in rivulets down her face, her back, everywhere . . .

She'd finally accepted that the tree wasn't going to survive. It had shown signs of disinterest in life some time ago. She had done what she could to mollycoddle it over the heat of the summer, but now there was nothing for it but to chop it down and use it for firewood. Often, they would keep fallen trees, and sometimes these would continue to bear fruit, but this was blocking the way so now, instead of an ancient apple tree, she had a beautiful pile of logs waiting to be stacked in the wood-store for drying.

She wasn't sentimental. She would replace it, get a new tree tucked safely into the orchard so it would get strong before the first frost and the onset of winter, which would be upon them before they were ready. It was always so hard to believe cold weather was on its way in the soft warmth of early autumn, with the trees and bushes and hedgerows heavy with fruit, gold and purple and deep red and orange.

She gathered up the last few logs, flung them in her wheelbarrow and laid her axe on top. She gave a loud whistle, and Poe — named by her cousin Georgia after Edgar Allan Poe, because his shiny coat was as black as a raven's wing — bounded back to her. He was a formidable ratter. Even though Dragonfly Farm wasn't a proper working farm — no cattle or sheep; no grain to store — the outhouses were still a draw for vermin.

She calculated there was enough time for her to go and have a long bath with a dose of Epsom salts to soothe her muscles before heading to the Swan. She'd worked there for seven years and she wouldn't give it up for anything. On the banks of the river Rushbrook that gave the village its name, the pub was unspoilt, cosy but comfy, with a good mix of locals and people from further afield who popped in regularly for one of her famous pies. She was part of the fixtures and fittings. She belonged there as much as the flagstone floors and the cases full of fish that had been caught in the river and the photographs of the Rushbrook cricket team going back to the 1800s.

The pie-making had started when the chef had gone off sick and Tabitha had stepped in: she didn't have the skills to cook to order, so she had taken the contents of the fridge and made a selection of pies. They had gone down a storm and were now the pub's speciality. Chicken and mushroom, steak and Stilton, venison, fish, spinach and feta, rabbit and mustard — she changed them according to the season. They were all topped with her shiny pastry, hand-decorated with lattice work and leaves and finally monogrammed with an entwined *TM* for Tabitha Melchior.

Today, she was spending the afternoon making pies before her shift behind the bar, which would finish about midnight. Then she would be up at the crack of dawn the next morning to exercise racehorses for Jimmy O'Gowan. It was hard work and not nearly as glamorous as it sounded, but she loved it: she was light but strong, and a fearless rider. Every week Jimmy would plead with her to come and work for him full time. 'Ah, come on now, Miss Melchior,' he'd say, his voice syrupy with Galway charm. 'You're the only person who never lets me down. I need you to run the yard. We'd win the Gold Cup every year with you at the helm.'

But she would laugh her refusal.

When people asked Tabitha what she did for a living, she was always amused by the look on their faces when she recited the list. She'd worked out a long time ago that she wasn't a career girl. She didn't want to be answerable to anyone. She was a pie-making/racehorse-exercising/cider-making/anything-else-that-came-her-way barmaid who by and large chose exactly how to live her life.

OK, so she didn't get sick pay or have much of a pension, and even lumped together her income wasn't huge, but she did what she loved with people she loved and she never got bored, and

5

what could be better than that?

It was flexible too: if she wanted to disappear off to Glastonbury for a week, she could. When she needed to take time off for the apple harvest and annual cider making, she could. And she was able to be spontaneous and indulge in passion projects.

The week before, the whole of Year 7 from Nettleford Community College had come to Dragonfly Farm for the day — a field trip for all the new children to get to know each other and have a riverside picnic. The ritual had been established by Tabitha's great-aunt, Joy. As a health visitor, community had been important to Joy, and Tabitha wanted to keep the tradition going.

The coach had arrived and the children tumbled out, prepubescent and unruly, oozing ennui yet secretly glad not to be shut up in the classroom but instead to frolic in the orchards and enjoy the last of the Indian summer. She'd taken them into the barn to make some juice using the first of the early apples and gave them all a taste.

'Can't we have some proper cider, miss?'

'I'm afraid not.' Tabitha grinned.

'My dad loves your cider. He asked me to bring some home.'

'I'm afraid last year's has run out. And we haven't started this year's yet. Not till next month at least.'

She felt a little glow at the recognition. Melchior Cider might only have a product reach of about three miles, but it had almost cult status. Some people had been drinking it for more than thirty years, from when Joy first began making it as a hobby, selling it at the farm gate. It was said that if you drank it during the full moon, you could make anyone you wanted fall in love with you. Tabitha had never tested the theory, but there had been several Melchior Cider weddings to her knowledge: couples who had met while under its influence and had ordered it to be drunk at the reception. It had given her an idea — something she was working on in secret: to produce a sparkling cider, a light, delicious, celebratory fizz filled with West Country sunshine.

Afterwards, the children had done a few worksheets, grumbling, then she had taken them down to the river. The autumn sun filtered through the trees over their heads as they sat on the grassy bank where the river widened out into a large pool and became still, and the weeping willows trailed their branches on the surface. They listened, wide-eyed, as she told them the dramatic history of Dragonfly Farm.

'This farm once belonged to the Culbones. That's their house you can see on the other side of the valley.'

They all craned their necks to peep over the tops of the trees. They could just glimpse the grey slates of Rushbrook House and a pair of tall chimneys.

'One night, my great-great-great-grandfather, Joseph Melchior, won the farm off Casper Culbone in a game of cards at the Swan. They'd been drinking cider all evening and were three sheets to the wind.'

The children were all agog. Even though they were bursting with hormones and their heads were filled with selfies and Snapchat, the magic of storytelling still worked on them.

'Next morning, when they'd sobered up, Joseph made Casper honour his gambling debt. There'd been plenty of witnesses in the pub. He moved into the farm that very day.'

There was a communal nod. The children all understood the etiquette of gambling, it seemed.

'The Culbones were furious but there was nothing they could do. And even now,' Tabitha finished, 'Melchiors and Culbones still don't speak. They cross the road if they see each other.'

She was exaggerating slightly. She couldn't remember the last time she'd seen a Culbone, as Rushbrook House was rented out. But she had been livid when the Culbones' solicitor sent a letter to her great-uncle just after Joy had died, offering to buy the farm back. Over a hundred years on and they were still sore losers.

She didn't tell them the rest of the story either. How Casper Culbone had taken his revenge by stealing the love of Joseph's life. The unhappy ending was a little too graphic for eleven-year-olds, she thought, although she suspected they might relish the ghoulish detail.

She looked at the still water of Eleanor's Pool, as it was known locally, and as always, her heart ached with sorrow for the lovesick girl who had taken her own life. Tabitha had vowed never to let any man manipulate her in the way Eleanor had been by Casper Culbone, nor lose her heart

8

to someone who would drive her to madness. Tabitha still put flowers on Eleanor's grave sometimes, when she went to tend her great-aunt's memorial in the churchyard.

Afterwards, she gave the children a picnic of craggy cheese and sourdough bread she'd made that morning, and slabs of cake thick with sultanas. They'd been wary at first. She could see them wrinkling their noses and looking at each other doubtfully. They were used to plastic bread and processed cheese and bags of crisps and additive-filled chocolate bars washed down with fizzy pop. But every crumb was gone.

It had been the warmest of September afternoons, when the sunlight trickles like honey onto your skin, a gentler warmth than the harsh glare of high summer. Tabitha wished she could let the children jump into the river, but there hadn't been a risk assessment so the teacher was reluctant.

She strode back through the orchard now, smiling at the memory of sixty eleven-year-olds shouting their thanks as they climbed back on the bus. The long grass swished at her legs as she pushed her barrow through the apple trees. She reached up to tug at an apple overhead — it was still slightly reluctant to come away, but she pulled it off then twisted it in half. Inside, the flesh was smooth and creamy, and the musty apple scent made her stomach flicker with anticipation. But the pips in the core were too pale: not the chestnut brown they needed to be. Not time to harvest yet.

She reached the sprawling courtyard of

outbuildings at the back of the farmhouse. She emptied the logs into the stone store that was easy to get to when Gum, her great-uncle, needed to nip outside for a fresh supply on a dark night. It was his nightly ritual, to set the fire in the living room. She stacked the logs neatly at the very back to dry out. They wouldn't be ready for a year at least.

Then she pushed her barrow over to the tool shed, leaned it against the wall, wiped her axe carefully and hung it back up. In here were tools that went back generations, and she knew she would always find whatever she needed. Loppers and secateurs, shovels, forks, long poles for knocking the apples from the highest branches, pruning knives. They were all kept immaculate, the blades oiled, the handles smooth, and hung up on hooks in their own particular place. She loved the smell in here. Slightly damp, with a base note of oil and a top note of wood, the smell of centuries of toil.

She locked the shed up and dropped the key in her pocket. They might live in the depths of the Somerset countryside, but you never knew when a light-fingered opportunist might wander by and help themselves. And to Tabitha these items were irreplaceable. The handles had been worn down by generations of Melchiors. No insurance claim could make up for their loss if they went missing.

The sun was high in the sky, burning rose-gold. She stood still for a moment to enjoy the peace and remember the people who had been in and out of this yard throughout her life

— the ones who were still here, and the ones who weren't. She still expected to see Joy bowling round the corner with a basket of eggs or an armful of cabbages, her cheeks pink and her hair wild. She had left Tabitha and Georgia a little bit of money when she'd gone. Tabitha had planted the field that ran down to the river with fifty new apple trees. Not the kind of apples destined for the fruit bowl, but small, tannic and bittersweet — the best variety for sparkling cider.

'That money was supposed to be spent on you,' Gum had chided her.

'This *is* for me,' said Tabitha, who loved the orchards more than anything.

Georgia had bought a top-of-the-range Mac-Book, which made perfect sense, as writing was *her* life. Tabitha sighed, thinking of her cousin, and wondered if their feud had gone on long enough.

She missed Joy and she missed Georgia. Only one of those things could she do anything about. But what? Perhaps she should swallow her pride and pick up the phone. Not now, though. There were pies to be made.

She slipped inside the back door, ran through the kitchen and up the narrow, winding back staircase to the bathroom, where she turned the hot tap on to full blast, stripped off her clothes and watched the mirror over the sink steam up and her reflection disappear.

2

The knife fitted into his palm perfectly, his fingers curled round the satin-smooth walnut handle. It was just the right weight: not too heavy, but solid enough to have authority, and perfectly balanced. Nothing could argue with a knife like this. The blade would slice through almost everything. He imagined it plunging through flesh and fat and sinew without effort. It would meet no resistance.

He held it up under the lamp which swung from the ceiling of the railway arch. A tiny stamp near the handle made him smile, as it always did: an angel with a halo. And underneath were his initials: GC.

He wondered where the knife would end up. He always felt a protective fatherliness towards his handiwork. He shuddered to think of it being misused: thrust into a dishwasher or left at the bottom of a sink of dirty water.

Some of his knives were bespoke, the size and shape of the blade made to the customer's exacting requirements, the wood of the handle carefully chosen for the way it felt against their skin. Knives were very personal. Everyone had their own preference, moulded to their habits and their environment. A chef in a busy restaurant kitchen had different needs from a keen home cook. But one thing was certain. Interest in bespoke knives had rocketed; knife makers were heroes. And Gabriel Culbone was gradually becoming a brand.

He laid his latest specimen down gently and wiped the sweat from his brow with the back of his arm. He flicked a glance at the clock: he should crack on with the next, he thought, and get as much as he could done.

Before he could begin a sudden coldness stopped him, a chill that made every hair on his body ripple. He stood still as it ran from his head to his toes, accompanied by the strangest sensation of loss. He frowned. He wasn't a fanciful man, but he felt as if he had been standing under a tap, or dipped into an icy lake in the depths of winter. Rather than feeling adrenaline, he felt as if his heart was slowing; as if his system was closing down.

As quickly as the sensation had arrived, it had gone.

He looked at the temperature gauge on the wall. It was no colder than usual in the workshop. It could be arctic in here in the depths of winter, before he stoked up the wood-burning stove, but it was only autumn.

He shivered as he looked around for an explanation — an open door, perhaps — but there was none. Unsettled, he analysed the feeling of emptiness he was left with now the coldness had gone. It was more emotional than physical, although he couldn't have described it. He tried to shake the feeling away.

His grandmother, Diana, would have said *somebody's walked over your grave*. Alarmed, he wondered if she was all right. He knew the home

13

would ring him if something happened to her. He was the first point of contact, after all, as there wasn't much point in them calling his mother in Pondicherry. Or was it Comporta? He couldn't keep up with Lydia's itinerary these days. She was very much in demand, bending people into impossible positions and gently anointing their temples with scented balm until they reached a state of bliss.

His phone began to chirrup and he stared at it across the workbench, wondering if this was the call he constantly dreaded; if the shivery feeling was presaging bad news about Diana. He lunged over the workbench and snatched it up, staring at the screen.

Lola.

'Hi,' he answered, relieved.

'Hey,' she said. She sounded anxious. 'Listen, the shoot's overrunning. I'm so sorry. One of the other models was late and we've only just started. There's no way I'll be finished until late.'

'Oh,' he said. 'Well, don't worry. I can pick Plum up.'

'Are you sure? I can ask the nursery to keep her?'

'No. I don't mind. You know I don't.'

He never minded being with his daughter. He would be with her every minute of the day if he could, but work was a necessity, not a luxury. They shared her care between each other and weekday mornings at Squirrel Nutkin's nursery. Sometimes their system ran smoothly; sometimes it didn't, like today. But when you were freelance, you had to be flexible and you had to compromise. For Gabriel and Lola, it was vital that it was never Plum who was compromised.

'You're a legend. You know that, right? I don't deserve you.'

'No, you don't.' He was laughing. 'You owe me.'

'I'm sorry. I know you're behind on your commissions. I'll have her at the weekend if you want to catch up?'

'The weekends are for the three of us,' he said firmly. 'Don't worry. I'll grab Plum and hang out with her this afternoon. Do your thing.'

He heard her give him a squeaky kiss and grinned. As he hung up, he could imagine her leaning against the bare brick of some studio wall, swathed in a scrap of silk that would command a huge price tag, her hair tamed into glossy curls, her feet in impossibly high heels. She looked so terrifyingly unapproachable in her photos, but he knew the truth about her soft heart; how she sometimes felt that her perfect body was a curse.

'Only it's not perfect, is it?' she'd said to him through tears, the last time the test had been negative.

'Shh,' he consoled her. 'We have to give it time.'

'But we don't have time! I never seem to be here. We completely missed our chance last month because I was away.'

'Don't get upset.' Gabriel hated seeing her so distressed.

'Plum's three! Soon she'll be too old for a little brother or sister.'

'No, she won't. She'll love it whatever. Whenever it comes along.'

'What if it doesn't happen?'

'It will.'

It was his job to reassure her, because she was convinced it was her fault, that it was all down to her punishing work schedule and diet and exercise regime. The fact she had got pregnant almost straight away with Plum didn't seem to console her.

'I shouldn't have gone back to work so quickly afterwards,' she said. 'I've probably screwed up my body by having to lose all that baby weight.'

'It could just as easily be my fault,' Gabriel said, but she looked doubtful.

There was nothing else he could do or say except try to keep their lives as stress-free as possible. But it was difficult, when he was still trying to establish himself. No matter how many hours he put in, he had to make enough to cover the rent and his overheads and materials before he put any food on the table. Lola could make in a day what Gabriel made in a week. She insisted she didn't mind, generous as she was.

'It's only fair,' she said. 'I'm living my dream. It's time for you to live yours.'

He was making headway, but maybe he would never be well-known enough for people to pay four figures for one of his knives. It was possible, if you were at the top of your trade. And he had a good following. He was friends with enough chefs he'd worked with when he was a restaurant manager. A business like his thrived on word of mouth.

Lola had been brilliant at helping him with the publicity. She'd taken a ream of photos of him at work, sparks flying, bare-chested and in skin-tight leather trousers. The pictures were pure Instagram gold: the steel knives juxtaposed against his sweating torso, the trademark angel-with-a-halo tattoo on his right shoulder, his long dark hair tied back with a bandana, his dark eyes scorched into his face. Of course, he didn't usually work topless — it was far too dangerous — but you never let truth get in the way of a good picture when it came to PR, Lola said. He'd been a bit embarrassed by the whole thing, but if Lola knew anything it was how to exploit your looks to sell things.

'I want people to buy my knives because they're the best, not because you've somehow made me look like a rock star,' he protested. She laughed.

'Gabe — you're smoking hot. Use it. It's great free publicity.'

She was right. There was a ripple of magazine articles in food magazines and Saturday supplements, and an uplift in orders he was now trying to fill. In the meantime, Lola was working as hard as ever.

Was that why nothing had happened still, after nearly a year? Was it too much pressure for her?

He hadn't time to reflect on it now. He didn't even have time to clean himself up properly. He would usually shower before going anywhere near Plum, washing all the sweat and dirt and grime down the plughole. He took off his protective clothing, peeled off his T-shirt and did

17

a strip wash in the big sink, sluicing it all away as best he could, towelling himself off then sliding his T-shirt back on again.

He picked up his jacket, phone and keys and made sure everything was turned off. He only had half an hour to get to Squirrel Nutkin's. He grabbed his bike: it was black, fleet and light, designed to cut through city traffic, and on the front was Plum's seat, so he could curl himself round her while cycling. He had never liked the idea of her on a seat behind him.

He shut and locked the door, wheeling his bike out into the cobbled street outside.

'You're off early.' Heidi, one of the twins from the bakery next door to his workshop, greeted him.

'Yeah. Lola's shoot's running late. I've got to go and pick up Plum.'

'Hang on two seconds.' She opened the bakery door and the scent of vanilla flooded out. She came out moments later with a little box. 'Blackberry and apple turnover.'

'Oh.' Gabriel was touched. He bought a lot of things from them, because of Plum's allergies. There was a code amongst the arches tenants that they didn't expect discounts from each other, nor did they have any obligation to buy things from each other, but most of them helped each other out. Heidi and Helga often gave him little treats if they had things left over.

'Have you seen the letter?' Heidi looked grave.

'Letter?' Gabriel thought guiltily of the untouched pile of post in the workshop.

'From the landlord. He's putting the rent up.'

18

'Oh, you're kidding.' This was a disaster. The rent was already monstrous, but he had fallen in love with Rockham Arches. The only alternative had been an anonymous unit on an industrial estate.

'Yep. He's putting it up more than ten per cent. We're going to have to do some serious thinking.'

Gabriel looked alarmed. He adored Heidi and Helga.

'Don't go. I can't survive without you here.'

'We can't make a profit if the rent goes up.'

'Well, no. Nor me.' He made a face.

'Apparently they've got a waiting list as long as your arm for units. People are queuing up.'

'Shit.' The world wasn't short of people with dreams, it seemed. He looked down gloomily at Heidi and Helga's entwined initials on the cake box: their dream. 'Thanks for this. Plum will love it.'

Gabriel went back to his workshop and dug out the letter from the landlord from the pile of unopened post, stuffing it into his pocket to read and digest later. He left with a heavy heart.

Rockham Arches was his spiritual home, shared with a bunch of like-minded people all striving to make a better life for themselves and to share their skills and talents. As well as Heidi and Helga's bakery, there was a craft brewery, a bloke who did MOTs and repairs on vintage cars, a bike shop . . . all of them knew everything there was to know about their industry and worked tirelessly. It was tough to be a success in this day and age, but it was possible, if you put in the hours and took the risks.

He loved it here, he thought, as he pushed his bike along the cobbles outside the railway arches. He loved the industrial architecture and the notion of creating something new from somewhere old, and most of all he loved the sense of community amongst the other tenants. There was always someone around to give you a hand or make a brew. They shared each other's passions and dreams; swapped notes and gave each other advice. There was no sense of competition, just camaraderie. When someone made a big sale or got a new contract or won an award, there was a celebration.

He reached the main road, then pulled on his helmet, swung himself into the saddle and insinuated his way into the afternoon traffic. There was no such thing as rush hour any more; it was constant chaos. The journey home would take him at least an hour if he drove, but on a bike you had the advantage of being able to weave round stationary cars or slink down rat runs. With a fair wind behind him, he'd be at Squirrel Nutkin's in less than twenty minutes.

3

Tabitha had hardly got used to the heat of her bath water when she heard the knocker go on the front door. She was tempted to ignore it. She wasn't expecting anyone or anything and nor was Gum, as far as she knew. She was about to disappear under the water and make it go away when it sounded again, even more urgent, and she could hear Poe barking in the kitchen.

She climbed out, grabbed a towel, wrapped it around her and made her way down the wider front staircase that led to the hall, being careful not to slip. She tugged at the door, which always stuck, especially after a warm summer. She stood in the doorway, her hair still dripping. There was a man standing there with a distressed look on his face.

She was on her guard immediately. She'd heard about scams where people feigned an emergency, bluffing their way into your home. Though he didn't look like your average con artist. He didn't look furtive or shifty. He was tall, with dark hair swept back off his face, a smattering of stubble and very thick straight eyebrows, dressed in jeans, a pale-brown sweater and waxed boots that, judging by their cleanliness, had been bought in London, not at the local feed merchants.

'I'm so sorry,' he said, and his voice was cracked with emotion. 'It happened so quickly.

There was nothing I could do — '

'Poe?' she said. 'He's in the kitchen.'

As if on cue, Poe began to bark again.

'Oh God.' His dark eyebrows closed together. 'I didn't mean the dog. The police are there, and the ambulance. I'm so sorry. His truck just . . . ' He indicated a sweeping motion with his hand. 'He cut right in front of me.' Tabitha was staring at him, trying to make sense of what he was saying. 'Your great-uncle. Somebody said . . . he's your great-uncle?'

Tabitha just stood there, clutching her towel. 'Gum?'

'He must have had a heart attack or maybe a stroke. I'm so sorry.'

'Is he . . . going to be OK?'

'I don't know. I really don't. He was unconscious. They've taken him to the hospital.'

'How am I going to get there?' Her face crumpled. 'He took the truck. I don't have . . . I'll have to take the bike.'

'That'll take hours.'

'Motorbike,' she corrected him. It was a vintage Indian which Gum had bought when he was at university, to get him to Cambridge and back. Restoring it was an ongoing project for both of them but they hadn't touched it for months.

'Look, I'm very happy to take you. Why don't you go and get dry and dressed?'

It was then she noticed the silver car. Low-slung, a long bonnet. Again, a London car. Not built for pitted tracks and potholes.

'I can manage,' she said. 'Where did it

happen? Are the police still there?'

But as she spoke, she could feel herself unravelling. She began to tremble. She couldn't control it. Her teeth were chattering. She was going to cry. In her towel, in front of a strange man.

'I think you might be in shock.' He reached out a hand to touch her. She jerked out of the way.

'I'm fine.'

'You can't ride a motorbike in your state.'

She flashed him a glance. 'I'm a good rider. And it'll get there faster than that.' She nodded at his car.

'I think you need someone with you. Please let me take you.'

His voice was firm. Tabitha stared at him. No one would usually dare suggest she needed looking after. Nobody who knew her, anyway. Her default reaction was to tell him to leave her alone. But she stopped herself. He wasn't being patronising, he was being kind. She was frightened. And she didn't know what to do. Maybe she did need someone with her.

And to be honest, despite her protestations, she wasn't sure if there was enough petrol in the bike, or even if it would start.

'OK,' she said grudgingly. 'Thank you.'

It felt strange, to relent like that.

He nodded. 'I'm Dash, by the way,' he said. 'Dash Culbone.'

She looked at him.

'Culbone?' she said sharply.

He looked taken aback.

'Is that a problem?'

She gave an impatient huff. 'Surely you don't have to ask?'

One quizzical eyebrow twitched. 'You're worried about something that happened over a hundred years ago?'

She glared. 'Your family tried to buy this place right after my great-aunt died.'

'Oh.' He nodded a concession. 'I think it was a fair price. Market value.'

'You were taking advantage of a vulnerable old man.'

He sighed. 'It was only an offer. Let's try for a temporary truce, given the circumstances.'

She hesitated. 'OK,' she said. 'I'd really appreciate a lift. I'll be five minutes. You better come in.'

She stood to one side to let him come past her and into the hall.

'Let me make you some tea while you change.'

He was, thought Tabitha, one of those practical types who likes to take charge. Under any other circumstances she'd get shot of him as quickly as she could. But, right now, she needed him.

'The kitchen's through there.' She pointed to a doorway at the back of the hall. 'Very strong with just a splash of milk.'

And with that, she ran up the stairs.

★ ★ ★

Dash had never been in a kitchen like it. It ran the length of the back of the house, with a vaulted ceiling, walls the colour of Dijon mustard and a flagstone floor. The units were ancient, circa 1974, in burgundy Formica, and several of the doors were falling off their hinges — the kitchen was even worse than the one at Rushbrook. Faded red-velvet curtains framed the three sash windows looking out onto the orchard at the back, and in front of them was a table covered in a snow-white tablecloth embroidered with birds and flowers. A pewter candelabra took centre stage, a lifetime of late nights pooling down its sides in waxen stalactites. A basket held a pile of silver cutlery with pale bone handles.

Every drawer seemed to be open; everywhere you looked, someone was in the middle of something. An old Singer sewing machine had a dress still clamped in it, as if the person sewing it up had just walked away. A loaf of bread sat on the side with two slices sawn from it. Next to it was a large jar of eggs floating in pale liquid, like something from a Victorian science lab. There was a rocking horse in the far corner which seemed to be used to hold coats. Clothes hung from a drying rack: two pairs of country corduroy trousers and a tattersall shirt which must belong to Matthew Melchior. Several towels. And a hot-pink bra. It was chaotic and shambolic and a potential health hazard.

Dash looked for the kettle. He found one so ancient it wouldn't be out of place in a museum. He filled it and plugged it in cautiously — if this was his house, the first thing he would do was have the place rewired — then rifled through all

25

the tins on the shelf until he found some PG Tips.

It felt a million miles from his bachelor pad overlooking Tower Bridge. All he'd had there was a steel-grey linen sofa and a coffee table and a telly, because he was hardly ever at home. He was either working late or travelling. All that was behind him now. As of this week, he was a country bumpkin. No more Addison Lee coming to pick up him at 5 a.m.

He shivered a little. This afternoon was not an auspicious beginning to his new life. He stood by the window to compose himself while the kettle boiled. He might seem calm and unruffled, but what had happened had deeply upset him.

The truck had come from nowhere as he rounded the corner. He knew he wasn't going too fast because he was still re-familiarising himself with the country lanes. Sometimes they were so narrow that his car sensors beeped frantically, the hedges either side reaching out to scratch his paintwork. He wasn't doing much over twenty, so he'd avoided a collision, but he'd had to slam his brakes on, then watched, aghast, as the ancient yellow HiLux cut straight across him.

He knew there was nothing much he could do to help the driver. He was unconscious; his pulse thready. Dash had called the emergency services, then pulled his warning triangle out of his boot and put it up to warn any other traffic. A passer-by had said it was Matthew Melchior; that he and his great-niece lived alone together at Dragonfly Farm. He could see the police were stretched when they arrived. There were only two of them on duty in the area, and calls were coming through for a factory blaze near Honisham, so he'd offered to go and notify the relatives. They had been pathetically grateful.

'If it's curtains,' they'd said, 'we'll be needing to talk to you again for the coroner's report.'

He walked over to another window at the end of the room, where a writing desk was jammed into the alcove. Someone was in the middle of designing a logo with a Rotring pen: *JOY*, it read, in art nouveau lettering, and underneath *Melchior Sparkling Cider — for celebrations*. Above it was an intricate drawing of a dragonfly coloured over in a pale turquoise ink wash with emerald green highlights. He lifted the paper to see if there were any more clues. He was intrigued. The sketches were accomplished and assured. The dragonfly was perfect: they were a part of the landscape here in the summer, looping their way through the skies like miniature mythical beasts, iridescent in the sunlight.

The kettle rumbled to a boil and switched itself off. He went over to pick it up.

'Let's go.'

He looked up to see Tabitha standing in the doorway, in skinny jeans and a black shirt and brown suede knee boots, her wet hair scraped back and twisted up into a knot. He couldn't tell yet what colour it was. Her eyes were navy, her cheekbones high and her mouth wide. She looked grave.

'You don't want — ?'

'There's no time,' she said, picking up a tasselled scarf from the back of a kitchen chair and winding it round her neck.

Dash guided her to his car as chivalrously as he dared, opening the passenger door for her. She climbed in without a word. He got in next to her and started up the engine, doing a three-point turn in the courtyard.

'Don't go on the main road, whatever you do,' she told him. 'You'll hit the school traffic. Have they taken him to the Cottage Hospital in Nettleford?'

'A & E in Honisham.'

'Oh.' She swallowed. 'Right. Not just minor injuries, then.'

Dash paused before answering. 'No.'

He didn't want to spell it out. That he feared hospital was just a formality. He was pretty sure Tabitha knew, though. She was blinking with the effort of not crying.

'Hey,' he said gently.

'Put your foot down,' she replied. 'What's the point of having a car like this if you don't put it to good use?'

4

'The thing is, we need to show Elspeth as tough but vulnerable. Her inner steel but her con — con — '

'Concomitant?' said Georgia. She knew full well that was the word Natasha was fumbling for because it was exactly the word Georgia had used yesterday, when they'd had a pre pre-meeting meeting. This was the pre-meeting meeting, before they pitched their ideas for a new lead character to the executive producer tomorrow.

'Concomitant Achilles heel,' Natasha finished confidently. 'Which as we all know is her kids. Her children. Her raison d'être. The whole reason she's in this job.'

Martin nodded in approval. 'Excellent, Natasha. That makes her three-dimensional. Not just a career bitch.'

'A velvet fist in an iron glove, if you like,' finished Natasha, leaning back into the tobacco-brown leather sofa, shifting herself so Martin could get the full benefit of her lissom limbs.

She was bloody clever, thought Georgia. She was almost quoting Georgia word for word, but by saying *we*, Georgia couldn't protest that these character traits had been her idea. Not without looking petty.

Martin was very insistent on teamwork. He had no truck with egos, he would tell them.

Except his own. His ego and, sadly, his libido were intertwined and influenced everything he did, although he would never admit it.

Georgia sighed and adjusted her tortoiseshell-framed glasses.

'Do you not agree?' Martin asked her, sensing dissent.

Georgia decided to change tack and throw a curve ball.

'I just think we've seen this character before. A hundred times. The tough female cop with a soft inside.'

Georgia had to stop herself smiling when Natasha looked daggers at her.

'So why don't we subvert it?' she went on. 'Make her outwardly soft and vulnerable; a total pushover. Sort of . . . mumsy, almost. Then when she turns out to be as hard as nails . . . it's a total surprise to the audience. And every week we get lulled into thinking she's some kind of Mrs Tiggywinkle. You know, when she brings them all in flapjacks and gives them a cuddle when they're upset. But underneath she's ruthless.' Georgia gave a shrug. 'Personally, I'm bored with seeing all these glamorised cops on our screens. All high heels and lipstick and salon hair. Surely this is more real?'

Natasha narrowed her eyes. 'Are we going for real, though? We can get real any time we like.' She waved a hand. 'Out there.'

Martin held up a hand. 'No, no, no — I like this. Go on, Georgia.'

'What if she'd joined the police really late? After she'd had her family? And turned out to be a genius. Got fast-tracked. As much to her surprise as anyone else's. So she's not traditionally ambitious. Just really good at what she does. And what she's really good at is running a team. Getting the best out of everyone. Because teamwork is crucial to every successful operation.'

She couldn't help flicking a glance at Natasha, who had no notion whatsoever of teamwork. Natasha was out for herself and no one else. Georgia had worked with her kind often enough. Absolutely no talent but no qualms about stealing other people's ideas. She would go far.

Georgia plunged on, improvising. 'And if we cast well, it could be a fantastic part for one of our older actresses. Someone with years and years of experience and household appeal, who's looking for a challenge.'

'Yes!' Martin clapped. 'Because we all know it's middle-aged women who control the remote. This woman is someone they can relate to. Someone who is getting up and going for it.'

'But who actually *is* this woman?' Natasha was determined to play devil's advocate. 'Do we believe in her?'

Martin beamed from ear to ear. 'We totally do,' he declared. 'She's my mum. She'd make a terrifying cop. She doesn't miss anything. And I love that idea. A totally ordinary woman who's just brought up her kids, maybe been a lollipop lady — yes! Lollipop ladies are on the front line. They know what's going on with everyone. They notice things.'

31

Georgia watched Natasha scoop her baby-blonde hair back behind her ear in a thoughtful gesture and lean forward, obviously panicking that she wasn't going to get credit for any of this idea.

'Or a dinner lady,' Natasha suggested. 'Maybe she's a great cook too? We could cash in on the whole baking thing. And that's what she does when she's trying to solve a crime. Gets out her mixing bowl.'

Martin pointed at her. 'Nice twist. Good thinking.'

Georgia could almost hear Natasha purr with pleasure at his praise.

'Natasha, why don't you pull some thoughts together along those lines?' asked Martin.

Georgia blinked. Given that it was she who had steered this away from cliché, shouldn't she be writing the brief? She opened her mouth to protest, then stopped. Natasha wouldn't know what to write. Six months ago, she had been Martin's assistant. Almost overnight (and there had definitely been a night or two involved) she had become a junior script editor on *The Beat Goes On*, a twice-weekly prime-time cop show.

Georgia had no objection to people starting at the bottom and working their way up. And there were no official qualifications for becoming a script editor. She herself had started as a script reader at an agency, a couple of years after she left university, ploughing through the slush pile of unsolicited submissions and providing a report for any which showed promise. And she herself had turned out to show promise.

She'd done her groundwork too, though, watching hours of reruns of successful TV shows, analysing them for their elusive characteristics. And she'd studied all the great scriptwriters.

But Natasha hadn't even heard of Dennis Potter. She'd looked blank when Georgia had referenced *The Singing Detective* yesterday. Who on earth wanted a career in television drama and didn't do their homework? It didn't take long — television had only been going since 1955, after all.

'Maybe we should try something Potter-esque, to give the show a lift?' she suggested now, keen to see if Natasha took the bait. The viewing figures had dipped a bit of late, so they were brainstorming to find ways to attract more viewers.

'You mean like . . . Harry?' asked Martin, looking puzzled.

'Dennis!' gushed Natasha. 'I think she means Dennis. But it's all a bit passé, isn't it? That musical theatre pastiche? I mean, you can't do better than Potter so why try?'

She was even more cunning than she gave her credit for, thought Georgia. She must have left the meeting and googled Dennis Potter straight away.

She could feel her phone vibrating in her pocket. She ignored it, but then it started again. And again. Martin hated people looking at their phones in meetings. Georgia respected his rule. She tried not to overuse her phone, but it was difficult. You only had to go up to the little café next door, and see everyone scrolling and clicking, to know how they were eroding communication. Ironically. You'd never get a meet cute in a café these days. No one would look up long enough to make eye contact.

It rang again. Who on earth was trying to get in touch with her? Maybe one of those people who tried to lure you into a 'No Win, No Fee' litigation procedure. They were doggedly persistent.

By the fifth ring, she felt anxious. She didn't want to lose points in front of Natasha. But someone wanted to get hold of her. One of her parents, from up in the wilds of Scotland? She couldn't really think of anyone else who might need her.

It certainly wouldn't be Doug. Would it? She batted his memory away. It still made her feel slightly sick, every time she thought of him. Nevertheless, it occurred to her that it was morning in LA. Perhaps . . .

Stop it! she told herself. Even if Doug was trying to contact her, she didn't want to know. He was dead to her.

It was vibrating again. She couldn't carry on ignoring it. She grabbed her bag with an apologetic smile.

'Excuse me. Too much Diet Coke at lunchtime.' She gave a *what can you do?* shrug.

Martin and Natasha looked at her. It felt like too much information but she didn't want them querying her.

In the corridor, she pulled out her phone.

Tabitha. Six missed calls from her cousin.

34

Georgia felt her heart drop into her boots. There was only one reason her cousin would phone her, after what had happened last time they met. She had Doug to thank for the fact that she and Tab hadn't spoken since. She missed her. They were closer than some sisters.

With a shaking hand, she pressed Tab's number.

'Georgie.' Tab sounded strangled as she answered. 'It's Gum.'

'Is he OK?'

'No . . . ' There was keening despair in her cousin's voice. 'I got here just too late. To the hospital. He's . . . ' She couldn't say the words.

'Oh no. Oh no . . . Oh, Tab.'

Georgia leaned back against the wall in the corridor and shut her eyes. Their great-uncle. Their darling Great Uncle Matthew, who they called Gum. Their rock, their confidant, their inspiration. The person who had always been there for them.

'What happened?'

'He drove off the road in the truck. They think he had a heart attack. They'll have to do a post-mortem.' Tab was choking on her explanation, fumbling over the words. 'I need you, Georgie. Can you get here?'

'Where are you?'

'I'm still at the hospital. In Honisham.'

'OK, darling. I'm on my way. I'm leaving right now. Hang in there. I'll be as quick as I can.'

Georgia turned and headed back to the meeting room. She didn't care about scoring points any more. This was important. This was family. Her cousin needed her, and her cousin meant more to her than anyone in the world, despite everything.

She burst back into the office. She hadn't even had time to process the news. She was propelled by adrenaline; grief hadn't found its way in yet.

'I've got to go.' She grabbed her leather jacket off the sofa she'd been sitting on. 'My great-uncle's been killed in an accident . . . '

As she said the words, the reality hit and her voice cracked. She didn't want to lose it in front of Natasha.

'Great-uncle?' said Martin, in a tone of voice that implied dead great-uncles really weren't worth leaving an important meeting for. Georgia saw Natasha flash him a glance. What was in it? Triumph? As if to say, *See? I told you she wasn't a hundred per cent committed.*

She didn't care. She didn't need to defend her departure. She wasn't going to tell them how Gum was like a grandfather to them, how she and Tabitha had spent nearly every summer at Dragonfly Farm when they were young, how it was a home from home for them. And what a support he had been to Tab when she'd been a troublesome teen with no prospects, and how he and Joy had taken Tab in without a murmur. Just thinking about it made Georgia well up and she was determined to get out of the office — and Martin and Natasha's scrutiny of her — before she broke down.

'We're a very close family,' she said, swinging her backpack onto her shoulder. 'I don't know when I'll be back. Sorry.'

36

'No, no, no — you go. That's fine,' said Martin with the assurance of someone who didn't want to get into trouble with HR.

'Don't worry. I've got your back,' said Natasha.

Ha, thought Georgia, you're more likely to put a knife in it. People like Natasha dreamed of opportunities like this. She'd step up her campaign, winkle her way in further, and Georgia would be lucky if she had a job to come back to.

Right now, she didn't care.

She ran past the open-plan reception with its smoked-glass desks and bare brick walls, down the stairs and out into the backstreet where the production offices were tucked away. The location was one of the reasons she liked working for them: Covent Garden with all its delights was on the doorstep, but they were in their own little enclave, off the beaten tourist track, with a cute Italian café that served the best toasted cheese sandwiches and much-needed Aperol spritzes in enormous glasses.

She raced down the street, working out what she needed to take with her, then deciding not to go home to fetch anything. She was wearing a polka-dot shirt dress with posh trainers and her leather biker jacket: that ensemble would be suitable for most eventualities, and Tab would have clothes she could borrow. Tab was five inches taller and a string bean, but she could breathe in, or go and buy something in Nettleford if she needed it. Time, not clothing, was of the essence. She'd go straight to the train.

At Paddington she called her cousin.

'I'm getting on the next train,' she told her. 'I'll be with you by supper. Are you OK?'

'I'm OK at the moment.' Tab's voice was small. Her fierce, stroppy cousin never sounded small.

'Have you called anyone else? Your dad? My mum?'

It was funny, she thought, how the impact of this crisis would fall upon them, and not the generation above. Not that her parents or Tab's wouldn't *care*, but she and Tab were particularly close to their great-uncle.

'I wondered if you could do it.'

'Of course. But tell me exactly what happened.'

'His truck left the road on the way back from Nettleford this morning. He was going to the bank and to pick up a prescription and that kind of thing. One of the . . . ' Tab trailed off for a moment, as if she was gathering herself. 'One of the Culbones saw him. Said Gum just slewed across his path and straight off the road without stopping.'

'One of the Culbones?'

'Yep.' Tab sounded distasteful. '*Dash*. I mean, for God's sake, who gets called Dash in real life? He came and knocked on the door.'

'Dash?' murmured Georgia. 'Sounds like a typical Culbone name.'

The Culbones lived on the other side of valley, across the river from Dragonfly Farm, but they might as well have lived on the moon for all they had in common. They were other-worldly, one of

38

those gilded English families, like something out of *Brideshead*. They were rarely seen these days, like butterflies on the verge of extinction.

'I know. Ridiculous, right? But he was kind, actually. He gave me a lift to the hospital. And he's taking me home.'

'Good. I don't want you on your own.'

'He was pretty upset by the whole thing.'

'I'm not surprised.'

'Oh, Georgie. I can't believe it.'

Georgia could tell Tab was on the edge. 'Just get yourself home. I'll be with you as soon as I can.'

There were so many more questions Georgia wanted to ask. Was Gum killed immediately? Where was he now? She wasn't sure if Tabitha was up to answering them. Not over the phone, anyway.

'I can't fetch you from the station. The police took away the truck.'

'I'll get a cab. It's fine.'

'I need you.'

'I know, darling.' In that moment, Georgia knew that their rift had been healed. They were both so stubborn, they'd each been waiting for the other to proffer an olive branch.

Gum had told her off, the last time he had come up to town. He always took her out for lunch somewhere glitzy in the West End. He came up to buy socks from Jermyn Street, books from Hatchards and to have his hair cut. They went to Brasserie Zédel — with its pillars and mirrors and retro-glam, it was the perfect contrast to Somerset, and he revelled in it.

39

'She misses you, your cousin,' he told her sternly as the waiter poured a very good burgundy for them to drink with the entrecôte they were sharing. 'She likes to make out she's tough, but she's as soft as butter.'

'I know,' sighed Georgia. 'But she said some awful things to me. And to Doug.'

She cringed at the memory of the evening. They were in the kitchen after a bit too much to drink at the Swan, scoffing cheese and drinking cider brandy. Tab always got tense when she knew Georgia was leaving to go back to London, and Doug had sensed it and gone right for her Achilles heel . . . Things had got very heated very quickly, and Tab had fought back. It was gloves off.

Even though everything Tab said about Doug had turned out to be true, Georgia hadn't quite forgiven her for saying them.

Gum didn't take sides or want details. He did, however, want his two favourite people in the world to be friends again.

'Don't let Doug come between you. That would be a terrible shame.'

Georgia sighed. 'It is a shame. But she went too far. I'm not ready yet. It's going to take a bit of time.'

Gum put his hand over hers and squeezed it. 'Not everyone has a cousin, you know. They are a luxury. To be enjoyed and looked after. Not like siblings, who can be a responsibility and a nuisance.' He smiled, and Georgia looked at his wise old face, handsome once, and knew he was right. Pride, however, was hard to swallow, and it

40

was difficult to undertake a rapprochement from a distance. Her workload was punishing. She couldn't see how she could get down to Dragonfly Farm. And it would be impossible to get Tabitha to London. She hated the city and rarely came up.

'She misses you,' said Gum. 'She would never admit it, but I know she does.'

Now, in her panic, Georgia's mind began to play tricks on her. Gum's death was all her fault. If she'd buried the hatchet with Tab, things would have been different. She could have altered history's course. But she'd been too bloody stubborn, too proud and selfish, to heed her great-uncle's words. And now she would never have the benefit of his wisdom again.

Georgia wiped away a tear as she pushed her ticket into the barrier. Then another tear fell from her other eye. And another. As she stumbled onto the platform, sobbing, she realised that at least now Gum had his wish.

Georgia and Tabitha were going to be reunited.

5

After her phone call to her cousin, Tabitha stood in the middle of the hospital corridor leading to A & E. She should phone her father, Robin — Gum was his uncle, after all — but she couldn't face hearing him trying to be helpful and reassuring and utterly failing. Robin didn't have a practical bone in his body. He would literally have no idea what to do.

'You can't stand here forever,' said Dash kindly. 'Come on. Let me take you home.'

Dead on arrival. Somehow those words only belonged on television, spoken in urgent tones by actors dressed in green with stethoscopes around their necks. Not by normal, ordinary people in Honisham hospital, with their glasses on a chain around their neck and a cold cup of coffee next to their paperwork.

There had been a flurry of information about post-mortems, organ donation, identifying the body. Forms to sign. And now — nothing. All Tabitha could do was go home and process what had happened.

She felt filled with anxiety and strange thoughts. She blamed herself for the accident. If she had driven Gum into Nettleford . . . If she had offered to pick his prescription up for him . . . If she had made him a cup of coffee and delayed his departure . . . Maybe she could have changed the course of events if she'd behaved differently.

She turned and stared at Dash. She'd almost forgotten he was still there. He'd waited for her. Which was thoughtful.

'I could have got a taxi,' she told him.

'I wouldn't hear of it. You need someone with you.'

She realised she was being ungrateful. 'Thank you. I'm sure you've got other things to do.'

'Nothing that can't wait. Come on. There's nothing to be done here.'

Tabitha shivered, suddenly realising that there were people milling past her in both directions and she was clogging up the corridor. She started marching towards the exit. 'You're right. I bloody hate hospitals.'

'No one's keen, are they?'

'I suppose not. I haven't been here since I had an argument with a chainsaw.'

Dash raised his eyebrows. 'Who won?'

'I've got a nice scar on my shin. My fault for using it in shorts.'

Dash winced. 'Ouch.'

Tabitha gave a glimmer of a smile. 'Just a flesh wound.'

'You're tough, then.'

They walked through the automatic doors and out past a trio of smokers.

'No,' said Tabitha eventually. 'Everyone thinks I am, but I'm not. Not at all.'

Her eyes filled and her chin wobbled. She wiped away a tear with the heel of her hand, then looked around the car park.

43

'Where's the car?' she said. 'I can't remember where we parked.'

She frowned with the effort of trying to remember. It had all been a blur, getting to the hospital.

'If you wait here, I'll go and get it for you.'

'Don't be ridiculous. That'll take twice as long.'

Dash looked at her and she realised how rude she was being.

'God, I'm sorry. I'm rude when I'm upset.'

'It's fine.' He pointed towards the far end of the car park. 'We're that way.'

'Have you got the ticket?'

He waved it and dug in his pocket for change. 'Yeah. And I've got change.'

'Can I owe you? I've come out without any cash.'

'Absolutely not. I won't hear of it.'

'We'll see.'

Tabitha headed towards the area of car park Dash had indicated. He followed in her wake, slightly bemused by her demeanour. He'd never met anyone quite so . . . He couldn't think of the word. Abrupt? Defiant? Prickly? Though to be fair, he hadn't met her under ideal conditions. Perhaps she was usually sweetness and light?

In the car, Tabitha stretched her legs out in the front seat. The leather was soft and enveloping, and she leaned her head back on the headrest, shutting her eyes with a sigh. Her fists were balled up, and she was rigid with tension.

'I don't know what I'm going to do without him,' she said as Dash navigated his way out of

44

the unnecessarily complicated one-way system.

'I'm guessing you were close?'

'Yeah. Just a bit. I know everyone thinks it's kind of weird, living with your great-uncle, but he was more than that to me. Much more of an influence than my grandfather — he died a long time ago. Or my dad, come to that.'

'I think that's quite charming. All my great-uncles are barking mad. Or drunk.' The car pulled smoothly out onto the ring road. 'But how did you end up living with him?'

Tabitha didn't look like a country bumpkin or someone who lived with elderly relatives. She had an energy to her; a wild beauty that spoke of adventure and risk.

'Mum and Dad split up when I was twelve. They were crazy in love but brought out the worst in each other. I didn't handle it very well. I blamed Mum, because it was Mum who went off with someone else, so I didn't think she'd tried hard enough. And I hated her boyfriend — on principle, not because he was a bad person.' She managed a laugh.

'I can imagine.'

'So I ended up going to live with Dad when I was fourteen, which was great because he didn't have a clue about bringing up children. Bedtimes or feeding or homework or any rules at all. I fended for myself most of the time.'

'Sounds like a dream come true for a teenager.'

'Of course, that's what I thought. I could do what I liked. My school friends were all green with envy. We lived in West London. He was away a lot. I went out every night. Hung out with the cool kids.'

'Oh.' Dash nodded. He could imagine her dancing in the streets at Notting Hill carnival or queueing up to get into the latest nightclub.

'I thought it was so glamorous. I was a bit of a wild child.'

'You look as if butter wouldn't melt now,' he teased her gently.

She managed a smile.

'Well, it wouldn't. I'm a paragon of virtue. I never do anything I shouldn't.' She turned to him, and her expression was bold, defiant. 'Anyway, I ended up getting thrown out of school. Mum was livid and said I had to go and live with her. I refused. In the end, I ran away to Gum and Joy. They were the only people who didn't judge me. They took me in, made me sign up to retake my A levels at the college in Nettleford. Gum taught me to drive. Joy taught me to cook. And here I still am. Nearly ten years later.' She shut her eyes and scrunched her face up. 'Only now they're both gone and I don't know what to do without them. Which is ridiculous.'

'Hey. No, it's not. It's totally understandable. It sounds like they were your rocks.'

Tabitha nodded but couldn't speak.

'And maybe you were theirs?'

She shrugged. 'I don't know,' she said. 'Now I think I didn't do enough. They looked after me but I should have looked after them. I should have taken Gum into town this morning — '

'Stop it,' said Dash. 'He doesn't sound to me

46

like the sort of man who needed mollycoddling. You're feeling guilty. Grief does that. Don't let it.'

She was surprised by the firmness of his tone. And he was right, of course. Gum had never stood for any fuss. She nodded.

'I suppose I'm trying to make sense of it.'

'You'll drive yourself mad if you try to make sense of death. It never feels right. How can it?'

He spoke as if he'd tried to make sense of it himself, but Tabitha didn't feel she should pry.

'I know he was quite old. But it's not fair. He was as fit as a flea. And sharp as a tack. He put me to shame most days, with what he got done.'

She felt tears well up and breathed them down. They were approaching the supermarkets on the edge of Honisham. Dash slowed down.

'Is there anything you need to pick up from the supermarket? As we're passing? It might be an idea to stock up. Saves you going out again.'

'Good idea. But I can't think what we need.'

'Sit here and I'll whizz round for you. Milk? Bread?'

'Milk, definitely. Not bread — I can make that. Cornflakes. Tomato soup. Digestives. I don't know what else . . . Maybe a chicken?'

'I'll use my common sense.'

'Pink Panther wafers.'

'What?'

'You know. Pink Panther wafers.'

Dash shook his head, bemused.

'Oh my God, you must have had a deprived childhood. Pink wafers, with cream in the middle? In the biscuit section. Actually, hang on.'

47

She undid her belt. 'I'll come with you. I'll just sit here crying otherwise.'

They walked together towards the supermarket entrance and Dash grabbed a small shopping trolley.

'Thank you for all of this, by the way,' said Tabitha. 'I really appreciate it.'

'Isn't that what neighbours are for?'

She took the trolley from him. 'You Culbones haven't been very neighbourly until now.'

'Maybe things will change.'

She looked at him. 'Are you living here, then? Not just visiting?'

Dash nodded. 'I am. As of this month, Rushbrook House belongs to me.'

He walked in through the entrance. Tabitha stared after him in surprise. For years, Rushbrook House had been rented out to a series of tenants who had taken less and less care of it, and now it was almost tumbledown, according to the postman. She presumed Dash must have been gifted the house in some sort of inheritance tax dodge. Classic, she thought disparagingly.

But perhaps she shouldn't judge just yet. He was being extraordinarily kind and helpful. So she followed him in through the door.

She wandered around the supermarket aimlessly. She felt cold and lost under the harsh lights and hoped not to see anyone she knew. Everything seemed slightly heightened; her head felt light but her heart heavy. It was hard to make decisions, but Dash steered her about, urging her to stock up.

'The next few days are going to be chaos. You'll have people in and out. The last thing you'll want is to go out to the shops.'

They piled the trolley with staples, and occasionally Tab remembered something she couldn't live without.

'Fish fingers,' she said at the freezer counter. 'We'll have fish-finger sandwiches tonight, me and Georgia.'

'Who's Georgia?'

'My cousin.' Tabitha sighed. She held up her crossed fingers. 'We're like this, but I haven't seen her since May. We had a bit of a fall-out.'

'Families, eh?'

'I feel as if it was my fault, because everything usually is. I'm not very good at keeping my mouth shut. She was going out with the most awful man and I told her what I thought.' Tab looked a bit shame-faced. 'In front of him.'

'Ah.'

'But he had spent half an hour telling me I was wasting my life.'

'That's rather rude.'

'Yes. And then he buggered off to Hollywood and started shagging his producer. So turns out I was right. But people don't always like it when you're right.'

'No . . . '

Tab looked sharply at Dash.

'Are you laughing at me?' she demanded.

'God, no. I can totally empathise. Families are a nightmare to navigate.' He spoke with true feeling. 'I think we should get you home — get your fish fingers in the freezer.'

He grabbed the trolley and pushed it towards the checkout.

As Tabitha lined up behind him in the queue, she saw a tall figure at the next checkout, dressed in a checked shirt and cords and a dark-green quilted waistcoat. It couldn't be? Or could it? Perhaps it had been mistaken identity? She started to run towards the man, but as he turned to put his items on the conveyor belt, she stopped.

Of course it wasn't him. It was a man with the same build, the same dress code, but a totally different face. It wasn't Gum at all.

'Are you OK?' Dash was next to her, looking concerned.

'I thought . . . ' She pointed at the man. 'I thought it was Gum.'

She felt weak with disappointment. Dash curled an arm round her and she crumpled. He was warm and smelled of sandalwood, and she just wanted to lean against him and fall asleep and wake up to find it had all been a dreadful nightmare. But the *bing-bong* of the supermarket PA system brought her to her senses. She broke away from him and headed back to her trolley.

What was she doing, snuggling up to a Culbone? Gum wasn't quite in his grave yet, but if he was, he'd be spinning in it. Once again, she remembered the letter from the Culbones' solicitor. Gum had thrown it on the fire and not even bothered to reply. Had Dash been behind that?

Driving into the yard at Dragonfly Farm that afternoon was discomfiting. It had always been her place of safety, somewhere that lifted her heart, but now it felt almost hostile, as if it was blaming her for Gum's absence.

'I'll carry your shopping in,' said Dash.

'I can manage,' said Tabitha.

'I'm sure you can,' said Dash. 'But it doesn't mean you have to.'

And, in fact, she did feel weary. The thought of lugging the carriers inside and unloading them suddenly seemed a gargantuan task.

'Thank you.'

Inside, he put all the bags on the floor of the kitchen.

'You've been so kind,' she said. 'But, really, I can manage now.'

'Are you sure?'

Her head was whirling with people she needed to speak to, things she needed to do, and an overwhelming need to lie down. And she thought perhaps she didn't want to be on her own. The kitchen too held a sense of foreboding that was unfamiliar. There was a chill in the air that made it feel like a slightly frosty person keeping her at arm's length.

'Actually,' she said, 'I know it's a massive cliché, but I could kill a cup of tea. I need to go and put the sheets on Georgia's bed before she gets here. There's nothing worse than having to make up a bed when you're exhausted.'

'No,' said Dash, who couldn't actually

remember the last time he'd had to change his own bed linen. 'You go ahead. I'll get the kettle on.'

Tab just about managed a smile. 'Thank you.'

* ★ *

Dash set about the kitchen as best he could, considering he was pretty undomesticated. He filled the kettle again and switched it on, then unpacked the bags, putting things away in the most logical places. Even if he got everything else wrong, the fish fingers definitely belonged in the freezer. There was a sinkful of washing-up, so he tackled it — it was only a few cups and plates and a soup bowl.

He found the teapot, which was big enough to bath a baby in, so he threw in three teabags and filled it with boiling water. As he worked he uncovered more layers in the kitchen that told him about the people who lived here: piles of old paperbacks with faded postcards as bookmarks, envelopes full of seeds marked up in sloping black letters, an encyclopaedia of apples, a beer mug filled with spiky dahlias in a rainbow of colours — pink and orange and purple and yellow — that was so full of joy and life he was reminded of the sharp contrast between this and the sterile environment he'd lived in up until now. There had been no clutter in his apartment because he never did anything there but sleep, take a shower and get changed, and any signs of his presence had been whisked away by a cleaner he had never met. He had a lot to learn, he reflected, as he poured a jarful of murky liquid down the sink. He wasn't sure what it was but it looked as if someone had kept their paintbrushes in it.

Now he had to find a way to slow down, enjoy life, embrace Somerset and its slower pace, instead of wondering exactly which time zone he was in. Although he couldn't let himself slow down too much. He had plans. Ambitious plans. He still couldn't quite believe what he'd taken on. He liked this life so far though. He liked seeing the same faces more than once; passing the same cars when he drove down the narrow lanes. He liked being called by his name when he went into the post office to collect his morning papers.

When he'd asked the woman in the post office what the people at Dragonfly Farm were like, she'd said, 'The Melchiors? He's a dream; she's a bit of a madam,' and made a face. But then from what Dash had seen of Tabitha so far, she didn't seem like the type of girl other women would take to. Far too self-confident, far too attractive without any attempt at trying, far too brusque.

That she adored her great-uncle, though, he didn't doubt. And now he'd never know for himself what Matthew Melchior was like. He'd been working up to introducing himself, in the hope of healing the long-standing rift that seemed to be based on nothing but a century-old legend. It sounded as if the Melchiors had objected to the Culbones' recent offer to buy the farm, too, which was a little odd. It had only been an offer, not a threat. He hadn't disclosed to Tabitha that it had been his idea. It had never occurred to him that the offer would hit such a raw nerve.

★ ★ ★

Tabitha stood in the doorway of the airing cupboard on the landing. Piles and piles of folded sheets and pillowcases surrounded her, flanked by blankets and eiderdowns and towels. There was a smell of lavender and warm bedding. She put a hand out to choose a set for Georgia's bed: heavy white linen, slightly yellow with age, embroidered at the edges. She buried her face in its softness and it soaked up her tears; the tears she hadn't let fall in front of Dash. She wanted nothing more than to crawl into the warmth of the cupboard, wrap herself in one of the quilts and fall asleep until everything was all right again.

She went into the little room where Georgia always slept. The wooden floor was wonky; the walls were painted pale yellow. William Morris Brer Rabbit curtains hung at the window, the indigo nearly faded to grey. She pushed at the window to let in the air — she would have to remember to shut it again in an hour or so or the temperature would drop too far. She made up the bed briskly, snapping the bottom sheet out with a flick of her wrist, smoothing it down and folding sharp hospital corners, finishing with the top sheet and two satin-bound merino blankets. Over the top went a dusty-pink quilt, plump with goose down. She smoothed it all out, then fetched a duster from the airing cupboard to get rid of the worst of the dust from the windowsill and the pine chest of drawers.

People often complained that Tabitha never sat still. That she was always doing. It was true, because doing things stopped you thinking about the things you didn't want to think about. Even now, her mind was considering what else was needed in the room — a bath towel, some fresh flowers, a carafe of water — instead of the ghastliness. She wasn't going to wail and wallow. What was the point of that?

⋆   ⋆   ⋆

Dash was just pouring tobacco-brown tea into a brace of mugs from the clean selection on the draining board when Tabitha came back into the kitchen. He'd even shaken a few of the Pink Panther wafers onto a plate.

'How are you feeling?'

'I'll feel better when Georgia gets here.'

He thrust a mug at her. 'I had a bit of a clear-up.'

She looked at the clean things on the side and turned to him, frowning. Had he overstepped the mark, washing up for her? Was she insulted?

'Where's my mother?'

'What?'

'My sourdough mother.'

He shook his head, not knowing what she meant. She grabbed the empty jar that was upside down on the draining board.

'It was in here.'

He looked guilty. 'Oh.'

'Where's it gone?'

'It . . . um. I threw it away. Down the sink. If you mean the grey liquid.'

Tabitha stared at him in disbelief. 'Tell me you're joking.'

'No. It smelt awful.'

She took in a deep, trembling breath, then fixed him with a look that made him quail.

'That sourdough mother is more than five years old. It came from my great-aunt. It was the one thing I had to remember her by. I make bread from it *every day*.' Her jaw was clenched as she spat the words out.

'Oh God. I had no idea. I was trying to help.'

'You *idiot!*'

'Honestly. It just looked like — '

'Everybody knows what a sourdough starter looks like.'

'Well, everyone except me.' He'd heard of sourdough, of course he had. It was on every menu of every place he ever ate breakfast, smothered in avocado. But he hadn't a clue how it was made, or what made it sour. 'Look, I'm sorry. I really am. Can I get you another one?'

'You don't get it, do you?'

'Not exactly.'

'You'd better just go.' Tabitha could feel fury and grief and despair welling up inside her chest. She didn't want him to see her at her worst. Her uncontrolled worst. 'Thank you for everything and you've been marvellous, but just go.'

Her eyes were shut and she spoke through gritted teeth, the garbled words fighting their way out.

'Are you sure you'll be OK?'

She nodded. 'Georgia will be here soon. I'll be fine. Please. I want to be on my own.'

She prayed he wouldn't try to take control and insist on making amends. She didn't have the strength to battle against him. She heard the click of his heels on the flagstone floor, heard the door creak as it opened and then shut behind him. Then the distant sound of the front door closing and the throaty rumble of his car starting up in the yard.

Only when she heard the car accelerate down the drive did she open her eyes again to find the kitchen empty.

She stumbled across the room and into the wing-backed armchair that sat by the fireplace. She sank into it and drew her knees up to her chest, curling herself into as small a ball as possible. She couldn't count all the emotions she was feeling. Despair and regret and fear and impatience and *fury* — how could Dash be such an imbecile? She curled herself even tighter in the hopes of squeezing all the feelings out. There just wasn't room for them all inside her.

She stayed there, not daring to unfold, as the clock on the wall ticked steadily: five minutes, ten minutes. She couldn't bear to open her eyes and find that Gum wasn't there, poking a long-handled teaspoon into the depths of the teapot, whistling 'Autumn Leaves' gently under his breath. She just couldn't. That was what he did every day at this time, but would never do again.

She knew what had happened. It had been two years now since Joy had gone, and every day she had seen him struggle. To an outsider, he was, on the whole, the trenchant Matthew Melchior, bearing his cross but going about his everyday life with that peculiarly English stoicism that comes with bereavement. Being a widower was no excuse for special treatment or shirking one's duty. He might be retired, but he still took part in local life. Normal service resumed no less than a month after Joy was buried: committee meetings, lunches, matches (he still played tennis twice a week and was a demon on the bowling green) — all appointments and invitations were honoured without complaint.

But it was Tabitha who knew the truth about how heavily Joy's absence weighed upon him. She who broke his reverie first thing in the morning when she found him staring out of the window in his dressing gown, the kettle whistling but unheard. She who saw him start awake when he fell asleep in front of the evening news, and the look in his eye when he saw Joy's vacant chair and remembered. She who heard the heaviness of his tread as he went up the staircase to bed, his footsteps slow as if he was dreading the emptiness he knew awaited him.

In the end, that heaviness must have taken its toll. Gum hadn't died of a heart attack. His heart had simply collapsed, unable to bear the weight

58

any longer, its walls crumbling in.

Gum had, decided Tabitha, died of a broken heart.

6

The kindly girl who ran Squirrel Nutkin's had brought Plum out to Gabriel.

'We've had a brilliant morning, haven't we, Plum? We did French, then dance. Sausage and mash for lunch.'

Gabriel laughed. He had thought it was crazy for a three-year-old to learn French, but she seemed to remember it, pointing at things at home and telling him and Lola what they were: *la porte, la pomme.*

He'd picked her up and held her to him. She was wearing a pink needlecord pinafore dress with a broderie anglaise blouse underneath and tiny Dr Martens. He pushed up her sleeve to check her little wrists for telltale signs of redness, but they were perfectly smooth and unscathed.

'Did you dance well, sweetheart?' he asked to distract her, and she nodded.

He was ever-vigilant for signs of the eczema that had ravaged her when she was tiny, before they had discovered her allergies. He had berated himself for not realising sooner and for letting the patches go raw before they had sought out the best dermatologist they could find. He found her bravery agonising; the way her little mouth would turn down and her chin wobble and her eyes brim with tears that she was determined not to let fall.

She was three years old and the bravest person he'd ever met.

'Hey, Plumble,' he said, and blew a gentle raspberry into her neck. She squirmed in delight. He fastened her helmet on and put on her high-vis jacket even though they had less than half a mile to go. He would never take risks with Plum.

Now back at home, they were making her tea together. He let her put her little hand on top of his while he chopped up an onion for a fresh tomato sauce, then got her to tear up strips of basil to sprinkle on afterwards. There'd be no cheese, as she was dairy-free. He made everything from scratch for her, to be sure of no cross-contamination.

The kitchen was the only place Gabriel exerted his influence. Lola had bought the flat eight years before, and it was decorated in her eclectic, glamorous, magpie style — lots of original artwork, bright splashes of colour and lush plants mixed in with some cool vintage pieces, including a white leather sofa from the seventies that was big enough to set sail on the open seas with them all on board. But he had taken over in the kitchen. Until he moved in she had lived off ridiculously priced ready-made deli food, and he loved to cook for them.

When they met, he'd been managing a trio of fish eateries that sat side by side in East London. Hook was a formal restaurant, Line was a buzzy bar with small plates, and Sinker was an upmarket chip shop. His salary had been healthy; his working hours not. Lola and her friends were regulars at Line: the small portions and the delicious cocktails were perfect for their needs. Gabriel always joked about how she had reeled him in — fish puns were inexhaustible, it seemed.

Now, because of her generosity, he was able to realise the ambition he'd been harbouring ever since he'd been on a work visit to a knife maker in the Forest of Dean and fallen in love with the process. The fierce heat of the fire, the roaring noise, the beauty and sharpness of the blade at the end of it all.

Six months after Plum was born, Lola had gone back to work and he had quit Hook, Line and Sinker, because they couldn't both work unsociable hours. He'd set up his workshop at Rockham Arches, and was on hand to look after Plum whenever Lola was away on a shoot. It worked well, except now he was beginning to realise that the business was close to costing them money rather than making it.

While Plum munched her way through her pasta, he looked at the letter from the landlord. He really couldn't afford a hike in overheads. He sighed, looking across at the blown-up black-and-white photo hanging over the table. In it, a life-size Lola was standing in the surf wearing nothing but a man's dinner jacket, bikini bottoms and an electric smile.

She was his star and he would do anything for her.

Next to the canvas hung the calendar Plum had brought home from nursery last Christmas. September bore a drawing of Lola in bright yellow crayon. Underneath, the days of the week were marked up with appointments, work commitments, Plum's play-dates. And there was a big red ring around today.

A big red O. For Ovulate. For Optimum. Tonight was the perfect night for them to get it on. No pressure there then. It was a bit hit and miss anyway, as Lola could be so irregular, probably because of her lifestyle. But Lola liked a plan and there the big red O was.

Six months with nothing happening hadn't seemed out of the ordinary. At nine, things started to get a little tense. Now, as they were heading for a year with no luck, they were both starting to worry. And Gabriel had begun to dread O day. Usually he would welcome any excuse to make love to Lola, but this was no longer making love. It was *trying*. *Trying* for a baby. And it was trying. Because they were failing.

He folded up the landlord's letter and put it away, frustrated. He wanted to be able to provide for her, so she could take the pressure off herself, relax enough to get pregnant and maybe have time to enjoy the next baby. He knew how much it upset her when she had to go away or missed key moments with Plum. He wanted to give her the chance to be a proper mum this time around, if that's what she wanted. He wanted to give her the option at least.

'*Clangers* or *Magic Roundabout*?' he asked Plum. They had a selection of vintage children's videos and an old VHS player. Plum answered with the noise of the Soup Dragon, falling about laughing. He hadn't realised he could love her more as he plopped her into the middle of a giant silver beanbag and put on the telly while he had a shower, mulling over his predicament.

He saw he'd missed a call from Lola when he came back into the bedroom. She was being press-ganged into going out for dinner with the crew. She sounded apologetic, but he didn't mind. It was part of the job, networking and socialising. He texted her back to say no problem.

He didn't mention the ring on the calendar. Neither of them did.

7

The station platform at Nettleford was so short you had to make sure you were in the right carriage, otherwise you'd end up on the track. Georgia knew exactly where to get off so she was by the red-brick ticket office. Hanging baskets swung in the evening breeze as she headed for the exit. She'd phoned ahead for a taxi because she knew there was unlikely to be one at the rank, and if there was she might have been beaten to it. She fell into the back seat. Only ten minutes' drive and she would be there.

'Rushbrook, is it?' the driver asked, pulling onto the main road that led out of Nettleford.

'Yes. Thanks,' replied Georgia. Usually she would chat away to the taxi driver, quizzing him about local gossip, but she didn't want to speak in case he asked her questions she didn't want to answer.

The journey had been a nightmare. The carriage had been crowded and she'd had to call her mother and tell her about Gum. She'd tried to be discreet but she'd started crying as soon as she heard her mum's voice. The other passengers had been kind, and one had gone to get her a cup of tea.

Nicola wanted to drive down from Scotland straight away, but Georgia told her not to worry.

'I'm nearly at Nettleford now. Can you ring Uncle Robin and tell him, though? I don't think

Tab has yet. You know what he's like.'

Nicola sighed. 'Yes.' Her brother, Robin, Tabitha's father, was a bit of a liability. A lovable loose cannon. 'Absolutely no use in a crisis.'

Not like Georgia's dad, Chris, who came on the line after Nicola and was so kindly and reassuring that Georgia started crying again.

As she hung up, Georgia thought how lucky she was with her mum and dad compared to Tabitha. For a moment she wished they were heading down from Scotland, but there wasn't much point just yet. Much better for them to come down for the funeral.

The taxi made its way through the town. *Blink and you miss it,* people often said of Nettleford, but it had everything in it that you needed for everyday life: a market and a bank and the usual smattering of independents (butcher, baker, florist) as well as a funeral director and a financial advisor. Two pubs, a tea room, a fish and chip shop and an Indian takeaway that, confusingly, also served Chinese and Thai, provided sustenance, as well as the Glorious Artichoke, an adventurous new restaurant. It was much the same as many other small market towns, but it was comforting because the names over the doors and the faces behind them by and large stayed the same over the years.

Georgia peered out of the window to see her own family name — Melchior and Sons — still over the solicitors' window. Both Gum and his brother Peter (Nicola and Robin's father, and her own grandfather) had followed in their father's footsteps and studied law at Cambridge,

66

then joined the family practice. At one time the three of them would have overseen nearly every will written in Nettleford, conveyanced every house sale and steered a path through every divorce as it became more common-place in the latter half of the twentieth century. Peter had gone on to open his own practice 'up country', but Gum had never had any inclination to leave.

Georgia had once flirted with doing law so as to carry on the family tradition, but her heart wasn't in it. She loved fictional worlds, where your imagination could take you anywhere, not rules and regulations and small print. Anyway, the practice had now been sold, and had lost its family connection and personal touch. Gum had stayed on for a while as a consultant but when it had become a burden rather than a distraction he had let it all go, including the freehold of the handsome building his father had bought.

'It is important to learn to let go in life,' he had said. 'Not just of things. But of people. And ideas. And what you think defines you, when it doesn't any more.'

Remembering those words now, Georgia reflected that it was easier said than done, sometimes, to let go. She tried not to wonder what Doug was doing. Lengths in his pool; a wheatgrass shot. Or his producer . . .

As ever, the thought made her feel both sick and angry. Now wasn't the time to think about Doug, though. The thought of poor Gum overshadowed Doug's misdemeanours, and she felt a lump in her throat. She had to keep herself calm, for Tabitha.

Tab would be distraught about her great-uncle. For all her upfront, feisty gung-ho-ness, Tab was vulnerable. She didn't really have a clue about how to handle her emotions, because she never read books or watched television, so when things happened to her, they took her by surprise. She had been beside herself when their great-aunt Joy had died two years ago, even though everyone agreed that it would have been cruel for her to have lasted much longer.

Joy had certainly been more of a mother to Tabitha than her own mother, Alison. Joy had rubbed off Tabitha's rough edges when she came to live at Dragonfly Farm, taming her by setting her to work in the house and garden. In less than two years, Tabitha could coax an egg from an egg-bound chicken, build a bonfire, prune an apple tree, dig over a vegetable patch. And she learned to make cider: come late autumn, the barn was a hive of industry as she and Joy made gallons of the golden nectar renowned locally for its sweet, heady strength: liquid sunshine, someone had called it. It was ready to drink in June; by the end of August, they had always sold out.

When Georgia came to stay after her A levels had finished, she found Tab in dungarees and wellies, a far cry from the high-fashion kit she'd sported in London.

'I'm so happy here,' said Tabitha. 'I never want to leave.'

And so far, she hadn't. After Joy died, friends and neighbours said that at least Gum had Tab to look after him, but Georgia knew it was the other way round, that Gum was Tab's rock. That although Tab took control of all the practical things that needed doing at Dragonfly Farm, Gum was there to catch her when she fell. Georgia knew the dynamics because she'd come down as often as she could, until —

Well. Until.

Eventually the taxi left the town, and the buildings on the outskirts dwindled to nothing, sliding between fields of grazing sheep, stone walls alternating with hedging, the rolling Chadwick hills looking down benevolently to the east. Georgia felt a sense of calm descend upon her, the tension of the city leaving her shoulders. Everything here was just as it always was and should be. Nothing ever changed, not a postbox or a road sign or a tree.

Soon they turned off the main road onto a narrow lane that wound its way past a sprinkling of grey stone houses that made up the hamlet of Rushbrook. As they passed a tiny church, Georgia couldn't look in the churchyard. She couldn't bear to think of Gum's name being added to the white marble stone with the black writing they had erected for Joy. There would be fresh flowers in the vase, she knew without looking. He brought them every week without fail.

'It's just on the left, if you start slowing down now,' she instructed the taxi driver.

It was easy to miss the entrance. There was the briefest of gaps in the hedgerow, no gateposts, and no sign either. Visitors to Dragonfly Farm would be told to look out for the milestone then

69

count five telegraph poles and turn left just after the bent hawthorn tree. If they hadn't been given instructions, then they probably weren't welcome.

'Here.'

The driver turned off and slowed down over the cattle grid onto the track.

'Lovely spot, isn't it?' he ventured.

'It is,' agreed Georgia.

'What sort of a farm is it, then?'

'Well, it's not a proper farm, really. I mean, no cows or sheep or anything. Just apple orchards. We make a bit of cider.'

'Ah!' said the driver, the penny dropping. He tapped his head and pointed at her, as if making the connection. 'Your name's Melchior.'

'Melchior-Hawkins,' Georgia corrected him. It was a mouthful, but she liked to acknowledge both her parents in her surname.

He nodded in approval. 'Melchior Cider. I've had a few drops of that in my time. Good stuff.'

He chuckled to himself, obviously remembering drunken misdemeanours. Most people around Rushbrook and Nettleford had got up to no good under the influence of Melchior Cider at some time in their life.

For the first fifty yards the trees were in a tangle overhead, the setting sun dappling through, then the drive curved round to the west and swept up through the orchards, lush with the emerald-green grass of late summer. They were planted out with serried ranks of apple trees, their gnarled boughs laden with fruit in varying stages of red and pink and orange — more

70

varieties of apple than Georgia could remember. Kingston Black, Sweet Alford, Crimson King, Brown Snout, Hangdown, Foxwhelp — she loved the poetry of their names, the images they conjured, the eccentric Englishness. Some were tart, some sweet, some both: the apples had grown here for over a century, the branches that bore them thick with green-grey lichen.

And there, at the top of the hill, looking down on the bounty, its silhouette against the blushing evening sky, its mossy tiles undulating in a sagging roofline guaranteed to strike doom and gloom into the heart of any structural surveyor, was Dragonfly Farm.

They pulled up in the cobbled yard. The farmhouse was low and wide, in pale-red brick with white painted windows and a canopy porch to the front door. Adjoining it were the outbuildings that had been added over the past two centuries: the cider house, the big barn and a mishmash of stables and workshops and sheds, some open-fronted, some topped with wriggly tin. By today's standards of magazine perfection, it was scruffy and dilapidated, with priority given to the useful rather than decorative, but there was a lived-in feel to it that made it welcoming; a harking back to the day when living off the land was a necessity, not a lifestyle choice made by disillusioned city dwellers who proceeded to Marie Antoinette everything up.

'Nice,' said the driver. 'Is this home, then?'

'Not exactly,' said Georgia.

But it was. Dragonfly Farm was more like home than anywhere else in the world. Sunshine and haystacks; sparkling frost on the hawthorn and crackling logs; big mugs of dark-brown tea, bowls of chunky home-made soup, clotted cream on scones: images of days gone by flashed through her mind.

She opened the taxi door and breathed in the smell of evening grass, ripening apples, sun on brick. And best of all the pungent scent of woodsmoke, cutting through the chill air.

Suddenly something large with a wide wingspan swooped right over her head.

'Zorro!' she cried. The barn owl who roosted in the barn. Gum had built a nesting box for him and his partner, and he had climbed high into the rafters to put it up while everyone shut their eyes and prayed he didn't fall off. Zorro didn't stop for pleasantries, just headed for his perch. The pair came and went, sometimes disappearing for months at a time, but the fact Zorro was here now showed that he knew they needed his reassuring presence.

No sooner had she climbed out than the front door burst open and Tabitha came flying through it, followed by Poe. Georgia thrust a twenty-pound note at the driver and told him to keep the change, then turned to embrace her cousin.

She held Tabitha as tight as she could. They didn't say anything. There were no words. They had lost their lodestar. Their Gum. The man who had taught them so many things: how to set a mousetrap, change a tyre, tie a proper knot, open a bottle of champagne. And, not least, how to be kind and how to love someone. His devotion to his wife, Joy, had been total, and it had been reciprocated. There had never been a happier couple, and now they were both gone.

The taxi drove away as the sun slipped down behind the trees and the cold grey of night stole its way into the farmyard, creeping round them, Zorro staring down at the two cousins, unblinking, as Poe gazed up, his tail thumping.

8

At eight o'clock, Gabriel put Plum into the bed he had built for her. It was like a mini Swiss chalet, with a roof and windows and shelves to put her toys and books on. A snug little den for her to hide in, but big enough for one of them to get in with her, to read to her or to comfort her if she had a nightmare or if her skin got bad. It was painted red and white, and it was piled high with pillows and cushions and duvets filled with the softest hypo-allergenic filling.

They read *Each Peach Pear Plum*, because Plum thought it had been written for her.

He kissed his daughter and pulled the duvet up around her then went into his own bedroom. He'd watch a bit of telly and have a beer, then get an early night. His work was physically demanding. It would be good to wake up refreshed.

When Lola came in just before midnight, Gabriel did something he had never done before. He pretended to be asleep. He felt her slide into the bed next to him, smelling of toothpaste and the lingering traces of Alizarin. She was naked, he knew, because she never wore anything in bed, but he could feel her hesitate, sense her anxiety, sense her visualising that ring on the calendar just as he was. They both knew what they should be doing.

But he didn't think he could do it. He was so

tense, so worried, that the very last thing he wanted was the pressure of *trying*. He genuinely didn't think he'd be up to the job.

He was just remonstrating with himself, telling himself he was being selfish and unfair to miss the golden window of opportunity, literally girding his loins, when he felt her sink into her pillows with a sigh. And he recognised it as a sigh of relief not disappointment.

She needed the respite as much as he did. It was so difficult, this scheduling, this waiting, this hoping. It was crushing her spark; the spark that had drawn him to her. She had an infectious energy that made you think you could do anything you wanted. Like taking the Eurostar to Paris on a whim and going to see your favourite band in a sweaty underground nightclub, then coming out at two o'clock in the morning, hand in hand, and realising you had nowhere to sleep. That had been their first proper date.

'Haven't you seen *Before Sunset*?' Lola had asked, not turning a hair.

Gabriel shook his head.

'Julie Delpy and Ethan Hawke?'

'No.'

'That is a serious character flaw.'

He drew her close and tucked her under his arm, to keep both of them warm. 'Tell me what happens.'

'They stay up all night in Paris.'

'And?'

She looked at him and he looked at her. 'You'll have to watch it.' Then her face clouded over. 'No, wait. It's Vienna they stay up all night.

That's *Before Sunrise*. In Paris they only have an afternoon. *Before Sunset*. I definitely need to see it again.'

'We can do that. When we're home.' He imagined them curled up with a bottle of heavy red wine with the curtains closed against the elements and the lights dimmed as low as they could go. He laughed at himself. He was a hopeless romantic. 'But what do we do now?'

'There must be a bar or a café or a club. This is Paris.' She threw out her arms. 'Come on!'

It was starting to rain. He looked at the drops sliding over her china-white skin, her black eyeliner smudging, her lipstick long gone, and thought he had never seen someone so beautiful.

They roamed the streets all night, seeing the sights in the shadowy half-light, for the street lamps didn't stay on. And when they caught the early-morning train, she slept all the way back to London with her head on his shoulder while he sat in silent awe.

Next to him now, her breathing had deepened. She was fast asleep. He reached over and pulled the curtain back to let the moonlight shine in through the window, turning her pale skin to silver. He brushed away a lock of dark hair that had fallen over her eyes.

He feared that spark inside her was starting to fade, and he couldn't bear it. He would do whatever he could to stop it going out.

PART TWO

9

Gabriel loved Saturday mornings. The slow start, the lack of pressure to get out of the door or remember Plum's tiny ballet slippers for her dance class or cycle through the rain that was getting more frequent now autumn was here. He always got up first and made everyone a drink: strong Turkish coffee for him, skinny chai latte for Lola and a raspberry smoothie for Plum.

He put the coffee pot on the stove to brew then nipped downstairs to the postbox in the hall. That particular morning there were no parking fines or speeding tickets or reminders for a dental check-up. There was just one letter for him on thick cream watermarked paper, with an engraved heading and a bold signature in black ink. He read it, his curiosity growing with every word.

He was summoned to a meeting the next Wednesday by a Mr Thomas Bickleigh to discuss the contents of the will of Mr Matthew Melchior, recently deceased.

Was this the equivalent of those spam emails you got from people declaring they had millions to put in your bank account if you could just part with the details? Was it an elaborate scam?

He flipped open his MacBook on the kitchen counter and did a quick search for Melchior and Sons. The company did exist, and the address at the top of the letter — Market Square,

Nettleford, Somerset — matched their website details. And there was a photograph of Thomas Bickleigh, one of the partners: fifty-something, round-faced, genial, seemingly trustworthy. But it was easy to put up a fake website, so he trawled through some recommendation websites to double-check. Melchior and Sons were reliable and trustworthy, according to online feedback, and they were there in black and white on the Law Society website. They were there on Google maps too, in the corner of the market square. He finished by phoning the number at the top of the letter — the dialling code matched the code for Nettleford, and the voicemail message was delivered by a girl with a warm Somerset accent: *Hello, this is Melchior and Sons. I'm afraid our offices are closed right now . . .*

It seemed genuine enough. But he was no less puzzled.

Perhaps, he thought, Mr Bickleigh had an admiring client who wanted to commission a knife? His knives were often given as presents for landmark birthdays or anniversaries, and he liked to think they were special enough to be considered heirlooms. But surely he would just telephone or email? Why did Gabriel need to go down to Somerset to discover the contents of Matthew Melchior's will?

He googled Matthew Melchior too, but there wasn't much. He seemed to be on the committee of the Nettleford Bowling Club, if it was the same person. He had no Facebook or Twitter or Linkdln, but people of a certain age often didn't have an internet presence if they hadn't embraced social media.

He folded up the letter and decided not to reveal its contents to Lola until he knew more. She didn't need anything to worry about at the moment. If it turned out to be something insignificant, she would be none the wiser. And if it was something big, he could think about how to present it to her.

He was just tucking the letter into his messenger bag, next to the bloody letter from the landlord which he'd been ignoring for more than a fortnight — it was turning into a bag full of secrets — when Lola came in.

'Hi,' he said, feeling guilty, then stood up as he realised she was tearful. 'Hey. What's up?'

He was halfway towards her when he suspected what the problem was.

'Oh, you can guess,' she said, her voice thick with unshed tears.

Not pregnant. Of course. He should have remembered when he got up. She bought the most expensive kit — the one you could use before your period was even due — but it hardly seemed two minutes since the last ring on the calendar.

'Oh, babe.' He took her in his arms.

'I don't know why I hope,' she said, sniffling into his chest. They were both mindful not to show their emotion too much as they could hear Plum in the bathroom — she'd be running in any minute, with her sunny beam and the cuddly ostrich she dragged around by one foot.

'Don't be daft. It's still early days.' Except,

81

almost a year in, it didn't feel like early days any more — but what else could he say?

'I'm worried that the more I worry the less chance I have. But I can't stop worrying.'

'I know . . . ' he soothed her. She did worry, much more than she had when he met her. Sometimes she would sit up in the night with a gasp, panicking about something she had forgotten or, more often, thought she had forgotten. It was motherhood that had changed her, which was understandable, for suddenly you were responsible for a small being and life was much more complicated. Plum's eczema had added to the unfamiliar pressure, but thankfully they had it under control. They should be enjoying life more, but now Lola was fixating on her fertility.

No, that wasn't fair — he understood her frustration, not least because he wondered where the problem actually lay — with her or him or both of them — or if there wasn't a problem at all.

'We weren't really on it, last month, to be fair,' he told her, remembering his feigned sleep and regretting it now. 'We obviously need to be more rigorous.'

She managed to smile at his choice of words. 'Yes,' she said, extricating herself from him and sliding into a high stool at the counter. 'Maybe we need to spend a week in bed.'

He pushed her chai latte across to her and she smiled her thanks, then sighed and put her head in her hands.

'Mummy, why are you sad?' They both turned

to see Plum looking at her mother, her little face anxious. She trotted over to Lola and patted her knee. 'Don't be sad.'

'Darling, I could never be sad with you in my life.' Lola bent down and scooped up her daughter. 'What shall we do today?'

'Squirrels,' said Plum, very definite. 'I should like to see some squirrels.'

The way she said the word twisted Gabriel's heart up into a knot of love. *Thkwiwelth*.

'We can do squirrels, no problem,' he said. 'We'll go to the park and then how about going to the Breakfast Institute for pancakes?'

'Pancakes!' Plum bunched up her fists and punched the air.

The Breakfast Institute was a ritual for them and their friends most weekends. Whoever was around would wander down there at about midday for piles of pancakes with bacon and maple syrup, and the first to arrive would commandeer the biggest table. They would all read the papers, the hard-core ones sipping on a Mimosa or a Bloody Mary, everyone else indulging in the excellent coffee or massive range of teas. They would mull over the events of the week, swap notes, make plans to watch the football or organise a ski trip. Those who had kids brought them along knowing that no one minded if their offspring were less than well-behaved.

'Is that OK?' He put a hand on Lola's shoulder, worrying for a moment that she might not want to see other people.

'That would be perfect,' she said, rising to the

83

occasion. 'Come on, Plum. Let's go and get dressed.'

Ten minutes later, they were waiting for him by the door. Plum was dressed in a Fair Isle cardigan, soft denim culottes, striped tights and red wellies. Lola was in layers of butterscotch cashmere and skinny leather leggings. He felt a burst of pride.

'I've got to pop down to Somerset next Wednesday for a meeting,' he mentioned casually as he looked for the keys. 'A possible new customer.'

'That's OK. I've got nothing booked in,' said Lola. 'I'll block it out and tell the agency.'

Gabriel pulled on his parka. He'd decided he was going to have a chat to a couple of his friends this morning. Josh, and maybe Carter. See if they knew of anyone looking for a restaurant manager. He'd rather use word of mouth to start with if he was going to give up his knife making. It was often a case of better the devil you know. He'd start putting feelers out.

It was a shame, he thought, but it wasn't the end of the world. He was lucky to have a career to fall back on — he'd been good at his job and there was no reason to think he wouldn't find another position. He had Lola and Plum, and yes, things were a bit tricky at the moment, but he was going to sort everything.

'Come on, then,' he said to his girls. 'Thkwiwelth and pancakes.'

'Thkwiwelth, daddy,' Plum corrected him, and Lola doubled up laughing and he thought he might die of love.

10

Chris put the cool bag in the boot of the car, next to the suitcase. Nicola had protested they could get food en route, but he didn't see the point of paying out for an egg sandwich when it only took ten minutes to rustle them up yourself. It wasn't that he was tight, just logical. He had the exacting mind of a scientist.

'Making our own egg sandwiches probably costs about 20p,' he said, standing in front of the cooker waiting for the water to boil, poised with a spoon in his right hand ready to drop the eggs in. He'd collected them from their own bantams first thing. Eight slices of bread lay ready-buttered on the breadboard. 'They're £3.50 each at the services.'

Nicola felt too frazzled to think about the price or provenance of their egg sandwiches. She stood in her bedroom, wondering if she had packed the right things, or enough things, to wear. She had a navy dress and boots for the funeral; jeans and sweaters otherwise. Apart from her funeral outfit, she wouldn't need anything smart. The Melchiors didn't really do smart. Georgia probably would, of course, but she was the dressiest of all of them. She felt a flicker of pleasure at the thought of seeing her daughter — it was the one disadvantage of living where they did, that they didn't see her often enough.

It would take them the best part of the day to

get to Dragonfly Farm. She had suggested staying overnight somewhere, but Chris had insisted he was happy to drive as long as she could post the occasional Twiglet or Twix into his mouth. He had packed a supply of those too, along with a thermos of tea, a thermos of coffee and two bottles of their own fresh spring water.

He was, she thought, not for the first time, both indefatigable and endlessly obliging. And she knew Georgia would be longing for his arrival more than her own. Not that Georgia didn't love her mum, but Nicola knew herself to be a slightly distant and detached sort of a person. It wasn't that she didn't care, she just wasn't very physical. She wasn't cuddly, like Chris, with his unruly mop and his untucked shirts and his insistence on sandals whatever the weather, even with long corduroy trousers and despite the fact everybody groaned when he trotted out in them.

Nicola had insisted on proper shoes for the funeral. She didn't often interfere with Chris and his ways, but there were limits, and sandals to a funeral was one. So he had dutifully packed his interview shoes, which as he hadn't had an interview since 1994 really wasn't saying a lot, but she knew she would be pushing her luck asking him to get a new pair. Obliging with streaks of obduracy: that was a better description of him. She smiled.

It was the brightest of autumn days, and she looked out of the window with regret across to the sparkling freshness of the loch. There was no time for her daily dip before spending the day in

86

the car. She still marvelled at how she had adapted to life here. She'd been a city girl, a North London convert, reliant on the tube and the buses and the convenience of a nearby Waitrose and an art-house cinema and a dizzying choice of affordable ethnic restaurants. Now she had none of that on the doorstep and she had never been happier. Who wanted Moroccan or Mongolian when you had eagles swooping overhead?

It was Chris who'd spotted the plot, in one of those 'What would £100k buy you?' features in the Sunday paper. A hundred grand wouldn't get them a parking space in their little bit of Islington, but in the outer reaches of the Scottish Highlands it would, apparently, get them a generous plot overlooking a loch with planning permission for a sustainable eco-house.

He became obsessed overnight. He sent off for the details, scrutinised the plans, researched building materials, produced a spreadsheet and crunched a lot of numbers.

Then he sat Nicola down and presented her with a beautiful brochure that he had designed, showing the intricate details of their dream house and the lifestyle they could lead.

'This is not me strong-arming you,' he assured her. 'I have no interest in doing this if it's not your dream too. But you could give up the nine-to-five and just do consultancy. We could be eighty per cent self-sufficient. We could do whatever we liked. Travel when we want.'

Nicola had leafed through the brochure in awe. The house he proposed was stunning, made of stone and wood and glass, using sheep's wool and car tyres for insulation. She couldn't pretend that her nerves were not at screaming point with her job, rehabilitating young offenders. Recent cuts had been savage and heart-breaking. She cried at night for the angry, disaffected youths she dealt with and their lack of a future, and the effect their frustration had on their lives and the people closest to them. She knew if she wanted to give up work she could, for Chris's work running a research team for an international drug company had been exceptionally lucrative. Now he had stepped back and was consulting — still lucrative — and played the stock market, with apparent success.

Nicola would have found it annoying in anyone else, but his childlike delight in his profits amused her. She hadn't given up work, of course, because she did it for the satisfaction of occasionally setting someone back on the right path, and what else would she do? She certainly wasn't a lady who lunched.

But perhaps it was time for a change? This was pretty drastic, although Chris's plan was to extend the mortgage on the house in Manila Road and rent it out to cover the cost of the build. Nicola was surprised at how well the figures stacked up. The scruffy little house in an unfashionable part of London they'd bought nearly thirty years ago was now one of the most sought-after addresses. If they wanted to buy it now, they wouldn't have a hope.

'We can make the house work for us,' said Chris. 'We can use all our equity to build a new life, but without burning our bridges. If we hate it up there we can sell the house when we've finished it and move back.'

When he'd put it like that it was a no-brainer. And now they'd been here nearly three years, and she was doing consultancy too, with a trip to London once or twice a month to keep up with old friends and see Georgia. Chris was a genius. A visionary.

She felt a surge of love as she heard him call up the stairs — love for his egg sandwich making and his sandals and his pioneering spirit and his scientific analysis of how to move forward in life. And with that surge of love came a frisson of fear.

She always felt unease when she went back to Dragonfly Farm. How could you love a place so much yet live in fear of what lay in the shadows? Her throat tightened. She hadn't seen enough of Gum since they had moved to Scotland, she knew that, and the guilt sat on her shoulder, whispering in her ear, reminding her of her shortcomings.

She tried to shrug off the self-loathing. Gum had understood, of course he had, and he'd been to visit, twice. And she had helped him with all the awful paperwork when Joy was ill — the minefield of what care she was entitled to, and what allowances, and what equipment. It was enough to drive any normal person mad, let alone someone living with the agony of someone they loved suffering. Gum had insisted that he wanted to look after Joy himself and he didn't care about the money. Nicola had lectured him.

He *couldn't* do it all, and if you were looking after someone who was terminally ill, whose kidneys were careering towards failure, you had to look after yourself first and that meant rest; that meant respite. And if they were entitled to funding, they should have it.

'Chop-chop!' Chris popped his head round the bedroom door. 'I thought we were leaving at eight?'

'We are. Sorry. I was away with the fairies.' Nicola picked up her scarf and looped it round her neck, then grabbed her glasses and her handbag.

Chris scooped her into his arms and kissed her on the ear. She rested her head on his shoulder for a moment.

'I know it's horrid,' he said. 'Everyone hates funerals.'

'Just don't say *he had a good innings*,' Nicola replied. 'I never understand why people say that.'

She was grateful for his comfort. He did, after all, know the root cause of her fears and guilt. Although she hadn't shared with him the other reason her unrest felt so tumultuous; why her nerves were jangling. Why she had barely slept the night before.

She followed Chris out of the bedroom, down the open-tread staircase that led into the expansive living area with its floor-to-ceiling glass, slate floor and Swedish wood-burning stove. If you'd asked her four years ago if she could have lived in a place as minimalistic as this, she would have said absolutely not. She still couldn't believe how much stuff they had got rid

90

of from Manila Road before moving up here. Chris had allowed them twenty personal items each, in addition to practical things like knives and forks and glasses, and in the end Nicola had struggled to bring even that much. It made for a much easier way of living.

She shut the front door behind her and stood for a moment on the doorstep, running through everything in her mind. Their neighbour's daughter was coming to do the chickens. There was nothing else to worry about.

She knew she was hesitating to leave because she was fearful that life might not be the same when they got back. When Georgia had phoned her that evening to tell her about Gum, it had been the mention of Dash Culbone that had sent a chill through her — how he had been at the scene, and had been such a help to Tabitha.

Nicola had gone to the internet straight afterwards to look him up. In five minutes she found out everything she needed to know and where he fitted in to the Culbone family tree. It made her feel sick.

Years ago, she had made Chris a promise. Their whole life together had been built on that promise, and breaking it was the last thing she wanted to do. But the presence of Dash Culbone might leave her with no choice. She hoped he would give up on Tabitha. That he would scuttle back to his side of the river and find someone else to lap up his attention.

Everyone knew that Culbones and Melchiors should never mix. It always ended in tragedy.

Nicola thought back to that long hot summer

of 1986, over thirty years ago. She should never have crossed the river. She had been tempting fate, thinking that she could ignore what had gone before. With the arrogance of youth, she had thought herself invincible, but looking back now perhaps there had been some sort of curse?

The legend of Eleanor. The hapless pawn being shuttled backwards and forwards between two households; between two men. Of course, everyone had their version of events, and chances were that no one had ever known the truth except Eleanor — how she felt, how she had been treated, why she did what she did.

Nicola shook herself and strode towards the car. What on earth was she thinking? She was a sensible woman. She didn't believe in curses or superstition. She was panicking, that was all. Her fears would not come to anything. The past would stay in the past, and everything would stay just as it was.

'Let's go,' she said to Chris, who was stacking everything neatly in the car, making sure the thermos of coffee was to hand so they didn't have to stop until lunchtime. God love him, she thought. She was the luckiest woman in the world.

11

At Dragonfly Farm, Tabitha locked herself away in the barn to make Gum's funeral wreath. She'd spent the morning gathering fruit and flowers and greenery. She finally allowed Georgia in to see it: clusters of sloes and blackberries and crab apples all tumbling out of a basket, trailing oak leaves and ivy and hawthorn and rosehips.

'You don't think it's too twee?' Tabitha was anxious.

'It's stunning.'

'Everything's from the garden or the orchards.'

'It's perfect, Tabitha.' Georgia hugged her cousin.

Tabitha stared at her handiwork. 'The undertaker's coming in a minute to take it. So they can put it on the coffin.' She gulped.

Georgia patted her. 'Gum would have loved it. He'd be very proud.'

Tabitha turned away. 'Right. We better crack on,' she said, abrupt. 'We've got the rest of the beds to make up before the grown-ups get here.'

'Grown-ups?' Georgia wrinkled her nose. 'I think we've been pretty grown up over the last couple of weeks.'

'Well, yes. And I can't ever call my dad a grown-up. He's *useless*.' Tabitha rolled her eyes. Robin was flying in to Exeter from somewhere no one could pronounce where he'd been taking photographs for a cycling magazine. 'He means well, but he's hopeless at organising anything.'

'And Mum's too far away to be much help. But it's much nicer to have them here for the actual funeral than all the ghastly stuff. Don't you think?'

'Definitely,' agreed Tabitha.

Georgia had been at Dragonfly Farm as much as she could, coming up and down on the train. The two of them had identified Gum together, clutching hands in the brightly lit morgue, holding on until they got back to the safety of the kitchen before they cried in each other's arms. There were forms to fill out, the coroner's verdict on the post-mortem, the stress of waiting for the body to be released. On top of everything, Thomas Bickleigh, the solicitor who looked after Matthew's affairs at Melchior and Sons, was insisting on them coming into the office the day after the funeral so he could discuss the will.

'Why can't you come to the house?' demanded Tabitha over the phone.

'I'd prefer it if you came to the office. I'll have all the paperwork to hand.' Mr Bickleigh was insistent.

Tabitha hung up in a huff. 'Bloody jobsworth. Doesn't he know who we are? For heaven's sake, it's still our name over the door.'

'He wants to keep it formal, I expect,' said Georgia. 'And it's not our family business any more, remember?'

'Far from it. Gum was always saying how corporate and faceless it's got. He always went to people's house to discuss their wills.'

'They probably don't have the resources or the time.'

'They could have if they wanted to,' grumbled Tabitha. 'No one's got the personal touch any more. No one cares.'

After they'd done the beds, they sat at the kitchen table, surrounded by final checklists and gradually nibbling their way through a tin of shortbread someone had left on the doorstep: Georgia realised it was all they had eaten today.

She had done a deep clean on the kitchen yesterday. Gum and Tabitha were always doing more interesting things than housework and it showed. She moved everything off the surfaces and went over them with bleach, had a thorough chuck out of anything that was looking past its sell-by date, washed the windows, changed the tablecloth and put all the tea towels in the wash. It had been partly therapeutic and partly emotional. She didn't want to throw away some of the things she came across: the copy of *Country Life* Gum had been reading; the seed catalogue he had marked up with a black Sharpie.

And there was the pot of his Gentleman's Relish that only had a spoonful left in it. She told herself that keeping a scraping of anchovy paste wasn't going to bring Gum back, that there were plenty of better reminders of his presence in the house. But still, putting the white pot in the bin brought a lump to her throat.

'It's been great having you here.' Tabitha reached across the table and grabbed Georgia's hand. She looked a bit uncomfortable for a moment. 'And I still haven't said . . . '

She paused, swallowing her words down as if they were a gristly piece of meat.

Georgia grinned. 'Said what?'

Tabitha cleared her throat. 'Sorry.'

This was true. Neither of them had mentioned the elephant in the room. The horrible argument that had kept Georgia away from Dragonfly Farm all summer.

'He doesn't seem to appreciate you,' Tabitha had told Georgia the first time she'd brought Doug down to Dragonfly Farm. 'And he definitely doesn't like it here.'

'He's a townie. He's not used to the countryside.'

Doug's biography said he was a Londoner born, bred and educated, but in fact he'd been brought up in Woking. 'That is London, to Americans,' he had defended himself. Tabitha had nearly choked on her cider.

'It's like saying you live in Bristol when you live in Weston-super-Mare.'

'It's just for convenience. And I do live there now.' Doug glowered.

'Is Isleworth London, then?' Tabitha was at her most antagonistic.

'Yes.'

'Guys, guys, it doesn't matter. Can we stop arguing and talk about something else?' Georgia was nervous. She wasn't sure who she would back in a fight between Tabitha and Doug. Tabitha had no boundaries but Doug was good with words, his rhetoric deadly.

The two of them had bickered all weekend. It

was usually Tabitha who started it but Doug couldn't let it go, taking the bait every time. They were a volatile combination: Doug thought he knew everything, albeit in a quiet, studious way, and Tabitha couldn't stand bullshit. Throwing them together highlighted their differences.

'Your cousin's got serious issues,' Doug told Georgia on the train ride home.

'She has, actually,' Georgia told him. 'She was majorly dyslexic at school and no one picked up on it.'

'Dyslexia doesn't make you rude, does it?'

'No. But it's made her very defensive.'

'I'd call it aggressive.'

Georgia sighed. 'I was hoping you'd get on. She's good fun. And she's a doer. She doesn't bang on about what she's going to do, she does it.'

Doug looked at her. 'Are you getting at me?'

'Now you're being paranoid,' Georgia laughed. 'No.'

But Doug had talked about his script a *lot* over the weekend. To be fair, that was what the two of them talked about most of the time, but it stood out when there was someone else in the mix, especially someone who wasn't in the business.

'I think she gets freaked out when we talk shop,' she said carefully. 'Because she doesn't really read or watch telly.'

Doug didn't actually say *philistine* but she could tell he was thinking it.

'Maybe we just got off on the wrong foot,' he said eventually.

97

Georgia felt a little leap of hope. She couldn't bear it if Doug and Tabitha didn't get on. The two people in the world most important to her.

'Honestly. Give it time. Everyone loves Tabitha once they get to know her.'

'It's never good when people say that,' he said. 'But I'll take your word for it. I'm sure one day Tabitha and I will be inseparable and I'll look back on this and laugh.'

Georgia gave him a hug. 'Other people's families are always a nightmare.'

Doug made a face. 'That's just it, though. Mine isn't,' he said. 'You couldn't not like my family. There's nothing to dislike. Which I suppose makes them boring. But at least you know where you are with them.'

What he said was true. Doug's doting elderly parents were kindness, patience, thoughtfulness and duty personified. When he had invited Georgia to Woking for Sunday lunch, she had been treated like a princess from the moment she got there. Nothing was too much trouble and she was waited on hand and foot, not allowed to lift a finger, which she found a little unnerving but not unpleasant. It certainly went a long way towards explaining Doug's view on the world: his confidence and assurance that everything would work out all right. She wished she had an ounce of his certainty.

People, she thought, were endlessly fascinating. How they were made up and how they reacted to their environment and the people around them. It was why she loved what she did so much. She was paid to study people, move them around the chessboard of life and see what happened.

It was Georgia's birthday weekend in May when it blew up. They had gone to Dragonfly Farm for the weekend; she always had her birthday there. Doug had wanted to take her to a show at the Donmar Warehouse as he knew someone in it and they could go on to a party afterwards, but Georgia, quite reasonably, said she didn't want to spend her birthday with people she didn't know.

Gum took them all out for supper at the Swan. Doug drank three pints of Inarticulate, the local bitter, and was even more argumentative than usual when they got back to the kitchen.

'I don't get it,' he said, looking at Tabitha. She was looking her most alluring, in an emerald-green dress that showed off her brown legs, and cowboy boots, her hair in a messy knot at the nape of her neck. 'You're so smart and talented. But you're stuck here in the middle of nowhere making pies. It's such a waste.'

'What?'

Georgia saw the flintiness in Tabitha's eyes. She patted Doug's knee under the table to indicate he should back off. But he went for the jugular.

'You're just being a coward. You have to take risks in life.'

'Really?' Tabitha's voice was icy. 'And what if I'm happy? Isn't that the point of it all?'

'I don't believe you are.'

Georgia cringed. Tabitha scowled. Doug

ploughed on, unaware he was heading into dangerous territory.

'I think you're too scared to get out of your comfort zone. You sit here knowing nothing is going to change, because nothing ever does in a place like this.'

'Doug!' Georgia gave him a warning glance. No one spoke ill of Dragonfly Farm or Rushbrook or Nettleford in front of Tabitha.

'I'm only saying it because I care and I think she's got potential.'

'*She?*' Tabitha leaned forward. 'At least I'm not hiding behind somebody else's talent.'

Doug gave her a polite, confused smile. 'Sorry?'

'You're using Georgia. Exploiting her. And because she's sweet and kind, she puts up with it.'

'That's not fair, Tabitha,' Georgia interjected. 'We're a team. We're collaborating.'

'Oh yeah? *My script. Me me me, I I I.*' Tabitha glared at Doug. 'I know how much work she's put in, but nobody else would guess.'

Doug had interest from a big-shot production company who had made some notes on his script. He and Georgia had been working hard to address the issues and had sent off a fresh draft the day before.

Doug pointed a finger. 'Maybe you shouldn't have a strong opinion on things you don't understand. I wouldn't tell you how to make a pie.' He managed to sound both patronising and withering. 'Georgia's my muse.'

'Ha!' Tabitha snorted. 'M-*use*. I rest my case.'

Georgia woke up the next morning to find Doug getting dressed and putting his things back in his rucksack.

'I think it's probably better if I went,' he said to her stiffly. 'I don't have to stay and be insulted by your cousin.'

Georgia sat up, still groggy with sleep and last night's alcohol.

'Don't be silly. Everyone had a bit too much to drink. We're making Sunday lunch.'

'I'm getting the 11.18. I'll call a taxi to the station.'

'Do you want me to come too?'

'Well, that's up to you.'

Georgia swung her legs out of bed and looked over at Doug. He looked pale and anxious and very upset.

'You look terrible.'

'I haven't slept. It really upset me. I've never been attacked like that before. She said that I was using you. That really hurt, you know? And I almost felt as if you agreed with her.'

'No! Don't be silly. Of course I didn't. I just know there's no point in arguing. I never argue with Tab. It all washes over me.'

'Washes over you?' Doug looked incredulous.

Georgia felt the panic of someone caught in the middle of two people who were as stubborn as each other. She was shocked by how crestfallen Doug looked. She knew Tabitha would be sleeping the sleep of the innocent, oblivious. She didn't feel fit to broker a reconciliation between the two of them. And she certainly didn't want it all starting up again.

101

'There's something else you should know. I wasn't going to tell you . . . ' Doug looked awkward. 'She cornered me in the corridor last night.'

'What?'

'When I went to the loo. She came up to me and said, 'Let's kiss and make up.' She was in her nightdress. Well, just about in her nightdress. There wasn't much of it.'

'Are you sure?'

'I didn't imagine it. She's got a dragonfly tattoo right here.' Doug indicated his upper thigh.

Georgia's jaw dropped open. It wasn't Tab's style at all, to be predatory. But how else could he have seen it?

'I think she was testing me. I think she wanted me to make a pass at her, so she could tell you.'

'That's not like Tab.'

'She does *not* like me. She'd do anything to get shot of me. She's jealous. She wants you to herself.'

'No. No, no, no. You're being paranoid. You're reading too much into it.' Underneath her strenuous denial, Georgia's mind was racing. Could Tabitha really have done that? 'What did you do?'

'I just smiled and said, 'No hard feelings,' and shot into the bathroom,' Doug laughed. 'And locked the door.' He looked at Georgia's anguished face. 'Don't worry about it. You're right. We all had too much cider brandy. Let's just get out of here and leave it behind us.'

'I'll have to go and tell Gum we're leaving. He'll be disappointed.'

'Blame me, if you like. Tell him I've got some rewrites to do for tomorrow that have just come in.' Doug wrote for quite a few television dramas and was in constant demand. 'I don't want to cause trouble.'

Georgia put her hands on her hips. 'I'm tempted to kick Tab out of bed and get her to come and apologise,' she said.

'Don't do that. Don't humiliate her. She won't thank you for it.'

'You're right. Oh, I'm so sorry. I wanted us all to have a lovely time. I wanted you to fall in love with Dragonfly Farm.'

'I have. It's Tabitha I haven't fallen in love with. But I think the feeling's mutual.' Doug made a rueful face.

Georgia sighed. 'It's a shame. I was looking forward to Sunday lunch.' She stuffed the rest of her clothes back in her bag and zipped it up.

'Why don't I take you for lunch at the Eagle? Then we could go for a walk on the river.'

'That sounds lovely.'

Georgia tried to sound enthusiastic. She loved the Eagle's Sunday lunches, and a spring walk along the Thames was always uplifting.

She went downstairs and found Gum reading the Sunday paper with a cup of tea in the kitchen. Next to him was an empty plate bearing traces of black pudding, fried egg and tomato, his habitual Sunday breakfast. He was dressed in cords, a tattersall shirt and a mustard cravat, ready to walk to Rushbrook for church. He wasn't religious, but it was a habit he had developed since Joy had died. A comfort, a chance to socialise and to replenish the flowers on her grave.

Georgia saw with a flash of guilt that he'd cleared up from the night before: he'd washed the empty glasses and the cheese plates and put the bottles in the big wicker basket that held the recycling.

'Gum . . . Doug and Tabitha had a bit of a row last night. He wants to go home. And to be honest, I don't blame him.'

He looked up at her, his brow slightly furrowed with concern.

'And do you? Want to go?'

She sighed. 'Not really. But I can't let him go off on his own. And Tabitha was really rude to him.'

Gum shut the paper. 'It will blow over. You know Tabitha. She won't apologise but she'll cook you lunch and that's her way of saying sorry.'

'She shouldn't speak to people like that. It's not acceptable.'

'She's very protective of you.'

Georgia wasn't going to tell Gum what Doug had told her about the inappropriate overture. She wasn't quite sure what she thought about it. It was obviously rooted in truth, because of the dragonfly tattoo, but she couldn't be sure what Tabitha's intentions had really been or if she'd just been winding Doug up.

Georgia frowned. 'Do *you* think he's using me?'

104

Gum didn't answer straight away. 'I under-stand teamwork. I'm not sure that Tabitha does.'

'I knew you'd understand. Because you and Joy were a team, weren't you? You always supported each other.'

'We did, darling.' A shadow flittered across Gum's face. 'And sometimes people don't like it when you're too close, as a couple. They can see it as a threat.'

'I can't imagine anyone finding you and Joy a threat.'

Gum smiled. 'Not anyone that mattered, certainly,' he reassured her.

For a moment, Georgia felt her great-aunt's absence more keenly than ever. Last night's altercation had upset her more than she wanted to admit.

'I'm so sorry we're going early. But I don't think I can face Tab this morning. Thank you for supper last night.'

'I'll give you a lift to the station if you like.'

'No, it's fine. Doug's called a taxi.'

'That's a waste.'

'I don't want Tab to think you're colluding.'

Gum chuckled. 'I can handle her.'

This was true. Gum was about the only person in the world who could wrangle Tabitha. Together with Joy, he was the one who'd tamed her, cured her of her wild West London ways. Georgia suspected it was easier if you were a step removed from someone; that it was easier for Gum as a great-uncle than either Robin or Alison, who couldn't cope with their unruly daughter. It wasn't that they didn't love her or care about her, they simply didn't have a clue how to go about managing her. Gum and Joy, despite never having had children of their own, or perhaps because of that, seemed to understand what Tabitha needed.

Georgia felt a mixture of sorrow and regret as she and Doug stood by the gate with their luggage waiting for the taxi. She leaned on the fence and looked across at the orchards either side of the drive. The pale-pink blossom that shrouded the trees danced in the slight breeze and teased them with its scent. She didn't want to leave.

'I do think this is the most beautiful place in the world.'

Doug slid an arm round her. 'I'm sorry. I feel rotten, dragging you away. We can stay, if you want.'

Georgia looked down the drive. She could see a green Nissan edging its way over the potholes.

'The taxi's here now.'

'We can get him to come back just after lunch.'

She looked down at the ground, drawing a circle with the toe of her boot in the dirt. She didn't want to go. She wanted to stay and have lunch with Gum and Tabitha at the kitchen table. She imagined the leg of pork being pulled out of the oven, its skin scored into tiny lines, the bed of apple and onion slices underneath, carved into thick slices and then served up on the huge willow-pattern plate and lugged to the table. But it wouldn't be the same if Doug was there too. There would be tension. Tabitha might not even join them. She might stay in her room or disappear off somewhere else. You could never tell what her mood might dictate.

Was this Doug's way of saying sorry, offering to stay? Or was it his way of forcing her into agreeing they should leave, so he could always say to her, 'I said we could stay'? Suddenly she wasn't as sure of him as she had been.

She turned to look at him. He was staring at her, anxious.

'Baby, I don't want this to spoil our weekend. I'm really sorry. I want to do what's best. But I don't think I can handle Tabitha. I know you can't see it because she's your cousin, but normal people don't cut up that rough. It's like she's feral.'

'Feral,' said Georgia. It was quite a good word for Tabitha. She was a bit like a wild cat. Sleek and beguiling but with a vicious claw if she was cornered. She nodded. 'I know. She went too far. And if I pander to her she won't learn. The trouble is, Tabitha's organised life to suit her and she never has to compromise. Which means if things don't go her way, or people see things differently, she can't handle it.'

'Well, I'm glad you can see that, and I'm sorry it happened.'

Georgia sighed. 'Maybe we've all let her get away with too much?'

'Maybe she needs to grow up?'

Doug strode across to the taxi, which had reached the yard. He put their bags in the boot, then opened the door for Georgia and waited while she got in. She hesitated for a moment, looking up at Tabitha's bedroom window, but her curtains were firmly shut.

Her heart felt heavy as the taxi drew away from Dragonfly Farm. Tabitha had been rude and wrong, and unkind to Doug, and it was unforgiveable, at least until she apologised. But Georgia had a feeling she wouldn't. She wasn't even sure Tabitha knew *how* to say sorry. She certainly had no recollection of her ever saying it to anyone.

Doug was right. Tabitha needed to grow up. Or at least learn how to treat people.

'Do you think Gum will be all right?' asked Doug. 'We've left him to deal with the aftermath.'

'Gum? Gum will be fine. He's pretty tough.'

She wasn't worried about leaving Gum at Tabitha's mercy. He was the one person in the world Tabitha respected and she would never dream of being rude to him.

Which just went to show that she could curb her tongue if she wanted to.

Georgia sat up straight, suddenly feeling entirely justified in their decision to leave. Tabitha could jolly well realise the consequences of her behaviour for once.

Two weeks later, Doug had sold his screenplay and was flying off to LA to meet with the production company. She'd driven him to the airport, hugged and kissed him at Departures and wished him luck. A month later he told Georgia he wasn't coming back. That he was staying in the Hollywood Hills, in a ritzy rented bungalow, to write the follow-up, because the producer wanted a sequel as soon as possible. And he wanted to do it by himself. He wanted a clean break.

'I don't want any distractions. This is important for me. I've got to get it right.'

Georgia had been crushed. Crushed that he hadn't acknowledged her contribution. Crushed that he didn't want her to be part of his success story. He hadn't even asked her out to celebrate; to loll by his pool for a week clinking champagne glasses. It had been their joint dream, but suddenly it had become his alone. All the hours they had spent discussing the plot, the character, the arcs, the journey. All the time she had put in reading draft after draft, marking cuts, places where he needed more or less exposition, more at stake, more emotion, a better joke. Yes, the original premise had been his idea, and it was a great elevator pitch — a young man cooks his way to stardom using his mother's handwritten recipes — but a pitch did not a screenplay make. It had to have structure. And heart. And teasing that out was Georgia's skill. Pushing the writer to dig deeper, cut, polish until the script shone bright.

She knew full well the script would have been left languishing if it wasn't for her input. But it was too late. She and Doug had no formal agreement. It had always been his name on the front. She'd never expected her name on it, or any payment, yet she had been happy to contribute, trusting him.

What *had* she expected, she asked herself? To be part of the adventure. To go out to Hollywood with him, work with him on the next script, enjoy the life, make contacts, develop her own ideas. Maybe even sell a script of her own. Yes, she thought, that was what she had imagined would happen. For like many script editors, she had ambitions to write. She didn't want to work on other people's projects for ever.

In the meantime, she tortured herself with Doug's Instagram pictures. Doug played the handsome, absent-minded English writer to perfection, with his dirty-blond dishevelled hair, his tortoiseshell glasses, the cords and jumper combo with the striped university scarf that looked as if it came from Cambridge even though Georgia knew he'd done media studies at a tiny university in Wales and had got the scarf in a charity shop. He'd modelled himself on Hugh Grant's bookshop owner in *Notting Hill* with a dollop of Harry Potter thrown in. He was catnip to any Anglophile female in Los Angeles. He even had a photo of himself at a proper typewriter as his profile picture, though Georgia knew he worked on a MacBook.

Doug's image was a bigger work of fiction than his script. But his producer didn't seem to mind. Far from it. For there she was, in more than half of his Instagram posts, curled up under his arm, working the Hot Librarian look with her red lipstick and her square, black-framed glasses. Did she know about Georgia? Or had Georgia been edited out in an early draft? Had he at any point said, 'Oh, my girlfriend, who had a huge amount of input into this project, is hoping to join me soon'?

No.

Now, Georgia had to acknowledge that Tabitha had been right all along. She was a little ashamed that she had stood by and let Doug attack her cousin, and not leapt to her defence. How could she have been so blind, while Tabitha saw him for what he was so clearly? She supposed it was because she had a tendency to be trusting, while Tabitha didn't. And, she thought with a slight blush, sex went a long way to covering up imperfections. Doug had been imaginative and surprisingly selfless between the sheets.

'We all make mistakes,' she said to Tabitha now, who grinned at her.

'Speak for yourself,' she said. 'I never do.'

Georgia wasn't going to argue that Tabitha never made mistakes because she never took risks when it came to affairs of the heart. She hadn't had a proper boyfriend since she'd moved to Somerset, as far as Georgia knew. She had a series of lovers — some secret, some not — to whom she made no promises. Georgia suspected that she deliberately chose men who were emotionally or literally unavailable and didn't need or appreciate endless texts or demands for affection. She was pretty sure one of them was Jimmy O'Gowan, the racehorse trainer, whose lifestyle had already cost him two expensive divorces.

'Have you heard from him? Doug the Bug?' asked Tabitha.

'He texts occasionally. But I don't answer.'

It took all her will not to.

'Good.' Tabitha fixed her with a stern stare.

Georgia swallowed. There was one burning question she had to ask. 'Did you . . . ' she managed, 'make a pass at him? Doug?'

'What?' Tabitha looked incredulous.

'He said you cornered him outside the bathroom and propositioned him.'

Tabitha crossed her arms. 'What? *He* propositioned *me*. He came slithering along the corridor and said, 'Let's kiss and make up.''

'He said that's what *you* said. And he said he saw your tattoo. That you had hardly anything on.'

'I was just in a T-shirt. But I don't usually find people wandering about at night. I can wear what I like to bed, can't I?' Tabitha was indignant.

'I thought you might be testing him.'

'In his dreams!'

Georgia began to laugh. She felt reassured. Doug's betrayal had shaken her confidence more than she cared or dared to admit, but she felt stronger than she had done for a while, back in the comfort of the kitchen, sitting opposite her cousin, and she didn't want to think about him. They had more important things to worry about.

'I don't think we should spend another second talking about him. He's the other side of the world, and he can stay there.'

'Agreed.' Tabitha lifted her mug of tea in a toast to Georgia's proposal. As they chinked cups, they heard the knocker go on the front door. Georgia glanced at the clock on the wall. Could it be her mum already?

112

The two of them headed out into the hall and opened the door.

'Mum!' Georgia rushed straight into Nicola's arms and squeezed her mother tight. 'I'm so glad you're here.'

'I beat the satnav,' said Chris cheerfully.

'He hardly let us stop. Only twice. And then only for five minutes for a wee. I'll be lucky if I don't get a bladder infection,' grumbled Nicola, but she didn't mean it.

'I wanted to get here in daylight.'

There was a flurry of coat removal and kisses and cold air as Chris brought the cases in. Georgia was about to shut the front door when another car came down the drive.

'My God, it's Dad!' said Tabitha. 'This must be the first time ever he's been on time. Nearly a day early, in fact!'

The four of them went out to greet him. Robin tumbled out of the taxi, pulling an assortment of cabin bags and camera cases with him. He was in too-tight faded cords, a leather jacket and desert boots, his aviator glasses a little superfluous in the approaching dusk.

'Christ, it's good to be back,' he said. 'I always forget how bloody wonderful this place is. And it doesn't change, does it? Hello, sis.'

He kissed Nicola on the cheek, then turned to Tabitha.

'Baby girl,' he said. 'I'm sorry I didn't make it sooner.'

'Hi, Dad.' Tabitha stood a little stiff at first, then relaxed into her dad's embrace.

'Um,' said Robin, rummaging in his jacket

113

pocket for his wallet. 'Has anyone got fifty quid I can borrow? I'm a bit short for the cab fare. I'll go to the cashpoint tomorrow.'

Chris paid the taxi driver, and when the car had gone they gathered there for a moment, the little cluster of Melchiors, as the sun started to go down and the sky turned coral.

'I keep expecting to see Gum,' said Nicola sadly, missing his reassuring frame ambling out of the front door.

'I still can't get used to it,' said Tabitha, her voice very small. 'I see him everywhere.'

Suddenly Tabitha felt uplifted by the arrival of everyone, even her feckless father. It was odd, she thought, how death recalibrated everything and brought people together.

12

At Rushbrook House, on the other side of the river, Dash Culbone was in a dilemma.

To attend Matthew Melchior's funeral or not? Out of respect he thought he should, yes.

On the other hand, Dash had been at the scene of Matthew Melchior's demise. So maybe his presence would be a reminder of that? In which case he should stay away.

But then the Melchiors might consider him rude. It might look callous, as if he didn't care.

But if he did go, later it might look as if he had been buttering the Melchiors up.

Then again, he didn't actually *need* their agreement or permission or approval.

Though it always helped to have your neighbours on side when you had a business proposition.

Back and forth he went, turning the matter over in his mind.

Before the accident, his plan had been to contact Matthew Melchior and chat through his plans in an open and friendly manner, listening to any possible objections and ironing them out. Dash wasn't crass enough to blunder on without considering his neighbours. He knew that approach wouldn't work in a small community; that arrogance and bullheadedness on his part would lead to problems — pettiness, unhelpfulness, hostility. Country people could be wily and cunning.

He sighed, laying his pen down on the pad where he'd written all the pros and cons of attending or not attending. Dash liked to look at things from all angles. His job had taught him to be thorough. He shivered. The kitchen was growing cold, as it did once the sun had gone. He was loath to put on the heating just for himself, as it drank oil from the tank in the cellar. The heating system was antiquated and inefficient. The lighting was harsh and unforgiving too. There was a lot of work to be done.

Rushbrook House had been neglected for more than thirty years, and the cracks were, quite literally, starting to show. After the summer that still no one spoke about, Dash's grandparents had retreated to London, abandoning the house, leaving it empty. After five years, it had been handed over to an agent and rented out. The Culbones might not want to live there, but they weren't so well off that they could ignore a significant rental income.

There had been various tenants over the years, and some had been more loving than others, but now the house was bordering on uninhabitable. The wind whistled through the sash windows, the lights tripped, there was a dreadful smell of damp. Yet it was still beautiful. The structure was still there. The soft pale-red brick, the classic Regency frontage, the verdant setting of rolling fields and woodland overlooking the Rushbrook river in the distance — it was most people's idea of the perfect English country house. It could be restored.

Yet again Dash wondered if he had made the

right decision. It was a risk, going from international investment broker to country gent. The only gates he knew were departure gates. He had been flattered when his grandparents had asked him to take over their property portfolio and look after it. Over the years they had made a cluster of shrewd investments, but it needed consolidating and streamlining. Some of the less lucrative properties needed selling off and the money reinvesting.

He had looked closely at everything and made recommendations. His first suggestion had been for them to sell Rushbrook House. It needed a vast sum spending on it to bring the rent into line with what the house was worth. He advised them to cut their losses. But Hugh and Clara had been adamant that the house should remain in the family, as it had been for three hundred years.

'It's part of your family history,' Hugh told him.

Yet part of that history was never mentioned.

Dash took the train down to Rushbrook without telling anyone. He looked at the house, the grounds, the farmland, and a plan had begun forming in his head. He'd been involved in raising funds for similar projects in Europe. He knew where he could get investment. And he knew many buildings like this increasingly relied on the travel and tourism industry to keep them alive. Not many people had the cash to run a household this size. He began to put together a proposal and look for someone to manage the project.

As his ideas took shape, he gradually began to realise something. He was falling under the spell of Rushbrook House and the land it was set in. He found himself drawn back there, telling himself there was some detail he needed to check, but deep down knowing that all he wanted was to wake up to the sound of birdsong and a tentative pale-gold sun edging its way in through the window along with a scented breeze; a counterpoint to his jet-set lifestyle, played out in departure lounges and hotel rooms. He was existing on a cocktail of caffeine, booze, sleeping tablets, antacids and beta-blockers to survive the pressure of his career, needing them to wake up, perform, wind down, switch off, sleep. He had an ulcer and he was only just thirty. At Rushbrook, he could fall asleep without pills and sleep like a baby, waking refreshed and calm.

Perhaps he was the man for the job?

He called a family meeting. He had a proposition. He brought along his plans, photographs, figures. His grandparents gave him their blessing, leaving his father, Bear, proud and envious in equal measure. Dash sold his Thames-side flat, and now, here he was. He had been in residence nearly three weeks, rattling around in the cavernous rooms. It was odd, waking up and knowing what time zone he was in. Even odder, eating eggs he'd bought from a farmyard just down the road.

And he had set off on the wrong foot with Tabitha almost as soon as he arrived. He had done his best to be gentlemanly and helpful, but it had backfired rather. He was intrigued by her.

She was so very different from the women he was used to, polished and assured career women, weight and image conscious, ruthlessly ambitious. Yet Tabitha was intimidating and assured in her own way. He wasn't sure how to put things right between them. He had kept a respectful distance since the accident, not wanting to intrude or distress her, and there seemed to be plenty of people coming and going from Dragonfly Farm. But he wanted to do the right thing over the funeral.

He looked down at the sheet of paper, the black bullet points he'd written with his fountain pen. In the end, he decided that the right thing to do would be to stand at the very back of the church then slip away once the service was over. Respectful but unobtrusive. He had already sent a wreath on behalf of the family.

He put the lid back on his pen, stood up and took his nightly turn around the house, lighting a fire, switching on lamps, drawing the curtains. They were getting to know each other, he and the house. At first it made him feel very small and insignificant, with its high ceilings and echoing rooms. But he was starting to understand its ways, and it was starting to cooperate with him a little more. He knew that if he turned the cooker hood on, the electrics tripped, so he didn't bother with it any more. He knew that the large bath in the master en suite drained the immersion tank and there would be no more hot water for hours, so he took to using the little slipper bath at the back of the house. He knew that if he unlocked the front door it was impossible to lock it again, so he used the back entrance. He knew that something was nesting in the chimney of the drawing room, as he had nearly smoked himself out when he had lit a fire.

Where to start? Plumber, electrician, carpenter, chimney sweep . . . ?

Yet the more difficult the house was, the more determined he was to solve the problems it threw up and the more he grew to like it. Each solution felt like a triumph. He wasn't particularly practical on the DIY front. He'd never had to be, for his apartments were always fully serviced. But he was learning. He had a scientific mind and he was dextrous. And in the cellar he had discovered just about every tool a person could need. Some he recognised, many he did not, but he adapted them to suit his needs.

At night, when he drew the curtains and turned on the lamps, he imagined voices. The voices of his grandparents, his own father, their many friends: he had seen enough photos to know this had been a house of entertainment. He imagined their laughter. The music they played. The tinkle of glasses and cutlery.

And the voice that was no longer here. The reason for all the sadness.

His father had spoken to him before he moved down.

'I'm proud of you for bringing the house back to life,' said Bear. 'It's what it needs. But it was always going to be someone one step removed who took it on. It's still too painful for any of us. I think it always will be.'

Upstairs was a room at the end of the corridor that had been kept locked. The tenants had been told never to go in there: it was the one condition of rental. A few days after he arrived, Dash had found a screwdriver in the cellar fine enough to undo the lock. The house was his now, after all. He needed to know its secrets.

He had stepped inside, his heart thumping. The walls were dark purple, almost black. The carpet was now threadbare. There was a bed with an iron bedstead, covered in a maroon striped bedspread, and a similar fabric covered the window. On the wall were posters: Jimi Hendrix, The Doors, Lou Reed. There was a sound system, big and chunky, and rows and rows of LPs.

He felt overwhelmed. It was almost a shrine, but he knew no one had been to visit it for years. It lay there, empty, unvisited, unmoving. Nothing had ever changed.

There was a strip of photos on the wall, taken in a photo booth. The light was glaring and harsh, but not strong enough to mar the beauty of the boy staring out. Bleached blond hair falling over his eyes, which were ringed with kohl. Sharp cheekbones. A full, half-smiling mouth. A fringed scarf wound round his neck. Dash could feel his energy, just in a tiny photograph. Mischievous, quixotic. Possibly slightly dangerous.

He wondered if he would have liked him. He had dared to ask his father, who had sighed, and said, 'Tarka was wonderful. Everyone loved him. But he was maddening. He did exactly what he wanted.'

121

That was all Dash knew about his uncle. Or the boy who had never had the chance to be his uncle, for he had died before Dash was born.

He never dared ask his grandparents about him. His languid, elegant grandmother, whose brilliant blue hooded eyes hid her sadness, who was painfully thin inside her Chanel skirts and silk blouses: it was Clara who couldn't bear to stay at Rushbrook House and was the reason it had lain unloved for so many years.

Clara had taken his face in her hands the day he moved down. 'You will make it a happy place again,' she told him. 'I know you will.'

He'd wanted to ask her about Tarka then, but he could see that he had stirred things up, that she was restless and filled with disquiet, and he didn't want to upset her more.

Every night he went into the room before he went to bed and wondered what to do about Tarka's things. He couldn't leave it as it was for ever. Surely it was time to move on from the tragedy? But was it his place to decide that? No one had told him what to do or insisted it should be kept as it was. It was as if everyone had walked away and pretended nothing had happened. They had simply not dealt with the relics of the person they had so loved.

He picked up Tarka's school tie, irreverently hung around the neck of a plastic skeleton, waiting for a message from him, some sort of signal that he was ready to be packed away.

But nothing came.

13

Tabitha woke on the morning of the funeral and pulled the duvet over her head.

She was terrified.

She was terrified of breaking down in the church. Terrified of what to say to people when they offered their condolences. Terrified of the thought of that hole in the ground, and how on earth she was going to bear it.

She asked herself what Gum would say. He would say just get through it, and take comfort from the fact that she had everyone she loved with her. She tried to remind herself how dignified he had been at Joy's funeral; how he had stood upright and true as she was buried. Tabitha had clasped his right hand in her left as they stood at the graveside, and he had squeezed it, not to comfort her but to draw strength, and she had been glad to be by his side.

Gum had lost the love of his life, the woman who had shared everything with him for nearly sixty years. If he could be brave, then so could she. She shut her eyes, knowing that the moment she got out of bed the horrible day would begin.

And if today was daunting, the future was even more so. Gum and Joy had always been there to catch her, when life got confusing and stressful. They had given her life structure. They had wrapped themselves around her to the point where she knew that nothing bad could happen.

Only now it had. Both of them had gone and she was on her own.

The phone on her bedside table rang. She emerged from her nest and picked it up in case it was the undertaker with a crisis, but it was her mother. She was tempted not to answer. But Alison would only keep trying until she did.

'Hi, Mum.'

'Darling.'

She could imagine her, on hands-free in her Audi, negotiating the London traffic, briefcase on the front seat. Tabitha knew she would be written into her day's schedule: *8.15–8.30 Call Tabitha*. Alison had every second of the day accounted for.

'I just wanted to tell you I'm thinking of you and sending lots of love. How are you feeling?'

'I don't know yet really. OK, I suppose.'

'You're bound to feel sad. Is your father there?'

'Yes — he turned up last night.'

'I hope he's being helpful.'

'Um — sort of. Yes.'

Tabitha wasn't going to give her mother any ammunition against Robin. She hated it when her parents criticised each other. It was all right for her to do it, but when they did it took her back to her unhappiest time.

'Now listen. I know we've talked about it, but if you want me there today I can drive down.'

As Robin and Alison couldn't remain civil in the same room, they'd agreed it was best if she didn't come. Tabitha had felt her mother's relief when they'd decided.

'I'm fine, Mum. But thanks.'

'Well, let's go away somewhere when it's all over. A girls' weekend in a spa?'

Tabitha rolled her eyes. Her mother had got her so wrong. A spa was the last place she would ever want to go. But she didn't want to sound ungrateful.

'That would be great.'

'I've sent flowers, of course.'

'Thanks, Mum.'

'I've got my phone with me if you need me.'

'OK.'

Her mum was really trying. Albeit ten years too late. Maybe if she'd had as much concern for her welfare when she was a teenager, their relationship might be better.

Tabitha hung up and stared at the ceiling for a moment. Talking to her mother always unsettled her. Her problems as a teenager had stemmed from her distress at her parents' separation. She knew they didn't belong together, but she had hoped she would be enough to be their glue. She wasn't. She had heard them arguing about her one night. She had thought they would both be fighting to have her. It turned out to be quite the reverse. She didn't fit into either of their new lives. She listened in horror as they argued about who she should live with. Her mother worked long hours and made more money, whereas her dad was freelance and had more time on his hands, so her mum basically paid her dad to take responsibility for her. She heard him negotiating. At two hundred quid a week, he finally agreed to have Tabitha in his tiny flat and look after her.

Was it any wonder she had gone a bit off the rails? Tabitha felt unloved and unwanted, unlooked-after. Her father had let her run wild until she got expelled from school and ran away to Somerset.

Joy and Gum had repaired the gaping hole inside her, filling it with patience and comfort and the simple things in life, like mealtimes and bedtimes. Morning cups of tea and bedtime cocoa, properly made beds, washing pegged out on the line. And they had made her contribute to the household too. They had given her jobs and responsibility, and that made her feel safer than she ever had done. Her parents hadn't ever made her do anything. They had given her no respect for herself or her surroundings, she realised later.

And now, it was the little things that would keep her going. She had to keep some structure in her life. Lying in bed with the duvet over her head was the worst thing she could do. So she forced herself to throw it back and got up. She drew the curtains and opened the window to let fresh air into the room, folding back her bedding to give it a good airing while she had breakfast, as Joy had taught her. She remembered when she first arrived at Dragonfly Farm she never bothered making her bed, leaving her duvet in a heap, the bottom sheet rumpled, the pillows askew. Joy had soon changed that, insisting that making your bed properly set you up for the day. Now she wouldn't dream of leaving her bed unmade, letting the sweet outside air through the linen for an hour first.

She pulled on her jeans, ran downstairs and

126

whistled to Poe. Together they walked outside to let out the chickens, who scurried from their coop with squawks of thanks, fluffy and aimless. She put their pale-brown eggs in Joy's old wicker basket then made her way to the orchards. She could see a trail blundering through the wet grass — a badger, she guessed. Fieldfares and redwings flittered around her on the hunt for insects and grubs. Poe bounded about, ever on the lookout for the rabbits he wasn't allowed to chase.

As she walked through the trees, she saw strings of cobwebs hanging from the branches: dozens of delicately woven threads strung with drops of dew that glittered in the sunshine. She wandered amongst them, ignoring the sting of the cold air on her skin, trying not to break the spiders' handiwork.

For a fleeting moment, she could imagine her plucky, redoubtable can-do great-aunt striding through the orchard in an old hand-knitted jumper and wellies, her hair wild and her skin weather-beaten, her cheeks rosy and her eyes bright. She had put as much care into the orchards as she once had her patients, nursing the sick back to health. She'd had green fingers, and Tabitha had tried to learn as much from her as she could about plants and how to nurture them. Joy taught her how and when to prune, and how to graft, but mostly when to leave things alone, for Joy was a great believer in letting nature take its course except in extremis. As a result, the orchards thrived, the trees blossomed and the fruit was abundant.

What was going to happen to them now?

She'd know tomorrow, of course, after they'd been to the solicitor. Who would Gum have left the farm to? All his surviving relatives? Her dad and her aunt and Georgia and her? Would she be able to stay on? Or would they have to sell? She couldn't imagine the others wanting to keep their money in a crumbling old farm in Somerset. Not her father, certainly, and probably not Nicola either. And Georgia could probably do with the cash. One thing was certain: Tabitha wouldn't have the money to buy them out. Not on her pie funds.

She shivered. Her feet were wet and a chilly breeze sliced through her thin jumper. Poe nosed at her leg, aware that she wasn't herself.

'Let's just stay here today, Poe.'

Oh God, wouldn't that be nice? To wander around with him in peace and quiet, without having to worry about anyone else. Everyone would be getting up soon, needing breakfast, wanting to talk. Being kind to her, which would make her want to cry. She couldn't run away. She had to face it head on.

She went inside to make the first pot of tea on what was going to be a very long day.

14

As soon as she saw the man in the blue overcoat at the back of Rushbrook church, Nicola knew it was Dash Culbone. It was his aura. The Culbone air: a way of standing that told everyone he belonged in this church, that it was part of his history. It wasn't arrogance. He looked perfectly humble and he wasn't trying to prove anything. His stance was respectful. He simply looked as if he belonged.

Which, of course, he did. Dash Culbone's ancestors were plastered all over the walls. Centuries of them. They went far further back than the Melchiors, who were newcomers in comparison, only appearing towards the end of the nineteenth century.

She could see the family resemblance. She had never seen him before, but she recognised the bone structure, the hairline, the lean build. He was his father's son, unmistakably. Even if she hadn't been expecting to see him, she would have recognised him. Beauty had been handed down to him like a precious cargo, seemingly undiluted.

Nicola turned back to face the front of the church. She could see Gum's coffin, with Tabitha's arrangement spilling over the sides in a tangle of autumn fruit and greenery. Her eyes blurred as she looked at the number for the next hymn, the black letters merging as the vicar announced they would now sing 'When a Knight Won His Spurs'.

Panic was making her lungs tighten. Her mouth went dry. There was a rustle of hymnbooks and orders of service. The organ started up, the tune achingly familiar from schooldays.

She tried to sing, but the words stuck in her throat.

> *He was gentle and brave,*
> *He was gallant and bold . . .*

How Gum. How very Gum. She felt proud of Tabitha and Georgia, and what a wonderful job they had done in arranging the funeral. They had struck the perfect tone: a little bit of Gum's spirit was in everything they had chosen, from the thick wax candles that burned bright to the orange and dark-red dahlias in the flower arrangements to the rousing, moving hymns they had chosen and the Robert Frost poem Georgia had read.

Nicola used the respite of the hymn to gather her thoughts and be logical. Perhaps Dash had come down to sell Rushbrook House? That must be why he was here, she told herself, and it gave her a fleeting sense of relief. She wondered how much the house was worth. It had been sorely neglected; you only had to pass the stone gates, crumbling and moss-covered, to know that.

For she had driven past. Of course she had. Surreptitiously, on the pretext of going for the paper that morning. She would always be drawn back. Always be tempted to reopen that wound and revisit the shadows. As long as Melchiors remained at Dragonfly Farm, she wouldn't be able to bury the past. She knew it was unhealthy, but she couldn't change what had happened. It was part of her.

But she wasn't going to let that part leach into the present. Which was why she was so unsettled by Dash.

What if he wasn't selling? What if he was here for good? He would press himself upon them, eager to be neighbourly. And her worst nightmare would start to unfold.

She looked at Chris next to her. He wasn't aware of Dash's presence, and she wanted to keep it that way, hoping that no one would mention him. She could smudge over his existence until it was time for them to leave.

'Let us pray,' said the vicar as the hymn finished, and she sank to her knees, resting her arms on the pew in front of her and burying her head in them. Nicola prayed that by the time the service was over, and they turned to leave the church and go to the graveside, Dash Culbone would have disappeared.

⋆ ⋆ ⋆

Dash was lucky not to have been to many funerals in his life: an old history teacher of whom he had been fond, and a friend's mother. Today's service moved him more than he had expected. It was a glimpse of someone he had never known, yet he felt he would have liked to.

131

The eulogy, the warmth of the vicar, the ranks of friends and family crammed into the little church: evidence of a life well-lived and a man whose relationships went deep. It was a lesson, he thought, in loyalty and kindness, as these two traits seemed to be a recurring theme.

There was a core of Melchiors lining the path outside the church entrance as everyone left. Tabitha was at the head, looking startling in a black velvet trouser suit and a wide-brimmed felt hat. Next to her was Georgia Melchior-Hawkins, the order of service had told him, who had read Robert Frost so beautifully: she must be Tabitha's cousin. She was much smaller than Tabitha, her dark hair fastened at the side with a black silk rose, dressed in a red swing wool coat and high boots. The two of them were very close, linking arms, hugging each other in between accepting condolences.

Next to the two girls were a woman and two men. Dash estimated they were all in their early fifties, but he couldn't quite discern which of the girls' parents were which.

'Please,' he said as he shook Tabitha's hand, 'do let me know if there is anything I can do.'

Tabitha nodded at him with a fleeting smile. Distant. Cool. He could see she was struggling.

'I'm Georgia.' Her cousin emanated far more warmth and graciousness as she shook his hand. 'Thank you so much for coming.'

Tabitha didn't introduce him, he noticed. Deliberate? Bad manners? Or the distraction of another fifty people to greet?

He wanted to engage more with both of them,

but the line was moving along and he found himself looking into the clear gaze of the woman he had guessed must be Georgia's mother. She had the well-cut steel-grey hair that was currently the fashion for women of a certain age — the cut showed off her cheekbones and the grey set off her slate-blue eyes.

'I'm Dash. Culbone.' He waved a hand behind him. 'From Rushbrook House. I'm so sorry about your . . . '

'Uncle,' she replied. 'He was my uncle.' She scrutinised him for a moment. 'Are you here long?'

'Well, yes,' he said. 'All being well. I'm hoping to breathe a bit of life into the old place.'

He smiled. She didn't. She nodded, murmuring a platitude, then turned away from him to greet the next person in the line. He had no choice but to move on and shake the hand of the man beside her, who looked as if he'd been up all night.

'Robin Melchior,' he introduced himself, oozing superficial charm and brandy. 'Thanks so much for coming to see the old boy off. It means a lot to all of us.'

'Dash Culbone,' said Dash.

Already Robin had withdrawn his hand and was looking down the line for the next person to greet. Dash stood still for a moment, not sure if he had been deliberately snubbed. He decided he had done his neighbourly duty. And although it had been made clear on the order of service, and by the vicar, that everyone was welcome to the Swan for a drink afterwards to toast the memory of Matthew Melchior, he had a sense that the welcome didn't extend to Culbones, even now.

* * *

Later that night, the Melchiors gathered in the kitchen, suffused with that post-funeral bitter-sweet comedown: relief that everything had gone well, and the comfort of having seen so many familiar faces, and some not so familiar, during the course of the day. The Swan had been bulging at the seams, the cider had been in full flow and Alan the landlord had done them all proud with his buffet tea.

Nicola had made sure that the close family left at six on the dot and drove them all back to Dragonfly Farm. They needed time to be alone together and share their own private memories. Being on show at a funeral was exhausting; the greeting and the chatting took it out of you without you realising, and somehow you never quite had time to reflect on what the day really meant.

She had put two chickens and a clutch of jacket potatoes in the oven and made a coleslaw. She also knew from experience that lack of food combined with high emotion and drink could spell disaster.

Everyone agreed the funeral had been a huge success.

'If funerals can be a success,' said Georgia. 'But it was lovely. So many people. And they were all so kind about Gum.'

'Just the solicitor to face tomorrow,' said Tabitha, laying out the knives and forks.

'We'll all go,' said Robin. 'Safety in numbers.'

'I think just Tabitha and Georgia have been asked.' Nicola heaved the chickens out of the oven and put them on a big platter.

'Oh,' said Robin. 'Right. Well. We all know what that means, then.'

Nicola elbowed her brother as she walked past. He glared at her.

'It's all right for you,' he said. 'But we haven't all made a bomb on our property.'

Nicola sighed. She loved her brother, but he did always get chippy about money when he'd had a few.

'You'll always be welcome here, Dad,' said Tabitha. 'Assuming he has left the farm to us. For all I know it's going to be a donkey sanctuary.'

'Thank you, darling.' Robin leaned back in his chair and drank from his glass of red wine. He was smiling, but his eyes weren't.

'I don't care about me,' said Georgia. 'But what if he hasn't left it to Tab? Where will she go?'

'Of course he'll have left it to Tab,' said Nicola. 'She's the one who looked after him. Him and Joy.'

'They looked after *me*,' said Tabitha, her eyes suddenly filling with tears.

'No, darling, you were fantastic to them. You looked after Joy when she was so poorly, right up to the end. Gum would have been lost without you.' Nicola could sense everything unravelling.

135

Food was essential if there weren't to be tears or, worse, arguments. She handed Chris the chicken platter. 'Chris, darling, could you carve?'

'Course!' said Chris, glad of a distraction. He always found the Melchior family banter bemusing, and he was wary of Robin. Robin could be the life and soul, but he had a side, and Nicola and Chris had never approved of how he had brought Tabitha up. They had discussed taking her in themselves, just before she had descended on Gum and Joy. Chris had been relieved that Tabitha had absconded to Somerset, for although he loved his wayward niece, he hadn't been keen on the idea of her influencing his own daughter. Georgia was nearly two years older, but far less streetwise than her cousin. He'd had visions of Georgia being dragged around nightclubs and introduced to unsavoury characters over whom Chris had no control. Every loving father's nightmare.

Now, at thirty-one, Georgia was perfectly capable of looking after herself and Tabitha had calmed down considerably. Chris had observed how close they had been all day, and how they had supported each other. As only children, they valued each other.

He finished carving the chicken, then tapped his fork on the edge of his glass.

'I just want to say,' he said, 'how proud Gum would have been of you all today. And as the only non-Melchior here, how proud I was to know him and how I know his generosity of spirit will live on in all of you.'

Oh God, thought Nicola, looking at her

136

husband and feeling her heart swell with love and pride for him. *Please don't let the past break up our future. We've all been through enough.*

15

The morning of his meeting at Melchior and Sons, Gabriel parked in Nettleford town square, in front of the medieval market with its rounded columns and Gothic arches. He'd been in the car just over three hours, finally leaving the motorway at Honisham to meander through the soft greyness of the Somerset Levels. The morning mists shimmered on the horizon then gradually cleared as the autumn sun broke through to reveal patchwork fields stretching away into the distance, their flatness broken by the occasional tor.

This was a mystical county, he knew, full of secrets and magic and myth. He wondered just what he was being drawn into, with this mysterious summons. He would know soon enough: he saw by the hands on the town clock he had twenty minutes before the meeting at eleven.

He pulled out the jacket he'd hung in the back of the car. It was so English, he thought, to feel the need to dress up like a solicitor for a meeting with a solicitor. He should be confident enough in his own skin to rock up in his usual plaid shirt and jeans. But in a funny way it was nice to be formal and dress up in the suit he rarely wore. He'd even put on a tie: a silk tie Lola had given him, burnt orange with black spots. It gave him confidence. He checked his appearance in the driver's window: his shoulder-length dark hair might be a tad unconventional for Nettleford, but he scrubbed up quite well.

Once, Gabriel thought, a small country town like Nettleford would have held no appeal for him. Provincial, slow, with no edge, no opportunity, no nightlife. But as he looked around today, he found himself wondering what it would be like to live somewhere like this. Not having to brave the London traffic and take your life in your hands every day. Being somewhere everyone knew your name, where the pace of life was gentler, and you chatted in the post office queue, instead of staring ahead and clutching your parcel to your chest, like he did when he sent a new knife off to a customer.

'For the purposes of safety, can you tell me what's in the parcel?' They always looked alarmed when he said it was a knife, but he packaged them up safely, in extra-thick cardboard boxes with his name printed on the lid in bold capitals.

He wouldn't be doing that for much longer, he thought gloomily. He'd given himself until the end of the year to decide on his next move. The rent wasn't due to increase till next April, which bought him a few months. By then, Lola might be pregnant. In the meantime, he had polished up his CV and was going to start sending it out. His mates were on the lookout — Josh knew of a few places that were looking to expand. And, after all, if he was offered a job, he didn't *have* to take it . . .

As he approached the offices of Melchior and

Sons, his stomach began to churn. Was it nerves about the upcoming meeting? He'd had no reason to suspect there was anything to worry about. At least he hoped not: you never knew in this day and age. Perhaps he was being sued by another knife maker who thought he had stolen his brand? But then Nettleford didn't look like somewhere that was harbouring a shit-hot intellectual copyright lawyer. And this was about a will, not a lawsuit. Though was that just a cover? Was he being paranoid?

Then he realised what was troubling him: he was uneasy about being so far away from Plum. Since she'd been born he had never spent any length of time away from her. Lola had, of course, when she went on shoots, but being this far away from her made him fearful. It was rather like homesickness. A kind of longing combined with loss. He looked at his phone. He couldn't call the nursery to check on her. That really was helicopter parenting. Lola was on it. He reminded himself that she had to go through this all the time, and she had been quite happy to be in the role of chief carer for once.

Reassured, he bounded up the steps of a handsome double-fronted building to the left of the marketplace with a pale-blue front door and pushed his way inside.

'Mr Culbone.' A young girl with a country burr like thickset honey smiled at him. She had bright red hair, a very tight houndstooth dress and fuchsia lipstick. He recognised her voice from the answerphone message, the day he had got the letter. 'I'm Lacy, Mr Bickleigh's

140

secretary. I'll be your first point of contact if you have any queries.'

'Thank you,' said Gabriel. He sat down in a leather club chair in the waiting area. The walls were dark red, hung with hunting prints, and there were copies of *Country Life* on the table. It smelled of polish, percolating coffee and money. Old money.

'Everyone imagines this is what probate solicitors do every day,' said Thomas Bickleigh as he ushered Gabriel into his office moments later. 'Sitting people down to tell them they've inherited an unexpected fortune. But this is the first time it's happened to me. Not that this is a fortune,' he added hastily. 'But you have been left a share in a local farm. A third share. Equally split. Between you and the testator's two great-nieces.'

Gabriel thought Mr Bickleigh was probably in his mid-fifties. He was looking at Gabriel's passport now with his horn-rimmed glasses for scrutinising the small print — he had been asked to bring photo identification with him.

'Are you sure,' said Gabriel, baffled, 'you've got the right person?'

Mr Bickleigh read out his name, age and address. 'This was the information given to me by Matthew Melchior.'

'Good,' said Gabriel. 'Because you never want to be left a farm one minute and have it snatched away the next.'

Mr Bickleigh smiled politely at his attempt at a joke.

'The good news is that Mr Melchior left

provision by way of a life insurance policy for the inheritance taxes on his estate to be covered. So there is no reason for the property to be sold in the first instance. You and Miss Melchior and Miss Melchior-Hawkins will own it outright, once probate has been granted. So it will be up to the three of you to decide what to do with it, between you.'

'Right,' said Gabriel. 'So where is it? What is it?'

'Dragonfly Farm is a small farmhouse set in about ten acres just outside a village called Rushbrook. Four miles from here. Outbuildings, a couple of apple orchards and a bit of pasture that runs down to the river Rushbrook.'

'Nice.'

'Very. Though I can't tell you exactly what it's worth yet. We'll have to have it valued for probate.'

'And what about the great-nieces? Would they have any idea why this has happened?'

Mr Bickleigh shrugged, spreading his hands and holding them upwards.

'I've asked them both to come in at two o'clock, so I can outline the contents of the will to them as well.'

'They're going to love me, aren't they?' Gabriel made a face.

'I expect you will come as a surprise.'

'So — do you know why I've been left this? I don't know Matthew Melchior. I've never even heard of him.'

'I'm afraid I can't throw any light on that. I was just taken on to follow Mr Melchior's instructions. And make the will watertight. Which it is.'

'You mean nobody can contest it?' Gabriel felt sure the nieces would want to when they found out about him.

'Mr Melchior was of sound mind when he made it. It was all done legally with witnesses. I'm the executor — my fee comes out of the estate. There are really no grounds for contesting it. Other members of the family who might have an interest have been given a small bequest in acknowledgement of their relationship with him.'

Gabriel looked at him. He suspected he knew more than he was letting on.

'Can you give me a clue?' he said. 'Am I a random choice? Or is there a reason?'

Mr Bickleigh's smooth round face became smoother and rounder with impassivity.

'Mr Melchior's affairs are completely confidential. My job is to oversee probate and distribute the estate as instructed.'

He seemed very keen to stick to the protocol and keep everything on a formal footing. Gabriel could see he wasn't going to winkle anything out of him.

Then Mr Bickleigh cleared his throat, as if he was about to divulge something of value.

'The name Culbone is a familiar one around here. They go back several hundred years. The family have a house on the other side of the river. Rushbrook House.' He paused for a moment, as if deciding whether to divulge more. 'Dragonfly Farm used to belong to them. More than a hundred years ago.'

'Oh.' That was interesting. 'Culbone is my grandmother's married name. She divorced my grandfather a long time ago — I've never met him.' He grinned. 'And I've never met another Culbone. It's a pretty unusual name.'

'Well,' Mr Bickleigh spread his hands. 'Your family might be able to provide some clues.'

Gabriel didn't want to mention that his grandmother probably wouldn't. It still saddened him to talk about Diana's condition. It was private. Not for strangers. Perhaps his mother would shed some light on the situation. For now, he was more intrigued about Dragonfly Farm.

'Do you think I'd be able to see the farm while I'm here?'

'I was going to suggest to the Melchiors that you visit later this afternoon.'

'After you've given them the good news they've got to share their inheritance with a total stranger?'

There was a glimmer of a smile.

'Yes.'

Gabriel nodded. 'OK. Well, I'll hang around then. Can you give me a ring to confirm it when you've seen them?'

'Of course.' Mr Bickleigh held his hand out for him to shake. 'Thank you for coming all this way. You'll have to come in and sign more paperwork as we head for completion. Are you a country person?'

'Not really,' said Gabriel.

'People are very set in their ways around here,' Mr Bickleigh warned him.

Gabriel couldn't help feeling that he was

judging the length of his hair and the brightness of his tie and the fact he was wearing blue suede shoes.

'I'm sure I'll cope.'

As he left the office, Lacy smiled at him brightly. 'All right?'

'A bit puzzled but . . . fine.' She was gagging for feedback. He wasn't going to give her any.

'Betwaddled, we call it round here.'

'Betwaddled. Yeah. That just about sums it up.' He smiled back at her. 'Is there anywhere good to eat nearby?'

'Well. There's the Golden Egg. Or the Nettleford Arms do a nice ploughman's platter.'

'What about the restaurant across the marketplace?'

'Oh, that's just for special occasions. The Glorious Artichoke?'

He loved the way her Somerset accent wrapped itself around the name.

'Well,' he said, 'I think being left part of a farm is a special occasion. Don't you?'

16

Tabitha slung the Land Rover into the last parking place in the market square. Gum's HiLux had been pronounced a write-off and Tabitha only had her treacherous motorbike for transport. She didn't really want the truck back, under the circumstances. She'd have to buy something new with the insurance money. Jimmy O'Gowan had lent her the Defender in the meantime.

'Don't think it will make me come and work for you,' she'd teased him. 'I'm not open to bribery.'

'Ah, no, I know. I'd do anything for you, you know that,' he admitted. 'No strings attached and you can have it for as long as you want. It's just our back-up vehicle. We can do without.'

People had been endlessly thoughtful. Because, thought Tabitha, they had loved Gum so much, and she was now reaping the benefits. It made her feel a bit of a fraud. As long as she lived, she thought, she would never be as kind or thoughtful as Joy and Gum. She could try, though . . .

Tabitha, Georgia and Robin clambered out and huddled in the market square. It was a dull day with a bitter wind, and the little town looked even greyer than usual.

'Jesus, it's brass monkeys. I'm going to go and warm up in the Nettleford Arms,' said Robin.

146

'Come and find me when you know what's what.'

'Yes, Dad,' sighed Tabitha, watching her father slope off to the pub in the far corner of the market square. 'Funny,' she murmured to Georgia. 'He never bothers with me most of the time. But now there might be money involved, he's all over me.'

'He does care. He's just not very good at dad stuff.'

'No. He never has been.' She sighed. 'Not like Uncle Chris. You have no idea how lucky you are.'

'I know.' Georgia never failed to appreciate her father.

'He was wonderful yesterday. He kept checking up on me. All Dad was interested in was flirting with any female mourner under sixty.' Tabitha laughed despite herself. 'Right.' She looked at the facade of Melchior and Sons. 'Are we ready?'

Georgia hooked her arm through her cousin's. 'Whatever we're about to find out, you should get Dragonfly Farm.'

Tabitha laughed. 'You are so much *nicer* than me. And that's rubbish. Dragonfly belongs to all of us. It's our home from home.'

★ ★ ★

Ten minutes later they were sitting in front of Mr Bickleigh. Never a relaxed man at the best of times, he was finding it hard to look them in the eye after delivering his bombshell. Beads of sweat

147

started to pop out onto his forehead as he shuffled the paperwork in front of him.

'Gabriel Culbone?' said Tabitha. 'Who the fuck is Gabriel Culbone?'

Georgia gave her a nudge with her elbow as Mr Bickleigh flushed raspberry and pushed a piece of paper across the desk.

'Here are his details. I've checked his identity and I'm satisfied he is the beneficiary specified in the will.'

Tabitha flicked the piece of paper away, impatient.

'Yes, but who is he to Gum? Why has he been left a third of the farm when we've never even heard of him?'

'I'm afraid I'm not party to that information.'

'You *must* know.'

Mr Bickleigh indicated the file in front of him.

'I am simply the executor on behalf of Melchior and Sons. As laid out in Mr Melchior's last will and testament.'

Tabitha gave a tut of impatience. He was obviously hiding behind protocol. 'Well, when was the will made?'

'It was drawn up eighteen months ago. Once we had settled everything in Mrs Melchior's will. Obviously her estate passed straight to Mr Melchior, as is customary. Apart from a few bequests — I believe you were both left small sums.'

He looked at the two girls.

'Yes. But he must have explained who Gabriel Culbone was?'

Mr Bickleigh shook his head.

148

'It's not our place to query our clients' wishes. As long as we are satisfied they are of sound mind and are not being unduly influenced.'

'But maybe he was? Maybe this Gabriel bloke was . . . I don't know. Blackmailing him?'

'I really don't think so.'

Tabitha crossed her arms. 'It just seems very odd, that's all. Especially when he's a Culbone.'

'You've got to admit it looks suspicious,' added Georgia. 'You know the history between the two families, don't you?'

Mr Bickleigh nodded.

'I know Dragonfly Farm once belonged to Rushbrook House. And it was won off the Culbones in a card game.'

'Yes. And ever since then they've wanted it back,' said Tabitha. 'Gum got a letter not long after Joy died, offering to buy the farm. And now somebody called Culbone gets a share of it? Don't you think that's suspicious?'

Mr Bickleigh stroked his chin, mulling over the information. 'I can see how you might think so. But when I spoke to Mr Culbone this morning, he seemed to have no knowledge of Dragonfly Farm or have any connection to Rushbrook House. And he'd never heard of Mr Melchior.'

'Well, he would say that, wouldn't he?'

Georgia put a hand on her cousin's arm to calm her, then turned to Mr Bickleigh. 'Did you say he was here? In Nettleford?'

'Yes. I suggested that he come and see you this afternoon at the farm. But, of course, if that's inappropriate — '

149

'I want to know more about who he is before he steps over the threshold,' said Tabitha.

'I can telephone him if it's not convenient. Or if you'd like to meet him here first on neutral territory . . . ?'

Mr Bickleigh was starting to realise he had underestimated the delicacy of this situation.

'No. I think we should meet him at the farm,' said Georgia. 'There's no point in delaying it. We need to get to know him, don't we?'

Tabitha was looking thunderous.

'Oh yes, let's invite him in and let him choose his own bedroom, shall we?'

Mr Bickleigh looked awkward.

'I'm sorry if this has come as a shock.'

'Of course it bloody has.'

'Well. Anything I can do to help smooth the process. I shall keep you abreast of probate. As I explained to Mr Culbone, the inheritance tax is covered by the insurance. So we should be home and dry by the New Year.'

Tabitha tried to smile.

'I hope no one else is going to pop up out of the woodwork?'

'I'm sure not.'

'Thank you,' said Georgia. 'Tell Mr Culbone we'll see him later this afternoon.'

She gave him an apologetic smile, trying to compensate for Tabitha's belligerence. Mr Bickleigh smiled back, looking rather relieved that they were going, she thought.

★   ★   ★

'Google him,' said Tabitha as she marched out of the office with Georgia in her wake, sweeping past Lacy. 'Google him on your phone. There can't be more than one person called Gabriel Culbone.'

Georgia tried to type his name into her phone while keeping up with Tabitha, who pushed her way out of the door and ran down the steps.

'Wait, will you?' She scurried to catch up then looked at her cousin. 'Tab. You're crying.'

'Yes,' said Tabitha. 'I always cry when I'm fucking furious.'

'Hey.' Georgia put her arms round her. For a moment Tabitha leaned into her. She was sobbing properly now.

'It's OK,' said Georgia. 'It's been a tough few days. You're allowed to cry. You have to grieve.' She hugged her tight, patting her on the back.

Tabitha looked up. 'I'm not grieving,' she said. 'I'm *betrayed*. Gum told me everything. We had no secrets from each other. I thought he trusted me. I was there with him when Joy died, for God's sake. But he kept this from me. How *dare* he?'

'Let's go and find your dad and have a drink.'

'Oh yes. Dad'll be a huge help.' Tabitha gulped and wiped her eyes on her sleeve. 'He'll be half-cut already.'

'We can talk it all over logically. Make a plan.' Georgia looked down at her phone. 'Oh my *God*! Is that him?' She held up a photo of a man stripped to the waist in front of a furnace, his body gleaming with sweat, his dark hair down to his shoulders. 'He is *hot*.'

151

Tabitha looked at the photo. 'Don't be taken in,' she said, dismissive. 'You can do a lot with Photoshop.'

★   ★   ★

When he was sure the girls had gone, Mr Bickleigh shut the Melchior file with a sigh, running a finger round the back of his collar. It was slightly damp with sweat from such an awkward situation. His duty was always to his client, even though Mr Melchior was now deceased. It was more than his job was worth to reveal anything confidential. The practice was scrupulous about things like that. It wasn't like the old days, when everything was done on a handshake and people turned a blind eye. He would certainly face disciplinary action if he revealed Mr Melchior's history.

'All right?' said Lacy, popping her head round the door, desperate for details.

'Yes, fine, thank you.' Mr Bickleigh shut the file firmly and handed it to Lacy to put away.

He had spoken time and again to Matthew Melchior about the delicacy of the situation, warning him that it might cause problems and pressuring him to leave some sort of explanation in the event of his demise. But Matthew had remained stubborn.

'It's not my story to tell,' he'd told Mr Bickleigh firmly. 'It's not my story to tell.'

★   ★   ★

'It's outrageous,' said Robin when he heard the news. He had commandeered a table by the fireplace in the Nettleford Arms. 'I think we should contest the will. I mean, he's a Culbone, for heaven's sake. We all know how Gum felt about them.'

'We can't contest it,' said Tabitha, sliding into the oak settle and readjusting the cushions to make herself comfortable. 'The will's completely watertight.'

'I can contest it,' said Robin. 'I've been left out. I could say I think I should have been in it.'

'You're only his nephew,' said Tabitha. 'You haven't got a hope.'

'What about if we get another solicitor? An expert?'

'It would be a waste of money. And time. You know what a stickler Mr Bickleigh is.'

'Let's wait until we've met him,' suggested Georgia. 'We'll have a better idea of what we're up against.'

'But we're still trying to recover from yesterday. We're not ready to talk to him. Tab definitely isn't.' Robin was being uncharacteristically protective of his daughter.

Georgia was trying to be the voice of reason.

'But it's much better if the whole family meets him while we're here. Who knows when we'll all be together again? Mum and Dad are hardly ever down from Scotland.'

'I can always come down,' said Robin.

'Yes, but we want their input,' said Tabitha.

'Why? Because they're sensible and I'm not?'

'Yes. They are sensible. They don't get

153

emotional about things. Or angry.'

Georgia cringed. If Tabitha got her emotional responses from anyone, it was probably Robin.

Robin swirled his drink around, scowling. 'Of course I'm angry. It's a ridiculous situation. Gum leaving our . . . *legacy* to some bloke we've never heard of.'

'If anyone should be pissed off about this, it's Tab,' said Georgia. 'Dragonfly Farm is her home.'

Robin looked at her. 'Exactly,' he said. 'This isn't about me, you know. It's about my daughter. I'm not totally selfish.'

'I wish you two would stop talking about me as if I wasn't here,' said Tabitha. 'I want to meet Gabriel Culbone and I want everyone there.'

'Come on, then,' said Georgia. 'Let's go and pick up some scones from the bakery. We'll stuff him up with a cream tea then go for the jugular when he's in a food coma.'

17

Gabriel treated himself to lunch at the Glorious Artichoke and was pleasantly surprised to find it was as good as any London restaurant. He had celeriac and porcini risotto and an affogato to perk himself up, and afterwards he chatted to the chef over a plate of Nettleford cheddar and quince cheese. It was early in the week and the restaurant was quiet, so they'd swapped notes over a glass of Amarone, and Gabriel had felt relaxed enough to tell him his conundrum: how he might have to give up his business and go back into restaurant management.

'That's harsh,' agreed the chef. 'But nothing beats being at the coalface. I love this business.'

'Yeah,' said Gabriel. 'I guess it will be about finding the right place.'

As he left, he felt a little cheered. Maybe his fate wasn't so gloomy after all. But first, he wanted to know more — about Dragonfly Farm, the Melchiors and his own family history: anything that might explain this mysterious bequest. And what would it actually mean to him and, more importantly, to Lola and Plum? Would today's revelation change their future? He decided he'd have a look at where his namesakes hailed from. If, indeed, he *was* one of the Rushbrook Culbones. It was an unusual name, but maybe they had spread their net more widely than Somerset.

He'd got the directions to Dragonfly Farm from Thomas Bickleigh.

'Don't follow the satnav or you'll end up on the other side of the river at Rushbrook House. That's the Culbone family seat. Though they haven't lived there for years.'

He drove out of Nettleford and followed the directions to Rushbrook. It was idyllic in the autumn sunshine: the twisting narrow lanes and the trees on the turn and the fields falling away either side of him. He slowed down as he came past the little cluster of houses that made up the village, and pulled into the car park adjoining the churchyard.

It was restful in the afternoon sun as he wandered amongst the gravestones, and he took off his jacket and tie. There definitely was a strong Culbone presence, he noted, and there were several impressive family tombs. They had been significant around here, although the most recent stone was dated 1986, more than thirty years ago. Tarka Culbone, he read — and saw that Tarka had been only twenty-three when he died. *A dearly loved son, grandson and brother*, read the simple inscription. He wondered what had happened: whether it was an accident or an illness. There had been no Culbone buried here since.

In the more recent section of the graveyard he saw what must be Matthew Melchior's grave. The earth was freshly dug with turf laid carefully back on the top, and there were piles of flowers. He read a few of the attached cards: the messages were all heartfelt and gave him a sense

156

of a man who had been loved and respected. It moved him, and yet again he wondered about their connection.

'What am I to you?' he wanted to ask, although he knew he would get no answer.

The stone next to it was marked with the name Joy Melchior, and underneath was written *Beloved wife of Matthew*. How sad, he thought, but at least they were together again. He moved away. He felt as if he was intruding, perusing the grave of a man who had only been buried the day before. The last thing he wanted was for a family member to visit the grave and find him rummaging about for clues.

Instead, he got back in the car and drove past the turning for Dragonfly Farm, up over the bridge that straddled the river, and left along the road until he came to Rushbrook House. He couldn't see down the drive as far as the house itself, but the gates were grand, albeit dilapidated. The grass was overgrown and the hedges either side were a mass of brambles, the blackberries plump and shiny with juice. Again, he didn't want to be caught snooping, so he turned in the road and headed back to his appointment with the Melchiors. He was still none the wiser, but his initial investigations were certainly intriguing. Two families, two houses, a churchyard full of graves, many of which bore his own name. How did he fit into the story?

The sun was starting to drop like a copper penny behind the trees as he turned into the driveway of Dragonfly Farm. He slowed his car down, unused to mud and potholes. Banks of hawthorn and beech and oak formed a tunnel of citric yellow, burnt orange and plum-coloured leaves illuminating the twisted trunks and branches.

Then he turned a corner and saw a long, low farmhouse sitting in the afternoon sun, with an open-fronted barn, wrought-iron gates, white painted windows and a rolling orchard to either side, thick with ancient apple trees.

'Bloody hell,' he thought as he parked next to a Defender and a Volvo estate.

In his head, Gabriel had imagined the Melchior cousins as two spinsters dressed in dowdy clothing in flat shoes, gilets and headscarves, anxious and wary, swilling back gin and smoking endless Benson & Hedges. He didn't know why: the image just seemed to fit the story. Part of him was still expecting to discover this was an elaborate scam; that he would be asked to part with his bank details any minute and then be lured to a remote outhouse to be chopped up and fed to the pigs.

Then the front door opened and out came two women, one tall and rangy with wild blonde hair past her shoulders, the other smaller, darker, glossier.

He stepped out of the car. 'Hello,' he said, a little unsure quite how to introduce himself. 'I'm Gabriel Culbone. I think you're expecting me?'

'Well, no. We weren't, actually. Far from it,' said the blonde one. Her voice was slow and languid; deeper than her slight frame suggested.

'I'm Georgia,' said the other girl. 'And this is Tabitha. Don't take any notice of her. We know

158

this is a surprise for you too.'

For a moment, Gabriel felt as if he was in a fairy tale. A picture-book farmhouse, two bewitching women, an unexpected legacy — and then an owl swooped down from a tree behind them and sat on the gatepost staring at them.

'That's Zorro,' smiled Tabitha. 'Welcome to Dragonfly Farm.'

There was still a wryness to her tone he couldn't miss. A certain irony accompanied by a slight raise of her eyebrow.

'You're right. This has all come as a total shock to me,' he replied. 'I really don't have a clue what's going on.'

Tabitha looked suspicious, while Georgia was smiling as if to reassure him.

'You'd better come in,' said Tabitha.

He followed them inside, wary. Was he going to prick his finger and fall into a deep sleep? Choke on a poisoned apple? Be eaten by a wolf?

In the kitchen were more people, a pot of tea and, thankfully, a stronger sense of normality. There were introductions and an invitation to sit at the table. He tried to work out who was what to whom. Nicola, a softly spoken woman with grey hair, seemed to be Georgia's mother; a kindly, bespectacled man her father, Chris. A dissipated younger man was either Tabitha's father or her boyfriend — he almost seemed too young for the former but then he stood next to the grey-haired woman and their resemblance became apparent.

'I'm Robin, Tabitha's father,' he said. 'You're very brave,' he went on. 'I don't think a Culbone

159

has been over this threshold for over a hundred years.'

Gabriel looked puzzled. 'Why?'

'You know that Culbones and Melchiors have been sworn enemies for over a century?'

'No.'

'But don't worry, we're not going to kill you. Yet.' Tabitha gave another twitch of her eyebrow.

'Listen,' said Gabriel. 'Whatever your problem with the Culbones is, it's nothing to do with me. It's just my name. Inherited from a grandfather I've never met. My grandmother left him before my mother was even born, as far as I know.'

He tried to keep his tone light. He knew Robin was teasing him, yet there was an underlying air of tension that probably came not from a longstanding feud, but the fact he'd just swiped a third of their inheritance from them.

'So you don't know the legend? Of Eleanor Culbone?' Georgia handed him a thick china mug of tea. 'There's scones. And clotted cream. And three sorts of jam. All home-made.'

'Wonderful.' Gabriel didn't mention that he was still full from the Glorious Artichoke, but started helping himself. 'No — I've never heard anything about a legend.'

'I suppose you would say that.'

Gabriel felt awkward, but also a little aggrieved.

'Stop it, you two. There's no point in dredging up the past right now. As you can imagine, Gabriel, everyone is a little taken aback.' Nicola came to sit at the table. It was as if she was taking charge. 'We need to make some sort of a plan. Dragonfly Farm has been very important to all of us. It's a home from home for me and Robin and Georgia. But for Tabitha, it *is* home. I can't pretend to understand why Gum has jeopardised that for her.'

'The last thing I want to do is make anyone homeless.'

'Let's be realistic. You own a third. Or will do, once probate has been granted. Unless we uncover something in the meantime.'

Gabriel frowned. That sounded like a threat. 'Like what?' he asked, drawing himself up a little. He wasn't going to let himself be bullied. And at the moment it was four against one.

'It's OK,' said Chris. 'Nicola's just being protective. No one quite understands why this has happened.'

'Me least of all,' said Gabriel.

'Why don't you tell us a bit about yourself? We don't know anything about you.'

Gabriel found himself warming to Chris. As the only other non-Melchior he was less defensive than the rest of the family.

'OK — so. I live in London. East London. I've got a partner — Lola. We have a little three-year-old daughter, Plum.'

'Oh!' said Georgia. 'Plum. That's the sweetest name.'

'She *is* sweet,' said Gabriel. 'And I would do anything for her.' He paused for a moment. What did you tell people about yourself in a situation like this? 'I'm a knife maker. I make bespoke knives for people — chef's knives, carving knives, whatever they want.'

'That sounds cool,' said Tabitha, warming slightly.

'Yes,' said Gabriel. He didn't mention that at the moment it wasn't particularly profitable, and he was on the verge of giving it up. He didn't want to look as if he had a motive for cashing in on Dragonfly Farm.

'Why don't we show you around while it's still light?' Georgia suggested, sensing he had been grilled enough.

'That would be great,' said Gabriel. He wanted to get away from the scrutiny. It was stifling in the kitchen, with the late sun streaming in through the window. He craved space and fresh air.

'You'll need wellingtons,' said Tabitha. 'What size are you?'

'Um — ten?' Gabriel looked down at his navy-blue suede brogues. Mr Bickleigh had been right to look at them askance. They definitely weren't suitable for tramping around a farmyard.

'Gum was a twelve, but I'm sure you'll manage.' Tabitha thrust a pair of boots at him. Gabriel put them on, the symbolism not wasted on him as he tried on another man's shoes for size. A dead man's.

18

The sun was low in the sky as Gabriel, Georgia and Tabitha left the house and clomped through the courtyard. Around him, he could see a range of outbuildings in various stages of disrepair.

'We'll walk the land first,' said Tabitha. 'We can do the house when we get back.'

He followed her through a gate to the first of the orchards, already damp with late-afternoon dew. She indicated to her left and right as she strode through the long grass and along an avenue of trees. 'Some of these trees are over a hundred years old. They did their own thing for years, but our great-aunt did a lot of work on them, especially in the last ten years. She started making apple juice and cider again because we had the old press in the barn. From back in the day when Dragonfly was a proper working farm. It hasn't been, not since the war.'

Gabriel looked at the rows and rows of ancient trees. There was an order to them, even though they were all different heights and breadths. Already he could see there were many different sorts of apple — some shiny, some waxy, some dull; green and orange and red and yellow. They looked comfortable in their landscape.

'So tell me this famous legend, then? About how you came by it.'

The two girls turned to look at him. He felt a bit uncomfortable under their gaze.

'Everyone still goes on about it, as if it's not really ours. But it was won, fair and square. Years ago, Dragonfly Farm used to belong to Rushbrook House.' Tabitha waved a hand over the horizon. 'It's on the other side of the river, behind those woods. It's the Culbone family seat. Local gentry. There's no title, but they act like the lords of the manor.'

'That's not totally fair,' said Georgia. 'They're hardly even around these days.'

Tabitha shrugged. 'One of the Culbone sons, Casper, was supposed to run the farm. But he was a drunk and a gambler and a womaniser, you name it.' She was giving Gabriel a more salacious version than she'd given the school-children. 'Anyway, he lost the farm in a card game at the Swan to our great-great-great . . .' She frowned. 'I can't remember how many greats, but quite a few — grandfather. Joseph Melchior. The Culbones tried to buy him off when they found out what Casper had done, but Joseph insisted that the debt should be honoured. He was just a tenant farmer from the other side of Rushbrook, so having his own farm was a dream come true. And so he moved in.'

'Fair enough,' said Gabriel. 'That's how gambling works. You have to honour your debts.'

'Yes. But the Culbones weren't happy. Especially Casper. He felt as if he'd been made a fool of. He went back to live at Rushbrook House, but he had it in for Joseph.'

Georgia took up the story.

'Then Joseph met Eleanor. She was a wool

164

merchant's daughter from Nettleford. Every man in the Somerset Levels was a little bit in love with her. Joseph would never have had a chance if he'd just been a tenant, but now he had Dragonfly Farm he had status. He could offer her a good home and a good life. They fell desperately in love and were engaged to be married.'

Georgia paused for a moment. Tabitha leaned in, her eyes glittering.

'Casper Culbone saw this as an opportunity to ruin Joseph's happiness. He had more money — of course he did — and the promise of a much bigger house when his father died, and he had the best horses in the county and he dressed in the height of fashion. He moved in on Eleanor. She wasn't the sort of girl he would normally bother with. He liked society girls from London who were worried about dowries and jewels and titles. Eleanor wasn't interested in that sort of thing, but she was dazzled. Casper was, by all accounts, very handsome and very charming.'

'It's a Culbone thing,' said Georgia. 'They're all shiny on the outside but not much inside.'

'Oh,' said Gabriel.

'I don't mean you,' said Georgia hastily. 'You seem very nice.'

'Anyway, Eleanor broke off the engagement. She went and married Casper Culbone, in Rushbrook church. And once they were married it all went badly wrong. Casper was a drunk and he hit her. Hit her so hard she fell down the stairs and lost their baby.'

165

'Oh God,' said Gabriel. 'How horrible.'

'She ran away that night. She ran to Dragonfly Farm, to plead with Joseph to have her back. She'd made a terrible mistake and knew he was the man she loved. She pleaded with him, right here, in this very orchard.'

Gabriel looked around, as if he could see the ghosts of Joseph and Eleanor amongst the trees. 'Did he have her back?'

Tabitha sighed. 'He couldn't. He was already engaged to someone else. He wasn't going to break off his engagement and risk breaking his fiancée's heart. He knew only too well how that felt. He loved Eleanor, but she had made her choice and they both had to stand by that.'

'He was a man of his word.' Gabriel nodded his approval.

'Eleanor couldn't face going back to Rushbrook House. And she was too ashamed to go home to her father. She couldn't bear the fact that she had been so foolish, had been taken in and had lost the love of a good man. She went down to the river . . . and drowned herself.'

There was silence as everyone took in the end of the story. The light was fading and the shadows were creeping in. Gabriel shivered.

'And from that day on,' continued Georgia, 'Culbones and Melchiors are daggers drawn. Joseph never recovered from her death. He swore that if a Culbone ever crossed the river and set foot on his land he would kill him.'

'And that's how we still feel about them,' said Tabitha.

'Not really,' said Georgia. 'We never see them.

166

And Dash was very kind to you when Gum had his accident.'

'Fair enough,' said Tabitha. 'But I'm pretty sure he was behind the offer to buy the farm from Gum. They can't let it lie, you know.'

The three of them looked out across the valley to the woods on the other side. There was no glimpse of Rushbrook House through the trees in the gloaming, but Gabriel could sense its presence. He could only imagine how furious the Culbone family would have been to lose the farm. Precious acres, precious protection.

And now the Melchiors were panicking. A Culbone was encroaching on their territory; clawing back their legacy. No wonder they were jittery.

'That story explains a lot,' he said. 'But I'm still not sure how I fit into the picture. I might have the Culbone name, but I don't have anything to do with Rushbrook House or Nettleford. As far as I know, my grandfather was a Culbone, and he and my grandmother lived in Kensington.' He frowned. 'But I can't ask her anything. She's got dementia. My mother might know something.'

He looked around him. The sky was layered up in shades of navy and orange as the sun set. The apple trees stood out against it, their branches spread protectively as if to keep the enemy away. Behind them, yellow light spilled out from the windows of the farmhouse and a plume of woodsmoke wound its way towards the rising moon.

Gabriel wasn't sure how to feel. This was a

167

magical place, but the story behind it was unsettling. Although not as unsettling as the reason for him being drawn into the present-day story. He was starting to suspect there were things he was going to uncover that he might not like. That he might have a fight on his hands when deciding what the farm's future was to be. A fight with his own conscience.

He looked up at the sky. It was nearly dark. Even if he left now he wouldn't be back until after Plum's bedtime. 'I better make a move.'

'Stay!' said Georgia. 'Stay for supper. We've only just met you. If we're all going to be owners of Dragonfly Farm, we need to get to know each other. Don't we, Tab?'

'There's no more room,' objected Tabitha. 'The bedrooms are all full.'

'He can have my room and I'll bunk up with you.'

'I suppose so.'

Tabitha didn't look all that enthusiastic. But Gabriel was tempted. He'd have to phone Lola, though. Find some explanation as to why he wasn't coming back.

'The thing is,' said Georgia, 'we need to talk everything over. Because how are the three of us going to share the farm? How would that even work?'

'I've got no idea,' said Gabriel. 'Until today I didn't even know it existed.'

'It's the most beautiful place in the world,' said Tabitha. 'And I would kill anyone who tried to take it away from me.'

She looked at him, her expression fierce.

168

'I can see how wonderful it is,' said Gabriel. 'But this is quite confusing for me.'

'Stay tonight,' said Georgia more gently. 'We can talk it all over. And Mum's done roast lamb.'

'And you'd better try some Melchior Cider,' added Tabitha. 'Once you've drunk that, you'll be completely in our power.'

She smiled, her eyes glittering.

'When you put it like that,' said Gabriel, 'I can't really say no, can I?'

* * *

Gabriel stood in the hall at Dragonfly Farm while he phoned Lola. It had a flagstone floor, rows of boots, shoes, coats and hats and a grandfather clock overseeing the comings and goings. He could hear the rest of the Melchiors chatting in the kitchen, no doubt speculating on his provenance but also what he might do with his share of the farm.

There was little point in them speculating as he had no idea either who he was to them or what he was going to do. All he did know was that he was already falling under the farm's spell. He had to keep his head, and not be bewitched. Yet he felt more at home here than he ever had anywhere. The house was mellow and warm and welcoming. Its walls rippled with unevenness; the plaster was soft to the touch; the wood of the beams and the staircases gleamed with patina. Even the glass in the window shone differently.

It was as if he was seeing everything through a filter, some magical candlelit glow. Or maybe

169

there had been something in his tea. Something that made him not notice the flaws and the cracks, the dust and the cobwebs. Even the ramshackle buildings outside had looked perfect to him. He longed to know what lay behind each door.

He squared staying overnight with Lola, equivocating slightly, telling her his meeting had dragged on and he felt too tired to drive back.

'If I stay the night here, I can stop off and see Diana on the way home tomorrow. I haven't seen her for a few weeks.'

This was a perfect plan, as his grandmother's nursing home was in Marlborough — he could easily divert through Wiltshire. He always felt guilty about not visiting more but it was difficult, with a job and a family and the distance: the Brambles was at least a two-hour drive out of London. This would assuage his guilt and he might be able to dig for some clues.

'No problem,' said Lola. She sounded very content. 'Me and Plum are having a lovely time.'

Then he dialled his mother, hoping she was in Comporta and not Pondicherry, otherwise he'd be waking her up in the early hours. It went straight through to her voicemail, as she never answered anyway. Use of mobile phones was generally frowned upon in the retreats where she taught, but she would get back to him eventually.

'Hey. It's Gabe. Give me a call when you can.'

He hung up, wondering if she would be able to shine any light on this mystery. Like him, Lydia had grown up the only child of a single mother. She'd had an anarchic streak, rebelling

170

and protesting at every opportunity, dying her hair, piercing her nose and holding up placards to bash the establishment. Gabriel had come along when Lydia was living in a squat in Camden. His imminent arrival meant his father, the leader of the squat, suddenly decided that the rabble-rousing rebel life was not for him, grew out his Mohican and set up as a kitchen fitter in his native Swansea.

Lydia didn't want to go and live in Wales. She finally managed to get her act together and trained as a yoga teacher. Gabriel loved his mum — her hennaed hair, her flowing, Stevie Nick's clothes, her misguided idealism and her chronic lack of self-awareness — but he recognised that, despite her obsession with karma, she was very good at putting herself first, before both him and Diana. He and his grandmother had always been quite close, though. Being one generation apart allowed you to be generous about people's faults, he had found. The things that grated on Lydia's nerves — Diana's obsession with her appearance and table manners and who was who — Gabriel just found endearing.

'Just remember,' Diana would say to him, 'the name Culbone can open doors.'

Was that why she'd kept the name, after she left her husband? There were so many questions.

As he put his phone back in his pocket, Gabriel wondered if trailing in the wake of his nomadic mother was what made him appreciate Dragonfly Farm. Somewhere that held the marks of generations of the same family and had evolved with them. Did he have the right to put his mark on it too? Where did he fit in to this puzzle?

He made his way back into the kitchen. Everyone had gathered round the table, except Nicola and Chris, who were putting the finishing touches to the food. It was cosy, with the overhead lights turned off and candles on the table, and while the overall feel was casual, even a bit scruffy, there were linen napkins at everyone's place, and crystal water glasses, and silver salt cellars at each end.

'Wait a minute,' said Chris. He stood up and went over to the kitchen drawer. He pulled out the knife he had used to carve the chicken the night before. 'Is this one of yours?'

He handed it to Gabriel, who nodded in delighted recognition. 'Yes,' he said. 'Look — there's my initials on the blade — GC. And an angel with a halo.' He put the knife on the table in front of him. 'This is one of the most popular knives I sell on my website.'

'Gum must have sent away for it,' said Tabitha. 'I think it's been here for a while.'

'I'll have a record,' said Gabriel. 'I keep a note of everyone who's bought one.'

There was silence for a moment as they all contemplated this twist in the story. Evidence of a conscious link between Gum and this stranger they had never known of until today.

Dinner was very jolly, all things considered. Admittedly, two large glasses of Melchior Cider helped Gabriel relax, then there was plenty of red wine with the lamb, served up with bowls of mashed potato and purple sprouting broccoli.

'Sorry it's not very elaborate,' Nicola said. 'Chris did the mash and he has absolutely guaranteed no lumps.'

'Five quid to anyone who finds one,' grinned Chris.

'I've got a lump in my gravy,' said Robin. 'What's that worth?'

'That's not a lump. It's a bit of onion.' Nicola cuffed the back of her brother's head playfully.

Gabriel observed the family dynamics and did his best to sum everyone up in his head: Nicola, reserved but protective; Chris, kind and practical; Robin, needy and provocative. Then the two cousins: Georgia was smart and funny; Tabitha was bold but, Gabriel suspected, the most vulnerable of all of them. He could see that she was a little adrift without her great-uncle, and that her father didn't even begin to serve her needs. The others were all mindful of her mood.

He suspected that while he had been out of the room making his call, they had all agreed to keep things amicable and superficial over supper. He didn't feel as if he was being grilled or analysed although he suspected they were all making notes for comparison later. Conversation flowed smoothly. They were all interesting and interested in him. Chris made him demonstrate how to sharpen a knife properly, and he enjoyed making a ritual of it.

At the end of the evening, a bottle of cider brandy was produced.

'This is made about ten miles away. We don't have a still here. It's nectar. But you might not remember anything tomorrow. And it might make you say things you regret,' warned Robin, pulling out the squeaky cork stopper and pouring a measure into each glass. It ran out, thick and amber. Gabriel took a sip, cautious — he wasn't much of a spirit drinker. It both burned and soothed his throat, smooth and fiery.

'Wow!' He put his glass down.

The brandy gave him a warm glow and a sudden rush of fondness for his newfound friends — or should that be family? That was alcohol for you, common sense warned him. Don't give anything away. Or make any promises you can't keep. The Melchiors looked beguiling in the lamplight: Georgia's wise and laughing eyes, Tabitha's huge navy-blue pools that sometimes reflected something darker and deeper. Robin had pushed open the window and was smoking a cigarette. Nicola was clearing away the cheese, helped by Chris. Gabriel suddenly felt very tired. It was gone eleven, he realised, and he'd set off very early that morning.

Tabitha was getting tearful. 'I don't want everyone to go tomorrow.'

'I have to,' said Georgia. 'That awful Natasha will pinch my job if I don't stand my ground.'

'I've got a gig in Munich at the weekend,' said Robin. 'So I need to get ready.'

'Oh, darling.' Nicola came round the table and gave her niece a hug. 'Come up and stay with us. A change of scene would be good for you.'

'I can't leave at the moment. I've got the apples to harvest soon. And who's going to help with the cider making? It was hard enough with just me and Gum.'

They all exchanged glances.

'I'll come down when I can,' said Georgia.

'There's masses of people who will help you. You know how much everyone loves you around here. They'll all muck in,' Nicola soothed.

Tabitha crossed her arms and nodded.

'I'll help,' Gabriel suddenly found himself offering.

'Yes,' said Tabitha, a little arch. 'Technically they're your apples too, now. So you better had.'

★ ★ ★

It was no surprise that the combination of rich food and the cider brandy and the day's strange events gave Gabriel disturbed dreams that night. He twisted and turned in the bed Georgia had sacrificed for him, getting tangled in the thick linen and heavy blankets, waking with a start. His mouth was bone dry, and he patted the bedside table to see if he could find the glass of water Nicola had handed him to take up to bed.

'There was a lot of salt in that mash,' she'd told him.

It was pitch black in his bedroom. There was no lamplight from outside. Nothing.

Suddenly he heard an unearthly screech. It made his blood run cold, and he remembered Zorro. It must be him. He bloody hoped so, anyway, as the screeching cut through the night once again, harsh and grating. Then it stopped, and he thought he had never heard such silence.

Blackness and silence. He swallowed, feeling a little unnerved. This was the depths of the countryside. He really was in the middle of nowhere.

He foraged in the fragments of dream that still hung in his head. Plum, on a swing in the orchard, her head thrown back, laughing. And Lola, on the banks of the river far behind them, reaching out a hand to a young woman. When she came out of the water, she was wearing a long white robe, clutching a casket. And when he turned round, the swing was empty and Plum was nowhere to be seen.

He told himself it was a jumbled-up load of nonsense. Snippets of everything that had happened stuck back together with no logical framework, but preying on his fears. That was dreams for you. But the images had been so clear, and the fear so tangible, he couldn't get back to sleep. He lay beneath the blankets. He couldn't get up and start prowling around the house. Maybe he should sneak away and drive back to London? But no matter how stealthy he was, he would wake someone, and it would be rude. He started to count sheep. It seemed the most logical thing to do.

★   ★   ★

Next door to Gabriel, Georgia was having a sleepless night too. Sharing a bed with Tabitha was torture: her cousin was restless and wriggly and took up more than her fair share of space. Georgia was feeling anxious, knowing she had to get back to work, knowing she had to say goodbye to her parents again, worried about

176

leaving Tabitha, worried about what on earth was going to happen to the farm. She'd just managed to fall into a fitful doze when her phone chirruped and she started awake, her heart thumping. She picked it up.

It was Doug. She felt a rush of adrenaline as she pressed on his text.

I'm so sorry about Gum. I know you thought the world of him. Sending you love. Xx

He must have seen her Instagram post of the funeral wreath Tabitha had made for Gum, with the words *Farewell to a wonderful man* underneath. Georgia knew it was oversharing at the time; a little bit mawkish and the kind of post she usually raised an eyebrow at. She had also been suspicious of her own motives. Had she been trying to smoke Doug out and elicit some sympathy from him? Was she really that needy?

She spent the night reading and rereading the text and wondering whether to reply. Was he using this as an excuse to get back in touch with her? Re-establish a relationship? She had noticed that his own Instagram posts had lessened of late; not so much poolside posturing, and no sign of the Hot Librarian. Had the heat gone out of Hollywood?

What if it had? It was what he deserved, ditching her like that, looking after his own interests when she'd been such a support to him. Georgia tried to remind herself how she had felt when he'd sent her the dumping email. Absolutely sick.

But she missed him. Even though he had betrayed her, she still thought about him. And she hated herself for it. Ugh — how could she be so wretchedly weak? What was wrong with her? But she remembered, despite his behaviour, how they had been on the same wavelength, talking for hours about films and books. Those weekend afternoons, drifting around bookshops and cafés, buying cheese and dark-red wine then going home and lying on the sofa, reading, eating, drinking then rolling slowly into each other, undressing, kissing . . .

She shivered at, the memory, blushing slightly.

At five o'clock, after no sleep at all, she gave in and texted him.

Thank you.

It had been a kind message and she was too well-mannered to ignore it. Though she had every right to. She bundled under the duvet and tried to snatch a few minutes' sleep — she needed to catch the train just after seven to get to the office in time for a script meeting. But it was hopeless. She got up and got dressed, packing as quietly as she could and taking her case down to the kitchen. She didn't want to wake Tab, who needed to sleep after the events of the past couple of days.

Poe jumped up out of his basket, happy to see her, then stood at the back door whining to be let out.

'Come on, then,' she whispered.

She took him outside into the orchard. The

moon was still hovering like a fat yellow pearl, lighting up the trees, and she thought of all the many hours she and Tabitha had spent scampering around the orchards as children, playing hide and seek, climbing up into the branches, making dens. Joy would bring them out apple juice and biscuits and they would lie on the scratchy red tartan rug that was still on the back of the chair by the fire in the living room. They would look up at the pale-blue sky and breathe in the blossom, and Georgia would make up stories about the wildlife they had discovered: voles and badgers and foxes and woodpeckers. And the dragonflies that hovered over them, zipping amongst the branches, shining with peacock blue and emerald green.

She wondered what the next instalment in the story of Dragonfly Farm was going to be. It seemed fated to be linked to the Culbones yet again. Would it never be free of them? She thought back to the legend, imagining the distraught figure of Eleanor running down to the water's edge. Had she meant to do what she'd done or had she fallen?

Day was starting to break, a milky mist rising up through the trees as Georgia walked Poe down through the orchards towards the river. Her heart was thumping as an idea began to form inside her head. Eleanor's story was the perfect inspiration for a film. How had she not seen that before? It had everything. Intrigue, rivalry, love, heartbreak. Beautiful scenery. Duelling men. A tragic heroine. A stunning period setting. A big house. A flawed family.

She had reached the bank of the river. The water rushed past her, no time to stop for pleasantries. It was bright and fresh and clear: she could see the stones at the bottom. She could imagine them beneath her feet, slippery with bright-green moss. She could imagine the cold taking her breath. She could imagine Eleanor slipping beneath the surface, desperate to escape her situation, a girl whose only mistake had been to fall in love. But then she had been tricked, blinded by glamour and glitter and money. She had forgotten what was important. She had forgotten to be true to her heart.

Georgia turned and ran back up through the orchards to the house. She burst into the kitchen where her mother was filling the teapot yet again — how many times had it been used over the past few days? The kitchen was filled with the quiet hush of early risers trying not to wake late sleepers, but in her excitement Georgia ignored it.

'I'm going to write Eleanor's story,' she told Nicola, who looked startled. 'I'm going to write the script. I need to start doing what I really want. I love my job but I want to write. Properly, not just rewrite other people's stuff.'

'Oh!' Nicola wasn't sure what else to say. 'That sounds . . . fantastic.'

'I want to work out what really happened. What she thought and how she felt. She's like a Hardy heroine. Tragic, like Tess. Her story's perfect for a screenplay.'

'It sounds brilliant, darling.'

'Imagine,' breathed Georgia, 'if it got made.'

'Keira Knightley!' said Nicola.

'She's probably a bit old now.'

'The next Keira Knightley, then.' Nicola smiled.

'Oh, I'm just dreaming, I suppose,' sighed Georgia. 'But I'm going to write it. At the very worst, it can be my calling card. It might even get me an agent.' She looked at her watch. 'Shit. Can you still give me a lift to the station? I'm going to miss my train.'

'If you don't mind me driving in my pyjamas?'

'Course not. Oh God, I'm going to miss you guys.'

'Me too.' Mother and daughter stood in each other's embrace for a moment, relishing each other's warmth, knowing it would probably be a while before they saw each other again.

Chris came in, fully dressed, dangling his car keys.

'Your taxi's here,' he grinned.

'Oh, are you going to take her?' said Nicola. 'I didn't think you'd be up in time.'

'Course I am. Are you ready, love?'

'Have you had breakfast?'

'No. I'll grab something on the train. It's way too early for food.' Georgia made a face. She picked up her bag. 'Say goodbye to Tab, would you, Mum? I don't want to wake her.'

'Of course.'

Nicola watched her husband and her daughter go, her eyes filling with tears. In the cold of the morning, still light-headed from getting up so early, the fragility of life came home to her more keenly than ever. She turned away from the window, not wanting to look down towards the river, with its dark history, its memories, the story that still ran through her no matter how far she tried to run away from it.

19

Gabriel woke with a start to find it was nearly ten o'clock. After all those sleepless hours, he had fallen into a deep slumber and woken later than he had done for months. He jumped up, a little embarrassed. It was rude to sleep in so late in someone else's house. He got washed and dressed as quickly as he could.

Downstairs, he found the house was silent. Everyone seemed to have vanished, even Poe. He stood awkwardly in the kitchen, not sure whether to just go and leave a note of thanks.

What he hadn't dared to look at in the dead of night spread itself before him: the silver mist curling around the tree trunks, the branches even more heavily laden with fruit than they had been the day before — or so it seemed — and a buttery sun venturing over the horizon, turning the silver to gold. How could he have been so afraid? He looked for Zorro, to chide him for his nocturnal screeching, but the owl was nowhere to be seen.

The back door flung open and Tabitha bounded in, bringing the cold air and Poe with her. She was wearing neon festival leggings and an army jacket, her hair tied up in an old silk scarf, carrying a basket of eggs.

'Morning,' she said. 'Everyone's scarpered. Chris and Nicola had to get back to Scotland; Georgia had to get back to work or she'll be sacked. Dad's still asleep but he's getting a cab to the station later. Thank God, because he drives me mad. He's great if it's a party but when it's real life . . . ' She rolled her eyes in fond exasperation.

'Will you be OK on your own?'

'Yes. There's masses to do. And I need to get back to work. The Swan are running out of pies.' She put her basket down. 'Let me give you a Dragonfly Farm party bag. To remind you what you're missing when you get home. You better take some eggs. And some cider.'

'I'd love that.'

'Come on. We'll go and grab some bottles.'

He followed her back out into the yard. 'Are all these buildings unused, then?'

'Some of them. We use the cider barn and a couple of the sheds, but the cattle shed's been empty for ages.'

The cattle shed looked pretty derelict, but on closer inspection it just needed some love and attention. Its walls were solid. They needed pressure-washing and a few coats of white lime. The roof could be easily replaced and a new door put on. Gabriel didn't need any imagination to see himself set up in here. He'd have far more room. No overheads. This space was perfect . . .

What was he doing, daydreaming like this? Life wasn't just about him any more. He couldn't drop everything and do what he wanted. He turned and walked back out into the courtyard and followed Tabitha across to where the cider was stored: an ancient building with stone floors and thick oak walls.

'Me and Gum had such exciting plans,' she said. 'We wanted to expand the business. I've just planted a new orchard. It's got another year or two before it's mature. But we were going to invest in a new bottling plant and a tractor. And employ someone to do some marketing for us. We're never going to be a household name. We haven't got enough land to be big. But it would be great to get Melchior Cider better distribution and maybe some press coverage. It's always been a hobby, but I think there's real potential.'

'Definitely,' said Gabriel. 'You've got the orchards and the premises and the passion, which is the difficult bit.'

'And then there's my secret project. I was keeping it from Gum because it was supposed to be a tribute to Joy. A kind of memorial.'

'Tell me.'

Tabitha's eyes shone as she outlined her vision.

'I want to make a sparkling cider. Something affordable that is really celebratory, with a proper cork, that people can pop open on special occasions. Instead of bloody prosecco, which is often horrible nowadays — bitter and cheap and nasty. This would be light and fresh and delicious. I was going to call it Joy.'

Gabriel nodded. 'That sounds wonderful.'

'We'd make it using the keeving process, which is traditional, but we'd need a lot of new equipment. So I don't know if that particular dream is ever going to come true.' She shrugged. 'I was thinking of crowdfunding. I was supposed

to be meeting a business advisor. But now . . . '
She sighed and pulled a couple of bottles out of
a rack. 'It's all a bit up in the air. If I'm not going
to be able to stay here.' She thrust the bottles at
him. 'Here.'

Gabriel took them off her. 'I need a bit of time
to take everything in. You do understand that?'

It made him feel awkward, knowing that he
had such an influence over what happened next.

Tabitha nodded. 'Of course. Come back down
for a proper visit. Bring your daughter. And — ?'

'Lola.' He stepped forward to give Tabitha a
hug. She tolerated rather than appreciated it; she
wasn't a very huggy person. 'I am really sorry
about Gum,' he told her. 'I just wish I could have
met him.'

She nodded. 'He'd have liked you.'

Her tone was gruff but Gabriel knew she
meant what she said.

'Thank you,' said Gabriel. 'And I'm sorry if I
came as a shock.'

'I never thought of Gum as having secrets,' she
said. 'But I guess everyone does.'

As Gabriel made his way to the car, he found
he didn't want to leave Dragonfly Farm. He
wanted to sit and drink a big mug of tea at the
kitchen table and talk to Tabitha more about her
ideas, perhaps explore the neighbourhood and
get the lie of the land. Even stop at the pub — he
knew it was within walking distance, and he
imagined an open fire, an oak settle, a dark pint
of something rich. But he needed to get on the
road if he was going to have time to call in on his
grandmother.

A frisky breeze fluttered around him, bringing the scent of grass wet with morning dew and the musk of the first windfalls that had thudded onto the ground. He stood and looked over the orchards for a moment, towards the flame-coloured woods on the skyline and the slate-grey river beneath, and the mysterious house across the valley whose chimney he could just glimpse, a thin trail of silver smoke etching itself across the sky. The house where his namesakes lived. Was part of his story locked inside the walls of Rushbrook House?

He had just pulled onto the motorway when his phone rang. His mum's name flashed up on the screen. Lola had insisted on all the bells and whistles when they bought the car, and he was glad now.

'Hey!' he said. 'How's Comporta?'

'Heaven on earth. You and Lola should come out.'

'Um — we have Plum, remember?'

'Bring her too!'

Gabriel rolled his eyes. He wasn't going to inflict a three-year-old on one of the tranquil retreats his mother taught at. They were thousands of pounds a week. He wasn't quite sure how Lydia had worked her way up to become an exclusive yoga teacher to the rich and burned-out, but she'd managed it. He had to admire her for harnessing her passion and making a living from it. Maybe he had something to learn from her.

'Listen — what do you know about your dad? Max Culbone?'

Lydia scoffed. 'Only that he was a beast. What kind of man treats his pregnant wife so badly she has to leave him?'

'Is that really what happened?'

'Yeah. Just before I was born. Can you imagine? The Culbones cut Mum off afterwards. As far as they were concerned she was dead to them.'

'So why did she keep the Culbone name? She could have gone back to her maiden name.'

'She was still in thrall to them, even after everything they did. You know what she always says: *The Culbone name opens doors.* Well, it doesn't. I can tell you that for nothing. Not at the DHSS when you're trying to get a decent place for you and your baby to live in.'

He remembered the unprepossessing flats they used to live in. No one had paid over the odds for yoga lessons in those days. There had been a lot of lentils. Not trendy delicious Puy lentils with sprigs of rosemary and garlic, but bowls of grey slop. He couldn't hold it against her. Lydia had done her best.

'Did she ever talk to you about Somerset?' he asked. 'Where the Culbones came from?'

Lydia sighed. 'She used to go on about some big house somewhere. *If I'd had any sense,* she used to say.'

'What was it called? Was it Rushbrook House?'

'Oh God, I can't remember. I used to hate it when she got maudlin.'

'Did she?'

'Sometimes, when it was bloody freezing and she didn't have enough money for the meter.

188

Being a single parent in the sixties was really tough, Gabriel. You and I had it pretty easy compared to Mum and me. Though I know it wasn't always ideal . . . ' She trailed off for a moment, her voice tinged with regret. 'Why all the questions, anyway?'

'Oh — somebody's got in touch on one of those genealogy websites, asking about me. Because my name's Culbone.' Gabriel was surprised at how glib he could be, how easily the lies came. 'I'm on my way to see Diana now, anyway.'

'Oh, send her my love, and tell her I'll be back at the end of the month.'

Gabriel didn't want to remind his mother that the news would mean nothing to Diana. Of course, Lydia knew that only too well: she was an expert in pretending everything was all right. He supposed that's how she had got through life.

He hung up, feeling none the wiser about his heritage. He put in a call to Lola, to tell her what time he'd be home. She had handled the latest pregnancy disappointment so well, though she still sounded a little subdued and not quite her usual sparkling self. He wanted to go home and tell her that it was all going to be OK. That she didn't have to work if she didn't want to. He'd estimated how much his share of the farm was worth. He'd looked at the value of similar properties in the area, hating himself for being so mercenary as he scrolled through the website. Even by his most conservative estimate it was enough money to cushion them nicely for the next couple of years if Lola wasn't working so hard. Enough to cover his rent rise so he could —

He told himself to slow down. There was a long way to go before the money was his. They hadn't even got probate yet. There was plenty of time to make the right decision. Plenty of time.

20

Georgia prayed that the train would get into Paddington on time so she wouldn't be late into work. She'd had more than her fair share of time off over the past few weeks. To be fair, it was compassionate leave, but she was aware she was pushing it a bit: Gum had only been her great-uncle, after all. But Tabitha had needed her, and for Georgia, family was more important than her career.

Now the funeral was over, she had to refocus. Natasha and Martin had assured her that everything was under control, and they could manage without her until she got back. That didn't comfort her, however. She was sure Natasha had made it her mission to ensure that Georgia wasn't missed. They hadn't phoned her once because of a script emergency while she was gone. Natasha would have made sure it was covered.

So it was about time she got back and re-established herself. She was Senior Script Editor, after all. She had read the latest scripts that had been delivered, comparing them to the storyline the writers were supposed to follow, tracking the dramatic arcs of each character. Balance. Writing was all about balance. And timing. Toying with the audience, teasing them, but also giving them satisfaction. Doug used to say it was like sex . . . Delayed gratification was always much sweeter.

She shook her head in irritation, cross that he had popped into her thoughts. Even crosser that she kept flicking glances at her phone every few moments, waiting for a reply to her reply, even though he would probably still be sound asleep at this time of day. She calculated how long it would be before he got up, then felt furious with herself. She shoved her phone in the bottom of her bag and got out her notebook. She wasn't going to waste any more time thinking about Doug.

She was going to think about Eleanor, and the best way to tell her story. She started making notes: a list of characters, their backgrounds, and sketching out the main plot points. The game of cards in the Swan, the Culbone fury, Joseph Melchior meeting Eleanor, Eleanor meeting Casper — it was like an elaborate dance, with everyone moving in and changing partners. She felt a fizz in the pit of her stomach as she wrote, the feeling she got when she recognised a good story, when every turn of the page revealed another twist. A perfect story was almost symmetrical, with the end resonating back to the beginning. With that in mind, she began the outline with Eleanor spying Casper Culbone swimming naked in the river and being transfixed. Was that a Levi's commercial cliché too far? It would do for now. She scribbled it down, visualising the scene in her head. Rock-hard abs and blushing pink cheeks . . .

Before she knew it, the train was sliding into Paddington as scheduled, the tube was on her side, and she was in perfect time for the ten o'clock script meeting, bounding up the wide wooden stairs to the open-plan office.

'Good to have you back,' said Natasha, who had a very confident air about her and a new black blazer that meant business. 'Don't worry if you're not up to speed.'

'I am,' smiled Georgia. She went around the meeting room, greeting the writing team, catching up on their news. She'd worked with them for three years now, so they were like old friends.

'Glad you're here,' said one of them, casting a meaningful glance at Natasha over Georgia's shoulder. She sensed unrest. Writers didn't care for change, or young upstarts.

She gave her notes at the meeting. They were astute, thoughtful, and she made sure that she came up with suggestions for any changes that needed to be made. She always thought things through carefully. She didn't just expect the writer to come up with solutions. Scriptwriting was collaborative. Teamwork was essential. That way you got the very best scripts.

Natasha seemed a little bit disgruntled. Her notes were far more critical and far less constructive. Georgia knew there really wasn't time on a show like this to tear scripts apart unless they were truly dreadful. You had to work together to hone them. This wasn't Chekhov; it was popular drama. And it was easy to criticise.

She was just sitting back at her desk when Martin came up to her.

'Coffee?' he said. It came across as an order,

not a suggestion. Georgia closed down her computer screen.

'Sure.'

The two of them walked down the stairs and out into the street, heading for the little Italian on the corner. She was a tiny bit nervous. Her contract was up shortly, and although she had assumed it would be renewed, you could never be sure.

'So — is everything OK?' Martin asked in a tone of voice that implied he hoped so, because he had something else to say she wouldn't want to hear.

'Well, it was sad, but it was wonderful to see everyone. That's the funny thing about funerals.'

'Every cloud,' smiled Martin. 'Anyway, it was interesting. Because in the past fortnight or so, Natasha has really stepped up. I've been impressed with her.'

'Right.' Georgia tensed. Surely he wasn't going to sack her?

'I think she could manage as Senior Script Editor.'

Georgia stared at him. He wasn't expecting her to agree, surely? To step aside and let Natasha take her job? She wanted to tell him the writing team didn't seem keen on Natasha, but that would be unprofessional.

'Don't look at me like that,' laughed Martin. 'I'm not getting rid of you. I've got a proposition.'

'What?'

He stopped at the counter to order their coffee then led her over to a table by the window. He sat down and leaned back in his chair.

'I think you should join the writing team.'

'Sorry?' This was the last thing Georgia was expecting.

'I've seen how you work. You're a very skilled storyteller. You come up with more new material in the story meetings than anyone, even our lead writers. And you mould those stories in your editing work. You're more than just a script editor, Georgia. That's not being disrespectful to script editors — far from it. It's a difficult job. It's a craft. But I think you'd be put to far better use as a writer.'

'Wow. Wow. I mean, yes. That's what I want to do. Be a writer, I mean. I didn't think I was ready yet.' Why did she suddenly sound so inarticulate?

'When is ready? There are no rules. I think you've got the talent. You've certainly got a holistic understanding of what is needed in a script. I've seen your dialogue, when we've had to improvise at the last minute. It's smart, funny, economical, bang on the money. And there's no doubt you can plot. Put it all together and what more do you need?'

Georgia shook her head in disbelief.

'So what do you think? Don't get me wrong — if you don't want to do it I'll happily renew your contract. But I think it's the right decision for you and for the show.'

Georgia was thinking as fast as she could. This could be Martin's way of getting rid of her. Perhaps he was trying to lure her with the offer of writing, then sack her off the show in three episodes' time. Perhaps it was something he and Natasha had cooked up. Surely he wasn't that weak? Or that taken in by Natasha? She waited until their coffees arrived, then gave her answer.

'I want a guaranteed number of episodes. At least six.'

He frowned. 'That's more than any of our other writers. We only ever guarantee four.'

Sometimes writers burned out or lost the plot and you didn't want to be over-committed.

'I want a year's work. That's how long my editor's contract would be if you renewed it.'

Martin looked at her in admiration. 'You're a tough nut.'

'I don't take unnecessary risks,' said Georgia.

'I'm the one taking the risk.'

'No, you're not. You wouldn't offer me this if you didn't think I could do it.' Where was all this confidence coming from? She felt a thrill from the power.

Martin gave a bark of laughter. 'You're quite the negotiator. Maybe writing's the wrong job?'

'Writers need to be able to negotiate. They need empowering. The script is the most important part of any drama, but somehow the writer's contribution gets overlooked.'

'Sounds as if I might be creating a monster.'

'Yep. Maybe.' Georgia did a monster face, waggling her fingers. 'Seriously, I would love to accept your offer. I didn't expect this at all.'

'I'd still like you on the end of the phone while Natasha settles into the driving seat. But you should get writing straight away.' Martin put a hand on her shoulder. 'I've thought long and hard about this. It's a selfish move. I want to be credited with starting you out on your writing career. I think you're going to be a star.'

Georgia looked a little shell-shocked. She had been tensed for a possible power struggle with Natasha. The last thing she'd expected was to be handed her dream on a plate.

Martin put two sugars in his coffee and stirred.

'And just for the record, I'm not taken in by Natasha. I'm a happily married man. I'm not going to sacrifice my marriage to be a stepping stone in someone else's career.'

Georgia gave a rueful smile. Were her opinions that obvious? She was never very good at hiding her feelings.

'She's very ambitious.' She didn't add that she was attractive too. It would be crass.

'There's nothing wrong with that. I'm going to channel it. She needs the edges knocking off her, that's all. Don't worry. In a year's time Natasha will have calmed down. She'll be less pushy and more confident.' He picked up his cup. 'You'd make a useless poker player, by the way. I can always see exactly what you're thinking.'

Georgia laughed.

'Thank you, Martin,' she said. 'I really appreciate your faith in me.'

'Don't let me down.' He grinned at her and took a swig of his coffee.

Georgia headed back to the office and sat at her desk. She wanted to tell someone her news but her mum and dad would still be driving home. Tab would be excited for her but wouldn't really understand the nuance of what had just happened. She had blind faith in Georgia's ability so she wouldn't be surprised.

She leaned back in her chair and let out a sigh. She knew what was bothering her. There was only one person who would understand the enormity of Martin's offer. One person who would be proud and who would congratulate her and probably rush out and buy a bottle of champagne. Only he was on the other side of the world.

21

Gabriel always thought the Brambles was as nice a place as any to end up. It was a rambling pile on the outskirts of Marlborough, inhabited by a dozen elderly residents kept in the style they had become accustomed to, even if most of them were unaware of their surroundings. The standards were high, the atmosphere convivial and the staff warm and kind: they worked hard to make their charges feel at home and assuage any guilt felt by relatives.

The Brambles welcomed guests with open arms and went out of their way to make their visits inclusive, offering drinks on arrival, the opportunity to share lunch or to take part in any of the activities. Gabriel was shown to Diana's room, and not long afterwards a steaming pot of real coffee arrived along with two bone-china mugs and home-baked shortbread.

Diana's room had thick damask curtains and a rich carpet, a bed piled high with the softest bedding, a flat-screen television, necessarily large but somehow discreet. Her paintings were on the wall and Classic FM floated out of a digital radio on the small table next to her reclining armchair. She sat, beautiful but vacant, immaculate in a pearl-grey sweater, a lilac tweed skirt and dainty pumps, her head wrapped in a velvet turban, for she had lost most of her hair. She had on powder and pink lipstick. He'd never seen her unmade-up.

'Hello, Diana.' Gabriel bent to kiss his grandmother's cheek and breathed in Arpège. She held his hand in two of hers and gazed at him. There was no recognition, but she nodded in approval at the sight of him.

He sat in the matching armchair adjacent to hers and chatted away for a while, to get her used to his presence. Her replies were non-committal and infrequent but she looked interested. Then he told her where he'd been over the past couple of days.

'I went to Somerset yesterday.'

She nodded, but he suspected she would have nodded like that if he said he'd been to Bucharest or the Vatican.

'To a little village called Rushbrook.' He paused for a moment. She looked at him, a little coy. 'Do you know a man called Matthew?'

She seemed to start in her chair, sitting upright, alert. She thought for a moment.

'Matthew Melchior.' She said it triumphantly, like a TV game show contestant giving the right answer to the jackpot question.

'Yes!' said Gabriel, astonished. He felt a leap of excitement at the connection. 'Do you know him?'

She looked at him, smiling. The name had lit something up in her eyes. He leaned forwards.

'Diana? Did you know him?'

She held his gaze, but as she looked at him, the light inside her eyes faded. He could almost see the name drifting away to a place she couldn't catch it again.

'Matthew Melchior,' he repeated 'Who is he?'

'Who?' She frowned, uncertain.

'Matthew.' He tried the word that had unlocked her. She put her head on one side, puzzled.

He mustn't put her under pressure. But the revelation that she knew Matthew Melchior was enormous.

'Matthew's very nice,' he tried, wondering if a more conversational approach might work. 'He lives at Dragonfly Farm.'

To his horror, his grandmother's eyes filled with tears.

'Oh, don't cry,' he said. 'Please don't cry.'

Diana started breathing heavily, as if to stop herself from breaking down into sobs. Her mouth turned down at the sides, then opened into a gape. A horrible mewling emerged.

Gabriel put his hands to his head. He'd been so crass. So insensitive. But how was he to know that a simple name would unlock such distress? He knelt down next to Diana and took her hands, talked to her, soothingly, stroking her skin, pearl-white with sky-blue veins.

'It's all right. You're safe here. It's Gabriel. Nothing will hurt you. We're at home, having a cup of coffee. It's Thursday today. I'm going to stay for lunch with you. I think it will be chicken. It smells like chicken.'

He carried on talking, hoping she would be distracted by something he said and forget whatever was causing her such anguish. Eventually the terrible noise subsided.

Gabriel felt relieved. He had been cruel,

201

blundering in like that with his questions. She was speaking, and he bent forward to catch what she was saying.

'I made a mistake,' she said quietly. 'I made a mistake.'

'No, darling, you didn't. It's all OK. You're all right.'

He wanted to steer her mind away from whatever was distressing her. Take her to a safer place, where she could feel settled. He chatted on for a few minutes about nothing in particular and it seemed to work. The tension went from her face and fingers.

She was calm eventually. A benign smile was spread across her face. Gabriel couldn't be sure if she was genuinely feeling at one with the world or if the smile was to guard her from more questions. He sat for a moment in the quiet of her room, holding her hand, his eyes roaming around. Everything she possessed was now in here. There was a wardrobe, a chest of drawers, a small dressing table with a chair which could double as a desk, a bookshelf holding a row of historical paperbacks — could Diana still read? Did that ability go with the disease? Or did she just stare at the words as they melted into meaninglessness? Perhaps he should read to her?

A care assistant popped her head round the door. 'All OK? We'll be bringing lunch in about five minutes.'

'Lovely. Thank you.'

The door closed. Gabriel looked back at Diana. Her eyes were shut and her breathing deeper. She seemed to have fallen asleep.

Would it be very wrong, he wondered, to look at her things and see what he could glean? He sat for a moment debating the morality. He was certain Diana held the key to his identity, but the answers were locked inside her. And it wasn't as if he was taking advantage of her by looking. He simply wanted to know why Matthew Melchior had included him in his will. And why Diana knew his name.

He folded his hands together as if in prayer while he thought. Diana dozed. He had five minutes to search for any evidence of a connection. He would be doing no harm, although he didn't care for the idea of someone finding him rifling through her drawers. Could he explain his position and ask permission? He thought it sounded dodgy no matter how he framed it.

He got out of his chair decisively. He had the code to the safe that was screwed to the wall behind her wardrobe: only he and his mother held it. Inside were Diana's documents. Passport, national insurance details, a marriage certificate. He spread the certificate out.

There was his grandfather's name, Max Culbone. And his date of birth. And the date of their marriage — 29 August 1957. And below that was the first indication that there was any link.

The church they had been married in was St Mary's, Rushbrook.

He stared at the words. Diana had been married in the little church he had visited on his way to Dragonfly Farm. She had been married within breathing distance of Matthew Melchior's home, in the church where he had been buried only two days before.

There was a divorce certificate from a few years later. Her will, leaving everything to his mother. He folded the paperwork back up and replaced it in the safe, looking inside for more clues. There was a silver-backed brush, mirror and comb set with Diana's initials — DMC — engraved on the back. Her married initials, Gabriel noted. Perhaps a wedding present from Max, before it went wrong? She had kept them, and no doubt she'd used them every day, passing the soft bristles through her hair. He thought it was a shame they weren't kept out for her to use now, but perhaps it was too much worry for the staff in case they were stolen.

Right at the back of the safe was a jewellery box. His fingers hovered over the dark-brown crocodile leather. Was this a step too far? This would definitely look wrong if he got caught. But in his mind's eye he imagined a locket, with Matthew's picture inside. Or some other love token that would prove a connection.

He popped open the clasp of the box and opened it to reveal a soft cream suede inside, with a padded tray. There were half-a-dozen rings, a string of pearls and some diamond earrings neatly stored in little sections. He lifted the tray gently, and underneath was a tangle of more earrings, bangles and several chains. He stirred the jewellery with his finger. At the very bottom was a brooch. It sparkled as he held it up.

A dragonfly.

It wasn't a valuable piece compared to what else was in the box. He thought it was made from marcasite. But it was dainty and intricate, designed in an art nouveau style, with delicate wings. He took it over to Diana and laid it on the arm of her chair. She started, opened her eyes and looked at the brooch but said nothing, then reached out with a finger and touched it gently.

'Would you like to wear it?' he asked. What was the point of having all that jewellery if it just sat in the box?

She nodded. She sat very still while he pinned it to her cardigan.

'It looks very smart,' he told her.

The door opened and an assistant wheeled in a trolley. There were two plates of chicken in mushroom sauce with rice and green beans. It looked delicious and fresh. The assistant pulled out a table on wheels to put between the two of them so they could eat together.

'I put Mrs Culbone's brooch on. She wanted to wear it,' said Gabriel. 'You might like to make sure it gets put away safely.'

'Oooh, she loves her bling,' said the assistant. 'She must have had a lot of admirers back in the day.'

Diana looked up and smiled. Gabriel felt his throat tighten with regret. All the things he didn't know about his grandmother. Not just the things that were relevant to his investigation, but the things that made her who she was. He hardly knew anything about her and it was too late now.

The motorway was predictably clogged on the way back from the Brambles. Gabriel could feel his stress levels rise as the traffic stopped and started. He couldn't help thinking that he would never have to experience this level of inconvenience in Somerset. He might have to stop to let some cows across the road occasionally.

Dragonfly Farm had got under his skin, he realised during the journey home. Images from the day before kept flashing into his mind as he inched round the M25. He couldn't help imagining his workshop transplanted into one of the outbuildings, the smoke from his furnace curling up into the sky; drying out dead branches from the orchard to make apple-wood handles. He began to visualise a special Dragonfly Farm knife: a multi-purpose chef's knife that could become a kitchen classic, like a Le Creuset pot —

Get real, he told himself. *You have responsibilities. Stop indulging in some idyllic hipster fantasy.* Lola and Plum were his priority. Making sure they were safe and happy and living their best lives. For if they were happy, then he was.

He got home just as Lola and Plum got back from nursery.

'Good trip?' Lola asked, and he couldn't help feeling she was a little cool with him. She was never cool. Was she annoyed he had stayed away for the night? Surely not. She'd sounded fine about it the night before.

'I think it was promising. I met some

interesting people.' None of this was a lie, but he felt bad not telling her everything. He didn't want to just yet. He didn't want to make promises he couldn't keep. He wanted to know more about why Matthew Melchior had included him in the will. There might be some awful condition attached that hadn't emerged yet. It might be a mistake. The Melchiors might contest the will, even though they'd been told they couldn't, and another lawyer might think differently. There were so many unanswered questions.

They had supper once Plum was tucked up in bed. Gabriel was tired from the late night and lack of sleep. He kept yawning. Lola frowned.

'I'm not used to all that driving,' he said, hoping to explain away his weariness.

She was toying with her food. She dropped her fork in her pasta. There was something the matter. Definitely.

'What is it, Lo?'

She sighed. 'Kitty told me you asked Josh if he knew of any jobs going.'

Gabriel sat back in his chair. He was pretty sure he'd told Josh to keep it quiet. But if he'd let it slip to his girlfriend, Kitty, she was bound to tell Lola. They told each other everything, those girls.

'I'm not making enough money. The land-lord's putting up the rent. I need to get a proper job.'

'You don't have to.' Lola put a hand over his.

'I was looking at options. I hate you having to work so hard. I can go back for a while, just to

207

take the pressure off.'

Lola looked away. He could see she was trying not to cry. Then she turned back.

'I love you for thinking like that,' she told him. 'But I have to work. It's what I do.' She laughed, but it was mirthless. 'It will happen eventually. It has to.'

'But maybe if you took some time off? Just for six months or so?'

'I can't afford to. It will be bad enough if I do get pregnant. It wasn't so bad when I had Plum but this time — I'm way older. I'll be over thirty. Past my sell-by date.'

'You will never be past your sell-by date.' He stood up and took her in his arms.

'Thank you,' she said. 'For offering. But I don't think you should give up the workshop. You've put so much into it.'

He had. He'd spent six months as an apprentice and spent a lot of money on equipment.

'I can always set up again in a few years.' He could just put it all on the back burner. It wasn't wasted. 'Anyway, I don't have to decide straight away. Let's talk about it when I'm less tired. I need an early night.'

He was exhausted by it all, and felt pulled in too many directions. He just needed to sleep. Maybe his subconscious would sort everything out and it would all seem clearer in the morning.

22

Georgia spent the rest of the day typing up the notes from the script meeting, flagging up any changes of location to the production team and notifying the casting director of new guest characters that would need finding. Running the scripts for a show was as much about logistics as creativity. You couldn't make things up willy-nilly without telling people. You had to have an eagle eye and make sure the scripts kept to the schedule and the budget. It wasn't just cutting to the chase and cliffhangers. She sent the notes off to all the writers on the team, then headed for the tube.

She was exhausted. She needed an early night. The emotion of the past few days was starting to take its toll, and she still hadn't really had time to digest today's work bombshell, let alone yesterday's news of her being left a share of Dragonfly Farm. She had assumed Tabitha would get it, as she was almost the daughter — or granddaughter — that Gum and Joy had never had.

She shut the front door, kicked off her boots and left them at the end of the line of shoes in the hall. She lodged with a friend of her parents who had been loath to give up her beloved Islington house just because she was retiring, so she rented parts of it out to 'like-mindeds' to justify staying on. Georgia was up in the attic, where she had a big bedroom, a tiny shower room and a boxroom she used as a study. She was very happy there. The landlady didn't mind what colour she painted the walls, or if she brought a friend or two back, and it meant there was usually someone in the kitchen when she went down to the basement to make herself something to eat, which was where she was heading now.

Tonight, though, the house was quiet. Georgia sat in the kitchen, waiting for the aubergine parmigiana she had bought from the deli on the way home to heat up. Her phone was on the table in front of her. She picked it up idly and sent a few texts. One to Tabitha, to check she was all right. One to her parents, to see if they were home yet. And one to Gabriel, to say sorry for leaving without saying goodbye. She had warmed to him, despite the circumstances. It seemed as if he was as surprised as they were by the contents of Gum's will.

If she was honest, the news about the will had been slightly overshadowed by Martin's offer to her. She was still dying to share her excitement with someone who would understand how important this was to her. There was really only one person. She looked at the time. It was just after lunch in LA. He was probably in a swanky restaurant somewhere. Or doing laps in his pool.

Her mental audience was screaming, *No! Don't do it!* But she knew she was going to. She began to text:

Hey. Guess what? I've just been commissioned

to write 6 episodes of The Beat Goes On. Hash-tag WTF?!!

She put the phone back down. Her mouth was dry. What was she doing, contacting him? She pretended to herself that she didn't care if Doug replied or not. She pulled the aubergine out of the oven and scooped it onto a plate. It was scalding hot so she would need to wait a few minutes for it to cool down if she didn't want to burn the roof of her mouth. She thought about pouring herself a glass of wine but decided not to. She didn't care for drinking on her own, and they'd drunk a lot last night. It would mean she'd wake up clear-headed tomorrow. She'd been in a bit of a fug today.

She had just finished her supper and was giving the kitchen a bit of a tidy when the doorbell rang. It was probably the other lodger who always seemed to forget his key. She ran up the stairs and along the hall, then pulled open the door.

On the doorstep was Doug, holding out a bottle of champagne. In the street, a black cab pulled smartly away. Georgia wondered if she was so tired that she was hallucinating.

'What are you doing here?'

'I thought we should celebrate.'

He had on a beanie and a big grey jumper over faded jeans, a scarf wrapped round his throat. He had a slight tan. He was looking good. Fit, healthy, confident. Cocky?

'You should be in Hollywood.'

'I'm back home for a few meetings.' He held

up the bottle. 'So can I come in?'

Georgia frowned. 'You *dumped* me.'

He looked down at the step, kicking the threshold with the toe of his shoe, nervous. Then he looked up. 'Yeah. I need to talk to you about that.'

Would she have sent that text if she had known he was in London? She had sent it as a kind of *fuck you*. To prove to him that she was OK and she was getting on and was going to be a success without him.

Or was this what she had been secretly hoping for? A reconciliation? Yes, Doug had his faults — as Tabitha had repeatedly pointed out — but who didn't? He had strengths too. And he was looking out at her from under his lashes, his dirty-blond hair curling out of his hat, that tentative, cheeky smile making her tummy fizz ever so slightly.

Tabitha would be incandescent if she let him over the doorstep. But Tabitha was miles away. She didn't need to know. And Georgia did want a glass of champagne to celebrate, if she was honest. It was no fun at all celebrating on your own.

She stood to one side. 'You'd better come in.'

He leaned in to kiss her cheek as he walked past. She shut her eyes, breathed him in, but didn't return the gesture. Not yet. Not until she was sure.

She took Doug straight down the stairs and into the kitchen. She knew if she took him upstairs it would give out the wrong message, and she didn't want to be at a disadvantage. She found two glass tumblers and Doug made a great show of opening the bottle with a flourish as if Georgia had just won the Monaco Grand Prix.

'Congratulations. It was only a matter of time,' he told her. 'You're hugely talented, Gee. You know that.'

She felt a flicker at the familiarity and fondness of his nickname for her: he used to call her Gee, or Gee Whizz when he was feeling particularly affectionate, and it made her laugh because he made the Americanism sound so English. The champagne was going to her head a little, and the kitchen was warm now the heating had come on. She felt herself relaxing, the memory of the hurt he had caused her receding as she basked in his congratulations. It was good to have someone to celebrate with.

She laughed. 'Let's see how I get on with these episodes first. I might not be able to hack it.'

'Gee.' He leaned towards her, his face serious. 'You're properly talented.'

'Thank you.' She wondered about telling him her film idea then thought, *No, keep your mouth shut, Georgia.* She still didn't know if she could trust him.

'Honestly. And that is part of the reason why I broke things off.'

'What?' Georgia was puzzled. Doug topped up their glasses again, then sat back in his chair. She noticed his abs looked flatter and his shoulders a little wider.

'What your cousin said,' he went on. 'About me using you. That really hurt me. Not just professionally. Emotionally. When I went to LA I wanted to prove I could do it without you. That I could write the next script on my own, without your help. Then I would be worthy of you. I'd be able to stand on my own two feet, hold my head up and come back and claim you.'

Georgia shrugged. 'Have you got any idea how I felt? I was devastated.'

'I'm sorry. I guess I wasn't thinking straight. Everything happened so fast. And *Take Two Eggs* was so important to me — the thing I really wanted to write. But it was you who put the heart into it. Not me. You brought it to life. You gave it a soul.'

'Well. Thank you.' It was true, she thought. The script had been a bit dry before she got her hands on it. She got him to put in jokes. Romance. Raise the emotional stakes. It was Georgia who'd thought of putting the timer shaped like a tomato in the corner of the screen, to denote time running out before the lead character could realise his dream. A silly motif, but it had made the script a little different.

'You should have got the credit, not me.'

She was surprised at his confession. But she wasn't going to be mollified that easily by a few well-chosen words of contrition. She knew him too well.

'What about the money?' she asked. 'That would have been nice too.'

He blinked. 'Oh, come on. You know those film deals aren't as much as they're cracked up to be. I had to spend the option on rent so I could stay in LA. There's nothing left.'

214

He was looking right into her eyes now. She took another gulp from her glass.

'I made a big mistake, cutting you off like that,' he said. 'It was the only way I could do it, though. Keeping a distance and giving myself time to find my voice. I prayed every night that you wouldn't find someone else in the meantime, because I always meant to come back to you when I'd cracked the sequel.' He laughed. 'Cracked it. Get it?'

The sequel was called *How to Make an Omelette*. Georgia gave a glimmer of a smile.

'Why didn't you say all this when you left? You could have explained. I'd have understood. It would have made it easier.'

'Because then I'd have been tempted to pick up the phone and talk things over with you. To get you to read stuff and tell me what you thought. It's been really tough, the sequel.'

He looked so disconsolate. He'd taken his beanie off and his hair was ruffled and falling into his eyes. Once, she would have reached across and pushed it out of the way with her finger. And that would have moved this from a catch-up chat and confessional to something much more intimate. It was very tempting to fall back into bed with him. He was that perfect combination of gentle but assertive, making her feel both cossetted but slightly out of control between the sheets . . .

She gripped her glass. She needed to be in charge here, not get swept away by her sex drive. It must have taken quite a bit of courage to admit what he had. It didn't mean he could have

215

her back, though. She needed time to think. Everything in her life was changing too quickly for her to trust herself to make the right decision.

Then she remembered the Instagram photographs. The bespectacled brunette.

'What about the Hot Librarian?'

'Who?'

'The girl in all your pictures?'

'Sandra?' Doug put his head back and laughed. A little too loudly. 'Let's just say I don't think I'm quite her cup of tea.'

'Oh,' said Georgia, doubtful. He'd looked very much her cup of tea in the photographs.

'You didn't think we were an item?' he asked, grinning.

She shrugged. 'I didn't think anything,' she said. 'I'd been dumped. You were free to do what you liked.'

'Listen, the past few months have been me and my laptop and nothing else.' He mimed typing.

She looked at him. She had no idea if he was lying or not. Or if she cared. She was too tired to think.

'So you've finished it?'

'Yes.' He nodded. 'I just need to sprinkle a bit of glitter on it. But the nuts and bolts are definitely there.'

She didn't reply. He cleared his throat.

'I was wondering . . . if you'd have a look at it. If we could be writing buddies. I'd happily look at your scripts in return.'

That would have been a tempting offer once.

216

Doug was a very experienced prime-time scriptwriter. His input on her first drafts would have been incredibly useful. But Georgia was not going to fall into the same trap. She knew his new script would probably be tightly plotted. But it would lack the emotional depth she had brought to the first one. The depth that had made it sell.

She looked at him. He was a sociopath, she thought. He didn't understand emotions. Life for him was a game of trades and one-upmanship and obliterating anyone who stood in his way.

She remembered his treatment of Tabitha. Tab hadn't suited his needs so he'd tried to get rid of her. She wasn't going to drag it up now. He would only deny everything. But the memory gave her the courage she needed.

'Sure, I'll take a look at it,' she said. His face lit up. 'Though I don't really need a *writing buddy*.'

She put her glass down and smiled at him.

'If you want me to do a pass on your script like last time, maybe you could get your producer to call me and we can talk about a fee? And a credit?'

Doug paled. 'What?'

'We should keep this businesslike. Then we both know where we are. No blurred lines. And then everyone knows who's contributed what.'

'I can't do that.'

'You must have explained to . . . Sandra? . . . that I'd had an input on the first script?'

Doug spluttered. 'I did say that you'd

suggested the tomato timer thing. They love that tomato thing.'

'Doug — I did way more than the tomato thing.'

Georgia was impressed with herself. Where was this confidence coming from? Her ability to stand up for herself? Was it because she was immune to Doug's charms and didn't feel beholden to him? Or was she simply more confident after today? She didn't know exactly, but it felt good, not to let herself be exploited. Before, she would have said yes, and she would have been working on his script before she knew it, giving it her all and letting him take the credit. And the money.

Doug looked thunderstruck.

'I don't know what's happened to you,' he said. 'You've been spending too much time with your cousin.'

'Well, yes,' said Georgia. 'Families do spend time together when there's a funeral.'

'Oh shit.' Doug squirmed. 'I am really sorry about Gum. I did text you.'

'Yep.'

He frowned. 'You've gone all frosty on me, Gee. This isn't like you.'

Because she wasn't doing what he wanted?

'I'm tired, actually. It's bedtime for me, I'm afraid,' she said, yawning and putting her glass down. 'Do you want to call a cab?'

'Oh. Right.' He got out his phone, unsure. He prodded at the Uber app.

'I'll finish tidying up while you wait.' She took their glasses over to the sink. There was an awkward silence. He walked over to her.

'Gee, I'm sorry if I've been crass. You're a star. A star in the making. I'm so proud of you.' He pecked at the side of her head but she jerked it away so he kissed the air beside her. Georgia could smell the Penhaligon cologne she had bought him last Christmas. It was so familiar and delicious and provocative: once it would have set off a pulse deep inside her — now it made her feel slightly ill.

She stepped away from him. She wasn't going to make a scene. She might need him one day. And his contacts. She smiled to herself as she squirted Fairy Liquid into the sink.

'My Uber's here,' he said, and his voice sounded very small.

'Bye then,' she said. 'And my offer still stands. Have your producer call me if you need me.'

23

Gabriel had just fallen into a much-needed and rather heavenly deep sleep when the bed-side light snapped on. Lola was sitting up with his phone in her hand. He hadn't heard the text come in. He didn't have a passcode because he didn't have any secrets. They always looked at each other's texts and messages. They had total trust in each other.

'Who is Georgia?' she asked him.

He sat up, confused. 'Who?'

'Georgia.'

'Oh! Georgia.' He nodded. 'She's one of the people I was doing business with.'

Shit. It hadn't occurred to him that one of them would text this late.

His blood ran cold as Lola started to read.

I'm so sorry I left this morning without saying goodbye. You were dead to the world. It must have been all the cider brandy. I know this is a tricky situation but we will sort everything out, so don't worry. See you soon. Georgia

'Oh my God. Baby. It's not what it sounds like,' said Gabriel, trying to take the phone off her. 'It really isn't.'

'Isn't it?' said Lola, sadly. 'So what is it, then?'

Gabriel looked down at the text. He was going to have to tell her. He couldn't think of any other way of explaining Georgia's message, which was actually rather kind and sweet when put into context.

'It's going to sound crazy,' he said. 'You're not going to believe it, because I'm not sure I do, yet.'

And he proceeded to give her an accurate précis of the past twenty-four hours. Mr Bickleigh, the churchyard, Dragonfly Farm, Tabitha and Georgia. And his visit to Diana. The dragonfly brooch.

At the end, Lola looked puzzled.

'Why didn't you tell me straight away? Why keep it from me, Gabe? Don't you trust me?'

'Because I don't understand. Because I've got too many questions. Because I need to find out why Matthew Melchior put me in his will. I didn't want to tell you until I had all the answers. Until it made sense.'

There was silence for a moment. Lola was quiet, her eyes large. She opened her mouth once or twice to speak and then she burst into tears and threw herself at him, flinging her arms round his neck.

'I thought you were going to leave us,' she sobbed. 'I thought you were going to leave me and Plum.'

'What? No!' Gabriel was horrified.

'I thought you'd had enough of the pressure. Enough of the baby thing.' She was almost hysterical. Gabriel was perturbed. He'd never seen her like this. But then perhaps he'd never given her any reason to doubt him before.

'Don't be silly,' he said, patting her back.

221

'I can see you looking at me all the time, worrying. And I try really hard to pretend to myself it doesn't matter if I get pregnant or not. But it does. And I feel like a failure. And every month I try to make it happen, but what can I do?'

'You're doing everything you can.'

'But I know how much you want another baby.'

For a moment, Gabriel didn't know what to say. They'd talked about it over and over and agreed it was what they both wanted. She shouldn't be going through this just for him. Of course he was longing for a brother or a sister for Plum, but not at Lola's expense.

'Sweetheart, you and Plum are enough for me. If it's not what you want — '

'But it is what I want! I want to get pregnant and get fat and not worry about losing all that weight. I want to be normal. And I want to be there. Here! For the baby and for Plum and for you. Not be stuck in some freezing bloody warehouse or on a plane or having to schmooze and network . . . ' She stopped, exhausted. 'I loved it yesterday and today, hanging out with Plum. It felt so right. So normal. I don't want to be Lola Koslovsky any more. I just want to be . . . me.'

He held her as tightly as he could, so she felt safe and secure. As tightly as he held Plum if she fell over and hurt herself.

'You can be you, my darling,' he told her. 'Whichever version of you you want to be. I'm going to make sure of it.'

24

Dash left it for a few days after Matthew Melchior's funeral before calling in at Dragonfly Farm. Enough time to be respectful but not neglectful. And from what he could see (not that he was snooping, but his binoculars were quite powerful) there was only the Defender in the driveway, which meant Tabitha must be on her own. And that must be horrible, especially as the weather had been grim: the brightness of early October had vanished overnight and dissolved into relentless rain, filling up the gutters at Rushbrook House so quickly they overflowed. But today the sun had ventured out again, and Dash decided to get some fresh air and do his neighbourly duty.

The walk to Dragonfly Farm took considerably longer than Dash thought it would. If he had walked across the fields behind Rushbrook House, through the woods and down to the river then across the fields on the other side and up, it would only have taken ten minutes. But the driving rain of the past few days had swollen the river. It was nearly bursting its banks, and he didn't feel confident about crossing it even at its most shallow. The stepping stones had completely disappeared.

So he'd had to walk down the drive, turn right then walk to the crossroads, turn right again over the stone bridge and go another half a mile down to the drive of Dragonfly Farm. It had taken almost half an hour. The rain had stopped and the sun had come out, and he could hear the raindrops falling from the last of the leaves. He was boiling.

It was good for him. There was no decent gym for miles. He remembered his old life, up at five to hit the treadmill in the brightly lit gym of whatever hotel he was in: it was impossible to tell where he was or what time it was, they were all so similar. His body was already missing the regime. He could sense a softening of his limbs. So he'd resolved to walk wherever he could to keep his cardio fitness up. He'd have to do something else to address the rest: his abs and biceps were definitely less defined.

He knocked on the front door, looking at the peeling paint, surveying the rotting wood of the windows, the moss on the roof. The soft red brick was the same as the brick of Rushbrook House: he supposed they had been built at the same time, the one to supply the other with milk and meat and grain. Now, three hundred years later, both houses were in a state of decay that rather suited them. This part of the country had no truck with shiny front doors, pointed brickwork and upright chimneys. Dishevelment was de rigueur, both in houses and people, he had noted. Unless your roof was actually caving in or your windows falling out, why bother going to the expense of keeping it shipshape?

There was no reply from within.

He looked down at the bag he was carrying, and the precious cargo inside. He couldn't leave it on the doorstep without an explanation. He should have brought a pen and paper to leave a note, he thought. He never carried a pen and paper any more, he realised. How was he going to let her know he had been?

Annoyed with himself, he turned to go just as Tabitha came round the side of the house. For a moment he was blinded by the newly washed sun behind her, all of her colours blurring. He was reminded of a song his dad used to play in the car. Something about a girl in a silk dress, coming out of the sun. Al Stewart, he thought, 'Year of the Cat'. He felt that momentary pang of nostalgia that songs often bring: a longing for a return to more innocent times, him clamouring for his dad to change the tape from his old fogey music to some thumping dance tunes. Now, he would love the soothing embrace of Al Stewart. Was he getting old?

'Hello?' she said in a hostile tone. He supposed they hadn't parted on great terms the last time he was here, though he had shaken her hand briefly at the funeral. He cringed at the memory of the sourdough fracas.

'I came to see,' he said, 'if you are OK, and if there's anything you need.'

'I'm all good,' she replied. 'But thank you.'

'Well, if you need anything, please just ask. I can give you my number.'

She managed a smile. 'Thanks.' She made no attempt to get her phone out, however.

'And I brought you a present.' He held up the canvas bag.

She reached out for the bag and opened it,

pulling out a Kilner jar. She frowned for a moment, then a smile spread over her face.

'It's a sourdough starter,' she said. 'Where did you get it?'

Dash looked proud. 'I made it myself. I looked it up. I went all the way to Dorset to get the best organic flour from a flour mill. I've been feeding it. It might not be ready yet.'

She began to laugh. 'You're mad.'

'I know. But I felt so awful. And I know it's not the same as the one I threw away, but . . .' He gave a shrug.

She inspected it more closely and gave a nod of approval.

'I've been meaning to start another one but there hasn't been time. Well, there has been time but I haven't been in the right headspace. So thank you.'

'I've got an ulterior motive. Of course.'

'Of course.'

Dash cleared his throat. 'I want to talk to you about my plans for Rushbrook House. So if you do have any objections or issues we can iron them out before I go to planning.'

She raised her eyebrows. 'You're not hoping to build a housing estate?'

'God, no. Nothing nearly so drastic.'

He waited for her to ask him in, but she didn't.

'I can either tell you here, on the doorstep. Or you can ask me in for a coffee and I can show you the plans on my iPad.'

She laughed, thawing slightly.

'You might as well come in. It's still a bit of a

tip. I haven't properly cleared up since everyone left.' She sighed. 'I haven't had the energy.'

'Has everyone gone then?'

She nodded. 'Yep. Life goes on, apparently. Gum's dead and buried and suddenly everything's back to normal.'

'I'm so sorry,' said Dash. 'It does feel as if no one has time for anything these days.'

'They all have their lives to be getting on with. And I don't seem to have the energy for anything. Apart from the stuff I *have* to do.'

'Why don't we go out for dinner?'

He couldn't believe he'd said it. It just popped out. She looked at him, startled.

'Dinner?'

'I'm going stir-crazy. I haven't eaten properly since I got here because I can't really be bothered. We could go to the pub and get something to eat?'

'I don't know about the pub,' said Tabitha. 'I've been playing catch-up on pies. I never want to see another pie again.'

'Oh.' He looked crestfallen. 'What about somewhere proper?'

She did at least consider his suggestion before rejecting it.

'I'm not sure I'm in the mood for proper. I might start crying into my soup.'

'Oh. No. I understand.' She was definitely mellowing a bit, he thought. 'Why don't I drive into Nettleford and pick up a takeaway? I could bring it round and we can go through the plans.'

She thought about it for a moment. 'Actually,' she said, 'I'd rather come to you. I've never been to Rushbrook House. I wouldn't mind a snoop round.'

'Oh,' he said, a little startled by her frankness. 'OK.'

He rather liked the idea of a guest. Apart from the odd workman, no one had been to the house since he'd arrived.

'Tandoori king prawn masala, peshwari naan, bhindi bhaji and some poppadoms.' She rattled off the list. 'I'll bring some mango chutney. I'll be there at eight.'

She turned and walked into the house, shutting the door behind her. Dash stood open-mouthed, then looked at his watch. He had some serious cleaning up and titivating to do. The house wasn't fit for visitors. It was cold and bleak and unwelcoming. It would take him ages to make it feel lived in.

Calm down, he told himself. This was a business meeting between neighbours, not a date. But he wanted to cheer Tabitha up, make her feel looked after and welcome. He could see she was putting a brave face on things. It was odd, though, because she didn't give off a need-to-be-looked-after vibe. Quite the contrary. She was refreshingly different from his usual type: they were feisty and independent in their own ways, yet also demanding and in need of constant attention. His last girlfriend had had high expectations, and Dash had found it exhausting, remembering to send flowers and choose the perfect present. In the end, there had been nothing spontaneous about their relationship. It had been something of a reign of terror.

228

He'd almost been relieved to have a reason to call things off when he moved to Somerset; he'd wanted a clean slate.

He turned and started to jog back down the driveway. Luckily he had trainers on and not heavy walking boots or wellies. As he dodged the puddles on the drive, he thought he would be as fit as a fiddle if he kept this up.

25

It hadn't taken Gabriel long to track down Max Culbone on the electoral register. It was an unusual name, and there was one roughly the right age living off Kensington Church Street. He sent him a very polite letter, explaining that he was Diana Culbone's grandson, and asking if they could meet. To his surprise, he received a handwritten reply on headed notepaper two days' later, inviting him to call in any afternoon between three and six o'clock.

Gabriel finished work early the next afternoon and made his way over to Kensington on the Tube. This part of London felt so different, with its elegant wedding-cake houses and air of discreet calm, compared to the edgy energy where he lived and worked. He loved this city, with its many sides. Like a complex person, it was full of surprises.

Like Lola. He had been surprised by her sudden vulnerability that night. He hadn't realised quite how much she hungered for normality. He was shocked that she could even think for a minute that he might have been unfaithful. It made him all the more determined to make things right for her. You couldn't plan a future together if one of you felt compromised. And he had long thought that her lifestyle wasn't sustainable. In a way, he was relieved she recognised it. They could start to build a life that was perfect for all of them. Recalibrate their careers, their finances, their dreams. He just had to figure out where Dragonfly Farm fitted into the puzzle.

He found the flat where Max lived quite easily, in a white stucco mansion block flanked by trees ablaze with autumn. He rang the bell. A brisk voice answered.

'I'm pushing the buzzer now. Come on up. Second floor, third on the right.'

Gabriel didn't take the lift, but went up the stairs two at a time, taking just a moment to catch his breath before knocking on the door.

He was greeted by a pair of cobalt eyes in a face that would once have been chiselled but was now rather gaunt. Max's head was topped with just a few fine strands of white hair. He wore moleskin trousers and a fine burgundy jumper with a yellow cravat tucked into the neck. He was over six foot though was now rather stooped. But he had presence, an aura of confidence and charm, as he ushered Gabriel into his flat. It was large, with high ceilings and big windows, the walls painted eau de nil, with a lot of rather dainty furniture and some very good paintings.

After rattling about in the kitchen for a few moments, Max brought out tea and shortbread and sat himself down in a green velvet armchair by the window, waving to Gabriel to sit opposite.

'So — Diana is your grandmother? And it's taken you this long to come looking for me?'

'I haven't had a reason to up until now.'

'I've not seen Diana for nearly sixty years. Ours was the shortest of my marriages. It turns

231

out that I'm not awfully good at them. Is she still alive?'

'Well, yes,' said Gabriel. 'But I'm afraid she has dementia. She's in a home.'

Max winced. 'Oh God.'

'A very nice one. My mother and I spent a long time making sure we'd found the right place.'

'How nice to be cared for so.' His tone implied that he wasn't, but it was wry rather than self-pitying. Then he sighed. 'I was a shit to Diana, but she was terribly tricky. We weren't suited at all. We should never have been allowed to marry. Are you married?'

'No,' said Gabriel. 'But I have a partner. And a daughter. She's three. Plum.'

'Plum. Plum Culbone?' Max rolled the name around his mouth and nodded in approval.

'Actually, she's Plum Koslovsky. After her mother. Lola's grandmother was Russian and she took her name for modelling because it sounded more glamorous than Lola Platt.' Gabriel smiled 'Plum should be called Koslovsky-Culbone but that seemed ridiculous, so I took a back seat.'

'Well. Perhaps you'll have a boy one day. You can keep the Culbone name going through him. That would seem fair?'

'Perhaps,' said Gabriel, and noticed his stomach flip a little at the mention of *one day*.

Max picked up his cup.

'I'm not proud of how I treated Diana. But we were both swept up in each other at the time. She was quite startlingly beautiful, you know.

232

Like Snow White. Black hair, red lips, pale skin like porcelain . . . Of *course* I wanted her in my possession for the rest of my life. But the ink wasn't dry on the marriage certificate before we were like Liz Taylor and Richard Burton. We scrapped from dawn until dusk. She threw tantrums; I threw my glass at the wall.' He made a face. 'Of course, by the end there was an added problem.'

'Ah,' said Gabriel. 'My mother?'

Max nodded, with a heavy sigh.

'Diana wouldn't even let me see her when she was born. Can you imagine? Not being allowed to see your own child?'

'I can't.' Gabriel was shocked. 'That's terrible.'

'Yes. Of course, I was painted as the villain; I thought that was particularly cruel. She left me a month before the birth and filed for divorce. I always thought she felt I had tricked her somehow.' He looked puzzled, and Gabriel saw a glimpse of the frustrated young man who couldn't live up to his bride's expectations. 'We'd barely been married eight months. I couldn't be who she wanted me to be. I was twenty-two. Selfish. Naive.'

Gabriel looked at the old man and felt a flash of pity.

'Surely you could have got joint custody, if you wanted to see the baby?'

'Oh, I don't think things worked like that in those days. I just found a way to forget.' He mimed drinking from a glass. 'So . . . your mother.' A flicker of something deeper than regret crossed his face. 'How is she?'

233

'Lydia? She's very well. She teaches yoga to wealthy bored women. They worship her. She's very good at what she does.' She was. He'd seen the testimonials on her website, the praise for her warm and nurturing nature. She had definitely mellowed in later years. 'She's in Portugal at the moment. She never stays in one place for more than five minutes.'

Max chuckled. Then he looked serious. 'I did always wonder,' he said, 'if perhaps Lydia wasn't mine. And if that was the real reason I was kept from her.'

Gabriel held his gaze. 'I was wondering that too.' He paused for a moment. 'I've been left a legacy. By a Matthew Melchior? A third of Dragonfly Farm, near Nettleford.'

Max's eyes looked bright with interest, as if his suspicions had been confirmed.

'The farm that used to belong to Rushbrook House?'

Gabriel nodded. Max thought for a moment.

'My brother, Hugh, inherited Rushbrook House from my grandfather. I'd been cast out of the family by then. No room for black sheep or drunkards or divorcees.' He leaned forwards. 'I was staying at Rushbrook House when I first met Diana. My grandparents had one of those ridiculous house parties they have in the countryside at Christmas time — when the soup's always cold and the hot water runs out but there's plenty of booze to make up for it. It was a *coup de foudre* for both of us. Eyes across a crowded room . . . '

He was silent for a moment, reminiscing.

Gabriel could imagine him, in a dinner jacket with a white silk scarf, a cocktail in one hand and a cigarette in the other, too young to handle his good looks without causing damage.

'We both went back to London afterwards. She was working in an art gallery.' He laughed. 'She left her job as soon as I proposed to her. We had far better things to do.'

Max shook his head with a smile, immersed in the memories of young love. But as he remembered more, he frowned.

'She would insist on us getting married at Rushbrook. She said she wanted a country wedding; a *family* wedding.'

'Perhaps that's when she met Matthew?'

Max frowned. 'She never mentioned him to me. But she wouldn't have dared, because we're like the Doones and the Ridds. From Lorna Doone. Have you read it?'

'No, I haven't. But maybe that made him even more attractive? The fact he was forbidden.'

'Perhaps. Women are attracted to strange things.'

'It would explain his bequest, if Matthew Melchior was my real grandfather.'

'Well, we won't be able to ask him, if he's six foot under.' Max gave a bark of laughter, but Gabriel felt his forced jollity was covering discomfort at remembering the past, and at being confronted with further evidence of the failure of his marriage. Evidence that he had been cuckolded, perhaps. 'We can never know.'

'Actually, there is one way we could find out,' said Gabriel, aware that what he was going to ask was delicate. It had been Lola's idea, when he'd explained the situation to her. She spent a lot of time between set-ups on shoots reading trashy magazines and watching daytime television. Gabriel still wasn't entirely comfortable suggesting it, but he had to admit it was a practical suggestion. 'Would you consider doing a DNA test?'

For a moment, Max turned to look out of the window. His face was impassive, and Gabriel wondered what he was feeling. Regret? Humiliation? Relief that he might not have been the villain of the piece after all?

He turned back, finally. He looked drawn and tired, as if the memories had leached the energy from him. He managed a resigned smile.

'As long as you're not expecting to inherit anything from me. There is nothing.' He waved his hand about. 'I cashed this in yonks ago.'

'No,' said Gabriel. 'I'd just like to know who I am. And why I've been left part of Dragonfly Farm.'

'It's all very *Great Expectations*, isn't it?' Max was rallying. Trying to make light of the revelations. 'Yes, by all means. Test away. What do I need to do?'

Gabriel felt awkward. It really was excruciating, asking someone to provide their DNA.

'I'll have the test sent to you. It's very easy. No blood. Just a saliva swab.' Even the word 'swab' made him cringe. It sounded both invasive and clinical. 'Then you send it off in a prepaid envelope.'

'Marvellous. Very *CSI: Miami*. Don't worry,

236

I'll follow the instructions to the letter. How soon will they tell you?'

'They'll email me the results within ten days.'

'And will you let me know?'

'If you'd like to know?'

'I suppose I would. Out of curiosity.'

'It's not a hundred per cent accurate. It gives you a likelihood score, depending on how much DNA we share.'

'Well, it'll be interesting. Probably the most interesting thing that's happened to me for years. It'll give me something to talk about at parties.'

Gabriel looked alarmed.

'Don't worry. No names.' Max got up and patted him on the shoulder. 'I'll be quite disappointed if you're not my grandson. You seem a splendid sort of chap.'

'Oh. Thank you.' Gabriel felt a flicker of affection for Max, who had been very generous and frank. 'And thank you for your time and being understanding. And for agreeing to do the test.'

'To be honest, I'm surprised I haven't been asked to do one before.'

He smiled at Gabriel, his eyes snapping with mischief, and Gabriel felt the full force of his charm; the charm Diana had no doubt been attracted to. He wondered if he had any of that charm in his own blood.

Or if Max Culbone wasn't his grandfather at all.

26

That afternoon Dash drove into Nettleford with an extensive shopping list for his emergency make-over. Candles, he knew, were essential for masking squalor. He could do with a tablecloth for the kitchen. Some decent wineglasses, not the ghastly Paris goblets in the cupboard that reminded him of a town-centre pub. Some decent wine. Flowers! They always provided a distraction.

Luckily the little town had some hidden gems. He found a dozen thick beeswax candles, a pale-grey French linen tablecloth and some glasses in a homeware shop. The florist gathered him together some autumn flowers in shades of deep rusty red, orange and yellow tied with raffia. He bought wine and a bag of ice and mixers and a bottle of local gin as well as half-a-dozen beers. He even remembered to get a decent corkscrew as the one in the kitchen drawer was useless.

He enjoyed the challenge, realising he had paid no attention whatsoever to his surroundings for the past five years: his environment had been attended to by an anonymous squad of maids and housekeepers and cleaners. But he quite relished the prospect of creating a homely welcoming atmosphere at Rushbrook.

He stopped off at the Maharajah and pre-ordered the food, adding in his own order to

Tabitha's, and some samosas and raita. He made arrangements to come back and pick the food up at seven thirty — it would give him time to get it home and put it in serving bowls. He didn't want to be pulling off cardboard lids and tipping everything out onto a plate when Tabitha arrived. It seemed too studenty.

Then he went home and set to work bringing the house to life with his new purchases, digging about in the cupboards for candlesticks and vases. Considering he didn't have a domesticated bone in his body, he didn't think he'd done a bad job. Candlelight did indeed go a long way towards covering up the eighties monstrosity that was the kitchen — limed oak with barley twists everywhere. The tablecloth and flowers transformed the rather orange pine table, and he borrowed cushions from the living room to make the chairs more comfortable. He stood his portable speaker on the side and found a French radio station that played atmospheric jazz.

'Good job, Dash,' he told himself. 'You'll be in *World of Interiors* next month.'

He was back from the takeaway by ten to eight and decanted the food ready to reheat in the oven. Then he remembered the reason for Tabitha coming over and rushed to the dining room, which he had appropriated as his office, making copies of the plans.

He stood for a moment looking at them, and yet again wondered if he was doing the right thing. He had wanted to do something meaningful, that gave him a sense of who he was, after the anonymous, soulless pursuit of financial

239

gratification of the past few years. Happily he had made enough to be able to secure his future, but it was still a risk.

Rushbrook House had meaning. It might not have been part of his childhood, but it was in his family and synonymous with the Culbone name. He wanted to invest in that heritage, to bring it back to life. He'd researched his idea, costed it out, got some investors on board and drawn up some plans. By next summer, with a fair wind behind him, the first phase of his project would be up and running.

He was just stapling the copies of the plan together when he heard the roar of an engine. He rushed to the dining-room window and pulled back the curtain. He could see a headlamp heading across the field behind the house, straight towards him. He peered more closely until he saw the figure of Tabitha astride an old motorbike, by now racing across the lawn and heading for the side of the house.

In the time it took him to leave the dining room, cross the hall and open the front door, she was parked up in the circular driveway in front of the house, pulling off her helmet and dismounting. She crunched over the gravel, smiling a greeting at him. She was in skinny jeans, a red polo-neck sweater and a combat jacket. Her hair was down and he thought she had on lipstick.

'I hope you haven't ruined the lawn,' he said in a teasing tone.

'Lawn?' she said. 'That hasn't seen a mower for months. It's more of a meadow.'

'I know,' he sighed. 'I haven't had time to get it seen to.'

'I'll do it,' she said. 'A hundred quid cash and it will look like Lords.'

'A hundred quid?'

'I'll bring my own ride-on mower for that. It's a labour of love, I can tell you.'

'How did you get across the river?'

'There's a narrow bit after the bend by the bridge. I just went for it.'

She strode past him and into the house.

'It's bloody freezing because the heating system's packed up,' he said, following after her. 'But the kitchen's warm because of the Rayburn. Come on in.'

She pulled a bottle out of the inside of her jacket and put it on the table, along with a jar of mango chutney.

'The wine's left over from the funeral,' she said. 'It's supposed to be quite good.' She sank into a kitchen chair. 'I think I'm ready for a drink now. I didn't drink much while everyone was here because it makes me too emotional.'

'Oh.' Dash feigned alarmed as he wielded the corkscrew.

'Don't worry. I won't snivel all over you. I just miss everyone and wish they were at Dragonfly all the time, but that's not how life works, is it? You can't keep all the people you love near you.'

'Well, no. I suppose there wouldn't be room.'

She looked around.

'There would here. This place is massive.'

'Massive but, my God, it needs work. I'm

241

beginning to wonder what I've taken on.'

'So . . . tell me the plans?' Tabitha was refreshingly to the point.

'I suppose the easiest way to explain is to give you this. It's just a mock-up, but it gives you an idea.'

He handed her a copy of the proposal. She put it on the table and began to read.

'*Luxury Somerset Safari Lodges: come and unwind on the banks of the Rushbrook in one of our six lodges, hand-built from reclaimed timber and nestled in a riverside glade amidst woodland bursting with flora and fauna. Get back to nature and stare at the stars with all the luxuries you would expect from a five-star hotel: exquisite bedding, beautifully appointed rooms and twenty-four-hour room service.*' She looked up at him. 'You've got to be kidding me. Have you got permission? You can't have. We haven't been notified.'

'We've spoken to the council and we're pretty confident they'll grant us permission. But I wanted to talk to you first. I'm certain it won't affect you. The trees between us will screen everything.'

'What about the wildlife?'

'We're working hard to put things in place to make sure nothing is disturbed.'

Tabitha snorted. 'Six lodges? That sleep how many?'

'Four maximum.'

'So that's twenty-four people camping out by the river?'

'They will be spread out. And we'll have strict

rules. This will appeal to people who respect wildlife.'

'I think you're being naive. Get a few bottles of wine down them and they won't give a stuff about the otters or the herons.'

Dash sighed. 'We're going to manage the woodland properly. And the river. We're employing conservation experts to make sure we don't upset the indigenous species.'

'Oh, I'm sure you've got everything you need on paper to convince everyone.' Tabitha tapped the paperwork. 'You won't have got this far without making sure you've got it in the bag. And I imagine the Culbone name still bears weight around here.'

'That's not fair. I'm not trading on my name at all.'

Tabitha flicked through the pages, filled with pictures of beautiful people looking at the stars from the middle of a wooden hot tub, fairy lights twinkling.

'In that case I might just nick your ideas and get in there first.'

'What?'

'Our side of the river is much nicer. It faces south for a start. But you know that already, don't you? As you offered to buy.' She gave him a saccharine smile. 'Those fields of yours get properly boggy in the winter.'

Dash swallowed. 'We have drainage experts.'

'Tell that to the river when it floods. It's your bank that bursts.' She picked up her wineglass.

'Are you going to object, then?' asked Dash. He was a little in awe of Tabitha. He suspected not a lot got past her, and that she could be a fierce adversary, as well as knowing a lot of people in the area. He really wanted her on side.

She shrugged. 'I can't stand in the way of progress. We've been lucky here so far in our little bit of Somerset. It's pretty unspoilt.'

'Our mission is not to spoil it. We'll have a strong eco message.'

'All those four-wheel drives charging around the lanes?'

'We're encouraging people to take the train. We'll collect them by minibus.'

'And what are they going to do when they're stuck in a field for a week?'

'The whole point is to do nothing. To relax. Have a digital detox. Get a massage. Go fishing. Mountain biking. Wild swimming.'

Tabitha's eyes widened at this. 'Not naked, I hope?'

He grinned. 'I didn't have you down as a prude.'

'No, but I like to have a choice about who I see with their kit off.' She held his gaze and he found himself flustered. She had a way about her that made him unsure and confused.

'Anyway,' he went on. 'The plan is to get the lodges up and running first. I'll live on site and manage it, and gradually restore this place, which will be the clubhouse. With a bar and a private dining room and a cinema.'

'Glampington House,' said Tabitha. 'Nice.'

Her tone was light, but he wasn't taken in.

'I have to admit,' he said, 'I'm a bit daunted. It's a massive project. This is supposed to be me having a less stressful lifestyle, but I'm not so sure.'

'How long's the house been empty? I know it was rented out.'

'Off and on, yes, for the past thirty years. Since before I was born.'

'It looks like it. This kitchen's even worse than the one at Dragonfly.'

'Nothing's been touched since my grandparents left. Since . . . you know.'

'Since what?' Tabitha shook her head.

'Since the river thing. The drowning.'

'Eleanor Culbone? That was yonks ago.'

'No. No, not Eleanor.' Dash's face clouded. 'My uncle. Tarka?'

'Oh.' Tabitha nodded. 'I knew there was some sort of tragedy. Back in the eighties? But I don't know much about it.'

Dash sighed. He poured himself another glass of wine, then topped up Tabitha's glass.

'Everyone pretends it didn't happen, that's why. I can't get my family to talk about it. Not even my dad. His brother.'

'Was it an accident?'

Dash sighed. 'That's what the papers said.'

'But what do you think?'

'That there was more to it.' Suddenly he wanted to tell her about Tarka's room. About the relics of the man he'd never known who had meant so much to so many people. 'But I don't want to ask my family. I don't want to upset my grandparents or my father. Everyone's pleased I'm taking the house on, though. At least it might make us some money, instead of falling down around our ears.'

'Well,' she said, 'I suppose it will be nice to have proper neighbours again.' She looked at him. 'Tell me something. Do you have a relative called Gabriel?'

Dash frowned, shaking his head. 'Not that I know of.'

She looked at him as if she suspected he might be lying.

'Honestly,' he said.

'Only here's a strange thing,' she said finally. 'My great-uncle left a third of Dragonfly Farm to a total stranger. A third to me, a third to my cousin, Georgia, and a third to a bloke called Gabriel Culbone.'

'Oh,' said Dash, surprised.

'We met him yesterday. We don't know what the connection is. Least of all Gabriel. It came as a total surprise to him. He says he got his name from his grandfather. Max Culbone? He was married to Gabriel's grandmother but they got divorced years ago.'

'Ah,' said Dash. 'That must be Mad Max. My grandfather's brother. He's a bit of a black sheep, by all accounts. A bit of a drinker and a player. He's probably got illegitimate children everywhere. We don't see him.'

'So he's still alive?'

'I think so. I can find out for you. But what's the connection to Gum?'

'That's the mystery. Our solicitor won't tell us, but he insists Gum was of sound mind when he made his will.'

'I can do a bit of asking around. My

grandparents might know.'

'Would you?' Tabitha looked at him, hopeful.

'It must be very annoying, especially if you were expecting to get all the farm.'

Tabitha sighed. 'Oh, I never *expect* anything from anyone. It makes life so much easier if you're never disappointed.'

'Right,' said Dash. 'Good to know.'

She grinned at him. 'I have high expectations of myself to make up for it.'

'But you're going to keep it? The farm, I mean?'

'I hope so.' She frowned. 'I mean, it's home from home for me and Georgia. But I don't know about Gabriel.'

'Not everyone wants a tumbledown farm in the middle of deepest, darkest Somerset.'

'Watch what you're calling tumbledown,' she replied. 'I think this place gets the prize for that.'

'Sorry,' he said. 'I didn't mean to be rude. But what if he wants his money out?'

'I can't think about it. There's no way me and Georgia could afford to buy his share.' Tabitha sat back in her chair, defiant. 'I'm going to have to make him fall desperately in love.'

Dash looked at her. Did she mean with her or the farm? He imagined that once Tabitha unleashed her charms, there wasn't much you could do about it.

★ ★ ★

It was half ten when they'd finished eating and Tabitha pushed aside her wineglass with a sigh.

247

'I'd better go.' They were halfway through their second bottle. 'I've got to be up at half five to ride.'

She got to her feet, picking up her combat jacket.

Dash stood up too. 'You can't ride that bike back. You've had far too much to drink.'

'No, I know. I'll walk.'

'But it's pitch black.'

For a split second, he toyed with asking her to stay. He wouldn't usually hesitate with a woman he found attractive, but something about Tabitha stopped him. He genuinely had no idea what her reaction would be, or even if she found him attractive in return. He couldn't read her. It was a first for him. He could always read the signals. He certainly wasn't going to make an overture unless he saw a green light. Tabitha was firmly on amber. Neither stop nor go.

She shrugged her jacket on, smiling her thanks, then pulled a head torch out of her pocket and strapped it onto her head. 'I never go out without this at night.'

'Even so, it's a long way to go in the dark. Let me call you a cab.'

'No! I'll be fine. I'll go over the stepping stones. I'll be home in ten minutes. There's nothing to be afraid of.'

Dash looked out into the darkness and shivered. Nothing would induce him to walk into that blackness and down to the river. 'Are you sure?'

'What's there to be afraid of?'

Ghosts. Spirits. Hands reaching up to pull you

down into the icy depths.

'Well, nothing, I suppose,' he replied, not wanting to admit his own fears, which were somewhat childish and based on superstition. 'Though will you text me when you get back? Just so I know you're safe and the evil pixies haven't got you.'

'You better give me your number then,' laughed Tabitha, pulling her phone out of another pocket.

'What else have you got in there?' he asked.

'Hoof pick. Hip flask. Plasters. Thermal gloves. And lipstick.' Tabitha gave a pout.

'There is this amazing invention called the handbag,' said Dash, keying his number into her phone, then handing it back to her.

She dropped it back into her pocket with a laugh.

'See you. Thanks for dinner,' she said, and disappeared out of the door into the night.

Dash sat at the kitchen table with the last of the second bottle and watched as her light zigzagged across the field and down towards the river. She was plucky all right, and he admired her nerve. He could handle the streets of any international city at midnight, but not that still, quiet blackness with eyes that watched you from the shadows.

The light disappeared for a while. He strained his eyes to see if he could spot it on the other side. The Melchior side. He waited for another ten minutes. It seemed like a lifetime. Was she all right? Should he go after her?

Then his phone pinged and he picked it up.

Back safe. No evil pixies. Thanks again. T

No kiss, but she definitely wasn't the text-kiss type. He saved her number and put his phone down, looking out across the fields again. He saw a light go on at Dragonfly Farm and felt comforted to see it. He started to clear away the plates. The room felt colder without her, as if she had taken the warmth and light with her. *You're smitten*, he told himself.

He batted the thought away. He had felt pretty isolated over the past few weeks, so he'd enjoyed Tabitha's company. That was all.

27

Autumn got her feet under the table at Dragonfly Farm. The days dawned bright and crisp with a swirl of mist; the sun felt under less pressure to supply heat and was content to throw a treacly light over the landscape; night galloped in bringing long shadows and damp chill. But the fields and hedgerows were still busy with sloes and rosehips and buzzards and hares, and the apples in the orchard grew heavier and heavier until the boughs groaned with the weight of them, creaking and waving in the breeze.

Tabitha found it harder to get out of bed in the mornings, especially on exercise days, when the horses' breath began to billow and they stepped out more carefully on the slippery roads. The grief inside her felt like a lump of cold porridge. It was heavy and could not be dislodged. She tried to keep busy. The pub was getting a little quieter as the summer receded, which was perfect as it was nearly time to harvest the apples: the first windfalls had begun to drop into the long grass.

And Gabriel called to tell her that he had tracked down Matthew's order for the knife they had found in the kitchen.

'He ordered it about eighteen months ago, and had it sent to Dragonfly Farm.'

'That must have been not long after Joy died,' said Tabitha.

'I've been to visit Max Culbone. The man I've always assumed to be my grandfather. He told me his brother, Hugh, inherited Rushbrook House.'

Tabitha felt her cheeks go pink. That must be Dash's grandfather, and Max was the great-uncle he'd mentioned.

'Max and my grandmother met at a party at Rushbrook. They fell in love and got married, but apparently my grandmother left Max before my mother was born. He never even saw the baby.'

'That's so sad,' said Tabitha.

'Yes. But they were different times. Anyway, Max has agreed to do a DNA test, to see if we are related. He always suspected that he might not be my mother's real father.'

'So what if he isn't your grandfather? Do you think Gum might be?'

Gabriel hesitated. 'I don't know. I don't know where we go from there. My grandmother can't tell us anything. But she knew him. When I went to see her, she said his name.'

'That's intriguing.'

'I know. But frustrating too.'

'Listen — why don't you bring Plum and Lola here for a visit? Come down for the weekend and we can start to gather in the apples,' Tabitha suggested. 'It's bloody hard work. But I think you'd enjoy it.'

This year's crop was looking promising. She couldn't wait to get the apples off the trees and into the cider barn for pressing. She needed something to take her mind off her grief.

252

Preferably something physical. Of course the different varieties ripened at different rates, but her eye told her that this coming weekend would be a good time to start gathering them in. It would be impossible to harvest both orchards all at once without a lot of help, and she certainly couldn't afford to pay for extra hands. But Gabriel would be useful, and hopefully Georgia would come down.

Gabriel paused for a moment before replying. He wondered if he should be keeping their relationship on a more businesslike level, but part of him longed to see the farm again. And it might do Lola good, to get away from London for the weekend. And Plum would be in heaven.

'I'd love that.'

'Bring suitable clothes. It can be cold and wet and muddy,' warned Tabitha before hanging up. She felt strangely cheered at the prospect of Gabriel and his family coming and filling the four walls with noise and laughter. The house felt so dreadfully empty with only her to rattle around in it.

Several times in the following days she thought about asking Dash over. She'd really enjoyed his company: it was unusual for her to meet a man who didn't seem daunted by her energy and eccentricity. But she was anxious about the future of the farm, and she knew that when she was anxious she was not always good company. She didn't want to jeopardise her relationship with Dash. If there was to be anything between them, she wanted to be confident and carefree, not stressed and preoccupied. She knew herself only too well: she was like one of the racehorses she exercised. If conditions weren't ideal, if something happened to spook her, she would overreact, rear up, bolt, and unseat her rider in a display that was totally disproportionate.

Instead, she decided she would make him some bread from the starter he had given her. She was profoundly touched by his gesture. He had gone to a lot of effort. It soothed her, measuring out the ingredients, mixing up the dough, then kneading it into soft, pliable balls and leaving them to prove. She breathed in the rich, yeasty fug, then slid the tins into the oven to bake.

The loaves were perfect. She broke one apart straight away, while it was still warm. The crust was firm, the inside chewy, the flavour rich and tangy. She smiled in delight, wrapped one of the loaves in a tea towel and put it in an old cake tin.

On her way into Nettleford, she stopped at Rushbrook House to drop the loaf off for Dash. There was no answer when she knocked at the door. Disappointed, she left the tin on the doorstep. She didn't leave a note. He didn't need to be Sherlock Holmes to work out who had left him a freshly baked loaf of sourdough, surely?

Later that night she had a text from him.

That is seriously good bread. Thank you! D

Tabitha sat in the kitchen staring at the phone. She had never stared at a phone screen in her life. But she was a tiny bit disappointed he hadn't said more or arranged to see her. Maybe it was her move? She chewed on her thumbnail. Should she ask Georgia? No. She wasn't even ready to admit her feelings to herself yet, let alone her cousin.

Feelings? What were her feelings, exactly? She tried to analyse them. She was intrigued by him, and his ambitions for the house. She respected him, which was unusual — it took a lot to earn Tabitha's respect.

She'd had to force herself to leave Rushbrook House that evening. She couldn't pretend that she hadn't been tempted when she had watched him across the room in the candlelight, knowing he had been on his own for a while, that he would have been open to suggestion . . . She'd thought about him that night in bed. Tabitha was quite red-blooded. Under any other circumstances Dash would have been a challenge she enjoyed. For the first time in her life she had exercised caution. Something had warned her to treat their relationship with a respect she sometimes didn't afford herself. Usually Tabitha only did no-strings sex — she didn't want her life cluttered up with demands and obligations — but she had a suspicion he might not be interested in no-strings.

Maybe she needed to text back? But she couldn't think what to say. Tabitha wasn't *playing* hard to get. She just was.

She stared at the phone again, willing a message to pop up.

How did people do this flirting/texting/dating thing? How did they stand it?

28

To Gabriel's surprise, Lola was up and ready to leave by eight o'clock on the morning they were going down to Dragonfly Farm for the weekend. She was dressed in skin-tight waxed leggings, a Belstaff jacket and a grey fedora with a jaunty feather in it.

'We're going to a farm,' she told Plum, who she had dressed in her own mini country outfit: a corduroy skirt, boots and a gilet with pheasants on it.

'Will there be a donkey?' Plum was obsessed with donkeys.

'I don't think so, darling,' said Gabriel, and her little face fell.

For a wild moment, Gabriel thought about phoning Tabitha and asking if she could find a donkey for Plum. He imagined taking her out to the orchard in the morning, holding her in his arms, telling her to look under the trees for a surprise. Tabitha seemed like the kind of person who could magic a donkey out of thin air. But it was a ridiculous idea. He never wanted Plum to be spoiled and indulged, but at the same time he wanted to give her the world.

I love you so much, thought Gabriel, looking at his daughter as he strapped her into her seat and she settled her cuddly ostrich onto her lap. *Whatever we do will be because it's right for you.*

Saturday in Somerset was bright and blustery, the sky a tentative duck-egg with chunky blobs of cloud bustling here and there as the car rattled up the driveway.

'Here we are,' said Gabriel. 'Dragonfly Farm. What do you think?'

He tried to see it through Lola's eyes. She was a city girl, through and through.

'It's so pretty.' Her eyes took in the orchards, the trees swaying slightly in the breeze. Some of the apples had already fallen into the soft grass below.

'There's a doggy!' shouted Plum, as Poe belted round the corner to see who they were.

They drew up into the farmyard. Gabriel was conscious that all the buildings were a bit dilapidated. That the farmhouse itself was rather scruffy. The bright sunshine was highlighting its faults rather than disguising them.

Tabitha came out of the house, dressed in scruffy jeans and what looked like one of Gum's old jumpers and a pair of wellies that had been cut down. A million miles from Lola's designer perfection, yet somehow it didn't matter.

'It's great to see you,' she said, hugging Gabriel, then she turned to Lola with a smile. 'You must be Lola. Welcome to Dragonfly Farm.'

'Hi.' Lola held out the bunch of lilies she had bought at her favourite florist: they were extravagant, tied with a large green bow.

'Oh. Gosh. You shouldn't have. These are beautiful. Come into the kitchen. Georgia's making coffee. Oh, you must be Plum.' Tabitha smiled as Gabriel lifted Plum out of her seat and

257

popped her on the ground. 'Now, Poe is very friendly but he forgets how strong he is, so don't let him knock you over.'

'Careful, darling.' Lola hovered anxiously as Plum patted Poe and squealed with delight at his wagging tail.

Gabriel ushered his family inside, realising how nervous he was. He wanted everyone to get on, but they were all so different. He had already seen Tabitha clock Lola's pristine boots and raise an eyebrow. He had no worries about Plum, who headed straight for the rocking horse in the kitchen and climbed into the saddle.

Georgia and Lola might have more in common, he thought. Georgia worked in media and had a more London air about her, in camouflage joggers and a sparkly jumper, her hair in a messy bun.

'Georgia's got some amazing news,' said Tabitha. 'She's been commissioned to write six episodes of her police programme thing.'

'Tab!' said Georgia. 'They don't want to know. Coffee or tea?'

'I've got water,' said Lola, brandishing her water bottle.

'I guess your body's a temple,' Tabitha grinned.

'Not really,' said Lola. 'But I'm mostly off caffeine and alcohol. We're trying for another baby.'

'Oh,' said Tabitha. 'Right.' She wasn't quite sure what to say. 'We might as well head to the orchard and get started. We've only got a few hours of daylight.'

The five pickers rambled up to the east orchard. It would be a month before all the apples were gathered in, but Tabitha was keen to make a start, especially as the weather was fine. There was nothing more miserable than apple picking in the freezing rain.

Brightly coloured tubs were put under the trees that were ready. Each variety needed to be kept separate until the time came to blend them. Gabriel and Plum were put in charge of the Somerset Redstreak, while Lola was to gather in Dabinett.

'They've all got different qualities,' Tabitha told them. 'Yours are both bittersweet, while mine is bitter-sharp. And Georgia's picking the sweetest variety — Ashmead's Kernel.'

They all set to work. As the sun rose higher, the long grass dried and the scent of apple became stronger. It was immensely soothing and satisfying, grubbing about for waxy-skinned fruit. Plum ran from tree to tree, helping different people, carefully picking up the apples from the ground and plonking them in the right bucket.

'Have you got a donkey?' Plum asked Tabitha, never one to give up.

'A donkey?' Tabitha knelt down beside her. 'Do you know, I haven't, but I think a donkey would be a fabulous idea. Do you like donkeys?'

Plum nodded. 'I want one.'

'Me too,' said Tabitha. She looked out at the orchard and imagined a long-eared grey donkey meandering about. It was just what the place needed, a living creature to liven things up.

Horses were too high-maintenance, goats were a nuisance, but a donkey would be sweet. She felt a little burst of something in her heart. Hope? Excitement?

Then she reminded herself she couldn't make plans. Certainly not ones involving a commitment like a donkey. The future of Dragonfly Farm was precarious. She had a long way to go before she could start indulging her fantasies.

Tabitha parked up Jimmy O'Gowan's Defender. As the tubs filled they were put into the back of the truck, and when the back was full she bounced over the tussocks to the farmyard and unloaded the buckets into the barn before coming back with more empty receptacles.

At lunchtime they piled into the kitchen. Tabitha had made soup and sausage rolls, and they all, sat around the table until every last morsel had been devoured. She'd even made Plum her own soup without cream and gave her a little plate of sausage and apple sauce, as Gabriel had forewarned her of Plum's allergies.

She slipped away at one point, after she had eaten. She felt overwhelmed by the situation, not least because she was so uncertain about what was to happen. In some ways she felt as if she was putting on a performance, trying to convince Gabriel that Dragonfly Farm was a dream come true, yet it felt so right, all of them sitting around the table, and everyone seemed to accept that she was mistress of the house. Not that she wanted to be in charge, necessarily, but it suddenly felt good, to summon people to the table and feed them, to make sure they were happy.

For a moment, she laughed at herself. She was going soft in her old age. She wasn't the welcoming, nurturing type, like Joy had been. Or was she? Had she simply needed to wait for the right time to assume that role?

She looked across the valley and wondered about asking Dash to come and join them for dinner. It was a hospitable and kind thing to do: he would probably be alone. And he would get on with Georgia and Gabriel. She frowned as she thought about how he would respond to Lola. She had a feeling shimmering, glamorous Lola would be Dash's type. She didn't particularly want to be in Lola's shadow.

And then there would be the whole Culbone question. Perhaps she needed to be a little more certain of the connections between them all before she invited Dash over.

'Come on, everyone,' she said, walking back into the kitchen. 'Let's get pressing while it's still daylight.'

In the big open-fronted barn adjacent to the house was all the cider-making equipment. Some of it had been here for centuries; some had been added to by Joy who had often lugged things back from auctions or farm sales. The apples were tipped into a big old cast-iron bath — the plug had been blocked up with cement — and hosed clean.

'Don't worry too much,' said Tabitha. 'Pull out any big twigs and leaves, obviously. But the alcohol will kill anything dodgy.'

Then the cleaned apples were thrown into a big crusher. It made a tremendous noise as it chewed up each apple then spat out a glutinous pulp. A powerful scent rose up, the air filled with a sweet pungency, rich and fruity.

'Now, this is the fun bit,' said Tabitha, taking a bucket of pulp over to the press. Gabriel ran his hands over the ancient oak, wondering about who had made it and the tree it had come from, admiring its simplicity. A layer of pulp was spread onto a pressing plate then wrapped in cloth. When a few of the plates had been piled up, a weight was placed on top and the giant metal screw was turned until the pulp began to release its juice. Amber-gold liquid poured into the bucket from a tap at the bottom.

'There we are,' said Tabitha. 'One hundred per cent pure.'

She dipped an old mug into the juice and passed it round for everyone to taste. They all laughed at Plum screwing her face up as it was more tart than the juice she was used to.

'Don't drink too much,' warned Tabitha. 'You'll get bellyache.'

They spent all afternoon pressing until everything they had picked was juiced and poured into plastic barrels ready to be stored in a warm place while it fermented.

'I love this,' said Gabriel to Lola. 'It's nature doing her thing, with no real intervention from us. It's bloody amazing.'

'This barn's beautiful.' Lola looked up at the rafters. 'It would make a great house.'

'Tabitha's hoping to start making sparkling

cider. Like an alternative to prosecco or cava.'

'An affordable celebration,' added Tabitha. 'I think it could really catch on, if we market it well. It would come in a proper champagne-style bottle.'

Gabriel was touched by Tabitha's enthusiasm. She wasn't by nature an effusive person, but he could see she was eager for Lola's reaction, hoping for approval.

'That sounds great,' said Lola. 'Like the countryside in a bottle.'

'Exactly. Though we'd have to get investors. There's loads of things we'd need. It's a different method from normal cider, so there's equipment we'd have to buy. And we'd need a big marketing budget.'

'It's a marketing dream, this place,' said Lola. 'It's like Instagram heaven. Everybody loves heritage products, especially if there's a family behind it. You could have great fun.'

Gabriel realised that Lola would be the perfect person to get behind the idea. She had such a good gut when it came to visuals. She understood branding. She could even be the face behind the campaign. He could see it already: a photograph of Lola in a flouncy off-the-shoulder maxi dress and cowboy boots, sitting on the back of a tractor, holding a bottle of sparkling cider.

But a warning bell told Gabriel not to get in too deep. He didn't want to compromise his relationship with Tabitha by getting overexcited, or let Lola think he was manipulating her.

'It could be a very quick way of losing a lot of money,' he said. 'Trust me — it's tough, setting

263

up artisan businesses. It takes a long time for the profit to show. You have to be able to ride that out.'

He saw a pained expression flitter across Tabitha's face. She looked as disappointed as Plum on discovering there was no donkey. She wasn't very good at hiding her feelings, he realised. He should tread carefully. It was a very attractive proposition on the surface, but he knew enough about running a business to know that there were endless pitfalls and potential expenses and the market would be a very competitive one.

Out of the corner of his eye, he saw Lola picking up Plum, whose little lips were starting to turn blue.

'Plum's getting tired and cold,' Lola said to Gabriel. 'I think I'll take her inside.'

He saw Tabitha's lips tighten as she turned away. He'd love to help make her dream come true, he thought, but he shouldn't give her false hope. He knew he held the key to the future of Dragonfly Farm, and it was a big responsibility. Everyone's future, everyone's dream. He felt for his phone in this pocket, the email he'd received yesterday afternoon. It hadn't helped him at all.

★ ★ ★

Dusk had fallen over the farm, a gentle grey cloak that darkened to navy blue. Gabriel looked up at the stars, which seemed to shine more brightly here: thousands of tiny pinpricks spread across the sky.

'Wow!' he said. 'In London the sky is grey sludge. We're lucky if we can see the moon.'

'We don't have any light pollution,' said Tabitha. 'It's one of the best places in the world to see stars. They're not competing with anything.'

He remembered the constellations from when he was a young boy and felt excited as he started to identify them. 'The Plough' he said, pointing upwards. 'And is that Orion's Belt?'

'Full marks,' teased Tabitha. 'We'll make an astronomer of you yet.'

They wandered back into the kitchen. Lola was snuggled up in the old red chair with Plum and was reading to her from the collection of 'Flower Fairies' books Georgia had found her: they had been in the house for as long as anyone could remember.

'We're trying to see if there is a Plum fairy,' said Lola. 'But we haven't found her yet. There's an Apple Blossom fairy, though. And Rosehip. And Acorn.'

Plum was staring intently at the book, turning the pages, leaning into her mum, resting her head on her arm. She looked very much at home. Gabriel felt his heart swell with pride at the two of them: Lola looked the most relaxed he had seen her in a long time. In the lamplight her sharp bone structure looked softer; there was a slight curve to her cheekbones; her dark hair, usually pulled up into an elaborate bun, was falling around her face and onto her shoulders.

This was a happy place, he thought, looking about him at the glorious chaos, breathing in the smell of cooking, feeling the warmth of the wood-burning stove, listening to Jacques Brel trickling out of the radio on the kitchen top.

No one dressed for dinner. They were all in slippers and big socks and sloppy jumpers. There was no standing on ceremony. Tabitha pulled a side of beef out of the oven and left it on the side to rest, then lit all the candles on the table. Gabriel offered to carve, using the knife they now knew Matthew had ordered from him, and he felt a connection to the man as the slices of pink meat fell away onto the platter.

Over dinner, Lola sang for her supper, regaling Tabitha and Georgia with behind-the-scenes stories and snippets of indiscreet scandal which they lapped up, wide-eyed. She was at her best tonight, thought Gabriel.

Before she had time to finish her crumble, Plum's lashes became heavy. She was almost asleep in her pudding.

'She's done amazingly,' said Georgia, stroking the back of her head.

'I'll take her up to bed and tuck her in,' said Lola.

But after twenty minutes she still hadn't come down. Gabriel went upstairs to find her. She was tucked up in bed with Plum, her arms wrapped round her, fast asleep.

He put a gentle hand on her shoulder to wake her up.

'Hey,' he whispered. 'Come back down. I'm going to tell them about Max.'

'Oh God, sorry. It's all that fresh air.' She clambered out of the bed. 'It's very special, this place,' she said to him as she tucked Plum's ostrich under the little girl's arm.

'I know,' he said.

They looked at each other. Then Lola shrugged. 'But it's like a holiday. It's not real. It doesn't fit into our lives. Does it?'

'Not really,' said Gabriel. Of course it didn't. But could it?

Downstairs, Tabitha had put a big piece of Somerset brie out with a pot of pear chutney. Gabriel poured himself half an inch of golden cider brandy.

'I got the DNA test back,' he told Tabitha and Georgia, pulling up the email on his phone. He'd paid for the premium service: the one that promised results in forty-eight hours. 'The results show the chances of me and Max Culbone being related are so small he can't possibly be my grandfather.'

Tabitha and Georgia looked at the graph showing Gabriel and Max's DNA.

'So do you think that means . . . maybe Gum is?' Tabitha managed at last.

Gabriel nodded. 'Diana and Max were married at Rushbrook Church. And my mother was born not long after. A couple of years before Gum and Joy were married.'

'So you think Gum and Diana might have had a fling? While she was engaged to Max?'

'There's something else that made me think it's possible.' Gabriel took out his phone. 'My grandmother had this in her jewellery box.'

He passed them a photograph of the brooch, pinned to Diana's sweater.

'A dragonfly,' said Georgia. 'It can't just be a coincidence, can it?'

'I don't know. I don't think it's worth much, but it was with all her valuable jewellery, so it must mean a lot to her.'

'So Gum might have been involved with a Culbone. That's scandalous!' Tabitha's eyes were wide with outrage. 'No wonder he didn't tell us.'

'But how do we find out the truth?' said Georgia. 'None of this is actual proof and there's no one left to ask.'

'It's obvious,' said Lola. 'Why don't the three of you do a DNA test? They can tell if you're cousins.'

Georgia frowned. 'But is that what we'd be? It's making my brain ache.'

'Me too,' said Tabitha.

'Second cousins,' said Gabriel. 'If Gum was my grandfather and your great-uncle, then we'd share a great-grandfather. Which would make us second cousins.' He grinned. 'Don't worry. I've done some research which is how I've been able to figure it out. I'm not an expert on these things usually.'

Georgia and Tabitha looked at each other.

'I think a test would be a genius idea,' said Tabitha finally. 'You *feel* as if you belong to us. So it would be nice to know for sure.'

Gabriel laughed. 'That's the cider brandy talking.'

'But what if it throws up something awful?' asked Georgia, who didn't look so eager.

'Yes,' said Lola. 'Some other terrible secret.

You see things on the television. Skeletons in the cupboard.'

'Yes. We're messing about with people's secrets. Things they don't want us to know.' Georgia still didn't look happy.

'Stop thinking like a scriptwriter,' Tabitha laughed. 'We're just trying to make sense of what Gum has done, that's all. If we are related, then we know he and Gabriel's grandmother were . . . ' She couldn't quite say the word.

'Lovers? We'll never know the full details,' said Gabriel. 'But if we are cousins — or second cousins — Gum's bequest makes more sense.'

'And it makes us family,' said Tabitha. She pointed at Gabriel. 'You're much better off being a Melchior than a Culbone.'

'But I'm used to being a Culbone,' protested Gabriel. 'We're not all bad.'

'We won't hold it against you,' said Georgia kindly.

'Maybe you've had a lucky escape.' Tabitha was teasing.

She didn't mention that she'd been fraternising with a Culbone. She hadn't told Georgia that she'd been to Rushbrook House. She wasn't admitting to herself how she felt about Dash, because she wasn't sure yet. But it wasn't entirely impossible that there might be some kind of truce on the horizon.

Their family history, she thought, was unravelling. Perhaps it was going to rewrite itself?

★ ★ ★

In bed later, Lola snuggled into Gabriel for warmth. Georgia had given them a hot-water bottle, but the heating was definitely not what it could be.

'Gabriel Melchior,' Lola mused. 'It's like going to bed with a new man.'

'Oh,' he said. 'Well, if you were bored with the old me . . . '

'Oh my goodness me — never!' she said, curling herself around him. 'It's just kind of strange, that's all. To think you've been someone else all this time.'

She was stroking his face, running her fingers through his long hair with a mischievous smile. He shivered with the pleasure of her teasing touch.

'I don't think I have. I'm certainly not changing my name. I'm still the old me. Sorry to disappoint you.'

He was smiling at her in the semi-darkness. They'd left the small lamp on in the corner of the room. He remembered how pitch black it had been the last time he stayed here. He supposed you got used to it eventually, but tonight he wanted that glimmer of light. And Lola had never looked more beautiful than in these half-shadows.

'What do you think of it here?' he said.

'Magical,' she said, and began to kiss him. She didn't want to talk about Dragonfly Farm. Her mind was on other things. And soon his was too. All thoughts of wills and bequests and probate melted away into the background.

And for once, they were relaxed. Neither of

them mentioned where they were in the cycle or whether it was an O day. For the first time in almost a year they were just making love, for the pure, simple, glorious pleasure of it.

29

Georgia got the late train home to London on Sunday evening, finding a place in a nearly empty carriage. She got herself a hot chocolate from the buffet, wrapped herself up in her winter coat and got out her laptop. This was the perfect opportunity to do some writing on her film script. She'd been so busy with work, trying to juggle the last of her script-editing duties at the same time as getting started on her first episode of *The Beat Goes On*.

There were so many things whirling around in her head distracting her. Should she give up her London rooms and go and live in Somerset, if she was going to be a writer? It was the perfect retreat. She wouldn't have to pay any rent. She could contribute to the running costs. She could sit in the corner of the kitchen, at the little writing desk. And if she needed to go to meetings, the train journey wasn't that bad. She'd done it often enough in the past month.

But then if Dragonfly was going to be sold in the end, what was the point? She and Tabitha had pulled out all the stops to make Gabriel welcome. They'd all had a wonderful weekend together, but had it been enough to persuade him to keep his share? Gabriel and Lola hadn't given anything away when they left. They'd seemed very loved-up — it was the Somerset air, she supposed — but no one had quite had the courage to mention the elephant in the room.

Georgia also worried that she wasn't being much help to Tab with the cider business. She had too much work of her own to get fully immersed. But perhaps if she moved down she could get more involved. The orchards were their heritage, and the cider was Joy's legacy. It was important to keep Melchior Cider going, though they would need serious money to expand. Money they didn't have.

Maybe she'd sell her film script for millions and she could invest it? That would be divine retribution, if the story of the Melchiors' and the Culbones' rivalry saved Dragonfly Farm. She smiled at the thought and it spurred her on to write a few more pages. She was fantasising, but she needed a calling card if she was going to make it as a screenwriter: a piece of original work as well as the episodes she'd been commissioned to write. Soon she was immersed in her tale of hot-blooded lust and cold-blooded revenge.

After an hour, she needed a break. She decided she'd call home. It was the perfect time for a catch-up, and she had lots to tell her mother.

'How did the weekend go?' asked Nicola.

'It was sweet. I think they enjoyed it. Gabriel found out he's not Max Culbone's grandson. They did a DNA test.'

'Oh.' Nicola sounded surprised. 'So do we know who his grandfather is?'

'Not yet. Obviously we think it might be Gum.

So we're going to do a test too. To see if we're related.'

'Who?' Nicola's voice was sharp. 'Who is?'

'Me and Tab and Gabriel. To see if we're cousins. Well, second cousins. Which is what we would be if Gum *was* Gabriel's grandfather.'

There was no reply. Georgia looked outside again to see if they were going through a tunnel.

'Mum? Can you hear me?'

'Yes. Why do you need to do that, though? I don't understand. I mean, it doesn't make any difference to the will whether you're cousins or not, does it?'

'It makes a difference to *us*, though. If we're cousins, second cousins, whatever, then we're proper family. We can decide what to do together.'

'I see.' Nicola didn't sound as if she did see.

'I kind of hope Gabriel is related. Though we're all a bit shocked. I would never have though it of Gum.'

Nicola was silent for a moment.

'I'm not sure digging about in Gum's past is a good idea. If he'd wanted you to know what happened, he would have told you. He would have left a letter explaining everything, surely?'

'I think he was ashamed. I think what he did was out of character and he was ashamed.'

'Well, then you should respect his privacy now he's dead,' said Nicola.

Georgia was alarmed by her mother's tone. It was rather judgemental, which Nicola was not. On the contrary.

'Mum — are you OK? Has something

274

happened?' She couldn't imagine what. Her mum and dad didn't do drama. They were reassuringly calm and free from histrionics, unlike Robin and Alison, Tab's parents, who were still in constant crisis.

'I'm fine. Just get yourself back to London and let's chat tomorrow. Will you be in tomorrow night?'

'Yes. I'm going to get into the habit of two hours' writing every evening.'

'I'll talk to you then.' Nicola seemed in a hurry to hang up.

'Bye, Mum. Love you.'

'You too.'

⋆   ⋆   ⋆

Nicola sat with her phone in her hand, her heart beating so hard she could almost hear it. She felt sick. She was curled up in the depths of the sofa next to the wood-burner, and the heat suddenly made her feel giddy. *Oh God*, she thought. They were too far away from everyone when things went wrong. What should she do?

She looked at Chris, sitting in his favourite chair, immersed in Simon Sebag Montefiore and completely oblivious to her dilemma. He looked up, gazing at Nicola with a vague smile. 'Everything OK?'

'Mmm.' Nicola gave a non-committal reply.

She couldn't bear the thought of the pain this was going to cause him. She loved him so much. She remembered meeting him in the kitchen of the student house in Bloomsbury on her first day at university. He had been making pancakes for everyone, and she was impressed that someone who looked so undomesticated could make them without even looking at a recipe. He flipped pancake after pancake for everyone as they arrived, most of them sick with nerves, and it had been the perfect ice-breaker. They'd been firm friends from that day on. She was the shy history student; he was the geeky scientist, the boffin with the photographic memory and the kind heart and the obsession with Led Zeppelin.

He was an unlikely heart-throb, with his unkempt hair and his thick black glasses and his Wolverhampton accent, but the girls in the student house adored him. He was benignly oblivious to their admiration. He was the peacemaker and the repairman — he could fix any electrical appliance — the midnight-snack maker and the one who jogged to the garage when they ran out of wine or cigarettes or chocolate. He sat up with Nicola all night when someone spiked her drink with a tab of acid. He refused to fix her puncture when she had a flat tyre but insisted on teaching her how to repair it herself.

She had treated him like a brother to begin with — he was far more attentive and helpful than Robin had ever been. She'd had no idea then what a big part he was going to play in the rest of her life.

She didn't want him hurt. She would do anything to protect him.

She needed to think. 'I'm going upstairs for a bath.'

He lifted up a hand to give her a wave, engrossed in his reading.

She ran upstairs and went to the bottom drawer of her dressing table where she had tucked the mix-tape next to her Walkman, the one she'd saved up to buy that summer. Now it felt old and clunky, but at the time it had been a thing of beauty. She put in a fresh set of batteries, then pushed the tape in, wondering if it would still work after all this time, and it did. She marvelled that the wafer-thin tape was still robust enough to hold the precious music after thirty years. She remembered careering along the lanes with her tape deck turned up to full volume, a mad mixture of punk anthems, power ballads, throbbing dance tunes and rock classics spanning the previous two decades, not just that week's *Top of the Pops*. Every emotion was covered, from first love to heartbreak. She rode the roller-coaster as she listened, remembering the boy in the seat beside her. He'd had a gruff but tuneful voice that played with the melodies. Sometimes he harmonised, and she loved to listen to it, wondering how he did it.

There hadn't been a list of songs on the cover. She'd identified them over the years when she heard them in other places, because she didn't want to keep asking him 'Who's this by?'

'Wild Horses', 'Because the Night', 'Ever Fallen In Love (With Someone You Shouldn't've)' . . .

Oh my God, yes, she thought. And the longing never really faded. It just lay somewhere deep inside her. Each of these songs went straight to it, bringing all the memories flooding back. His smell, his touch, his smile. She remembered how he would sometimes lace his fingers in hers while she was driving. For miles she wouldn't change gear, not wanting to let go, driving with the other hand on the wheel, wanting to bring his hand up to her lips so she could kiss his palm. Eventually she would have to let go, but her hand would tingle for ages afterwards. All of her would tingle at the thought of him.

Tarka Culbone.

The name still made her shiver. She must not fall apart. In a way, she had been steeling herself for this for years. She had always known the secret couldn't stay locked away, any more than her feelings could ever fade.

Eventually, she got up off the bed and went back downstairs. She hovered in the doorway. Chris looked up.

'Everything all right, love?'

'We have to tell her,' she told him. 'We have to tell Georgia the truth.'

PART THREE

1986

30

When Nicola was twenty-one years old, after three not-terribly-serious boyfriends, two one-night stands and two holiday flings, she came to the conclusion that the kind of love you read about in books or saw in films really was a fantasy. She was happy with that conclusion, for it made life an awful lot easier. You didn't waste energy looking for true love, with the added bonus that no one could break your heart.

How very wrong she was.

She was spending the summer before her final year at university doing admin for her dad's brother, Matthew, at Melchior and Sons and living at Dragonfly Farm. Her father Peter had his own legal practice in Guildford, but Nicola didn't want people to think she was getting preferential treatment because she was the boss's daughter, so Nettleford seemed a good compromise, and definitely less claustrophobic than living at home with her parents.

Matthew and his wife, Joy, seemed happy to let her do her own thing and were kind and easygoing. So far, the summer had been uneventful and she had managed to accrue quite a nest egg and buy herself a little Mini from a garage in Honisham. September seemed a long way off, when she was due to return to London and move in with three of her friends: they had grown out of university accommodation, and it was exciting to think they would have their own place.

She was driving back from Netdeford on a July evening when she saw him, barefoot and bare-chested, in a pair of Levi's and a cowboy hat. She could tell he was drunk, for he was weaving across the road in an aimless zigzag.

She slowed down, winding down her window.

'Do you want a lift?' she asked. 'Your feet must be burning.'

He knelt down and crossed his arms, resting them on her sill. She found herself looking into a pair of indigo eyes. Well, indigo and red — the whites were shot to hell. The reek of cider was overwhelming, but explained his beatific smile. If he hadn't so obviously been a boy he could have been a girl, with his perfect skin and heart-shaped face.

'They moved my house,' he said. 'It's not there. It should be . . . right here . . . '

He nodded towards the field behind them. He must be one of the Culbones. They seemed to come and go from Rushbrook House at random: she sometimes had to slow down for a Land Rover or a sleek silver Jaguar.

'You've taken the wrong road. Hop in and I'll drive you back.'

'How do you know where it is?'

'Are you looking for Rushbrook House?'

He nodded, standing up, swaying, putting his hand on the Mini roof for balance. Nicola tried not to laugh. He was comedy drunk.

'Go on. Round the passenger side,' she urged him. He managed to walk round the front of the car, and she took in the perfect triangle of his torso, the smooth chest, the brown skin that had caught the sun that blazing hot day. He must have been in the beer garden of the Swan all afternoon. He pulled open the door and fell into the passenger seat. He tipped his head back with a groan.

'Can you put your seat belt on?'

'I never wear seat belts.'

'You do in my car.'

She leaned across him and grabbed the metal tongue then pulled the belt across him and snapped it into place.

He turned to her and gave an angelic grin. 'Thanks, nanny.'

For a moment she stared at him, mesmerised. How could anyone be so beautiful, she wondered. She wanted to put a finger inside one of the bleached blond curls tumbling from underneath his hat.

'Have you got a ciggy?' he asked. His eyes were closed. His profile was perfect: a straight nose over full lips as plump as marshmallows. His forehead was damp with pearls of alcohol-infused sweat. Nicola should have been repelled.

'I don't smoke,' she said, aware how prim she sounded.

He laughed. 'Of course you don't.'

'Well, it does give you cancer. So why would I?'

'Because everyone who's interesting smokes.'

'Are you calling me boring?'

'So far.' He opened his eyes and looked sideways at her.

'Cheek!' She put the car into first and drove off. He leaned forwards and pulled open the glove compartment, rootling through her cassettes.

'Billy Joel? Simply Red?' he said with distaste.

'What's wrong with them?'

'No soul.'

'I like them.'

'No Bob Marley? Scritti Politti? Clash?'

'Nope.'

'What's your name?'

'Nicola.'

He laughed.

'How is that funny?' She scowled at him, annoyed.

'Nicola.' He imitated her, sounding formal and uptight.

'It's my name. Don't be so bloody rude. What's yours?'

'Tarka.'

She snorted. 'Tarka? Like the otter?'

'Yes. My mum's favourite book.'

'You're lucky it wasn't *Winnie the Pooh*.'

'Otters are vermin, did you know that?'

'They're cute, though.'

'Have you seen them? In the river?'

'No. I thought they'd all disappeared?'

'Not if you know where to look. I could take you.'

Nicola smiled to herself. This was a first: the most beautiful boy she'd ever seen offering to take her otter spotting.

'I'd love that.'

He put a finger to his lips. 'You mustn't tell

anyone, though. It's a secret.'

'I won't tell a soul.' She pulled up outside the gates to Rushbrook House.

'Take me up the drive. It's bloody miles,' he grumbled.

'You could do with walking off what you've drunk.'

'Don't nag. It's very unattractive.'

He made no sign of getting out of the car so she drove carefully in through the gates and up the long, meandering driveway. It was lined with oak trees, and as she rounded the last bend the house was in front of her, a perfect manor house in pale-red brick with sash windows and white shutters, blushing in the late-afternoon sun.

'What a beautiful house,' breathed Nicola. It had always lain on the other side of the valley from Dragonfly Farm, but she had never been here before.

'I'm stuck here for the summer,' grumbled Tarka. 'They don't want me in London.'

'Who don't? Why not?'

He wouldn't answer. Instead he gestured for her to get out.

'Come inside. I'll play you some decent music.'

Her throat felt tight. With panic and something else she couldn't identify, though if it was anything to do with the swirling in her stomach and her pulse rate, it was desire.

'OK,' she said, unsure that she would be welcome. 'Won't anyone mind?'

'No!' He smiled at her. 'They'll be delighted to see me with someone so sensible.'

Nicola felt a little put out by this assessment of her, but she couldn't resist. She got out of the car and followed him across the circular drive and in through the front door, across a light and airy hallway and up a red-carpeted staircase. There didn't seem to be anyone else in.

He led her along a corridor. She glimpsed inside a bedroom, decorated in cream with floor-length curtains covered in blue and yellow flowers and a very large bed with a matching counterpane, perfectly made. At the very end of the corridor was his door. He ushered her inside.

The room was painted purple, with dark velvet curtains, and the walls were covered in black-and-white photos and posters. There were records everywhere, empty cans of Red Stripe with cigarettes stubbed out in them. A record player was flanked by huge black speakers. An elegant mahogany chest spilled out clothes. In the middle of the bed lay a Persian cat, which stared at Nicola in disapproval.

'Sit down.' He nodded towards the bed and she blushed. She went and perched on the end, stiff with self-conscious embarrassment. He threw off his hat and she saw his cloud of white curls, almost shoulder-length. He looked like a cherub. He grabbed a record, tipping the vinyl disc out of its sleeve and taking it over to the record player.

'Roxy Music,' he told her. 'Your musical education starts here.'

He put the record carefully onto the turntable and moved the needle across.

''In Every Dream Home a Heartache','' said

Tarka, moving across the room and throwing himself onto the bed behind her. 'How ironic.' He patted the space next to him. 'Come on. Lie down and listen.'

She edged backwards until she was lying near him but not near enough to touch. He had tucked his arms behind his head and seemed unaware of her presence. He was lost in the lyrics and the music; the tremulous voice and the swirling keyboard. Nicola lay there, feeling the heat of his body inches away from her, not daring to move.

'Thank you. For bringing me home,' mumbled Tarka next to her, reaching out and feeling for something. She held out her hand for a second then realised it was the cat he was looking for. He hooked a hand under its stomach, lugged it onto his own and moments later he was asleep.

Nicola lay there until the record ended, then wasn't sure what to do. Tarka was spark out. She doubted if he would wake up until the morning. She slid off the bed and crept out of the room, along the corridor and down the stairs, praying that no one would see her.

She was out of luck. A man walked out into the hall from another room just as she reached the bottom stair.

'Hi,' he said, unperturbed. This must be the kind of house where you came across strangers and didn't ask questions.

'I . . . gave Tarka a lift home. He's fallen asleep.'

'God, he's so rude. Sorry. That's kind of you.' He held out his hand. 'I'm Bear. Tarka's big brother. Has he been a nuisance?'

Bear? Maybe their mother's favourite book *had* been *Winnie the Pooh* after all. Bear was older than Tarka, broader, darker — or at least he hadn't attacked his hair with peroxide. Not as pretty, though attractive by most people's standards. Next to Tarka, anyone would look ordinary.

But he had much nicer manners and didn't make her feel wary or unsettled.

'No. He's been fine.'

'I suppose he's bladdered?'

'Um . . . a bit. Maybe.'

'Have you got far to go?'

'Not too far.' She didn't want to tell him where she was from.

'Well, thanks. Mum would have made me go and get him so you've done me a favour.'

'It was no problem.'

He raised a hand and wandered past her, not remotely concerned that she might have it in mind to pinch the family silver.

Nicola crossed the hall and slipped out of the front door. She stood between the pillars at the top of the steps for a moment, looking down the drive, the swathes of pasture either side, the great oak trees standing guard, and wondered what it would be like to be brought up here.

Why, for all his beauty and privilege, did Tarka seem broken? There was something not quite right about him. A devil-may-care self-destruction. Perhaps he thought nobody cared about him? He had seemed pathetically grateful for her concern.

She looked up to see if she could see his window. She had lost her bearings in the house and wasn't sure if his room was at the front or the back. There it was, on the top right, if the drawn curtains were anything to go by. She pictured him lying on his bed, in a deep cider slumber. She had a strong suspicion that he might not remember her when he woke. He might have a dim memory of a girl in a battered Mini stopping for him, but he would probably have no recollection of her name or even what she looked like. She, after all, did not have the looks to stop someone in their tracks. She was anonymous. Unmemorable. She sighed and shivered a little as the sun slipped behind a cloud.

The next evening when she got home from work, Joy handed her an envelope.

'I found this on the doormat.'

It had NIKKI scrawled on it in red crayon. Inside was a cassette tape and a note:

Some proper music, to start your musical education.
T

'Cheek!' said Nicola, echoing what she'd said to him in the car. But she was smiling. She rushed up to her bedroom and pushed it into her Walkman.

She nearly wore out the heads playing the tape over and over again. Every song made her feel something different. Some of them were dark and unsettling. Some were pure emotion.

Some made her smile and lifted her heart. She realised that the music she had been playing so far in her life was just wallpaper; something to make your toes tap. No wonder he had been so disparaging.

All of them made her think about him. Those blue eyes, that mouth, his hair, the very smell of him that if she shut her eyes was there in the room with her, a spicy sharpness, musky, animal, the smell of sex.

How had he known where she lived? She was certain she hadn't told him. All she had told him was her name. Had he known who she was all along? He must have done.

She would have to go up to Rushbrook to thank him. She would have to be brave. She wasn't going to let him slip through her fingers. He was extraordinary. He was going to change her life. He was going to turn her from dull, boring, sensible Nicola into Nikki — someone confident and wild and interesting.

It took all of Nicola's courage to drive to Rushbrook House the next evening. The house seemed to be staring at her, the little stone canopies over the top-floor windows like raised eyebrows. Her mouth was dry as she walked up the stone steps to the front door and rang the bell.

A woman answered. She was in a pink pencil skirt with a flowery shirt tucked in, her slim brown feet tucked into loafers, her blonde hair cut short like Princess Diana, a pair of discreet diamond studs in her ears that matched the diamond in her engagement ring.

Nicola felt hefty and dowdy in her stone-washed jeans. She'd hacked the sleeves off her blue-and-white striped T-shirt to give a ragged edge and backcombed her hair. She'd felt pleased with her appearance earlier, but now she felt silly.

'Hello?' the woman said politely.

'Is Tarka in? Please?'

The woman hesitated. She seemed to be looking at Nicola as if to judge her suitability.

'Well, yes,' she said doubtfully.

Nicola held out her hand. 'I'm Nicola.' She wasn't sure where she had got the courage, but she felt it was important for this woman to know she was well-mannered. 'He gave me a present and I wanted to say thank you.'

'Oh. Well. I'm Clara. His mother.' Clara gestured for her to come in. 'He's upstairs.'

Oh God. She would have to go up the stairs and along to his room and knock on his door. Would he want to see her or would his face fall?

'Oh good,' said Tarka when he saw her. 'I was just about to die of boredom. All anyone in this house can talk about is the party.'

'What party?' asked Nicola as he drew her inside.

'Mum's fiftieth.'

'Your mum's fifty?' Nicola was astonished.

'Yes. She's having a big black-tie bash in the garden. With a band and a marquee.' Tarka rolled his eyes. 'I don't want to go but I've been told I've got to.'

'I'm sure it'll be fine.'

'Will you come?' He laughed. 'I'm allowed to

291

bring a friend. As if I'm six years old.'

'If you're sure they won't mind.'

He looked a bit baffled by this. 'Course not.'

'I came to say thank you,' said Nicola. 'For the mix-tape.'

'Did you like it?' He brightened. 'You're never allowed to play Billy Joel again.'

She thumped him on the arm. 'I will if I want.'

'Not if you want to be my friend.'

He looked at her, laughing, and her stomach turned over and she thought, *Oh God, I want to be so much more than that . . . I want to mean the world to you.*

They became as thick as thieves over the next two weeks. Mostly it consisted of Nicola driving Tarka to the pub — either the Swan or one of the pubs in Nettleford — while he got slowly drunk and she kept him out of trouble. She didn't mind, for she was besotted. He was affectionate and sometimes protective if someone got lairy and made a pass at her. But although he hugged her a lot, and sometimes kissed her on the shoulder or the cheek or the head — never the mouth — it hadn't led to more. Which was fair enough, because she was nothing like as attractive as he was. People usually matched up with people who were a similar level, physically, she found. And she was in competition with every girl in North Somerset. Heads turned wherever he went. Eyes glazed over with lust. He seemed to want to be with her, but never more than that.

Her uncle Matthew raised an eyebrow when she told him and her aunt about Tarka. She didn't mention being in love, but perhaps, in retrospect, it was obvious, given how she talked about him non-stop. They didn't interfere, though. They weren't interfering types.

One weekend, the Culbones went up to London for the weekend. A party of some sort.

'Another black-tie job,' Tarka had grimaced. 'I hate all of that stuff.'

Yet he seemed to go along with it. For a rebel, he seemed to conform to what his parents wanted of him. Why couldn't they just leave him behind to do his own thing? He was twenty-three, not twelve.

Nicola spent the weekend in agony. Over and over she imagined all the long-limbed shiny-haired girls that would be there in their silk gowns and Barbados tans, crowding around Tarka, smiling and laughing, drawing him in. She imagined a large London townhouse in a leafy square, and Tarka kissing a girl outside on the balcony, the glittering city lights behind them, and everyone inside chattering and drinking champagne whilst the two of them fell in love. He wouldn't come back. She would never see him again. She couldn't bear it.

She sat in the kitchen after Sunday lunch trying to read Georgette Heyer, who always gave her comfort. She had picked at her food, barely eating anything. There was no room in her stomach for chicken and potatoes, not even a pea.

'Sweetheart.' Matthew put a hand on her shoulder. 'Don't make yourself miserable. The Culbones . . . ' He paused for a moment to give

293

his words some thought. 'The Culbones are a different species. I'm not saying they are bad people, but they don't . . . *care* about things as much as the rest of us. They're . . . gilded.'

Nicola thought about his words. Gilded was the perfect description. Tarka was golden; he bathed her in a warm light. She put down her book.

'He makes me feel . . . ' There were tears in her eyes as she tried to describe it. 'He makes me feel. That's it. He makes me feel.'

Before Tarka, she hadn't felt anything. She had been on automatic pilot. She had been quite happy, and enjoyed things, and liked things, but there had been no depth or texture to anything she experienced. Now, music felt three-dimensional, books had hidden meaning, even a painting could move her to tears. She was hypersensitive to everything around her. She felt as if she never slept, just fell into a state of semi-consciousness where her dreams were in technicolour and shimmering underneath every-thing that happened in them was Tarka.

Matthew sat at the table opposite her. He looked grave.

'Can I give you a piece of advice?' he asked, and Nicola nodded. 'Don't fall in love with someone who makes you feel as if you're going mad. Someone you have no control over. Someone who makes you feel . . . ' He bunched up his fist and held it over his stomach. 'Someone who makes you feel anxious.'

Nicola stared at him. How did he know that's how she felt? He smiled at her, and there was a lifetime of wisdom in that smile. He had felt like her once, she realised, and she knew it wasn't Joy who had made him feel that way.

'Fall in love with someone who makes you feel safe. And warm. And like yourself. Not someone who makes you want to be someone or something else.'

He patted her on the shoulder again, then stood up and went over to the sink. His stance told her not to ask any questions.

Nicola stared at her uncle's back as he started the washing-up. How did he know? How did he *know*?

★   ★   ★

Matthew scrubbed at the casserole pot with a metal scourer. He always did the mucky stuff: the roasting tins with the baked-on remnants of meat, the greasy frying pans, the potato-encrusted saucepans. He loved to restore order and make them gleam, and he wasn't in the least bit worried about the state of his hands.

He felt unsettled by Nicola's meeting Tarka Culbone. The ghosts and the skeletons and the secrets had been firmly locked up for nearly thirty years, and that's where he wanted them to stay. But it was difficult when they were right on your doorstep. The remnants of them, at least.

He'd kept away from them as best he could, without actually running away. It had never occurred to him to leave Dragonfly Farm because of what happened. Far from it. Dragonfly was his. All of theirs. It was where

295

they belonged, the Melchiors. If he had his way, they would be there for ever.

He wasn't going to put too much pressure on Nicola. He knew full well that was probably the quickest way for her to fall under the Culbone spell. He would watch, and wait, and be there to catch her if and when it all went wrong.

★   ★   ★

Nicola was on her way up to Tarka's room one afternoon — she came and went from the house now, confident she was welcome — when Clara intercepted her in the hall. She was in a blue-and-white striped shirt with the collar up and white jeans. Tiny, elegant. Even her perfume seemed too heavy for her.

'Could I have a little word?'

Nicola stopped at the bottom of the stairs. She immediately felt guilty, as if she was going to be accused of something, though she couldn't think what.

'Of course.'

She followed Clara into the drawing room. Clara didn't comment, just patted the sofa next to her.

'I don't know how much Tarka's told you about things,' said Clara, and in her face Nicola saw the steel of a mother determined to protect her offspring.

'What things?' Nicola was wary.

Clara breathed in, obviously debating how much to tell Nicola.

'Tarka is very fragile. I'm telling you because I

want you to understand, and to keep an eye on him for me. There was an incident before he left art college last year. He didn't realise quite what he was doing. He was drunk, of course, and someone had left out some pills . . . '

She looked away, clearly hoping that Nicola would work out what she was trying to tell her without actually having to say the words.

'He tried to kill himself? Is that what you mean?'

'It was a silly thing. There was some sort of falling-out with someone and . . . ' Clara finally managed to look her in the eye. 'You do understand that he's a little unstable? That he feels more than normal people. And that makes him do things on impulse sometimes. It's why he's here, at Rushbrook. Until he gets stronger. So I don't want him upset.'

'I'd never upset him. I think the world of Tarka.'

'Oh, I know, dear. I don't mean you.' Clara leaned forward and put a hand on Nicola's. 'Tell me . . . if you think there is anyone. If you suspect there's anyone who might hurt him. And if you do, would you let me know? We have to protect him.'

'Of course.'

Afterwards, Nicola realised that Clara meant that she, Nicola, would never break Tarka's heart. That it would be impossible for her to be the one that destabilised him. That she wasn't the sort of girl who would drive him to the edge or make him do something stupid.

Later that afternoon, Tarka took her down to

the river to see the otters. They walked across the land at the back of the house, down through the woods and along the bank to a place where the river widened out.

'You know where this is?' he said. 'This is Eleanor's Pool.'

'Yes. Where Eleanor Culbone drowned herself.' They looked at the water, deep and silent. It was sinister rather than tranquil, the trees overhead casting it into shadow.

'Sometimes,' he said, 'I understand how she felt. Knowing the man she loved didn't want her.'

'She was used,' said Nicola. 'That's what drove her mad, I think.'

Tarka was staring down into the dark-green stillness. He seemed a world away, lost in some reverie.

'Tarka?' Nicola touched his arm, concerned, particularly in the light of what his mother had just told her.

He turned and looked at her, and for a moment his face was filled with such sadness she didn't know what to say. And then he smiled, and the sadness melted away, and his face was alive again with excitement and mischief.

'Come on,' he said. 'They're further down here, the otters.'

They walked along the bank, leaving the menace of the pool behind, until he gestured to her to sit in the shade of a weeping willow. Here the sun found its way through the leaves, throwing speckles of light onto the ground.

'That's their slide,' he whispered, pointing to

the other side of the river where she could see a distinct groove in the muddy bank. 'We have to be very quiet.'

They sat for nearly two hours, waiting. Tarka fell asleep, as usual, and then Nicola found that she did too, overcome by the warmth of the sun. She woke to find him patting her arm gently, holding his finger to his lips and pointing to the river.

There they were, two white otters, frolicking in the river, writhing and twisting and moving through the water like little furry torpedoes. Nicola could barely breathe for the excitement of seeing them. They sat with their backs against the willow tree, watching. She grabbed Tarka's hand and held on to it as tightly as she could.

Then, in a flash, the otters were gone. Perhaps they had sensed they were being watched.

'Oh,' said Nicola, disappointed.

Tarka lay down, resting his head in her lap, looking up at her, half smiling, his eyes searching her face. She stared back. She could barely breathe. She felt the warmth and heaviness of him on her bare thigh. She didn't know what to do with her hands. She wanted nothing more than to let them drop into his hair, to entwine her fingers in his curls. Her blood was rushing through her, faster and louder than the river beside them. Surely he could hear it? Was he enjoying tormenting her, knowing full well both how uncomfortable and desperate it made her feel? Or was he oblivious? He probably did this all the time, breaching the bounds of etiquette and decency by getting dangerously close to people.

The sky was reflected in his blue eyes, making them shine even more brightly. She half closed her own, drowning in desire and confusion yet too petrified to speak or move as he turned his head to kiss her thigh. He traced his way upwards with his mouth and she felt the warmth of his lips on the pale soft skin under her denim skirt, his fingers reaching up to push aside the cotton of her knickers. She had no time to think about what he was doing and no inclination to protest. How could she object? It was as if he was eating a peach, relishing the sweetness of a summer-ripe fruit as he found the very core of her, teasing with his lips and his tongue. Currents of silver zipped through her like lightning, flashing faster and faster until —

'Oh God. Oh. Oh my God!' She arched her back, then looked down at Tarka's angelic face smiling up at her from between her thighs.

'Got you,' he whispered.

She wanted to laugh and cry. She wanted him to do it again. She couldn't speak.

'I wish I was good enough for you, Nik,' he sighed.

'You are,' she breathed. 'Of course you are.'

'No.' He shook his head. 'I would spoil you. Not in the good sense of the word. I'd *ruin* you.'

She didn't care about being ruined. She longed for it. She dug her fingers into the earth as her heartrate began to subside. A dragonfly hovered just near her eyeline, its wings thrumming as fast as the pulse inside her. Then it flew away, taking her hope with it.

Sometimes, Tarka's mood blackened when they were together. For no apparent reason. Suddenly the light went out in him, just as it had on the river bank that day, and he sank into gloom. He wouldn't speak. She couldn't cajole him out of it. Once or twice she left him to it and went home, because she couldn't bear it. It made her want to cry, because he wouldn't tell her what was the matter or let her cheer him up.

One afternoon, Nicola was at Rushbrook House when Bear and his girlfriend, Zanna, arrived for Sunday lunch with her parents and brother, Jamie. Bear and Jamie and Tarka had been at school together, and Jamie had introduced Bear to Zanna on a skiing holiday. Nicola had seen the pictures of them all together, clowning about on the slopes in Val d'Isère. She couldn't imagine what skiing was like. Another world she would never be a part of.

As soon as Nicola realised she was intruding, she went to leave, but Tarka insisted that she join them for lunch and Clara didn't seem to mind. Nicola felt self-conscious at the table in her jeans and sweatshirt. All the women were in jewel-bright silk dresses and court shoes, their hair streaked with blonde. Lunch was chicken breasts in a white sauce studded with green grapes followed by a raspberry pavlova: a trial for the upcoming birthday party.

Tarka didn't even pretend to be polite. He rolled his eyes at most of the conversation and even yawned at one point, and Nicola had to jab him with her elbow. He was being impossibly rude. It was an excruciating wait until after the cheese, when Clara looked at her son and gave a nod, as if to say *you can get down now* to a naughty young child who was itching to leave the table.

They went upstairs. Tarka put Lou Reed's *Transformer* on the record player. When 'Perfect Day' came on, Nicola was surprised to see tears rolling down his cheeks.

'What is it?' She rushed to his side and started hugging him. 'What *is* it?'

He shook his head. For a moment he was too choked to speak.

'Never,' he finally said, 'fall in love with someone you can't have, Nik. Never.'

Suddenly the penny dropped. He was in love with Bear's girlfriend, Zanna, Nicola realised. That explained everything. His disinterest in anyone else. His black moods, for of course it could come to nothing. His bad behaviour at the lunch table. His tears. His tears for a girl who was already taken, by his own brother. And she wasn't surprised. Zanna was luminous, bright, confident, accomplished. Everything Nicola was not.

Nicola thought how cruel the world could be in matters of the heart. It would be so simple if he could only transfer his passion from Zanna to her. But she knew that was impossible, and that wasn't how it worked, and it was why the songs he played her had been written, for if everyone loved the people who had fallen in love with them, there would be no heartache. No heartbreak.

Tarka got up to change the record. His face

302

was like thunder and he turned the volume up so the angry guitar reverberated through the walls of the house. Nicola picked up the sleeve to read the words: 'Ever Fallen in Love (With Someone You Shouldn't've)'.

'I'm going home,' she said. 'I don't know how to make you happy, so I'm going home.'

'Fine. Leave me then.' He was sulky, and it didn't suit him.

She ran down the stairs, hoping that none of the lunch party would spot her leaving or try to talk to her. They were all in the drawing room. She could hear the clink of coffee cups and the murmur of polite chatter.

'She seems sweet, Tarka's little girlfriend.' She heard a voice float out into the hall.

'Oh yes,' said Clara. 'She's very sensible, thank goodness. She seems to have calmed him down a lot.'

Nicola frowned. Why on earth did they think she was Tarka's girlfriend? She supposed that for an outsider it might look as if they were together. They spent enough time with each other, after all. And no one else was to know that, apart from the afternoon on the river bank, they had no physical contact.

'It must stop you worrying about him so much.'

'Nothing,' said Clara, 'stops me worrying about him.'

Unless it was because Tarka wanted them to think she was his girlfriend. She was a distraction from his real feelings. His real feelings for Zanna. He was using her. She was a cover-up.

She felt sick, the grapes and chicken roiling in her stomach.

'Is she coming to the party?'

'Yes. She can keep an eye on him.'

She shot out of the door before she could hear any more and ran down to the river, not much caring if they saw her from the drawing-room window. She splashed through the water over the stepping stones and ran up the slope on the other side.

Of course, she didn't have the strength to stay away from him for long, or the courage to accuse him of using her. He came looking for her a few days later, his mood much brighter, and he asked her forgiveness for being a grump.

'Bear used to be fun, that's all. Now he's obsessed with Zanna. I've got a horrible feeling they might get married. I can't stand the thought of it.'

'Everyone has to grow up. Even you.' Nicola prodded him. 'You're not Peter Pan.'

And she suddenly realised that their relationship was just like Peter Pan and Wendy's: her fussing over him and Tarka refusing to take any responsibility for anything more arduous than ordering a drink or turning over a record. No wonder he wouldn't grow up. Everyone was so busy wrapping him in cotton wool and keeping him away from reality. He was going to stay how he was for ever if they weren't careful.

'Mum wanted me to give you this.' He proffered a white envelope. Inside was a thick invitation with silver cursive writing. An invitation to the party.

'Oh!' she exclaimed. She was surprised, but then she began to panic. What would she wear? Who would she be sat next to — she knew there were already ructions about the seating plan. Would she have to dance? She couldn't bear the thought of having to dance in front of all of them.

'I've told them to sit you next to me otherwise I won't go,' said Tarka.

'What am I? Your babysitter?' laughed Nicola.

'Something like that,' said Tarka with a smile. He was lying on the bed next to her, twiddling her hair. The touch of his fingers made her scalp tingle. She rolled over so she was almost on top of him.

'No, really,' she said. 'What am I?'

He looked at her, frowning. 'You're you. The sweetest girl.'

It was the title of his favourite song.

'I don't know what that means,' she whispered. 'I don't know what I mean. To you.'

'Everything, Nik, I promise you that.'

The warmth of him against her body was making her melt. She wanted that feeling again, the feeling he had given her on the river bank. She slid his T-shirt up and ran her fingers over the velvet heat of his skin. She wanted to feel every inch of it on hers.

'Don't,' said Tarka.

'Why not?' She could feel his hardness, hot through his Levi's, and she pushed herself against it, its confirmation making her bold.

'I don't want . . . to hurt you.'

'I'm not a virgin, you know.'

She wasn't to realise that he meant a different kind of hurt. She leaned down to kiss his neck and he let out a groan of desire, sliding his hands onto her, pulling at her clothes.

It was even better, that feeling, with him inside her.

31

Nicola spent a good chunk of her summer wages on a dress for Clara's party, telling herself that she would be able to use it for job interviews once she'd graduated. It was electric blue with a ruffled peplum and a tight pencil skirt. She felt sleek and sophisticated for the first time in her life, especially when she put on the matching court shoes. Perhaps not as sleek as Zanna, but not bad.

Tarka had asked her to come to the house before the party started at seven. Nicola parked round the side of the house so as not to clutter up the drive with her little Mini. Her high shoes were in a bag on the back seat, and she had on a pair of flat ones for driving. The front door was open, ready for the caterers to bring food through to the kitchen before serving dinner in the marquee.

She had never seen such preparations as over the past few days. Gardeners and flower arrangers and cleaners. A cake in three boxes had arrived the day before. Crates and crates of champagne and boxes of glasses.

'The thing is,' Tarka explained, 'Mum hasn't got daughters so she's never going to be able to arrange a wedding here. This is to make up for it.'

'Do people really care so much about things like that?'

'Oh yes,' said Tarka. 'They really do. It's all about appearances. Everything has to be perfect.'

Afterwards, she was to remember what he'd said, but at the time, she laughed. Who was she to judge if Clara wanted to put on a display of wealth and good taste?

The house was quiet. The calm before the chaos. She walked in through the front door and was just starting to go up the stairs when she saw Jamie and Tarka in front of the big mirror at the top. She paused on the half-landing: they hadn't seen her yet. Tarka was tying Jamie's bow tie for him. She watched as he wrapped the silk round Jamie's neck, tying it with a flourish. He patted the knot into shape, then looked up at him.

Something stopped Nicola from calling hello. She watched as Tarka reached up and touched Jamie's cheek. The two of them didn't take their eyes off each other. Then Jamie raised his hands and put one either side of Tarka's face, drawing him towards him until their lips met.

There was a hunger and a familiarity to their kiss that showed it wasn't their first. Eventually, Tarka pulled away, but his gaze was locked on Jamie's, daring him. They stared at each other, breathless, then Jamie put up a hand to Tarka's chest, pushing him away.

'No.' His voice was low, but definite. 'No more, Tarka. We're over.'

Tarka flinched and turned away. He walked to the top of the stairs, then stopped as he saw Nicola staring up at them. He smiled his brilliant smile.

'Nik!' he said, not missing a beat, as if nothing

had happened. 'Thank God you're here. Mum wants me to go into Nettleford for more Pimm's. Let's go.'

In the car, Nicola gripped the steering wheel tightly.

'I saw you,' she said. 'I saw you kiss Jamie.'

Tarka just shrugged.

'Are you . . . ?' She wasn't sure of the best word to use. An adjective or a noun? Queer? Bent? A homo? Nothing she thought of seemed very polite and she didn't want him to think she was prejudiced. Even though she was shocked.

Tarka sighed. 'Oh, darling,' he said. 'I'm not anything. I like everyone, you see. Boys. Girls. Men. Women . . . Anyone who'll have me . . .'

He laughed, but it was an uneasy sound.

That must be everyone, thought Nicola. Who on earth would be able to resist Tarka?

'You mustn't say anything.' Tarka's voice was level, but his fists were clenched tightly with tension. He wasn't as insouciant as he pretended to be. 'It would kill Mum.'

'*That's* why you've let them all think I'm your girlfriend.' Nicola felt mortified as the truth finally filtered through to her. She pulled the car over to the side of the road. 'I was your cover. How could you do that to me?'

'Nik — that's just not true. I never told anyone you were my girlfriend.'

'But you let them think I was. That's why I'm coming to the party. Admit it.'

'You're coming because you're my best friend.' He put a placatory hand on her arm and she shook it away.

309

'I'm not coming,' she said. 'I'm going home. You used me, Tarka.'

'It's you who tried to make this something it's not,' he shot back.

She winced at the cruelty of his words. He put his face in his hands.

'Oh God, I'm so sorry,' he said. 'I can't lose you as well. I can't bear it. You're the only person who cares about me.'

'That's not true. They all care, your family.'

'You've got to come to the party. Please. I won't be able to get through it without you next to me.'

Nicola didn't reply. How could she have been so stupid? How could she have thought he was in love with his brother's girlfriend? Of course he wasn't. He was in love with Jamie.

'When did it start?' she asked. 'You and Jamie?'

'Oh God. Skiing. When he introduced Bear to Zanna. We'd known each other at school. We were together for a while. But he broke it off. He couldn't admit that he loved me. To himself. Or anyone else. Or even me. It's not the *done thing*, you know.'

'Is that why . . . ?' Nicola remembered what Clara had told her. About the pills. 'Your mum told me. About your overdose.'

'I didn't think I could live without him. It was too much. If I could have had a clean break, maybe I would have been OK. But with Zanna and Bear together he was always going to be on the edge of my life. And to see him in our house . . . ' His voice faltered. 'I don't know how

310

I'm going to manage the party.'

Nicola sighed. 'It's OK,' she said. 'I'm here. I'll look after you. I promise.'

She got him ready in time for the family photograph on the stone balcony. Hugh, Bear and Tarka were devastatingly handsome in their dinner jackets, and Clara was magnificent in ice-blue taffeta, diamonds sparkling at her throat. The perfect family. Proud parents. Dutiful sons.

Over dinner, she watched with increasing alarm as Tarka got steadily drunk, sloshing wine into his glass haphazardly. Jamie was, thank goodness, on another table. She tried to distract him, tried to get him to eat, but he became more morose.

'People will notice,' she hissed at him, and he started to put on an air of forced jollity that was worse than being gloomy, telling awful jokes and laughing loudly.

'You're ruining the party. Can't you think about your mother? She's worked so hard to make this a perfect day.'

'A *perfect* day,' said Tarka with a sardonic smile.

'Today,' said Nicola, 'is not about you. You're being thoroughly selfish.'

Tarka raised his glass. 'Cheers. Thanks for the vote of confidence. Love you too.' He smirked at her, and Nicola thought how desperate he looked. She wasn't sure what to do. She couldn't make it right for him, but she didn't want him to make a scene and she didn't trust him not to, the way he was drinking.

'Why don't you go up to your room?' she said. 'Have a sleep. Things might seem better afterwards.'

He stood up and looked at her, swaying slightly. His eyes were bloodshot, the way they had been the first time she'd met him. His smile still made her heart twist. He was so beautiful with his bright ringlets, standing there in a white shirt untucked from his trousers, his buttons undone to his chest, his bow tie hanging round his neck, the bowl of his wineglass cupped in his right hand.

'Good idea,' he said. 'I'll get out of everyone's way, shall I? I think that would be best.'

'Yes,' said Nicola, and watched as he wove his way between the guests, back up through the French windows and into the house.

She moved around the party for a while, feeling slightly self-conscious. The guests were mostly the Culbones' friends from London and she didn't feel confident enough to start a conversation. Then Bear, lovely kind Bear, saw her and asked her to dance with him. The floor was filling up, and there were enough people on there for her to be able to merge into the crowds. Bear was a good dancer, and a chivalrous one: he made her feel as if she was good too.

'Thanks for looking after Tarka this summer. Mum really appreciates it, you know,' he said to her as they left the dance floor. She opened her mouth to reply but couldn't think what to say. She gulped down another glass of wine and felt the memory of earlier receding. She went back onto the dance floor. She lost herself in the beat and realised she was enjoying herself, that she didn't feel self-conscious dancing along to 'Eye of the Tiger' with everyone else — it didn't seem to matter if you didn't have anyone to dance with.

An hour had slipped by and darkness had fallen. She thought she had better go and check on Tarka. He'd be in one of his drunken stupors, she supposed, but she ought to wake him up and get him to come back down or people would think he was rude. He'd have slept off most of it. She ran up the stairs, trying not to think about what she had witnessed earlier as she passed the mirror on the landing.

His room was empty. There was no sign of him at all, except the turntable spinning round and round, aimless. On his pillow was a note. She grabbed it.

I can't pretend any more.

For a moment she was paralysed with panic. She looked around for clues — bottles, tablets, anything that might suggest what he had done. What would he do, if he was desperate? Not a gun — there had been no gunshot. There was no blood anywhere.

Then she remembered what he had said the day they'd been to see the otters. What he had said as he stared down into the water.

Sometimes I understand how she felt. Knowing the man she loved didn't want her.

Eleanor's Pool. She felt a chill as cold as the water itself. She ran back down the stairs, kicking her shoes off at the door, then outside and down the side of the house, down to the woods. She ran, stumbling over the rough ground, the full moon only just giving enough light for her to make her way to the river. She prayed for the first time in her life. Prayed that her premonition was just her being fanciful. Prayed that Tarka would be in some pub in Nettleford shovelling ten-pence pieces into the jukebox and playing The Clash, getting longing glances from the girls and murderous glares from the blokes, crashing into people and saying sorry. Tarka spent his whole life saying sorry.

The moon lit up the river. Its surface shone black and hard and unforgiving. It wasn't going to give up its secrets easily. The night was still. Not a rustle of leaves. Not a living creature. There was no sign of life. But no sign of death either. No body floating in the pool. Nicola let out a sigh as sweet relief flooded through her. Her heart was thumping as she looked around to double-check, peering into the shadows, not wanting to think what else might be lurking. Rats. Murderers. Ghosts.

Did a body float or would it sink to the muddy bottom?

Or would it get washed downstream?

Her heart in her mouth, she moved along the bank, taking care not to trip over the roots of the trees on the edge, unease replacing the initial relief. She had been too quick to assess and assume. Twice she slipped on the mud, her heart lurching each time. Her legs were trembling: they felt as useless as if she were in a dream, as if

314

they were made of jelly.

As the river narrowed again, to the spot where the water began to tumble over the stones and run more freely, she saw what she had dreaded. He was there, face down in the water, stuck at the bottleneck. He looked small. Fragile.

Fragile. That was what Clara had called him, she remembered.

Nicola could hear herself screaming his name as she scrabbled down the bank and leaped into the water. The river wasn't deep here, but the bottom was slippery and the water was freezing. She pushed through it as quickly as she could, gagging on her own sobs. She fell, and her sobs turned to gasps as the icy water enveloped her. She heaved herself up, pushing through the shallows.

At last. She was by him. She reached down to curl her arms round him and turn him over, praying that she wasn't too late. But, of course, she was. She could tell by his weight; the lifeless weight of him. Death, it seemed, made you lumpen and awkward. She didn't have the strength to pull him out and onto the bank. She knelt next to him, working out what to do. Her teeth were chattering with cold and fear and shock as she felt the last vestiges of hope slither away. He wasn't going to cough and splutter and come back to life. His eyes weren't going to sparkle and his beautiful mouth wasn't going to turn up at the corners and she would never hear his laugh again.

She let him fall back into the water. She was freezing and exhausted. She had to get back to

Rushbrook. The party would be coming to an end soon. What was she going to say? For a moment she was tempted to flee across the fields, run to the sanctuary of Dragonfly Farm, curl up in her bed and shut everything out. But she couldn't. She had to rescue Tarka. She wanted him dried and wrapped up in warm soft blankets. She wanted him safe.

She didn't know how she made it up to the house. She stood at the entrance to the marquee, barefoot, drenched and bedraggled, searching for someone to tell, someone who would understand and take charge.

If she shut her eyes, then opened them again, perhaps it wouldn't have happened. Perhaps she would see Tarka on the other side of the marquee, throwing back a glass of champagne, flicking his ash onto the coconut matting, laughing, dazzling some girl who wouldn't be able to take her eyes off him, who would be wondering if she had any chance, any chance at all, of keeping his attention for more than two minutes . . .

But when she opened them, her eyes met Bear's. Oh God. Not Bear. He couldn't be the one she broke the news to. She saw him walk through the crowds towards her, frowning. She leaned against the side of the marquee, limp with grief and fear. He began to run. He knew. He could see from her face what had happened.

'Nicola?' He was right beside her. He grabbed her, half to hold her up, half to shake her into a revelation. 'Nicola — what is it?'

What words to choose? She didn't want to

316

speak them aloud. 'He's in . . . the river. He's . . . '

She collapsed against Bear's chest.

'Where? Whereabouts? Somebody call an ambulance!'

People were noticing now. They crowded around her. It was important to pull herself together. This was not her tragedy. It didn't belong to her, not really.

'He's . . . I think he's dead. I couldn't get him out. I tried. I really tried.'

Her voice didn't seem to belong to her. She hated herself for the thin desperate wail that was spooling out of her mouth. She wanted to be strong for everyone. She wanted to make it all right. There was a hubbub around her, urgency that segued into panic. Someone appeared with a coat to put round her. And over and under it all, the thump of the bass and the sound of 'Tainted Love' by Soft Cell, until someone managed to tell the DJ to turn it off. The sudden silence felt shocking.

As the news flickered around the marquee, Nicola wanted to shrink and disappear. She couldn't leave. She knew the police would be here soon. That she would have to speak to them and tell them what she had seen. She hoped beyond hope they wouldn't need her help to find him.

Someone was leading her out of the marquee, up the steps at the back of the house, through into the drawing room. Bear, his arms on the mantelpiece, his head nestled inside them. His father, Hugh, next to him, rigid and grim. Then

317

Clara in the doorway, framed by the French windows, screaming, screaming, screaming, stumbling into the room and falling into Hugh's arms.

A trio of male guests were taking charge. Between them they had sobered up and were making a plan, practical, subdued, tight-lipped. Hugh was talking to them. There was an altercation. She guessed he wanted to go with them to retrieve the body, but they were telling him no.

She pulled the coat round her shoulders and made for the hall, keeping her head down. She needed to step away from the chaos. She needed to clear her head. As she slipped through the doorway, someone was about to come in. She looked up. It was Jamie. His hair was dishevelled; his jacket undone.

For a moment they locked gazes. She saw in his eyes a flicker of fear underpinned with doubt. He knew something was amiss. He knew it was something to do with him. He put his hands up to his mouth and shook his head.

'This is your fault,' said Nicola.

Jamie grabbed her shoulders. 'You mustn't tell anyone. No one must know. No one will understand. Clara would never forgive me.'

Nicola looked at him, appalled by his cowardice. She drew herself up.

'What a waste,' she said. 'What a bloody awful waste.'

She saw Jamie's face melt in front of her, his mouth turning downwards, his eyes drooping, despair rearranging his features. She didn't want to console him. She wanted to berate him.

'You kissed him, Jamie. I saw you.'

'He kissed *me*.'

'You gave him hope. You know how he felt about you.'

'The thing is,' Jamie went on, his voice thick with anguish, 'Tarka made you lose your senses. There was a time when I'd have done anything for him. But he could be cruel. He used people.'

Had he used her, wondered Nicola? Or had he needed her?

Jamie's jaw was rigid with the effort of not breaking down, and his fists were clenched.

'Don't tell anyone,' he begged. 'Don't tell anyone.'

Nicola shut her eyes. Everything was closing in on her. She had to get away. She couldn't stay here a moment longer. She put her hand up to her chest: it was so tight she could hardly breathe.

She ran to the telephone in the hallway and dialled with shaking hands.

'It's me,' she said. 'Can you come and get me? From Rushbrook House. Can you come and get me now?'

'Of course, love,' said Uncle Matthew. 'I'm on my way.'

32

The Culbones closed ranks. The gates of Rushbrook House swung shut and were locked tight. All the guests had left. Only the police and the local doctor were allowed in and out. Everyone prayed that the good weather they had longed for that weekend would leave: the news and the heat combined were too awful to bear. At night, sweat and tears mingled on sheets and pillows, salty and sticky. In the shops and the pubs, the tragedy was dissected. Too much money and not enough discipline was the verdict, but there were people who vouched for Tarka's sweet nature; girls who sobbed at the memory of his lips on theirs. And there were others who stayed silent. No one liked rumours; no one wanted to be suspected of anything untoward.

Nicola was interviewed by the police, gently and kindly, at Dragonfly Farm. She told them that Tarka had been upset about something that evening but she wasn't sure what. She didn't mention Jamie or the note she had found on his pillow. She had taken the note with her when she fled, but she must have dropped it when she found him. It must have floated off, his secret borne away by the river. She wasn't going to betray Tarka by revealing the truth or explaining why it was he felt he couldn't pretend any more.

What would be the point? She knew

instinctively that it would be no consolation for Clara and Hugh to know the turmoil he had been in, although she suspected they did know. It had been Nicola who had been naive.

There was an inquest, a verdict of accidental death: Tarka had been impossibly drunk when he drowned. The level of alcohol in his blood would have rendered him insensible.

She received a stiff little note from Tarka's mother.

Thank you for being so kind to Tarka this summer. I know he valued your friendship. The funeral will be family only. I do hope you understand our decision and will respect our need for privacy.

She was not needed or welcome at Rushbrook. She certainly didn't feel entitled to ignore their wishes and intrude on their grief. She saw Bear the day before the funeral, buying cigarettes in the village shop, dark rings under his eyes. They had hugged each other, wordlessly.

'I'm so sorry,' he whispered as he let her go. 'About the funeral. But Mum . . . we have to do what Mum wants.'

'Is Jamie all right?' she asked him, on impulse.

Bear hesitated for a moment. He wouldn't quite meet her eye. 'Well, of course he's dreadfully cut up. We all are.'

'Is he going? To the funeral?'

Bear looked stricken. 'He's Zanna's brother. He's . . . family.'

He looked at her as if to say *please don't ask me any more.*

He didn't ask why she was concerned about Jamie, in particular. Which meant he knew.

She could see how the Culbones worked. They were the kind of family that turned their backs on things they didn't want to acknowledge. If it didn't fit into their picture of how life should be, it hadn't happened. Perhaps an ounce of understanding or compassion would have saved Tarka? They had gathered around to protect him and look after him that summer, but only the version of him they wanted. They didn't want the real Tarka.

There was no point in saying this to Bear. She suspected it was Bear who was holding things together at Rushbrook House. He had strong shoulders, but he wasn't strong enough for the truth. It wasn't his fault. It was how he had been brought up. Nicola turned and left the shop because she didn't know what to say.

She didn't know how she lived through such darkness in the blinding white August heat. She stayed in her room, the curtains drawn against the sun. Her parents came down to comfort her, together with a shocked Robin — they didn't know how to help her. It was Matthew and Joy who understood what she needed: a week to sleep, deeply, with a little help from something supplied by the same doctor who had been to Rushbrook House. Then she was made to get up, to eat a little, to walk in the fresh air. Her limbs felt stiff and bruised from the exertion; her mind played tricks on her, visions of what had happened flickering in and out of her consciousness, like a television trying to find its signal.

She worked with Joy in the vegetable garden, picking beans and raspberries that she never ate. She fell asleep in the orchard under a tree and woke to the sound of Joy calling her name, her voice sharp with panic until she found her.

Her father spoke to the dean of the university. They would understand if she didn't want to go back; if she wanted to defer for a year. She didn't think she could fit the Hundred Years' War into her brain along with her grief. She needed distraction, but not anything complicated. Menial work that occupied her mind but wasn't too taxing.

'I want to go back to London,' she told her parents. 'I'll live in the flat, and I'll get a job. I can't do nothing. But I couldn't write an essay, let alone a thesis.'

It was time for her to leave Dragonfly Farm. Matthew and Joy had been wonderful, but it was too close. At night she could hear the river, chuckling over the stones. She drowned it out by playing the tapes he had given her, drifting away on the lyrics.

'The Sweetest Girl' — that's what he had called her. 'You're the sweetest girl,' he'd whispered to her, and now she realised what he meant. That she was naive and innocent and without a clue.

In September, she went up to London as planned, moving into a flat in Maida Vale with three of her university friends. Chris was in the kitchen, just as he had been on her first day in the student house. This time he was making dahl, grinding up the spices and measuring them out in his exacting, scientific way. As she walked in, he wandered over and gave her a tight squeeze then went back to crushing cardamom pods. It was fleeting, but so comforting. It said *I am here* but didn't cause her to have to explain anything or go through what had happened. It was what she wanted, for her grief to be acknowledged but for her to be allowed to be normal.

'Here,' he said, dolloping out spoonfuls of spicy yellow dahl. 'Comfort food. I'll put the rest in the freezer and you can bung it in the microwave whenever you want.'

He portioned up the remains into individual sandwich bags. She smiled. It was so Chris. Organised, logical — why fork out for an Indian takeaway when you could have the fun of making it yourself and live off the leftovers?

She got a job waitressing in an American-style diner in Covent Garden. It was a popular cocktail and burger joint, always full to the brim with loud music and a buzzy atmosphere. While she was at work, she never had a second to brood as it kept her on her feet day and night.

She was a month into the job, serving up two king-size cheeseburgers with French fries and root beer floats, when the nausea hit her. She threw them on the table and fled to the staff toilets. She knew she hadn't eaten something or caught a bug. She thought fleetingly of the risk she had taken with Tarka then pushed it to the back of her mind. Trembling, she rinsed her teeth, told the supervisor she needed to leave and ran home to the flat.

324

Chris came back and found her sitting at the kitchen table with the washing-up bowl in front of her.

'I'm pregnant,' she told him.

'Crikey,' said Chris. 'I didn't know you were seeing anyone.'

'I'm not,' said Nicola.

'Oh!' Now Chris did look shocked. 'You mean . . . ?'

She had told him a little of what had happened in Somerset. Enough for him to glean that there had been something more than just friendship between her and Tarka.

'Yes,' said Nicola, gulping back the nausea. 'Oh dear.'

Chris sat down opposite her, concerned.

'Don't decide anything for at least a week. You don't need to do anything yet.'

He was so wise. So gentle. She put her hand on her chest, feeling her heart flutter with panic.

'Breathe,' he said. 'You're not breathing. You need to breathe, you know.'

This made her laugh. Chris was funny, a bit of a boffin, with little concern for his appearance — he wasn't unattractive, he just wasn't very good at clothes or haircuts, with his dishevelled mop and his uniform of jeans and baggy shirts, the big old jumpers he got from Oxfam and his square black NHS glasses. He was, she knew, destined for great things, but he wore his genius lightly.

'I don't think,' she said, 'I can face any more sadness.'

'Maybe this is a happy thing?' he said.

She looked at him, puzzled. She didn't have a proper job or any money. She couldn't bring up a baby in this flat. Her room was only ten foot by ten foot.

'It's only a baby,' he said. 'People do this all the time. Just not in our rarefied, middle-class world of university and gap years and milk rounds and career ladders. Having babies is totally normal.'

She opened her mouth and shut it. That was the last reaction she'd expected from him.

'My mum was a single mum,' he went on. 'She was brave enough to have me, in Wolverhampton in the sixties, when it made you a social pariah. Her parents kicked her out. My dad didn't want to know. I am forever grateful for her bravery.'

'Oh, Chris. I had no idea.'

'That's not emotional blackmail, by the way. You must do whatever you think is right. I'm just saying that maybe one of the options isn't as hard as you think.'

Despite his reassurance, she felt a wave of despair. She put her head in her arms. Chris rubbed her back.

'Whatever I can do,' he said. 'You just tell me.'

'Thank you,' said Nicola, her voice muffled. 'I need to get a proper test.'

'I'll come with you.' He laughed. 'If you can bear the ignominy of everyone thinking I'm the father.'

She tutted. 'Ignominy.' Only Chris would use a word like that. 'It would be the luckiest baby in the world, to have you as its dad.'

He looked at her for a moment then looked away.

★ ★ ★

As promised, Chris came with her to the Family Planning Clinic. They sat in the brightly lit waiting room, looking like a normal couple, reading leaflets on herpes. The clock ticked on. Her appointment was long overdue. She looked at the other women in there, wondering what their stories were. She was dreading the conversation with the nurse. Dreading having to articulate her situation and being given a due date, and having the options outlined to her. Then having to make a decision.

'Nicola Melchior?'

She stood up. Chris stood too. She looked around the room, at the other women waiting their turn, waiting to make their decisions. He slipped his hand into hers.

'Come on,' he said. 'Let's get all the info.'

At the end of her internal examination, and after peeing into a plastic tube that was whisked away, the nurse looked up from filling out her paperwork.

'April 10th,' she said. 'If your dates are correct.'

There was only one date that was a contender, so Nicola nodded. Though she thought she might have to fudge the details a bit when she told everyone.

'A spring baby,' she said. 'That will be nice.'

Chris looked up at her in surprise. The nurse smiled at Chris.

'Well, this is all very exciting, isn't it, Dad?'

Chris opened his mouth and did something waggly with his eyebrows and caught Nicola's eye and they both collapsed laughing. The nurse looked slightly put out, not sure what was quite so funny, but she put it down to nerves and gave Nicola her next antenatal appointment.

From that day on, Chris barely let her out of his sight. Of course, he had to, because he had to go to university and she had to go to work, battling her nausea to keep on serving up gastronomic excess to hungry tourists. But he made her jacket potatoes with beans and grated cheese, because that's all she wanted to eat, and brought her home Double Deckers to put in the fridge. He forced her to go out walking when she wailed about how fat she was getting.

'You'll thank me for it,' he told her as she trudged behind him along the Regent's Canal all the way up to Camden Market. He took her to jazz at Ronnie Scott's in Frith Street, and every Thursday they went to the cinema and she fell asleep after five minutes and he would fill her in on the plot on the way home.

At five months, when she was starting to show and it didn't just look as if she had been eating all the customers' leftovers, she dissolved into total hysteria at the thought of what she was doing.

'I'm going to have to tell my parents.' She'd avoided it until now. 'And my aunt and uncle.'

She was sitting in the biggest chair in their lounge in front of *Neighbours*. It had become her daily habit, and she joked the baby would come out singing the theme tune. But she couldn't get up out of the chair and suddenly everything seemed too much.

'Would it be a crazy idea,' he asked, looking at her as she sobbed, 'if we got married? Would that stop you panicking? I mean, I'll probably end up earning quite a bit, between you and me. And — ' He paused for a moment, frowning, as if what he was about to say had only just occurred to him. 'I can't think of anything I'd like to do more than look after you and baby Charlene for the rest of my life.'

'Baby Charlene?'

He nodded at Kylie Minogue on the screen. 'Isn't that what you'll call her? If it's a girl?'

Nicola burst out laughing. And she felt something well up inside her. It was, she realised, a kind of love.

Her love for Chris in no way resembled what she had felt for Tarka. That had been dark and terrifying and all-consuming. It had gnawed at her and left a jagged hole. And the feelings she had for him had never been reciprocated. She had been a friend, someone Tarka had found solace in temporarily. She knew if things had turned out differently he would have moved on and forgotten her.

But her love for Chris was sweet and gentle and comforting, like a warm blanket on a cold day, a blanket that she knew was with her all the time. She never feared waking and finding it gone. She knew it would be there for ever, whatever.

'Do you know,' she said, 'I would love that. I

really think I would.'

They went down to Guildford to tell her mum and dad, who seemed a little bewildered that she and Chris had made such a commitment to each other so young, but after everything that had happened in the summer it seemed like nice news, so they offered their support.

She telephoned Matthew and Joy to tell them.

'What you said to me,' Nicola told Matthew, 'about falling in love with someone who makes you feel safe? Someone who lets you be yourself? That is Chris, exactly.' She smiled. 'Chris is my Joy.'

Everyone seemed very happy that she was in safe hands with the father of her baby after such a terrible tragedy. A baby, they all agreed, would help her forget.

33

It was a Sunday evening, and Chris and Nicola were eating tomato soup and white-sliced toast covered in butter and Marmite, because on a Sunday evening you always thought you were full from Sunday lunch and couldn't eat another thing, but come eight o'clock it was usually time for a little something.

The toast stuck in Nicola's throat along with the words she was longing to say. She knew if she didn't say them tonight, the week would get underway and the chance would be lost.

'I think,' she said, 'we should tell Georgia the truth. Before she starts school next week.'

Chris put down his spoon. 'Tell her?'

'That you're . . . ' She couldn't say the words. It sounded so brutal. *Not her real father.*

He didn't say anything for a moment. 'Do we have to? Do we really have to?'

'We can't lie to her for ever.'

'But there's no reason for her to know. Not really.' Chris pushed his soup bowl to one side. 'She's too young to understand the biology. We don't want to go into all of that, surely? So how would we explain it?'

'I just feel now would be the right time. Starting school is a big step. She should know who she is.'

Chris stared at her. His eyes were wide, his lips pressed together, his chin trembling. He looked like a distressed owl, and Nicola's heart twisted inside her. Every bit of her moral fibre told her it would be wrong to stay silent, to keep Georgia in the dark about her paternity.

But the face opposite her told another side of the story. She couldn't ignore Chris's point of view because he was 99.9 per cent Georgia's dad. The 0.1 per cent was a technical detail. Did she have the right to turn everyone's life upside down on a technicality?

'Only we know,' Chris was saying. 'Nobody else has any idea. You've never told anyone.' He looked closely at her. 'Have you?'

'No!'

'Not even Matthew? Or Joy?'

'Definitely not. Why would I?' Nicola was shocked that Chris thought she might have.

'I don't know.' Chris's shoulders slumped as he spoke.

There were two meanings to the verb *father*. One was simple science: a nanosecond when the egg was fertilised by a microdot. The other was all-encompassing. An ongoing state that took time and energy and care and *love* — eternal, everlasting, enormous amounts of love. Love that Chris had dispensed without question and with all his heart.

'I couldn't bear it. I couldn't bear it if she thought differently of me because she knew I wasn't her real dad. Because as far as I'm concerned I couldn't be more real. I feel as if she is part of me and I am part of her. She's in my blood and my bones and my heart and my soul.'

Nicola's skin prickled with anxiety. She

understood what Chris was saying, and it was all true. He could not have been a more wonderful or devoted father. He went above and beyond, she knew he did, because so many of her friends complained that the men in their lives didn't engage with their kids, not really, only under sufferance and in ideal circumstances.

Did Georgia ever need to know? Chris was on her birth certificate. Of course, she didn't look anything like him, but she didn't look much like Nicola either. But not so extraordinarily unlike them to arouse suspicion. Georgia looked like herself.

If she made a pact with Chris now, they could never go back on it. Their secret would be buried deeper and deeper as the years went by. There was no reason for it to be uncovered. The three of them, by chance, had the same blood group. There would be no desperate search for a kidney or bone marrow that might flag up an anomaly. Unless —

'What if there's something in her medical history? Something she should know about?'

She could see Chris, the scientist, weighing this up. Then she realised that of course he had thought about all this before, and what he was weighing up was how to respond.

'I think the chances of her inheriting a genetic disorder are pretty slim.'

'Are they?'

'She's a happy, healthy girl. If anything changes, we can think again.'

In all the years of love and loyalty and support and kindness, Chris had never asked anything of her until now. And so she agreed to keep their secret. It seemed to be the least she could do, to repay what he had done for her, and she had no right to break Chris's heart. He was Georgia's father and that was the end of it.

PART FOUR

34

The moon was still lording it over the loch just before dawn, throwing silver across the water like a beneficent dowager throwing coins for the poor. It was possible to imagine that you were the only person in the world, looking across the expanse of still, shining water into the darkness of the mountains beyond. But he wasn't the only person in the world, far from it. How much easier would that be.

If Chris had been a betting man — actually, he sometimes was, when the odds really were in his favour — he would have said they could have kept their secret for ever, with just the two of them knowing. He hadn't counted on Gum's intervention from beyond the grave. Had Gum guessed the truth, and this was his way of ensuring it came out? But why would he do that? And it was far too complicated a means. Gum was a man of integrity: open and honest. He would have just said to Chris, 'I know you're not Georgia's dad, and I think you should tell her.'

Although now it seemed as if Gum had secrets of his own. So perhaps not so honest after all.

He sighed.

'Are you awake?' A gentle voice came from across the room. 'So am I. We might as well get up and go.'

He walked towards the bed and sat down

beside Nicola. 'Yeah. I haven't slept, really. All of it going round in my head.'

She sat up, leaning her back against the headboard. He could just make her out in the paleness of dawn.

'Nothing might come of it. They might not even do the wretched DNA test. But I couldn't bear for her to find out some other way. If there was someone else on the database she matched with and it all came out. It's so much better if we tell her the truth.'

'I agree. I absolutely agree. We should have told her years ago. I was wrong.'

'No. No, Chris. You love Georgia. That's why you wanted to keep it from her.' Nicola pushed her hand into his and held his fingers. 'I'll tell her it was me that didn't want her to know. That I was ashamed.'

'No,' said Chris, vehement. 'No way are you taking the bullet.'

'You covered for me, all those years ago.'

'I want to tell her the truth. All of it. That's the right thing to do and the easiest.' He stood up. He managed a smile. 'I'll go and do some sarnies, shall I? And the coffee.'

Nicola watched him go, and her heart ached for him, her kind, brave husband. It would be OK, she told herself. Georgia wasn't the hysterical kind.

She bit her lip as she thought about the ramifications of revealing their secret. There were other people who should know the truth as well, perhaps. They might not be as accepting. But that was not a problem for today.

★ ★ ★

'Oh, Mum!' said Georgia that evening, her face wet with tears.

They were sitting in the kitchen of her house. She had been so anxious to know why they had driven all this way and appeared on the doorstep that she hadn't even made a cup of tea. She was desperate to be sure that one of them wasn't ill or leaving the other one. What she had been told was the last thing she expected.

Nicola looked at Chris. She wasn't sure if the exclamation was reproach, or shock, or dismay. She'd left out some of the detail — it was a distressing story, after all — but she could talk to Georgia in more depth some other day, when she'd had a chance to take it in.

'I really hope you can understand why we did what we did,' she said.

'It's my fault we didn't tell you before.' Chris looked gaunt with the worry and the long drive. 'But I want to tell you what it was like, the day you were born. There you were, wrapped up in a snow-white blanket, and as soon as I saw you I recognised you. You were mine. My beautiful, perfect blue-eyed girl. I loved you with every cell in my body from that moment. You belonged to me. Me and Mum. You were *our* daughter.'

He put his face in his hands for a moment, and when he looked up there were tears in his eyes.

'It was very wrong of me. You had a right to know the truth long before this. But there never seemed to be a right time, and you seemed to be

339

more mine than ever as the days went by. Sometimes I completely forgot you weren't technically my daughter. Oh God, this makes me sound crazy and possessive and weird and controlling . . . '

'No, it doesn't.' Georgia shook her head. 'None of this makes any difference to me. You're right. You are my dad. I belong to you. Tarka . . . ' She stumbled over the unfamiliar name for a moment. 'Tarka is just a technicality. He is nothing to do with us. We are a family. And if anything,' said Georgia fiercely, 'his story makes me love you even more. I don't care that I don't have your blood. I've got your love, and that's what makes me yours. All yours.'

Chris reached out and took her hand in his. 'Thank you,' he said. 'That means the world to me.'

'And Mum — I can't believe what you went through. And poor Tarka.' Georgia stopped. She had questions, but they were not for now. They were for a day with just her and Nicola together. She was curious, of course she was, but she was mindful of Chris's feelings. Today was about the three of them, not about ghosts.

Chris cleared his throat. The emotion was all a bit much for him. 'I think I'll get the case in from the car.'

Georgia was giving them her bed for the night and sleeping in her little study. It was too far for them to drive straight back home. She watched him as he left the room, smiling fondly at his retreating back, his rumpled clothes, his scruffy hair. Her dad.

'Thank you for being so kind,' said Nicola. 'Though I knew you would be.'

Georgia frowned. 'It's all so complicated, isn't it? There are so many people involved. For me, the only one who really matters is Dad. As long as he knows how much I love him.'

'I agree, that's the most important thing. But do you want to tell anyone else? Tab?'

Georgia put her hands behind her head, pulling her hair up and clasping her fingers together. She sat like that for a few moments while she thought.

'It's all or nothing,' she said. 'Either we tell no one, or everyone. And I've got a feeling it would be best to have everything out in the open. I don't want to spend the rest of my life worrying about letting it slip by accident. And it's not as if anyone has done anything wrong. You and Tarka were so young. It was an awful situation. No one has anything to be ashamed of.'

'I did what I thought was right at the time. And I was so lucky to have your father. I couldn't have managed without him. And you have brought us such joy.'

Georgia walked over to the fridge.

'I need to think it through for a while before we make any decisions about who to tell.'

'Of course. It's been a secret for long enough. A little while longer won't hurt. Though there are Tarka's parents to consider too.'

Nicola remembered Clara, beautiful, glacial Clara, who had so clearly worshipped her son and feared for him. And her worst nightmare had come true.

'I was saving this,' said Georgia, pulling a bottle of champagne out of the fridge. 'For when I finished writing my first episode, but I think we need a glass now.'

She opened the bottle and poured a glass for her mother. As Chris walked back in she handed him a glass too.

'What are we celebrating?' he asked.

Georgia held her own glass up.

'I want to propose a toast. To Tarka, the father I never knew. And to my *real* dad. My proper one hundred per cent real father.'

Chris was openly crying now. 'It's happy tears,' he said, half laughing. 'I never cry, for heaven's sake. I'm a scientist. I don't get emotional.'

Nicola laughed. 'He's such a fibber. He bawled his eyes out the day you were born.'

The three of them clinked glasses.

And in his head, Chris did an extra little toast to Tarka, the man who had given him the centre of his universe but who'd never had a chance to meet her himself.

35

After they got back from their trip to Dragonfly Farm, Gabriel noticed a change in Lola over the next week. She was quieter than usual, more reflective. Not depressed, but she seemed weighed down by her thoughts. It was time for them to sit down and have a proper conversation. They'd avoided talking about the future of Dragonfly Farm, because in their hearts they both knew the answer. They'd had a wonderful time there. They both understood how special it was. But it was time to get real.

He sighed. 'Let's do one of those spreadsheets,' he said. 'Pros and cons. Put all the figures in.'

He pulled out a chair for her and sat down next to her at the table. She looked nervous, chewing on the side of her thumbnail.

'What? What is it?'

'There's something you need to know before we start. And I know it might feel as if I'm trying to hijack the situation, but I think the one thing we both want is another baby.'

'Yes. Of course it is.' He'd never been in any doubt.

'So I think we should go and see someone.'

'See someone?'

'Just for a consultation. I've had a recommendation for a fertility specialist who's treated a few of my friends. I think it would be a good idea to

343

have a few tests. See if there's anything obvious.'

Gabriel nodded. 'OK. Well, we can certainly go for a consultation. That won't do any harm.'

'Then if there is something wrong, we can start treatment. I know it would be expensive, but if we can get help, then why not?'

'Let's see what the specialist says. There might not be a problem.'

'No, but if there is, we can start straight away.'

Gabriel nodded. It was all moving rather fast, but what could he say? She was right. If there was a problem, they could get help. It was better than this cycle of hope and disappointment, and the frustration and the worry.

'Then there's this.' She pulled her iPad towards them and brought up the details of a house on the screen. 'It's a bit further out from here but it's really cute. And it has a workshop. And three bedrooms. Which, if we have another baby, we'll need.'

Gabriel looked at the details. It was the sweetest little house, with an old stone workshop at the bottom of the garden.

'You want to move?'

'I've been thinking and thinking and thinking. I loved Dragonfly Farm. Of course I did. It would be wonderful if we could keep it, as a weekend place. But we can't afford to. This way, we get everything we want.' Lola started to list on her fingers. 'Another baby, hopefully. A place you can work where you're not paying extortionate rent. We get to keep our friends nearby. Plum doesn't have to change nurseries and the baby can go there too. I can still work, but I won't have to take every job that comes along . . . '

Gabriel started to nod. If she had outlined this scenario to him a couple of months ago, he would have jumped at it.

She looked over at him. 'Please don't think I'm being controlling or manipulative. I'm trying to stand back from it all and get us the life we really want. I know you'll feel that you're letting Tabitha and Georgia down, but this is your inheritance, to do what you want with.'

'I know you're right,' said Gabriel. 'But it breaks my heart a little bit.'

'I know, baby. But you know what? Those girls are smart. They'll figure it out. Maybe they'll be able to get a mortgage? They have loads of equity in that farm. They'll have to make it work for them.' She scrolled through the house details on the iPad. 'I know I sound hard, but I haven't got where I am without having to fight and make tough choices.'

She looked at him and he saw she was about to cry.

'And I can't take much more of the hoping and the waiting. I need to do something. I'm not leaving it to chance.'

He leaned back in his chair and looked up at the ceiling. It was because he didn't want her to see his own tears. They were there for all sorts of reasons. Sadness that he hadn't yet been able to give her what she wanted so much: another baby. Regret that he was going to turn his back on people he felt drawn to. Frustration that Dragonfly Farm was going to slip through his fingers when he had seen so much potential. Shame that they were going to get everything they wanted, perhaps at the expense of Tabitha and Georgia.

But he knew Lola was right. And he knew that if he dug his heels in and fought for something different, they might fall apart. And he didn't want that.

He put his hand over hers. He didn't want her to feel as if she was forcing him into something he didn't want to do.

'You're totally right,' he said. 'Book a viewing. Book the consultant. And let's get this on the market. I'll tell the Melchiors.'

He walked away before he could change his mind.

★   ★   ★

It was with a heavy heart that he arranged to go down to Somerset a few days later for a meeting with Thomas Bickleigh and Tabitha, to sign the paperwork for the impending probate that was edging its way towards completion. The farm had been valued — the best of three valuations from local estate agents — and he was surprised at its worth. But he felt sick that the high value meant Tabitha and Georgia couldn't afford to buy him out. They would probably have to sell.

The drive down to Somerset was gloomy and grey. A persistent rain had set in, making visibility on the motorway poor, and the little roads that led to Rushbrook were shrouded in mizzle. He had arranged to pick Tabitha up from

346

Dragonfly Farm so they could go in together. He felt like a traitor as he turned into the drive.

For a moment, he felt furious with Gum. Why had he embroiled him in this? Gabriel would never have known, would have carried on in blissful ignorance, if he'd left him out of the will and left the farm to Tabitha and Georgia to share. Gum might have salved his conscience, or repaid some lifelong debt with his gesture, but it was causing more trouble than if he hadn't bothered. They still hadn't solved the mystery, but there was little point now.

The farm looked different from the last time he had been. The branches were bare of fruit now. Spindly and grey, they reached up into an even greyer sky. The wind whipped across from the east, malicious, causing doors to bang shut unexpectedly.

November had arrived to extinguish the optimism of October: those bright days made for squirreling and gathering and storing. November reminded you to make repairs and batten down the hatches. November was Eeyore, gloomy and dreary and doom-laden.

Poe was barking at everything in a fit of uncharacteristic bad temper. The hens wouldn't come out of their coop. Zorro was nowhere to be seen. Every creature with any sense was snuggled up keeping warm.

Except Tabitha. Tabitha was in the orchard, trying to get on with the arduous task of pruning now the last of the harvest was finished. She knew this was the optimum time to get the trees into shape, to cut out the clutter to let in the

347

light so the sun could touch the fruit next year. But it was hard work, in the wind and the cold. She had wrapped up as warmly as she could, but she found it impossible to prune wearing gloves.

As Gabriel arrived her fingers were starting to go numb, so she threw the last of the branches she had snipped down to the ground and climbed down the ladder to greet him.

'It's bloody Baltic,' she said.

He should be helping her, he thought. He wanted to help her. He loved the idea of removing any dead or damaged wood to keep the trees healthy; learning how they grew and helping them to maximise their crop. He so much wanted to be part of this process.

But the orchards would be nothing to do with him now. He was going to cut himself off from the dream. Melchior Cider was heading into his past as quickly as it had arrived.

Tabitha took one look at his face and frowned. 'What is it?'

'I'm really sorry, Tabitha.' He stuck his hands in his pockets and looked down at the ground. 'Lola and I have had to make a difficult decision.'

'You want your share of Dragonfly Farm.' Tabitha's voice was flat.

'I'm so sorry. I'd give anything to hold on to it and be part of Melchior Cider with you. But we've been trying for another baby for nearly a year now.' He paused, struggling to find the right words. 'We're going to a specialist. If we do need treatment, it will be expensive. We don't know

348

how many attempts we might need.'

He felt like a traitor. He felt as if he was using emotional blackmail to explain his decision, for how could Tabitha object to his argument without looking like a monster? It was all true though, he reminded himself. He wasn't making it up.

Tabitha looked back down at the orchard. At the trees she was nurturing. She knew how each of them grew, every twisted trunk, the thickness of every branch.

'You know this means we'll probably have to sell. Neither me nor Georgia have got the money to buy you out. Not even close.'

'I'm so sorry.' Gabriel didn't know what to say. 'Honestly, if we could afford to keep it, we would. I love it here. I'd love to get involved with the cider making. All your ideas are wonderful. We'd have made a great team. But . . . '

He shrugged helplessly. Tabitha looked at him.

'Family comes first,' she said.

'Yes,' said Gabriel, relieved she understood.

'I guess that's what Gum was thinking when he left you your share. That he was doing what was best for his family. Though we'll never know now. There's not much point in doing a DNA test, as it doesn't seem to matter. *Our* side of the family doesn't seem to count for anything.'

Her words cut him more than she could possibly know. She walked past him, her pruning knife still in her hand. Poe slunk past him too, looking up reproachfully.

'You better see Mr Bickleigh on your own. I'll sign the paperwork another time.'

And she walked away without even saying goodbye.

Gabriel was left standing in the orchard. He felt gutted. He had effectively ruined Tabitha and Georgia's future, while securing his own. What sort of a person did that?

He didn't want to think about the lucky people who would end up with Dragonfly Farm. Probably a couple like him and Lola who would renovate it lovingly. Maybe they'd even go into business making cider and make a small fortune. He would see a feature on them in the weekend papers and think *That could have been us.*

He walked back up to the yard. The wind whipped into his face, vicious, bringing tears to his eyes. He wiped them away with his sleeve and climbed into the car. He drove back down the drive without looking back.

36

Tabitha hid in the house until Gabriel had gone. She couldn't bring herself to speak to him. He was a traitor. He'd played her like a fool, pretending to be interested in all her ideas, encouraging her, making her believe in herself and the farm's future.

After she heard his car pull away, she went back out into the yard, walking into the barn. She'd pictured the farm in two years' time, the new orchard coming into fruit, new machinery installed, gleaming bottles of sparkling cider waiting to complete their fermentation before being sent off to weddings, landmark birthdays, anniversaries . . .

Joy would have become synonymous with celebration and happiness. Now her dream was never going to see the light of day. Someone else would realise it. It was all there, waiting for someone to make it happen.

Form an orderly queue, she thought wryly. In a few weeks' time no doubt there would be potential buyers traipsing through the house and grounds while she looked on. She saw Zorro peering down at her. Tears blinded her. What would happen to Zorro when someone bought this place? Would whoever bought it tear down all the old farm buildings? They were pretty ramshackle, though she could imagine some sort of expensive renovation job done on them, all glass and exposed beams. Either way, it wouldn't stay how it had been for the past century

She felt a surge of anger. This place had been her sanctuary. It had saved her. She was in no doubt she would have come to a sticky end if Gum and Joy hadn't taken her in. She had been wild and out of control. She had thought she would be safe for ever here. Now she was going to be cast out onto the street, she thought melodramatically. Yes, she'd get some money from the sale, but she guessed it would only be enough to buy a small flat in Nettleford, some anonymous little dwelling on the outskirts. She wouldn't wake up to the view over the orchards any more. She walked over to the fence and leaned on it, gazing at the trees she had nurtured, that Joy had nurtured, that her ancestors had nurtured. Joseph Melchior had probably planted the first one when he had arrived. What would he think if he saw it now?

She could see, over the tops of the trees, a murmuration of starlings gather. This was the first she had seen this year. They began to swoop in, hovering over the reed beds in the distance, thousands and thousands of black specks peppering the sky. She watched as they swirled in a graceful torrent, ebbing and flowing in tune with some hidden piper, an extraordinary feat of nature. More and more joined the cluster, choreographed with precision, each single bird focused on its own trajectory, gliding in and out, never seeming to collide.

She began to feel calmer. It was a lesson in life, this display. A lesson that while everything changed it nevertheless stayed the same; that everyone was on their own path but had to take into account what was around them.

She shivered as the sky grew dark and the birds seemed to melt away, though no doubt they were roosting in the trees below, ready to start another day.

'Hey.'

She nearly jumped out of her skin as Dash came up behind her.

'You scared me!'

'Sorry. I did call but you didn't answer.'

'Oh — I haven't got my phone on me.'

'Did you see the birds?'

'Yeah.'

'Amazing. I've never seen anything like that before.'

'Oh. It's a thing down here. People come for miles to watch.'

'They do?'

'The murmurations . . . '

'Sounds like a band name.'

She tried to smile at his joke. He frowned.

'What's up?'

She thought she probably shouldn't be divulging her business when she hadn't even had time to discuss it with Georgia yet. But she hadn't the heart to call her cousin yet. She wanted to feel robust when they spoke, not crushed.

'So,' she said, 'it turns out that Gabriel — your great-uncle's interloping descendant — has decided he wants his money out.' As soon as she spoke, she knew she sounded bitter. Well, she was bitter. 'Where am I supposed to get that kind of money from? Because although the farm's tumbling down around our ears, it turns out to be worth quite a bit. Just the kind of doer-upper that every bloody artisan hipster in London wants to flee to. Except Gabriel Culbone.'

'Oh.' Dash grimaced. 'Well. I suppose it's difficult, if he's got his life set up in London. Maybe he can't just drop everything?'

'It's not funny, though,' she protested. 'This is my home. This decrepit old dump means the world to me.' She looked down at the ground. 'They need the money for IVF. What can I say? How can I begrudge them that?'

Dash came in close to her. 'I'm sorry,' he said. He hesitated for a moment, then put his arms round her. To his surprise, she leaned against him rather than resisting. He held his breath, not sure whether to hold her more tightly or just give her a quick reassuring squeeze and let her go.

'I don't know what I'll do. Where am I going to live? I don't want to move. I mean, I could live in the quarters above the Swan with the other staff, I suppose. I'm certainly not going back to my dad or my mum. I could move in with Georgia, perhaps — but London doesn't suit me. It really doesn't.'

To her fury, tears were springing from her eyes. How dare they?

'I'm not crying,' she said. 'I'm not.'

'No,' said Dash, gently brushing her tears away with his finger. 'I can see you're not.'

She looked at him for a moment. It might be

354

nice, she thought. He might take her mind off it. Shit — had she made her bed that morning? She should have done. She usually did. She moved in closer. It was so nice to feel another human's warmth, to be cuddled. Jimmy O'Gowan was great in bed, but he didn't do cuddling.

Mind you, neither did she, really. But this felt good. They were pressed right up against each other. Tabitha felt herself defrosting.

'I'm thinking out loud here,' said Dash, his heart thumping as she snuggled into him. 'And I haven't thought it through. But what if I bought Gabriel's share?'

Tabitha leaned back and stared at him. 'What?'

'You said yourself your side of the river is nicer than ours. If I could expand onto that side — '

Before he could finish Tabitha wriggled out of his embrace.

'You've been waiting for this, haven't you?'

'What?'

'The minute you knew Gum was dead you knew I was vulnerable.'

'Hang on a minute — '

'You knew you only had to wait until I was on my uppers then swoop in with an offer.'

Dash looked horrified. 'Tabitha — that's a really awful thing to say.'

'It looks a bit suspicious, don't you think?'

'No! I thought I was doing a nice thing, offering. But forget it.'

'I don't trust you. You're a Culbone through and through. It goes right back to Casper and Eleanor. You lot can't bear anyone to have something you think is yours.'

'I don't know where all this is coming from.'

Tabitha pointed at him.

'I'm not sitting here and letting Dragonfly Farm go back to you. I'd give it away before I'd let that happen. You can get off my land. Right now. I never want to see you set foot on it again.'

She stormed across the yard towards the back door. She yanked it open and the handle came off. She stared at it in disbelief, hurled it across the concrete and stepped inside, slamming the door behind her. It bounced back open again.

★ ★ ★

Dash ran down over the fields, unable to get away fast enough. He couldn't believe what he had heard. He went over and over it all. He supposed, if he had been a different person, that Tabitha's wild imaginings could have some substance to them. If he had come down here with a predatory plan. But he hadn't. All he had wanted was a quiet life, and a project to keep him from boredom.

He felt stung by her words. Deeply hurt. He had thought there was a connection between them, a spark that he had been hoping would grow into something more. Now, he wasn't sure he could handle her. He'd been out with tricky women in his time but Tabitha took it to a new level.

He'd better forget about her, he thought, as he stumbled back through the river. Shit. The water had gone right over the top of his boots. His feet

356

were soaking. It didn't matter. He never had to cross over this bloody river again.

37

At Melchior and Sons, Lacy took Gabriel's coat and hung it up.

'Brass monkeys, isn't it?' she said brightly.

'Mmm,' said Gabriel, not in the mood for polite chit-chat.

She led him into Mr Bickleigh's office. Mr Bickleigh shook his hand.

'Thank you so much for coming down to sign. It speeds the process up no end.' He was presumably looking forward to having his bill settled, once the probate was completed. 'Everyone thinks solicitors hold things up so we can charge more, but bureaucracy is never profitable. Don't get me started on conveyancing.'

He threw his hands up in mock despair, then indicated the paperwork on his desk and held out a pen for Gabriel to use.

'Is Miss Melchior not coming in too?'

'Before I sign,' said Gabriel, 'I ought to tell you that I want to sell my share of the farm. I thought it was best to inform you at this stage, as it might affect the disbursements. And if we do sell, your firm might as well do the conveyancing, if you want the job. Obviously I'm yet to discuss this with the Melchiors properly, although I have told Tabitha.'

Mr Bickleigh looked surprisingly upset.

'Oh,' he said. 'Oh. That is a shame.'

'Yes. But it doesn't make sense for me to keep

my share. I mean, I have no sentimental attachment to the place really. I don't even know why it was left to me. We were going to do a DNA test to see if we were related but . . . '

Mr Bickleigh cleared his throat. 'So . . . none of your relations could throw any light on it? Your grandmother? You thought there might be a connection?'

'My grandmother . . . ' Gabriel sighed. 'There's definitely something. She recognised Matthew's name. She seemed to know who he was. Just for a split second. Then it was gone.'

Mr Bickleigh looked puzzled. 'Oh.'

'She has dementia. It's been pretty rapid. Not so very long ago she was driving, playing bridge, surfing the internet . . . ' He shrugged. 'We had to put her in a home in January. It's been pretty distressing.'

'Right.' Mr Bickleigh looked down at the Dragonfly Farm file. He seemed to be turning something over in his mind. 'I had no idea. This . . . changes things. A little.'

'How?'

'I've been mulling this over for some time. Wrestling with my professional standpoint. You must understand that client confidentiality is paramount at Melchior and Sons.'

'Of course.'

'Mr Melchior came to see me to rewrite his will after his wife died. That was when he included you in the beneficiaries. I've been aware of your existence for as long as I looked after his affairs. But he insisted that it was not his place to reveal the reasons he wanted to leave you part of the farm. He respected your grandmother's need for confidentiality. He maintained it was up to her to tell you her side of the story.'

'Up to Diana?' Gabriel frowned.

'But what you're telling me changes everything. If she has dementia . . . perhaps there is no need for confidentiality. I feel in this situation there is no obligation to keep the information from you any longer. On the contrary, I think it might help you. It might even change your mind.' He leaned forward, and he was smiling. 'Call me sentimental, but I would really like to see Dragonfly Farm stay in the family.'

'I'm not sure I totally understand.'

Mr Bickleigh stood up. 'Would you bear with me for a few moments?'

He picked up the file and walked out of the office. Gabriel sat in the plush silence, waiting. Was Mr Bickleigh going to reveal something that made any difference to his decision? Would he be better off not knowing? Should he walk out of the office right now, leave all of it behind? Leave instructions for the money to be sent to him when everything was wrapped up, and forget the Melchiors of Dragonfly Farm?

No. He wanted to know. He wanted to know where he fitted in with Tabitha and Georgia, whether he shared their blood. He wanted to know his grandmother's story — why she had cried at the mention of Matthew, and why she had the dragonfly in her jewellery box . . .

Eventually Mr Bickleigh came back in. He held a box file which he put carefully in front of Gabriel.

'Matthew Melchior was your grandfather. All the information you need is in there. I don't know if it will have any effect on your decision, but I hope it might. You are very welcome to stay here and read it. Or you can take it away. These copies are all for you.'

Gabriel opened the lid. Inside was a sheaf of correspondence. Letters. Bills. Invoices for school fees. Photographs and school reports. Copies of payments and cheque stubs. A report on him — including details about his business.

And on the top, a copy of a letter. Addressed to his grandmother at the house she'd lived in before she moved to the Brambles. Just before they had begun to realise how much she had deteriorated.

Gabriel smoothed out the pages and began to read.

PART FIVE

1957

38

Diana and Nancy Hillier blew in to Dragonfly Farm on the back of a gentle blizzard that Christmas. They whirled in with Matthew's uncle, Roland, in a flurry of snowflakes and exclamations.

'Nancy's a widow,' Matthew's mother, Catherine, told the family while preparing the house for the guests. 'Her husband was killed in the war. Roland met her at a private view. He seems very taken.'

Matthew's father, John, rolled his eyes. 'When isn't he?'

Uncle Roland was a bit of a ladies' man. He was always dashing off in a sports car to the Amalfi coast, or skiing in St Moritz, even though he earned little money as a picture restorer. He was very handsome, which went a long way, and had no responsibilities so could do what he liked with his spare time. And this year, instead of heading off somewhere glamorous, he had chosen to spend Christmas at Dragonfly Farm and was bringing Nancy and her daughter.

'We want a good old-fashioned country Christmas,' he declared. 'Roaring log fires and roast goose and long walks.'

Matthew, who was home from his first term at Cambridge University, had to move into his younger brother Peter's bedroom so Roland could have his, and Nancy and Diana were to

365

share the spare room.

That was the first thing that was changed. Seamlessly, by Nancy, who was one of those women who got her own way without even having to say what she wanted.

Matthew found it rather disturbing to think that Diana was in his room, in his bed. She was perhaps a little older than him, about twenty, and the most beautiful girl he had ever seen. Her skin was creamy with the faintest of pink blushes on each cheek, her eyes snapped with mischief, her hair was a halo of black curls, her mouth . . . well, he couldn't think about that too much.

She worked in an art gallery in Mayfair. He was certain Roland had got her the job as a favour to Nancy. He could imagine her gliding amongst the paintings then sliding off for lunches with prospective clients, bewitching them over veal escalopes into parting with more money than they meant to.

She was the kind of girl who made you do things you had sworn you never would. Even though she was coated in an air of wide-eyed innocence, there was something very knowing about her. It clung to her like the scent she wore. She left a trail of heady Moroccan rose wherever she went. You could tell where she had been just by breathing in the air.

Next to her, Matthew felt like a shadow, a whisper, a nobody. She was nothing like the girls he'd met at Cambridge, who were robust, intense, sometimes jolly but never glamorous. He was quite popular with them all, being good-natured, nice-looking (if not handsome), well-mannered, thoughtful — and not arrogant like some of the students. None of them had captured his imagination or his heart as yet. But Diana . . .

He was spellbound. Even though he told himself that everything he liked about her was superficial there was nothing he could do. She had possessed him, somehow. He was on edge all the time, ready, waiting, alert. Oddly, instead of making him tongue-tied and nervous, she made him confident. He felt as if he had finally made the step from boyhood to manhood as he prepared the cocktails before dinner, went out to de-ice the car before the inevitable shopping trips, lugged the Christmas tree in for his mother and wrestled it into position next to the fireplace in the drawing room. His table conversation was lively and interesting; his laugh louder than it ever had been. He was debonair, like his uncle. He had the world at his feet.

She took notice of him. He had thought she would be unapproachable, but she seemed to enjoy his company. If anything, it was Nancy who seemed lukewarm about their friendship. She steered Diana away from him at every opportunity. He supposed she thought he might make an improper advance. She was just being protective. Doing her maternal duty. As a widow, she was probably more cautious than she would have been had there been a man in her household.

On Christmas Eve, he took Diana down to the river to see if it was frozen hard enough to skate on — sometimes it was. The ground was smothered with frost, and she held out her hand for him to hold as they edged down the slopes. The sky was pearl grey, the air thick with tension and icy breath. The trees reached up their bare branches, black against a blank canvas. Everywhere was silent, until they reached the river bank, when they heard the sound of hooves.

A man astride a huge horse the colour of pewter thundered towards them, drawing to a stop just as Matthew thought he was going to mow them down. The horse wouldn't stand still, dancing on the spot and tossing its head, snorting and huffing. Everything gleamed — the horse's coat, the saddle and bridle, the man's boots. And his eyes, when he saw Diana staring up at him, her cheeks pink as Turkish Delight.

'You're trespassing,' he said.

'We're not,' said Matthew. 'This is our side of the river. I think you'll find *you* are.'

The man sneered.

'We can hunt wherever we like.'

And with that, he whirled his horse round, kicked its side and jumped over the river.

Diana stared after them, transfixed.

'Who was that?'

'One of the Culbones, I expect.' Matthew kept his tone level. 'We don't mix.'

'Why not?'

'There's a long-running feud between the two families. Going back generations.'

'Tell me.'

So he told her the legend. 'We're not far from the very spot where Eleanor threw herself in. It was an ice-cold winter's night. Some say she froze to death before she drowned.' He was embellishing the story with detail he couldn't know, for effect. 'Poor girl. She preferred to die than go back to her husband.'

'They can't still be like that, the Culbones.'

'I believe they are,' said Matthew.

'I should like to meet them.'

Matthew didn't reply. He looked at the river instead. It was covered in a thin layer of silver ice. He prodded it with his foot and it shattered instantly, water seeping through the cracks.

'Not frozen hard enough to skate, I'm afraid,' he said instead.

That night, they all went to Midnight Mass. Matthew had hoped it would snow again, and everyone would vote to stay inside by the fire instead, for he knew the Culbones would all be there, on the other side of the church. But it didn't. The weather was against him.

Diana had on a white rabbit-skin coat and matching hat. She would not have looked out of place on the top of the tree, he thought. A fairy with a magic wand, casting her spell over anyone who looked. Nancy, who was stunning by anyone's standards, faded into ordinary next to her daughter that evening.

The Melchiors sat at the front of the church on the right, as they always had. The Culbones sat on the left. There were more of them than ever this year, taking up the first three rows in their overcoats and hats, velvet and fur, signet rings and jewellery flashing, all smiles and laughs and kisses and handshakes. There must have been at least four generations, Matthew estimated, from the current incumbents of Rushbrook House down to a clutch of tiny ones who must be great-grandchildren.

And amidst them, the man who had been on the horse. There were two brothers about the same age. Hugh and Max, according to the order of service, for they both did a reading. Matthew thought this was a bit of a cheek considering they didn't actually live at Rushbrook House with their grandparents and were just there for Christmas, but the vicar was happy to indulge any Culbone whim. He knew who kept his roof in good repair.

Their rich, deep voices rang out in the little church, and Matthew noticed Diana didn't take her eyes off Max for a moment.

'God Rest Ye Merry Gentlemen', everyone sang as the service came to an end. Afterwards, everyone clustered in the churchyard in the cold air, chatting and wishing each other a very merry Christmas, and Diana and Nancy insinuated themselves amidst the Culbones, introducing themselves, radiating charm and laughter. They were a practised double act and quite shameless.

'Those two are terrible social climbers,' remarked Matthew's mother. 'I would watch that one if I were you.'

Matthew was shocked. His mother never said anything nasty.

Diana, Nancy and Roland ambled back over to the cars.

'Max lives in Kensington,' Diana was saying excitedly. 'Not so very far from us.'

Nancy and Diana lived in shabby Earl's

Court, but they liked to imply their flat was in Kensington. They were always a step away from who and where and what they wanted to be.

'We shall ask him for dinner,' said Nancy. 'As soon as we get back.'

She had the look of a mother determined to make a good match for her daughter.

On Boxing Day, Matthew woke to find that everyone was dressing up warmly to go to the hunt meet in Nettleford. His mother had dug out her old fox fur, whether in competition with Nancy or inspired by her, he couldn't tell. Nancy and Diana had certainly raised the bar in the house — everyone was a little more excited, a little more eager to socialise and have fun, a little more reckless.

'Do you want to come to the meet, darling?' his mother asked him. 'Because if you do we'll have to take two cars. We can't all squeeze into one.'

Diana was looking in the hall mirror, setting a red velvet beret onto her curls.

'I might stay here and do some studying,' Matthew replied.

'Oh, you are a stuffy old thing,' said Diana, poking him in the ribs. 'Come!'

The last thing Matthew wanted to do was stand in the marketplace and watch Max Culbone prance about on his steed, with Diana gazing up at him in admiration.

'No, thanks. It's too cold.'

He turned away from her and walked up the stairs.

'If you're staying, you could put the baked

potatoes in. We'll be back about one,' his mother called up after him.

He forgot the baked potatoes, of course he did, because he spent the time lying on the bed staring at the ceiling and thinking about Diana, so everyone was cross. Or at least he felt as if they were. In the end his mother did mash to go with the stew because no one wanted to wait another hour.

Diana seemed warmer towards him after the Boxing Day meet. As if by not going with them he had piqued her interest. Over the next few days, she drew him out: they played cards, walked to the Swan, and one day she insisted on making lunch to give his mother a rest. The two of them, under Diana's instruction, made cream of (tinned) asparagus soup and roast beef and a trifle with (tinned) pears and ladyfingers and piles of (tinned) custard with chocolate grated on the top.

It was rather fun, made even more gratifying by everyone enjoying the fruits of their labour. Matthew drank a little too much wine which gave him a surge in confidence and once or twice he thought he came close to being, if not witty, quite droll. Diana laughed, certainly.

After lunch, the grown-ups decided they would walk off their indulgence. Diana gave him a glance across the table.

'Matthew and I will stay here and do the washing-up,' she announced.

His heart gave a little skip, like a lamb in springtime, and he felt peculiar: the wine in his veins and the thought of her meant he could hear his own pulse whooshing in his head.

As soon as the grown-ups had shut the front door she took his hand and led him upstairs, to his own bedroom. His throat felt tight with panic and pleasure. They'd both had more wine than usual.

'I've got an idea.'

Her eyes were dancing and Matthew felt slightly alarmed. He knew she wasn't going to suggest another game of cards. There was too much mischief in her face.

She sat him down on the bed and stood in front of him.

'Let's have a go at . . . doing it.'

'What!'

'You and me. Why not? I mean, we're good chums. We're both not bad-looking. It wouldn't be too ghastly for either of us, and it would be good practice. So that when we find someone we really want to do it with, we know what to do. I'm a firm believer in being prepared for things.'

'You're mad.' Matthew was half laughing.

'Say yes!' Her fingers were in his hair, twirling it into curls, making him shiver.

'We can't . . . '

'Of course we can. People do it all the time. It's not difficult, I don't think. It can't be.' She put her head to one side and looked at him. 'And I know you'd be gentle.'

She was so close to him. The scent of roses filled his head. She came in closer and he could feel her laughter in his ear. It made him giddy. Her hands were on his waist, touching him, pulling his shirt up, her warm fingers on his bare skin.

He groaned. How could he walk away from this? He could feel his body responding, saying yes on his behalf. Before he knew it, his hands were on her hips, touching the silk of her dress. Her fingers were undoing the buttons, and she took hold of his hand and slipped it inside so he was touching her breast.

She gave a little moan of pleasure. 'Oh, Matthew,' she breathed. 'If I cry, you will be kind to me, won't you?'

She didn't cry. Far from it.

Afterwards, Matthew didn't quite know what to do with himself. All he could think about was Diana, and his need to touch her again, to feel her skin against his. But once everybody got back, she treated him as if it had never happened. She sat in the drawing room pouring the tea for everyone as if butter wouldn't melt.

She wasn't rude or nasty, just very matter-of-fact. That sense of camaraderie, of the two of them being the only people in the world, had gone. There was no whispering or cajoling or touching. He wondered if he had dreamed it. It seemed impossible to believe that an hour before they had lain naked together; that she had stroked his forehead gently with her fingertips afterwards and whispered, 'Thank you. I'll never forget this.'

And he had no idea what to say to her, or how to recapture what they'd had — the secret bond. He knew it had been an experiment, but for him, it had been momentous. Perhaps it hadn't been for her? Perhaps he *had* hurt her or frightened her and she hadn't wanted to admit it? Should he ask if she was all right? He should, he decided. It was the gentlemanly thing to do.

'Is everything . . . are you . . . all right?' he asked the next morning. She had asked him to pass the marmalade at breakfast as if they had barely met. He was worried that she was upset. He was worried that she regretted what they had done.

She stared at him with a bright little smile. 'I'm absolutely fine. Why wouldn't I be?'

The next day, Nancy came back from shopping in Nettleford with talcum powder, a brace of pheasant and an invitation. She had met Louisa Culbone, the doyenne of Rushbrook House, in the butcher's. She had invited them to a party to celebrate the impending New Year.

'It's practically open house,' she declared. 'We can all go.'

'Well, we shan't,' said Catherine, looking at Matthew's father for confirmation. She had already planned a cold salmon and board games. 'I've got nothing to wear. And I wouldn't feel comfortable. Not unless I'd had a proper invitation.'

It was funny, thought Matthew, that Nancy didn't push her further.

'Count me out too,' said Roland, and Matthew saw Nancy shoot him a look of panic. He laughed. 'Don't worry. I'll drop you two girls over and pick you up just after midnight. You go and have fun.'

No one had asked Matthew if he wanted to go.

It was simply assumed he wouldn't. He would stay at home with his parents and younger brother, and they would probably be in bed by half past ten.

On New Year's Eve, the house was filled with sartorial anxiety as Diana and Nancy prepared their outfits for the party, rushing about for safety pins and using up all the hot water. He glimpsed them through the doorway of his bedroom, Nancy standing behind her daughter, wrapping her hair round a pink curler with determination on her face.

'The Culbone name opens doors,' he heard her say. 'Marry a Culbone and you'll be set for life.'

Diana nodded. The room smelled of burnt hair, Parisian perfume and ambition.

At seven o'clock, everyone gathered in the hall to admire them. Matthew gripped the banister, wishing he was there, debonair in a dinner jacket, wrapping a shawl around Diana's bare shoulders, escorting her out to the car . . .

When Roland came back from dropping them off, he threw himself into the chair by the fire with a groan of relief. Matthew was the other side, pretending to read but wondering if Diana was already with Max.

His uncle surveyed him, twirling a whisky and soda in his right hand. Eventually he spoke, but his tone was kind.

'Don't torture yourself, Matty,' he said, using his childhood nickname.

'What do you mean?' Matthew looked up from his book, startled. Roland leaned forward, resting his elbows on his knees, clasping his glass in his hands. He surveyed Matthew for a moment, considering what to say.

'The trouble with women like that,' he said eventually, 'is they are only after one thing.'

Matthew felt his cheeks warm. He knew what Roland was alluding to. He had seen Nancy nudge Roland after lunch, lure him upstairs for a 'lie-down'.

'Do you mean,' he asked, 'sex?'

He coloured again at the mention of the word. Roland threw back his head and roared with laughter. Matthew felt a bit hurt. It wasn't that funny, surely?

'Not sex,' Roland explained through his mirth. 'Money. All they are interested in is money. Though they use one to get the other. And very good at it they are too.' He paused for a moment, reflective. 'We're not for women like that. They like men like us, though, because we are always there to pick up the pieces.'

'Is that why Nancy's with you?'

'Nancy's not after money any more. She knows she's missed her chance. She's far too old. She likes me because I'm fun and I don't care if she flirts with other men. But she's very ambitious for her daughter.'

He saw Matthew's face, longing written all over it. He smiled kindly.

'Oh, Matty. Diana's not the girl for you. She would make you dreadfully unhappy.'

After supper, Matthew went to fill his motorbike up with petrol from the spare can they kept in the barn.

'I'm going back to Cambridge in the morning,' he said to his mother. 'I need to get to the library.'

His mother was upset that he was leaving before she expected, but he couldn't bear another moment in the house. On New Year's Day, he left before Nancy and Diana had surfaced. He didn't want to hear a word about the party or see the dreamy look in Diana's eyes. He was superfluous to requirements.

39

It was easy to pretend none of it had happened once he got back to Cambridge. His freezing cold room in Fitzwilliam College, the horrible food, the endless amount of information he needed to absorb, the jolliness of the pubs and the warm beer and the camaraderie of his fellow students — he kept his mind busy with tort and conveyancing so there was no room for the memory of soft skin and dancing eyes. It was a battle just to keep warm. Who couldn't be happy in Cambridge, with its spires and thick stone walls and tiny streets and cobbles and latticed windows and people who were so brainy you wondered how they could ever sleep with all that information buzzing around?

His mother wrote and told him, rather gleefully, that Nancy and his uncle Roland were no longer an item.

I think Nancy did what she came here to do. I gather Diana is romantically attached to Max Culbone. They shan't want for anything if she gets married to him. I'm glad Roland is free of her, though. She's the sort of woman who values money over everything, and I fear she instilled that in her daughter. Which is a shame, because she was a pretty girl. It never does to have an avaricious parent and good looks.

379

His mother wasn't to know that her words made his stomach burn with jealousy. Or maybe she did? Maybe his mother was wiser than she seemed. Matthew scrumpled up the letter and threw it on the fire in his room.

One night, on the way home from a spirited evening in the pub, he came across a young girl in a coat too thin for February. She was staring up at a back window of the nearby nursing college.

'Are you all right?' he asked her.

She shook her head, shivering.

'Matron's locked me out. She jolly well knows I'm late. If I can just get up there, though, I could shin in. We always leave it wedged open, but I'm such a shrimp I can't reach.'

She was, indeed, a shrimp. Tiny, with large grey eyes in a pale face and a heavy dark fringe.

'I'll give you a leg-up,' offered Matthew.

'Oh, thank you! I'm already on a warning. I can't afford to get kicked out.'

He bent down obligingly and she scrambled onto his back and then his shoulders, reaching up and pushing the window open. He gave a final heave and she pulled herself onto the windowsill. He could just see a pair of skinny little legs flailing about as she tried to get purchase. A moment later she had disappeared inside. Then her face appeared again, wreathed in a smile.

'What's your name?'

'Matthew,' he whispered back. 'Matthew Melchior.'

'I'm Joy,' she said. 'Thank you. I don't know

how I'll ever repay you.'

She waved and shut the window.

He smiled. Her mischief and pluck had touched him. A big spirit in a little body.

Two days later he got home to his rooms to find the porter had left a package on his bed. It was half a pound of best bacon, wrapped in greaseproof paper and tucked in a brown bag, on which was written *Thank you for saving my bacon*.

He laughed for days, for longer than the bacon lasted. He cooked it on his fire and ate it between slices of thick buttered bread. It was delicious.

He hoped he would see her again but he didn't have the nerve to go knocking on the door of the nursing college: he felt sure matron would give him short shrift. But he didn't come across her, and soon he got swallowed up by his end-of-term exams and he had no time to wonder about her, let alone look for her.

And then his mother wrote to tell him the news that Diana was to marry Max Culbone that August, at the church in Rushbrook, and he felt sick thinking about it. He wanted to go abroad to France grape-picking but the friends who were going had no room in their car so he went back to Dragonfly Farm.

Everywhere he went, people were talking about the wedding. Everyone was going except the Melchiors, it seemed. Diana was spoken of as if she was a debutante Max had met in London. No one seemed to have any idea that she'd spent last Christmas at Dragonfly Farm. Matthew was cross with himself for minding.

He was alone in the kitchen the day before the wedding, absorbed in his books. It was baking hot, and he drank thirstily from time to time from a glass of water at his elbow. He heard a knock at the kitchen door — timid at first, then louder.

She was on the step outside, in a yellow dress and sandals, looking like a schoolgirl. An anxious schoolgirl.

'Diana!'

'Can I come in?'

His mother was in Nettleford, helping at his father's office for the day.

'What are you doing here?'

'It's my wedding tomorrow.'

'Yes,' said Matthew drily. 'I had heard.'

'We're staying at Rushbrook House. My mother is driving me mad. Max's mother is driving me even madder.' She looked at him. 'I think I've made a terrible mistake.'

Closer to her now, he could see the dark shadows under her eyes.

'It's just last-minute nerves, that's all,' he said. 'Everyone feels like that.'

'You're a good man,' she said. 'I fear I am not marrying a good man.'

'He's what you wanted, Diana.'

If he sounded harsh, it was because he was trying to protect himself.

She looked as if she was going to cry.

'My mother,' she said, 'gave me no choice. Max Culbone was what *she* wanted. Not me. She painted a picture of this gilded life I'll have with him. I'll never have to worry again, she told me. And maybe I won't. Not about money. But . . .'

She sighed.

Matthew didn't speak. The house was unnaturally quiet and it seemed hotter than ever. Outside, the trees and grass were motionless. Even the river was still, shrunk to almost nothing, the water lilies wilting. There wasn't a breath of wind or a ripple on the water's surface. He heard a cuckoo in the distance; it was past time for it to fly to warmer climes, but it must have been fooled by the weather. Was it warning him? Or was it mocking him, reminding him that he had been used?

The cuckoo then, on every tree,
Mocks married men; for thus sings he,
'Cuckoo;
Cuckoo, cuckoo!' O, word of fear,
Unpleasing to a married ear!

He might not be married to Diana, but she had taken what she needed from him and gone to another man.

As he looked at her, though, his heart softened. She was miserable and frightened, not the girl so full of life and vivacity who had burst into his world last Christmas. This was his chance to rescue her. He could have her for himself. He could snatch her from the arms of Max Culbone.

But what then? He was a law student, with no home to offer her, no money. He had plans to go and work for his father in Nettleford, and perhaps he would get a small flat there. He knew that was not the life Diana had planned for herself. Nor Nancy. He didn't fit their profile. He would not be a suitable consolation prize if Diana fled the altar. He remembered Roland's warning: *We're not for women like that.*

'I'm sure it will be fine,' he said kindly. 'Soon you'll have a house of your own, and you'll have a family. You'll be looked after.'

She stepped towards him and put her arms round his neck.

'I don't know that I will,' she said.

She was so warm. He wanted to protect her, of course he did. He wanted to say 'Marry me instead' but that was ridiculous. Even if he scooped her up and swept her away, after a while she would realise he wasn't the right man for her either. And he couldn't bear the thought of being rejected.

She was whispering in his ear.

'I think of you sometimes,' she said. 'I think of what we did. Do you remember?'

How could he forget? He didn't want to think about it now, because it made him even more aware of her proximity.

'Of course I remember,' he whispered back.

All he meant to do was kiss her. Just to give her reassurance, because it seemed to be what she needed. He didn't mean for it to go any further. He really didn't.

★   ★   ★

The next day, Matthew could hear the church bells begin an hour before the ceremony. The Rushbrook bell ringers loved a chance to show off their skills. The sound taunted him across the fields. He had hardly slept the night before, and now he couldn't study.

He was worried about Diana. He should have taken her more seriously. He should have offered to rescue her. She had fallen asleep in his arms, then peeled herself away from him in alarm when she realised the time.

'I must be back for tea. They'll be wondering where I am.'

She dressed and fled before they'd had time to discuss her plight any further. He needed to know she was all right. He looked at the clock. He raced up to his bedroom and found the little velvet box he had hidden in his dressing-table drawer. He ran back down the stairs, out of the door, across the yard, down the field, over the river and up the field on the other side.

He walked along the terrace at the back of Rushbrook House. There were people every-where preparing for the wedding breakfast afterwards. If anyone stopped him he would say he was delivering something. No one would recognise him, except Diana's mother. He would just have to hope he didn't cross her path.

He slipped in through the French windows. Through the drawing room. Into the hall. He paused for a moment at the bottom of the stairs, then ran up them. He walked along the corridor looking into each bedroom until he found her.

She was in a silk dress the colour of clotted

cream. It was cut off the shoulder with a tight waist and a very full skirt that trailed behind her. She had diamonds hanging from her ears. She looked at him, startled.

'What are you doing here?'

'I came to make sure you're all right.'

'I'm absolutely fine,' she said. 'Why wouldn't I be?'

It was the same thing she had said to him the first time. With the same bright smile. As if nothing had happened between them. He realised he was not her rescuer. She wasn't going to plead with him to take her with him. He wasn't going to lift her up in his arms and carry her away.

'You need to go,' she said, *sotto voce*. 'Everyone's at the church already. I'm to leave in five minutes. My mother — '

He put his hand in his pocket and drew something out.

'Here,' he said. 'This is for you.'

It was a tiny brooch: a dragonfly. It wasn't precious — not diamonds, just marcasite — but it was pretty. He had bought it in Nettleford just after Christmas, when in a fleeting moment of foolishness he had thought . . .

'I can't take this,' she said.

'It will look after you,' he said, pinning it to her dress, turning the clasp so it stayed fast. 'I'll always be there, if you need me. Always.'

There were tears in her eyes as she looked at him.

'My mother will be here in a moment,' she whispered. 'Please go. You've got to go.'

He heard the bells ringing out, even more insistent this time. As he left the room, he imagined the church, the pews filling up with guests, the scent of pollen from the flowers heavy in the air.

And Max Culbone at the altar, waiting for his bride.

40

When he went back up to Cambridge for the Michaelmas term, the first person he bumped into was Joy, standing in the queue for a bun at Fitzbillies, the bakery. She was with two other trainee nurses, and greeted him with glee.

'This is my knight in shining armour,' she told her companions. 'Old Bootface would have given me the heave-ho if it wasn't for him.'

'Thank you for the bacon,' he said to her, and her friends looked at the two of them knowingly as they smiled at each other. He loved the way her whole face lit up with mischief when she smiled; the way she seemed genuinely delighted to see him.

The queue was getting shorter. They were nearly at the counter. This was one of those moments, he knew, when what he said and did would affect his future.

'Would you like to come to the cinema one night?' he asked.

He didn't think her face could light up more, but it did.

'Oh yes,' she said. 'Oh yes, I'd love that.'

'Thursday?' he said on impulse, not having any idea what else he might be doing but knowing that whatever it was he would cancel if necessary.

'Joy! What do you want?' Her friends were at the counter.

'A sausage roll!' she called, then turned back to him. 'Thursday. I'll meet you outside the cinema at half past six.'

They went to see *The Bridge on the River Kwai*. But neither of them really took in what was happening on the big screen. They were both too aware that this was the first day of the rest of their lives together. There was no dramatic moment, no crashing music, no passionate screen kiss. It was an unspoken agreement. They felt like two slippers that belonged together, comfortable, content, cosy. As their hands joined as the credits rolled up, they looked at each other.

'Drink?' asked Matthew.

'Lovely,' said Joy.

Yet again, he had to let her climb on his shoulders to get back in and avoid the wrath of matron.

Life unfolded itself in front of them. Matthew graduated, Joy passed her nursing exams, and they got married in the chapel at his college and moved back to Nettleford. Matthew was to work at Melchior and Sons, for his father, and Joy joined the hospital in Honisham as a nurse. They rented a dear little cottage at the end of the high street and settled very quickly into small-town life.

There was only one sorrow. Month after month, there was no sign of a baby on the way. It was what they both wanted. They had everything planned. Matthew's mother had promised that she would help with childcare if and when Joy wanted to go back to work at the hospital, though Matthew assured her that he would be earning enough if she wanted to stay at home. But it never came to that.

Matthew found his heart breaking over and over again. He couldn't bear Joy's distress every time it was evident she wasn't pregnant.

'What's the matter with me?' she asked him, bewildered. 'I don't understand.'

'Perhaps it's not you,' he reassured her. 'I expect it's me. I'm so sorry.'

How long did you go on torturing yourself? After five years, they accepted the fact they would be childless. Joy plunged herself into her work and took up a role as a district nurse. Matthew took on more responsibility at Melchior and Sons. They were familiar and popular figures in the town, integrating themselves into the community. They played tennis, went to concerts, supported the local amateur dramatics and spent a lot of time with his parents at Dragonfly Farm.

It was a bleak November afternoon when Matthew's secretary led his next client into his office. He looked up to see Diana standing in front of him, buttoned into a black coat with a fur collar. She looked painfully thin and drawn, her hair teased into a beehive. Beautiful, but her eyes were dead.

'Oh,' he said, as she sank into the seat in front of him.

'I have nowhere else to turn,' she said. 'Trust me, I wouldn't be here if I had any other option.'

He swallowed. His mouth was dry. He felt unsettled — he could sense danger. He was immediately on his guard. He could smell her perfume, so familiar, but it was stale.

'You said you would always be there. If I needed you.'

She was not going to spoil what he had, he told himself. She was not going to walk back into his life and cause trouble. But he had made a promise. He couldn't deny that.

'Of course. What can I do for you?' He stayed polite but formal.

She put her gloved hands in her lap and looked down. He was shocked by her demeanour. She looked beaten. Downtrodden. There was none of the spirit or vivacity he had been drawn to.

'I've struggled for as long as I can, but I need help. For me. And my daughter, Lydia.' She put a hand up to smooth her already perfect hair. 'I had to leave Max before she was born. He's a drunk.'

'I'm very sorry.' Before the baby was born? What kind of a man was he, to drive her to such lengths?

'He's a drunk and a coward and a bully.' Tears came into her eyes. 'I tried to make the best of it. I *am* a good mother, believe it or not.' She looked a little defiant at this. 'But I've run out of ideas and I'm terribly tired and I'm terribly frightened. Sometimes I have people coming to the door to ask for their money — I've no idea what the debts are, but it seems that as his wife I'm accountable even though he is nowhere to be seen.' She grimaced. 'These aren't the sort of people who are worried about small details. They just want their money back.'

'This is very unfortunate,' Matthew agreed. 'But how can I help?'

'I need money.' Diana drew herself up and suddenly he saw some of that old energy. She looked him in the eye. 'And I've come to you because . . . ' She faltered for a moment. Even she had a modicum of shame. 'Max is not Lydia's father. Max is *unable* to father. Perhaps it's the drink, or perhaps that's why he drinks, who knows? Everyone called her a honeymoon baby and congratulated him. But if it was up to Max, I'd still be a virgin.'

Matthew had never felt fear like it. Perhaps only once, when he had overtaken a car on his Indian motorcycle without noticing another car coming towards him. That same spike of adrenaline coursed through him now. Panic and terror, made worse by the knowledge that the danger he had put himself in was entirely his own fault.

'Lydia is your daughter.' Diana's voice was soft now. 'She is six years old, and she deserves better. She deserves a good school, because she's a bright little thing. I'm guessing she has your brains, not mine.' She gave the ghost of a smile. 'As I said, if I could think of another way out I'd take it.' She leaned forward. 'My mother brought me up to believe I could have a fairy-tale life — the life she'd always wanted. That I could charm a handsome prince into marrying me and live happily ever after. I made a mistake,' she said, echoing the words he remembered from the day before her wedding day. 'I made a terrible mistake.'

Matthew put his hand over his mouth. For a moment, he thought he was going to be sick. He tried to think it through logically. He thought she was telling the truth. In a way, he hoped she was, because if she was lying, that made her even more calculating. And if he was the baby's father, he had a duty to her. Of course he did. He could not stand by and let his own child suffer because of some other man's cowardice. Matthew might be a fool, but he was not a coward. And he was certainly a better man than Max Culbone.

But there was one thing more important than the well-being of Diana and the child he hadn't known about. He was going to protect Joy for as long as he lived. After all, he wasn't foolish enough to think that Diana had come to his office for *him*.

'I'm so sorry for what has happened,' he said. 'And of course I'll help you. But there must be conditions.'

Diana just nodded. She was, he could tell, used to conditions. Everything in her life had been conditional upon something.

'My wife and I have been unable to have children. If your daughter *is* mine — '

Diana looked up sharply. 'She is. I promise.'

Matthew put a hand up. 'I'm not disputing that. I just mean that if she is my daughter, it means our misfortune is . . . not of my making.'

Diana thought through the implications of his words. 'Oh.' There was a flicker of sympathy in her face for the childless Joy.

'I will never, ever let my wife know that. I will never, ever let her think it's her fault that we can't have children. It would break her heart.'

To his surprise, there was a tear trickling down Diana's cheek.

'No one must ever know I am Lydia's father. That is my condition. I'm sorry, because in any other circumstance . . . ' He trailed off, not wanting to think about the position he was in too closely. 'But my wife comes first and always, always will.'

Diana was trying to wipe away her tears. 'Of course,' she said. 'And I'm so sorry.' She put her face in her hands. 'I am so sorry. I know what a wonderful father you would be.'

Matthew flinched at her words. They were sincere, which made it worse. He hoped he was doing the right thing. Doing his duty, while protecting the woman he loved. He wasn't going to sacrifice Joy to protect Diana. He felt a pang of regret for the child he would never meet, but he knew he could never be a proper father to Lydia. That wasn't what Diana wanted.

Again, he remembered his uncle's words: *We're not for women like that. They like men like us, though, because we are always there to pick up the pieces.*

He opened his drawer, pulled out his chequebook and took the lid off his pen.

'I'll give you a monthly allowance for Lydia. I'll pay for her to attend a private day school — I'll pay the fees directly to them.'

He started to write Diana's name, then hesitated. 'Is it still Culbone?'

She nodded and gave a wintry smile. 'The name is always useful for opening doors.'

'If you need anything else for her, just write to me care of this office and mark it confidential. And perhaps let me know of her progress every now and then.'

Diana sat still, her head bowed. He could feel her shame, and he was sad that she felt that. He understood she was here out of desperation, not calculation. The clock on the wall ticked solemnly. Matthew's pen hovered over the blank space on his chequebook and he filled out a generous sum.

His pen moved smoothly over the cheque as he signed it. He tore out the cheque and pushed it across the desk. She took it without looking at the amount, folded it and put it into her bag.

'Thank you,' said Diana softly. 'Thank you . . .'

She stood up and walked over to him, taking his hands in hers.

'You are a good man,' she said. 'Your wife is the luckiest woman in the world to have you.'

And she turned and left the office.

★   ★   ★

Many years later, Matthew sat in the same office, on the same side of the desk as Diana had, and gave his final instructions to Thomas Bickleigh. The file sat on the desk between them. It was filled with bills that Matthew had paid, copies of letters sent to Diana from Melchior and Sons, and letters from Diana to Matthew telling him of their daughter's progress. There was the occasional photograph, mostly of Lydia, but including one of Lydia's son, Gabriel.

'You're quite sure this is what you want to do?'

'Yes.'

'And you don't want to leave an explanation in your will?'

'No. It's not my story to tell. It's up to Diana to explain it to her grandson if she wants to. I don't want to break her confidentiality. She kept mine for many years. I've written to her explaining that.'

He pushed the letter across the desk. Mr Bickleigh picked it up to read it.

Dear Diana,

I hope this letter finds you well. I am sad to say that my beloved wife, Joy, passed away recently and I am now putting my affairs in order. I inherited Dragonfly Farm from my parents, and I intend to leave it to my two great-nieces, for as you know, Joy and I had no children. It was our greatest sorrow.

I feel strongly that it is the next generation who should benefit from my bequest. At the moment I am in full health, but I'm writing to let you know that on my death our grandson Gabriel will receive an equal share in Dragonfly Farm together with my great-nieces, Tabitha Melchior and Georgia Melchior-Hawkins. I have seen what he is doing with interest. He seems a fine young man. *I will leave it to you to explain our connection if and when you see fit. I think it's probably far too late for an introduction, but if you think he would welcome it, please get in touch, and I also include a letter for you to pass on to him if you wish.*

With my warmest wishes,
Matthew Melchior

Dear Gabriel,

We have never met, but I am very proud to be your grandfather. I am also proud to be the owner of one of your knives, and I am in great admiration of your craftsmanship. I am leaving you a share in Dragonfly Farm — one third, to be shared with my great-nieces, Tabitha and Georgia. I hope this news will be welcome and that Dragonfly Farm will bring you great joy, as it did my wife and me. I wish you every happiness.

Your grandfather,
Matthew Melchior

PART SIX

PART SIX

41

Gabriel closed the box gently. He leaned back in the chair, absorbing all the information in the hushed quiet of Mr Bickleigh's office, surrounded by files containing the last wills and testaments of most of Nettleford: legacies that might spark surprise or outrage or disappointment. Wills were a complex layering of duty and whim, nuanced by long-hidden secrets and moral obligations.

He felt his heart break for his grandmother. Now everything that had happened in their last conversation made sense. Her tears for Matthew, her declaration that she had made a terrible mistake, the dragonfly brooch. He didn't know quite how she had come by it, but she must have clung to it as a talisman of what she had lost over the years. And the letters that had arrived too late, just as all her memories began trickling away? Had she meant to act on them, and then forgotten? Or perhaps they had been swept up and thrown away with all the other unwanted post that arrived on her doormat, demands for charitable donations and adverts for hearing aids and reading lamps.

He felt sad for his mother, too, for perhaps more than anyone she had been the victim in all of this without a father figure, but he thought she had come out of it all right in the end. Lydia had always been very determined and independent, and Gabriel felt sure that she was happy.

He said his goodbyes to Mr Melchior and Lacy and hurried to his car, putting the box file on the front seat. As he started the engine, he realised that he wasn't a Culbone any more. He didn't have a drop of Culbone blood in him. He was a Melchior. At least, a quarter of him was.

And Tabitha and Georgia were officially his second cousins.

He wanted to drive to Dragonfly Farm and share his news. He wanted to sit in the kitchen and celebrate being part of the Melchior family. But he knew he wouldn't be welcome. He pictured Tabitha's crushed expression earlier, as she took in the implications of his decision. If anything, the revelation they were blood relatives would only rub salt into the wound.

As he drove, he thought about his grandfather. How he must have known how it felt to be disappointed month after month. It must have been far worse for him, for at least Gabriel and Lola had Plum. Matthew and Joy had borne their sorrow, but had still found it in their hearts to be loving and generous. And Matthew had kept his secret, for a whole lifetime, for the sake of his beloved wife. But now he was making things right.

Surely, thought Gabriel, he should be doing the right thing too?

⋆   ⋆   ⋆

It was dark when he got home. The flat was warm and welcoming. Lola had spent the last

402

week getting it ready to go on the market. Everything gleamed. It smelled delicious, of sandalwood and coffee beans and fresh laundry. She put her arms round his neck as he came in through the door and hugged him extra tightly, knowing he had hated what he had set out to do.

'How did it go?' she asked.

'Well.' Gabriel wasn't sure where to start. 'I think maybe you need to read these.'

He passed her the copies of Matthew's letters.

They went and sat on the sofa, his arm curled around her shoulder as she read them through. Her eyes were wide as she looked up.

'So he *was* your grandfather.'

'Yes. And I really do wish I'd had the chance to know him. He must have been wonderful.'

'*I hope this news will be welcome and that Dragonfly Farm will bring you great joy,*' read Lola.

Hearing his grandfather's words, Gabriel began to realise he belonged to Dragonfly Farm. He belonged to the Melchior family. He couldn't force his cousins to sell and break up years of happiness. That wasn't what Matthew had intended at all. But it wasn't up to him. He had his own family to consider — their needs. He couldn't force his wishes onto them.

He looked at Lola and was shocked to see tears running down her face, and he was touched at how moved she was by the letters. But she was smiling too. Laughing. Why was she laughing?

'It already has,' she said. 'Brought us great joy.'

'What?'

'It was Dragonfly Farm,' she said. 'I felt the

magic that night. Didn't you?'

'What?' What on earth was she on about? 'I don't understand.'

'I went for an initial consultation today. With the specialist.'

'You didn't tell me you were going.'

She waved a hand.

'Just to get the boring stuff out of the way, like blood tests. Before we go together.' She looked into his eyes. 'The first thing they do is a pregnancy test.' She was laughing again, wiping away tears.

Gabriel grabbed her arms. 'Lola. Lola, for God's sake. Tell me.'

'I'm having a baby,' she told him. 'We're having a baby.'

That night at Dragonfly Farm. She was right, it had felt special, somehow. It had been magical.

'This does change everything, you know,' she told him. 'I'd already been thinking about it all afternoon. Ever since I found out.' She picked up the letters. 'And now I've read these, it all makes sense. What if we sell this place and get a smaller flat? Then maybe we could convert one of the barns at the farm into a house. And you could move your workshop down there. We can live there, most of the time, but we'll have a bolt-hole here, for when I'm working.'

She wasn't sure he was listening. He was staring into space. She ploughed on.

'I think Plum would love it down there. I think it would be a wonderful place to bring up our little family. I know it will be strange for me. I don't know one end of a chicken from the other.

But I want you to have your dream too.'

Gabriel took her hand.

'It's got to be *our* dream, Lo. I can't force you into it. I don't want a scenario where I'm down there and you're up here and we drift further and further apart and I start spending too much time in the pub and it all falls apart.'

'I know. I get that. But I can start thinking about new projects. I can spend more time helping you. And I can help with Melchior Cider too. I know all about building a brand and product launches and getting a buzz going — maybe I'd be good at that?' She laughed. 'I'm telling you — I got so many likes on my Instagram from that weekend we spent down there. People go mad for that country-life fantasy.'

Gabriel started to smile. 'You could be the face of Melchior Cider. I can see you lying in a haystack with a bottle of cider in your hand.'

'Cider with Lola,' she said, in a mock West Country accent.

'Are you absolutely sure about this?' he said. 'Are you certain this is what you want? Do you really think it would work?'

She nodded. 'I'm a bit scared, because I don't know anything about the countryside. But we get the best of both worlds this way. And I think it would be the best thing for . . . the children.'

'The children,' echoed Gabriel. He could see Plum racing around the orchard, a baby lying on a blanket waving its little feet in the air. He felt choked.

'Thank you,' he said to Lola. 'I can't tell you

how much this means.'

'I know exactly how much this means,' she replied. 'That's the point.'

She put her arms around his neck and he pulled her close. And he thought with pride how his grandfather was going to live on, in Plum and the new baby. And then he remembered Tabitha and Georgia, and grabbed for his phone.

'I need to call Tabitha,' he said. 'And tell her what we've decided. Tell her Dragonfly Farm is safe.'

42

At Rushbrook House, Dash was freezing and furious. Freezing from his wade through the river. His feet were like blocks of ice, and he felt chilled to the bone. And furious with Tabitha. He was still reeling from the way she had turned on him. She had totally misinterpreted his actions.

Forget her, he told himself, as he tried to get warm by the Rayburn. The bloody Melchiors weren't happy unless they were feeding the rift between them and the Culbones. They seemed to thrive on it. It was almost as if they wanted the families to be divided.

Well, that was fine by him. They could coexist with the river between them. He could get on with his project. The plans were being finalised next week, the drawings tweaked. They'd be putting in their application right away and hopefully he'd get permission early in the New Year. He couldn't wait.

He got up to make a cup of tea then sat down to look through all the figures one last time. He knew there would be hidden costs when he started work. There always were. But he had left a margin for error in the budget. Hopefully that would cover any anomalies.

As he worked, he couldn't stop thinking about Tabitha. So many times he was tempted to pick up the phone and ask her opinion on things. How much did housekeepers expect to get paid around here? And gardeners? Who was the best supplier of fresh fruit and veg? Was there a decent wine merchant? She had a wealth of local knowledge as well as experience of catering and hospitality and the kind of clients he was hoping to attract. Her input would be useful.

He tried to stop thinking about her. He told himself he was just looking for excuses to get back in touch. She'd give him short shrift if he asked for her advice now.

As the shadows grew longer and the light faded, he started to realise something. He didn't need to ask her advice. On the contrary. He needed to tell her how he felt.

He knew he was right about her. He could tell, by other people's reactions, how special she was. He'd spent enough time in the Swan to know that Alan the landlord depended heavily on her, and that Jimmy O'Gowan thought the world of her too. He had seen the trainer's eyes follow Tabitha around the bar when he'd popped in there for a pie: there was adoration and respect and a certain amount of longing. He clearly worshipped her.

Yet Tabitha seemed to have no idea of her worth.

It was up to him to tell her how priceless she was.

He grabbed his keys and ran out to his car. He wasn't wading through that river again, not even for Tabitha. He accelerated down the drive and out into the lane. She better be in. Of course she'd be in. No, what if she was working tonight? Which nights did she go to the pub?

His car bounced through the potholes of the drive to Dragonfly Farm. He came to a halt in front of the house. He could hear Poe barking. Was it a warning or a welcome? He ran to the front door and banged on it as loudly as he could.

It took for ever for her to answer. Or it seemed to. She stood in the doorway, bathed in the light from the hallway behind. She was wearing a green velvet dress and what looked like Gum's fishing socks pulled up to her knees. And a bobble hat. She looked . . .

'What?' she snapped.

He pointed at her. 'You need to listen.'

'Don't threaten me,' she said, and Poe growled.

Dash put his hand down. He hadn't meant to look aggressive.

'You have got me so wrong,' he said. 'I don't give a stuff about that bloody legend and who owns what, and whether Dragonfly Farm really belongs to us. I made you that offer because I cannot bear the thought of looking out of my kitchen window and that light — ' he pointed behind her — 'that light not belonging to you, but belonging to some stranger. I want to know that you are on my doorstep. I want to see your light, Tabitha. And if that makes me sound like some kind of creepy stalker neighbour, I'm not.' He stopped for a moment. 'I don't care about Dragonfly Farm,' he reiterated. 'I care about you.'

Tabitha stood stock-still, staring at him. Poe sat down beside her, his tail thumping, waiting for the next move. A hundred emotions flickered over her face, but he couldn't identify them. How was she going to react? Was she going to laugh? Slam the door in his face?

Eventually, she spoke.

'I look for your light too,' she said. 'I can just see it from my bedroom. It makes me feel . . . safe. Knowing you're the other side of the river. I mean, I know I can look after myself — '

'God, yes,' said Dash with feeling. 'You're like . . . Boudicca.'

'But just sometimes I want to feel looked after. There's nothing wrong with that, is there?'

She smiled at him and he thought, *Oh, you glorious, vulnerable, invincible, wonderful woman.*

'We all need to feel looked after,' he said. 'Isn't that what love is?'

'Love?' she said, her eyes wide.

Dash quailed for a moment. Had he gone too far? Was he going to scare her off with his declaration? He didn't care. He'd never felt like this about anyone before.

'Yes.' He felt brave enough to step forward and take her in his arms. 'Yes. I think that's probably the best word for it.'

As she started to kiss him, Tabitha could hear her mobile phone ringing in the kitchen. *It can wait,* she thought. *Whoever it is can wait.*

43

Georgia hadn't spoken to anyone about her parents' revelation since they had been down to see her. She had been so busy with writing her script, she hadn't had a chance.

Now it was Friday, and she was going to go down to Dragonfly Farm for the weekend. They were all gathering to celebrate the news that the farm was safe. And to figure out just how Gabriel and Lola would fit into life there. They were very insistent that they didn't want to intrude on Tabitha and Georgia, for Georgia had decided she was definitely going to move to Somerset full time. She felt more confident about the idea now she'd got a proper commission under her belt. She'd delivered her first draft of *The Beat Goes On* to Martin earlier that week and he had phoned her to say how much he loved it.

'Bang on the money, Georgie Girl,' he told her. 'I'm so frickin' clever, it hurts.'

'*You* are?' she laughed. He was conceited, but it was endearing.

'I knew you would nail it. I've got a few notes, but nothing you can't handle. You better get on with the next one.'

With that affirmation, she felt confident making the leap from script editor to writer, and embracing the freelance lifestyle. She wondered about commandeering one of the outbuildings as a little office. Working in the kitchen was all very well, but she needed a whiteboard to plot out her scenes. This was a business, not a hobby. She had to be professional and take herself seriously.

It had taken a while, but she also felt ready now to tell Tabitha about Tarka. She wanted her advice: to ask whether she thought they should tell Clara, Tarka's mother, the truth. Her gut was telling her they should, but she wanted Tabitha's opinion. She felt too close to be objective and she knew her parents were too — their own emotions and needs might get in the way of the decision.

She was just putting the last of her clothes into her weekend bag when her phone rang. The number was withheld, but she answered anyway.

'Georgia Melchior?' a female voice asked with a transatlantic twang.

'Yes?'

'Hi. It's Sandra Sorelli here. I'm the producer of *Take Two Eggs*?'

'Oh. Yes. Hello.' Georgia was wary. The Hot Librarian.

'So Doug has delivered his first draft of the sequel, *How to Make an Omelette*.'

'Yes . . . '

'OK, so I looooove the script. I think it's really tight. The only thing is, it's just not as cute as the first script. And we want to make sure they're both tonally the same before we start to shoot.'

'Of course.'

'So Doug told me you did some work on the first script.'

Georgia wasn't sure what she was supposed to say.

'Um. A little bit. Yes.'

'And you thought of the tomato?'

'It was just a silly thing.' She realised she was doing that self-deprecating English thing. This was Hollywood calling. 'Silly, yes. But genius.'

'It *was* genius. We're using it again in the sequel.'

'Oh. Great.' Where was this conversation going?

'So I was wondering if you would do a pass on the second script? There's something missing and my gut instinct is maybe it's what you brought? So I wanted to come to you first. How are you fixed?'

Georgia told herself not to rush into anything. Not to sound too keen.

'I have a commission for a police drama I'm working on at the moment.'

'Do you think you could take a look, though?'

In true Hollywood style, Sandra was persistent.

Put your business head on, Georgia.

'I guess we need to talk about a fee? And a credit?'

'Do you have an agent? I can discuss it with them right away.'

Shit. She didn't. Not yet. It was on her list of things to tackle in the New Year.

'I'm between agents at the moment.' She put on her most confident voice. It was nothing to be ashamed of.

'Well, why don't I email you the script and

413

have my contract department call you?' Sandra sounded very persuasive. 'Doug insisted that you should be brought on board. And this project means a lot to us. It is such a cute premise. But it needs more jokes. And more romance.'

'So — romantic comedy, then?' Georgia cringed. Did she have to sound so uptight and English? But Sandra just laughed.

'Oh my God — you are so funny already. Yes. Yes! That's exactly what we want.'

Five minutes later, after she'd given Sandra her email, Georgia hung up.

People always surprised you. She would never have guessed that Doug would admit she had contributed. Maybe he had a bigger heart than she thought? Or maybe he knew that she was going to save his ass. Either way, it didn't matter. She had a Hollywood script commission.

She picked up her phone. She was pretty sure he had more sense than to be using this as a way to lure her back. She and Doug were over. But it didn't mean she couldn't acknowledge his gesture. She typed a quick text.

Thank you. That means a lot. I won't let you down. G

A minute later he texted back. A thumbs-up, a wink emoji and a movie reel.

He understood the deal. They were good.

She grabbed her coat and her bag, ran down the stairs and out of the door. She saw a cab and put up her arm. She wasn't going to go by tube. She wanted to get to Paddington as quickly as she could. She couldn't wait to get to Dragonfly Farm.

She couldn't wait to get home.

44

'Listen, I don't have to be here when Georgia
gets here. You probably want to talk to her on
your own . . . ' Dash was panicking. He didn't
want it to look as if he had got his feet under the
table or was unduly influencing Tabitha. Not that
it was possible to influence Tab in any way. He'd
learned that fast enough, but it was what he
loved best about her.

Tabitha was putting the finishing touches to a
coq au vin. She came over and put her arms
round his neck from behind, bending to kiss the
tip of his ear.

'No! It's great that you're here.'

'As long as she doesn't think I'm intruding.'

'It's not like you to be so insecure.'

'I think I'm just a bit jittery. I put the planning
application in today.'

He'd finally taken the plunge and pressed
'send' and was surprised at how nervous he was
about the outcome. He prayed the council would
see his vision and would pass the plans. He
couldn't wait to get his teeth into the project.
Tabitha had helped him with all the details. She
had a much deeper understanding of how things
worked around Rushbrook, and her input had
been invaluable in the end. A little local
knowledge went a long way.

'Hello!' Georgia appeared in the doorway.
She'd arrived without anyone hearing and let

herself in. She saw Dash and did a double-take. 'Oh. Hello.'

She looked at Tabitha, who looked defiant.

'You've met Dash. Briefly. At the funeral.'

'Yes, of course,' said Georgia, shaking his hand. She looked at Tabitha again, who smiled brightly. There was definitely something going on.

'I hope you don't mind welcoming a Culbone into your house?' Dash said.

'No. Not at all.' Georgia's mind was racing. She hadn't expected this.

Tabitha looked at her. 'Honestly, Georgia. He's OK. He doesn't bite.'

'It's not that.' Georgia put her bags down and went to sit at the table. 'Um — could I have a drink? Only I think I need one. I've got something to tell you.'

'Are you OK?' Tabitha gazed at her cousin with concern.

'Yeah. Yes. It's . . . It might be a bit of a shock, that's all.' She glanced at Dash. 'To both of you, actually.'

'Me?' Dash looked worried. 'In that case, maybe we should all have a drink.'

Georgia was impressed to see him take charge, gathering glasses and opening the bottle. He was a good host: the kind of guy who just got on with it and didn't make a big deal of things. She noticed him plant a kiss on Tabitha's shoulder as he passed her and saw Tabitha blush. Blush! She had never seen Tabitha blush in her life.

'So go on,' said Tabitha, looking serene as she slid into the seat next to her cousin. Dash brought over the drinks and sat opposite them.

'So,' said Georgia. 'I'll give you the short version first.' She cleared her throat. 'In 1986, my mum stayed here for the summer with Gum and Joy. She was at uni, and she was working for Gum in Nettleford. And while she was here, she met your uncle.' She looked at Dash.

'Tarka?' said Dash. 'I never met him. He — '

'Drowned, I know. The thing is,' Georgia carried on, 'my mum fell head over heels in love with Tarka. They had a summer fling. And then the tragedy happened.'

'She's never spoken about it,' said Tabitha, indignant. 'She never told us she fell in love with a Culbone!'

'Shh,' said Dash, who could sense there was more to the story. 'Go on.'

'Mum was pregnant,' said Georgia, and she felt tears prickling as she always did when she thought about how sad it all was. 'Mum was pregnant with Tarka's baby.'

'Oh, poor Nicola. What happened to it? Did she give the baby away?' said Tabitha, then looked at Dash, who had caught on much more quickly. 'Oh!'

'The baby was me,' said Georgia. 'I'm Tarka's daughter. Tarka Culbone was my dad.'

And Georgia shut her eyes, overwhelmed with emotion. It was almost too much, being here in the very kitchen where Nicola must have sat when she realised she had fallen in love. Being here with Dash, Bear's son and Tarka's nephew. Her cousin. And as a tearful Tab took her in her arms, she began to cry too, for both her fathers, and for Gum, and for Joy, and for everything that had happened, and for the fact they were still here, together, and that Dragonfly Farm was safe.

★ ★ ★

Dash was wonderful. He was so understanding, and gave Tabitha and Georgia some space to go over the rest of the story together: how Chris had scooped Nicola up and taken on Georgia as his own. And the next morning, he took Georgia over to Rushbrook House and showed her Tarka's room, showed her all the relics of the man who was her father. Everything that was still there and was still so much part of him. And she pressed his clothes to her face, and listened to the records, and looked at the photographs, and cried for the beautiful boy she would never meet.

'Do you think,' she asked Dash, 'your grandmother would like to meet me? I don't want to upset her.'

'I think she'd like that very much,' said Dash. 'But I can talk to her, if you like. It might make it easier. It will come as a shock, but I think it might be a comfort to her, to know about you.'

He was so kind, thought Georgia. Dash was kind and strong and funny and gallant and absolutely bloody perfect for Tab.

Culbones and Melchiors. Melchiors and Culbones. It was all whirling around in her head. But it didn't matter, she realised. It didn't matter which you were. They were one big family now.

45

It was pitch black and freezing when he got the nudge in the ribs from Tabitha.

'Hurry up!' she whispered. 'Everyone's in the living room.'

What bloody time was it? Only just gone six? Were they really all up? It was madness.

Why on earth had he agreed to it? Because it was her mad idea and he loved her, that's why. Because it was Christmas. And because everyone adored Plum, without exception. Especially Tabitha: the two of them were firm friends, always getting up to mischief and making silly plans. They'd spent all afternoon yesterday making a gingerbread house that looked just like Dragonfly Farm, and a load of gingerbread people to go with it. Plum had decorated them to look like each member of her new family, though nobody was quite sure who was who out of the half-a-dozen wonky gingerbread blobs, apart from a particularly wonky one with four legs which must be Poe.

Dash threw back the duvet then pulled on his jeans and a jumper and made for the back stairs. Then he ran back into the bedroom. Santa suit and beard. Tabitha had insisted. He scrambled into it, rolling his eyes.

He crept downstairs into the kitchen then out of the back door and across to the outbuildings.

There were already plans afoot to renovate the

yard. Tabitha had contacted the architect who was working on the development at Rushbrook House, and she had set up a meeting in the kitchen where everyone had thrown their ideas into the pot. The current plan was for Lola and Gabriel to convert the biggest barn into a house and apply for permission to build a brand-new purpose-built unit for cider making. And they were going to convert one of the stables into an office and a writing room for Georgia. No doubt the plans would change endlessly before they made up their minds, but it was exciting.

It was that stable he was heading to now. He slid back the bolt.

'Come on then, you.'

Five minutes later he tiptoed through the front door and into the hall.

'This way,' he whispered to his companion, and they crossed the hall to the doorway of the living room.

There they all were, gathered around the fireplace, the flames crackling in the grate. Lola had hung up velvet stockings for them all, each one emblazoned with an initial. There was even one for Dash. He loved the fact he had been included — he really felt as if he belonged now. His parents were coming down on Boxing Day and were going to meet Georgia. It was going to be emotional, but it felt right, and he was glad they were returning to Rushbrook after all this time. The house deserved to come back to life.

Plum had already had her heavy stocking lifted down and was sitting on the rug surrounded by wrapping paper as all the others looked on.

Tabitha, in a red flannel night-shirt and Gum's socks. Georgia, in tartan pyjamas. Lola, lounging in cream yoga pants and a cashmere hoodie. Gabriel, the only one who had noticed him, grinning like a lunatic and giving him the thumbs-up.

Dash cleared his throat but no one paid any attention.

'Ho ho ho,' he tried.

'Plum,' said Gabriel. 'Look.'

Plum's little head whipped round. Her eyes grew wide with disbelief at what she saw. Father Christmas in the doorway, holding a rope, and on the other end of the rope, looking quite at home, as if she wandered in and out of people's houses every day —

'A donkey,' Plum whispered. 'He brought me a donkey.'

★ ★ ★

As daylight eventually broke on Christmas morning, frost sparkled on all the branches of the apples trees. Mistletoe clustered high up in the hedges, its berries fat and white. On the front door hung an extravagant wreath of holly, ivy and bright pink roses tied with a golden ribbon. The turkey was already in. Tabitha had made cinnamon buns stuffed with plump cranberries to keep everyone going.

'Come on,' said Dash, impatient. 'It's time for your present.'

'Well, what is it?' Tabitha looked up from peeling potatoes in anticipation.

'It's outside. You have to follow me.'

'It's not another donkey?'

'No,' he grinned as they headed out into the fresh air.

'Well, what is it?' She looked around but couldn't see anything that was a suitable gift. Had he bought her a tool for the orchard? A tractor? She'd quite like a tractor.

'Come on.' He started off down the slope.

Her present must be at Rushbrook House, Tabitha realised, and ran after him through the field. She could hear the crunch of frosty grass underfoot and the rush of the river below.

They carried on down until they reached the bank, at the point where the river was at its most narrow. The water scurried past them, clear and bright. And there, right in front of her, was a bridge. A bridge about three feet wide and twelve feet long, made of clean, new wood cut in a gentle arch, with criss-cross supports and curved handrails.

'Who made this?' she gasped.

'Well,' said Dash, 'I'd like to say it was me, but I'm not that great a carpenter. So I had it made. To my exact specification.' He smiled proudly. 'It's to bring us together. Our two families. After all these years. Because I'm tired of getting my feet wet every time I come to see you. It's your Christmas present. I couldn't exactly wrap it.'

'It's amazing,' said Tabitha. 'It's the craziest, most perfect present I could ever imagine.'

'Will you walk over it with me?'

They stood in the middle of the bridge, the river running beneath them. They could see the chimney of Dragonfly Farm over the brow of the hill on the right, and the pale-pink facade of Rushbrook House through the trees on the left.

She took Dash's arm and felt her heart lift. At long last they were united, the Culbones and the Melchiors. For a moment, she dared to think of a horde of children racing over the bridge, secure in the knowledge that they belonged on both sides of the river, that they were welcome at Rushbrook House and Dragonfly Farm, that they could roam as far as the eye could see without fear.

That all this land was theirs. That it was where they belonged. Their home.

Acknowledgements

Huge thanks to Julian and Miranda Temperley for their kindness and hospitality whilst showing me their orchards at Burrow Hill. Their cider is the nectar of the gods, and as for Somerset Cider Brandy — you will never be the same again! Visitors are welcome so do drop in and see them if you are ever in Somerset on a sunny afternoon.

Thanks also to Debbie Kingsley and Andrew Hubbard for a wonderful day picking apples and making cider at South Yeo Farm. A real treat for someone who spends 99% of her life sitting at a laptop!

One day I will have my own orchard and put everything I learned to good use.

This is my 20th novel so I want to say thank you to those people who have kept my mind, body and soul together and helped me reach this landmark.

And the biggest thanks of all to my readers. You inspire me every day.

Finally, I'd like to dedicate this book to my dear editor Harriet Bourton — HB, this one is for you!

Credits

Veronica Henry and Orion Fiction would like to thank everyone at Orion who worked on the publication of *A Home from Home* in the UK.

Editorial
Harriet Bourton
Clare Hey
Olivia Barber

Copy editor
Karen Whitlock

Proof reader
Francine Brody

Audio
Paul Stark
Amber Bates

Contracts
Anne Goddard
Paul Bulos
Ellen Harber
Jake Alderson

Design
Rabab Adams
Joanna Ridley
Nick May

Helen Ewing

Editorial Management
Charlie Panayiotou
Jane Hughes
Alice Davis

Finance
Jasdip Nandra
Afeera Ahmed
Elizabeth Beaumont
Sue Baker

Marketing
Sarah Benton
Lynsey Sutherland
Amy Davies
Tanjiah Islam

Production
Ruth Sharvell

Publicity
Maura Wilding

Alainna Hadjigeorgiou   Frances Doyle
Georgina Cutler

Sales

Jen Wilson   **Operations**
Esther Waters   Jo Jacobs
Victoria Laws   Sharon Willis
Rachael Hum   Lisa Pryde
Ellie Kyrke-Smith Lucy Brem

We do hope that you have enjoyed reading this large print book.

Did you know that all of our titles are available for purchase?

We publish a wide range of high quality large print books including:
**Romances, Mysteries, Classics
General Fiction
Non Fiction and Westerns**

Special interest titles available in large print are:
**The Little Oxford Dictionary
Music Book
Song Book
Hymn Book
Service Book**

Also available from us courtesy of Oxford University Press:
**Young Readers' Dictionary
(large print edition)
Young Readers' Thesaurus
(large print edition)**

For further information or a free brochure, please contact us at:
**Ulverscroft Large Print Books Ltd.,
The Green, Bradgate Road, Anstey,
Leicester, LE7 7FU, England.
Tel:** (00 44) 0116 236 4325
Fax: (00 44) 0116 234 0205